To Rebecca Schaeffer,
who was there for me the whole way
as I transformed from statistic to survivor
strong enough to write this story

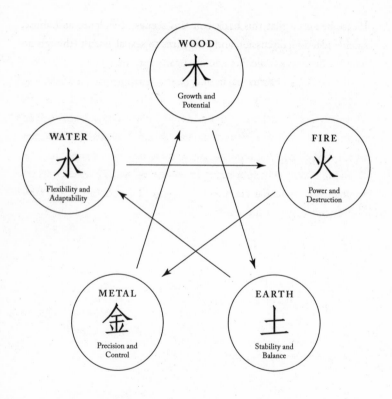

TYPE ADVANTAGE

Please be aware that this book contains scenes of violence and abuse, suicide ideation, discussion and references to sexual assault (though no on-page depictions), alcohol addiction, and torture.

This book is not historical fantasy or alternate history, but a futuristic story set in an entirely different world inspired by cultural elements from across Chinese history and featuring historical figures reimagined in vastly different life circumstances. Considerable creative liberties were taken during the reimagining of these historical figures, such as changing their family upbringing or relative age to each other, because accuracy to a particular era was not the goal. To get an authentic view of history, please consult non-fiction sources.

PROLOGUE

The Hunduns were coming. A whole herd of them, rumbling across the wilds, stirring up a dark storm of dust through the night. Their rotund, faceless bodies, made of spirit metal, glinted under the silver half-moon and sky full of glittering stars.

A lesser pilot would have had to fight off nerves to go meet them in battle, but Yang Guang wasn't fazed. At the foot of his watchtower just outside the Great Wall, he compelled his Chrysalis, the Nine-Tailed Fox, to launch into action. It was as tall as a seven- or eight-story building and bristly green. Its metallic claws pounded across the earth, shaking it.

A Chrysalis was no ordinary war machine. Yang Guang didn't maneuver it with steering wheels or levers, like he would an electric carriage or a hovercraft. No, he *became* it. While his mortal body sat dormant in the cockpit, its arms around the concubine-pilot he'd taken to battle tonight, his mind psychically commanded every part of the Nine-Tailed Fox, making it pounce toward the incoming herd on the horizon. Far out on

either side of him, the silhouettes of other active-duty Chrysalises raced forth as well.

Through hair-thin acupuncture needles along his pilot seat
that bit into his spine, Yang Guang channeled his qi, his life
force, to power the Fox. Qi was the vital essence that sustained
everything in the world, from the sprouting of leaves to the blazing of flames to the turning of the planet. Not only did he draw
on his own, he reached across the Chrysalis's psychic link and
sapped up his concubine-pilot's as well. Her mind wasn't strong
enough to put up any resistance as he did so; it was lost deep
inside his. Pieces of her memories flurried through him, but he
did his best to ignore them. It was best not to know too much
about his concubines. The only thing he needed was the inter-
action of her qi with his own, which multiplied his spirit pressure,
making it possible for him to command a Chrysalis so large.

Trickles of common-class Hunduns reached Yang Guang
first, like oversized metal bugs eager to burrow into the Fox
and kill him. Their various colors were dull under the starlight.
But some lit up, shooting weaponized qi out of their bodies in
luminous blasts or crackling bolts. If Yang Guang had faced
them as a human, they'd have loomed as big as houses and
vaporized him instantly, but when he piloted the Fox, they
were too small to hurt him. As he smashed them with the Fox's
claws, bursts of foreign emotion shot through him—grief and
terror and rage, as riotous as static. He didn't know how exactly
Chrysalises were made from Hundun husks—only the highest-
level engineers were allowed to know—but even centuries of
improving their craft hadn't vanquished the kink that made
pilots feel whatever the Hunduns felt when they pierced a
Hundun's hull.

Pilots didn't talk much about this in public, but resisting these
distracting emotions was a surprisingly rigorous part of battle.

Yang Guang was one of the most powerful pilots alive precisely because he could detach from them so well. Powering through the mental onslaught, he kept pummeling the Hunduns. The Fox's nine tails swished and creaked behind him like nine new limbs, slapping larger Hunduns away with resonant clangs.

Yang Guang had no pity for them. The Hunduns were invaders from the cosmos who'd pulverized the height of human civilization some two thousand years ago and shattered humanity into scattered tribes. If it hadn't been for the Yellow Sovereign, a legendary tribal leader who'd invented Chrysalis crafting with help from the gods, civilization would never have recovered, and the planet would have belonged to the Hunduns by now.

Camera drones whizzed around the Fox like red-eyed flies. Some of them belonged to the Human Liberation Army; others were from private media companies, broadcasting the battle to all of Huaxia. Yang Guang stayed hyper-vigilant, not letting himself make a mistake, lest he disappoint his fans.

"Nine-Tailed Fox, there's a Prince class in the herd!" an army strategist shouted through the speakers in the Fox's cockpit.

Yang Guang jerked alert. A Prince-class Hundun was a rare opponent, the same weight class as the Fox. If he took it out with minimal damage, it could be made into a new Prince-class Chrysalis, or be offered to the gods in exchange for some major gifts, such as manuals for ground-breaking technology or medicine. And the win would give a massive boost to his battle rank. Maybe he'd finally shoot past Li Shimin, that convicted murderer who did not deserve to be Huaxia's top pilot.

For a clean shot, Yang Guang would have to shift the Fox into a more complex form.

"Xing Tian, cover me!" he called to his closest comrade through the Fox's mouth, his qi broadcasting his voice across the battlefield. "I'm going to transform!"

"Got it, Colonel!" Xing Tian yelled from the Headless Warrior, a Chrysalis with shining yellow eyes where its nipples should've been and a mouth glowing on its gut. It stomped in front of the Fox, battering the swarming Hunduns with a giant spirit-metal ax. They died in splatters of light.

Assured, Yang Guang propelled his qi through the Fox with the most forceful spirit pressure he could generate. Radiant cracks fissured across the Fox's bristly green surface.

Chrysalises might have been constructed from Hundun husks, but they were superior in every way. The Hunduns were so mindless, they couldn't unlock the potential of the very spirit metal they were made of to become anything other than rotund blobs.

But humans could.

Yang Guang imagined the Fox's Ascended Form, and it morphed into being. The Fox's limbs thinned and lengthened, its waist drew in, and its shoulders rolled back, making it slightly more humanoid. Its nine tails became as sharp as lances, and they fanned out from the base of its back like sun rays, the way real nine-tailed foxes perked their tails up to intimidate enemies. He raised the Fox upright; with his qi conducting at a higher spirit pressure, he had enough control and finesse to balance it on two legs. That set the Fox's front claws free to fight with a weapon.

With an over-the-shoulder reach, Yang Guang fused a claw around one of the Fox's tail lances and snapped it from its back. He barreled through the roiling herd of differently sized Hunduns until he spotted the Prince class, then he sank low and leapt from the ground. The lance arced through the night, hurling a gleam of moonlight, before piercing the Hundun's round body, featureless except for its six tiny bug-like legs. Spirit metal shattered with a spectacular sound, like a whole warehouse of porcelain exploding. Yang Guang braced against the flood of the Hundun's rage and dread as the light of its qi-filled core sputtered and dimmed.

The other Chrysalises fending off the sea of glinting Hunduns hooted in delight. Camera drones closed in on the Prince-class husk, and Yang Guang could imagine commoners cheering across Huaxia behind their screens. Exhilaration thrilling him, he bounced backward in the Fox, scraping the lance out of the Hundun. However, even after he removed contact, a foreign fear lingered in his mind.

It came from his concubine now, cresting through him like a wave.

This was the point where he always knew a concubine's mind would not make it back to her own body. He was now sub-consciously controlling everything about her, down to her heartbeat. The moment he disconnected, there'd be nothing left to keep her heart pumping, and she'd pass into the beyond. There was no way around it.

The important thing was that her family would receive a nice compensation. Her soul would rest well in the Yellow Springs, knowing that.

He didn't remember her name. He'd tried not to. He went through so many concubine-pilots that it would be a paralyzing distraction to keep track of them. And he couldn't afford to be distracted. He had a world to protect.

She had known what she'd be getting into. She had made the decision to enlist for him.

Yang Guang focused on crushing and spearing the rest of the herd, reassuring his fans that their homeland would continue to be safe.

The concubine's noble sacrifice would not be in vain.

PART I

WAY OF THE FOX

There is a kind of creature in the mountain,
with the look of a fox with nine tails, whose sound
is like an infant's cry. It feasts on human flesh.
—*Classic of Mountains and Seas (山海经)*

CHAPTER ONE

A BUTTERFLY THAT
BETTER NOT BE MY DEAD SISTER

For eighteen years, my unibrow has saved me from being sold into a painful, terrifying death.

Today is the day I'm releasing it from its gracious service.

Well, *I'm* not doing it. Yizhi is the one manning the tweezers my sister left behind. Kneeling on the bamboo mat spread beneath us over the damp forest soil, he lifts my chin while ripping out bristle after bristle. My skin burns as if it's slowly incinerating. The ink-black rivulets of his half-up hair swish over his pale silk robes as he plucks. My own hair, way more matted and parched than his, sits in a messy bun under a tattered rag. Though the rag smells like grease, it keeps the stray strands out of my face.

I've been trying to act nonchalant. But I make the mistake of gazing at Yizhi's gentle, focused features for too long, wanting to inscribe them in my mind so I'll have something to hold on to in the last days of my life. My stomach twists, and hot pressure surges into my eyes. Attempting to squint the tears back only breaks them free down the sides of my nose—seriously, that never works.

Of course, Yizhi notices. Stops everything to check what's wrong, even though he has no reason to believe it's anything more than a reaction to the assault on my pores.

Even though he has no idea this is the last time we'll see each other.

"You all right, Zetian?" he whispers, tweezing hand suspended in a gossamer swirl of humidity from the waterfall not far from our hiding place. The rushing creek beside the low-growing trees we're huddling under drowns his voice from anyone who might discover us.

"I sure won't be if you keep taking breaks." I roll my swollen eyes. "Come on. Just let me power through."

"Right. Okay." His frown twitches into a smile that almost breaks me. He dries my eyes with his fancy silk robe sleeves, then gathers them back near his elbows. They're rich-people sleeves, too long and floppy to be practical. I make fun of them every time he visits. Though, to be fair, it's not his fault his father doesn't let him and his twenty-seven siblings leave their estate in anything not luxury-branded.

Lucid sunlight, freshly broken after days of rain, streams down in shafts through our secret world of damp heat and swaying leaves. A patchwork of light and shadow dapples his pale forearms. The bursting green scent of springtime presses against us, rich enough to taste. His knees—he even sits in a prim and proper kneel—keep a tiny yet insurmountable distance from my carelessly folded legs. His designer silk robes contrast absurdly with the weathered roughness of my homespun tunic and trousers. Until I met him, I had no idea fabric could be that white or smooth.

He plucks faster. It really does hurt, like my brow is a living creature being frayed bit by bit into two, so if I tear up again, it shouldn't be suspicious.

I wish I didn't have to involve him in this, but I know that, past a certain point, it would be too painful to face my reflection and do it myself. All I would see is my big sister, Ruyi. Without the overgrown hairs that have kept my market value low, I'll look so much like she did.

Plus, I don't trust myself to landscape two matching brows out of the entity I've got. And how am I supposed to sign up for my death if my eyebrows are uneven?

I distract myself from the scalding ache by scrolling on the luminous tablet in Yizhi's lap, reading the notes he's taken in school since he visited me last month. Each tap feels more scandalous than being alone with him on a frontier mountain, shrouded by greenery and spring heat, breathing the same thick eddies of earthy, intoxicating air. My village elders say girls shouldn't touch these heavenly devices, because we would desecrate them with, I don't know, our wicked femaleness or something. Only thanks to the gods in the sky was technology like these tablets reconstructed after humanity's lost age of cowering from the Hunduns. But I don't care how indebted I am to the elders or the gods. If they don't respect me just because I'm from the "wrong" half of the population, I'm not respecting them back.

The screen glows like the moon against Yizhi's leaf-shadowed robes, enticing me with knowledge I'm not supposed to have, knowledge from beyond my measly mountain village. Arts. Sciences. Hunduns. Chrysalises. My fingers itch to bring the tablet closer, though neither it nor I can move—a cone of neon light is spilling from an indent on the device, projecting the mathematically ideal brows for me onto my face. Yizhi and his dazzling city gadgets never disappoint. He whipped this up mere minutes after I lied about my family giving me a "final warning" regarding the unibrow.

I wonder how much he'll hate me after he finds out what he's really helping me do.

A droplet shivers out of the branches over our heads. It skims his cheek. He's so engrossed he doesn't notice. With a curled knuckle, I brush away the wet dash on his face.

His eyes startle wide. Color blooms into his pampered, almost translucent skin.

I can't help but grin. Turning my hand to touch him with the pads of my fingers instead, I wink. "Oh, my. Are my new eyebrows already irresistible?"

Yizhi breaks into a louder than usual laugh, then smacks his fingers over his mouth and glances around, even though we're decently hidden.

"Stop it," he says, quieter, laughter turning feather-light. He ducks away from my gaze. "Let me work."

The rising, undeniable heat in his cheeks singes me with a flash of guilt.

Tell him, my mind pleads.

But I just drop my hand as casually as possible and flick to a new section in his school notes, a social studies topic about the statistical dynamics of Hundun attacks.

Why should I endanger my mission by telling him? However Yizhi sees this relationship we have, I've never made the mistake of taking it too seriously. He's the son of literally the richest man in Huaxia, and I'm a random frontier girl he met by chance while getting some peace and quiet in the farthest place he could go on his hovercycle. If someone caught us together, he's not the one who'd get stuffed into a pig cage and drowned in the name of his family's honor. No matter that we've never crossed any lines we shouldn't.

My attention drifts to his lips, straying over their delicate curves, and I'm brought back to the time I marveled out loud about how soft they look. He admitted it's thanks to a four-step exfoliation and moisturizing routine, and I laughed so hard there were tears in my eyes as I touched his lips, and then I wasn't laughing anymore, just staring into his eyes, too close to him.

Then I immediately drew back and changed the topic.

A raw, tender part of me aches at what I will never have with him, but I have not and cannot rule out the possibility that this is nothing but a game to him. That I'm not the only peasant girl he visits on his break days. That the moment after I give in, he'd fasten the silk sash of his impeccable robes and laugh in my face, laugh about how something could mean so little to him but be life or death to me, yet I could still be hypnotized into it by his soft smiles and whispered words.

Maybe my caution is what's made this all the more thrilling, what's made him show up at the end of every month for the last three years.

I can never know his true motives. Which is fine. As long as I do not give in to my emotions, I cannot lose any game that might be being played.

Though, realistically, even if my entire village stumbled upon us this very second, my family wouldn't drown me now. I'm finally doing what they want: prettying myself so they can sell me to the army as a concubine-pilot. Just like they did my sister.

Obviously, they don't know about my bigger, deadlier plans.

As Yizhi moves on to the undersides of my brows, my finger lingers over a picture of a Hundun-Chrysalis battle in his class notes. The Chrysalis, the White Tiger, is so shapely and vivid in color that you'd never guess it was once a round, featureless Hundun husk. Pictured in its Heroic Form, its highest transformation, it looks like a humanoid tiger warrior made of smooth, milky glass. Its armor-like pieces are edged with radiant green and black lines, the colors blurring with motion as it raises a dagger-ax taller than a tree. It's a favorite of the army to use in promos, and I actually feel comfortable looking at it. The boy-girl pair mentally connected to it are a Balanced Match. There's little risk of the boy's mind consuming the girl's and killing her once the battle ends.

Unlike the female pilot in most other cases.

That's the way I feared Big Sister would die when our family forced her to enlist under a Prince-class pilot, the second most powerful rank. But she never made it to the battlefield. The pilot killed her the traditional, physical way. For what, I don't know. Our family only got her ashes back. They've been devastated for eighty-one days now . . . because they didn't get the big war death compensation they were banking on.

It's funny. Big Sister spent her whole life being *cared* about.

When is Ruyi getting married?

Is Ruyi going to enlist instead?

My, has Ruyi been sitting in the sun too much? She's getting a little dark.

But the moment news of her death spread, no one brought her up again. No one even asked what I did with her ashes. Only Yizhi and I know she's been carried off by the creek beside us. A little secret between him, me, and her.

I lift my eyes to an actual butterfly chrysalis dangling on a branch behind Yizhi. The Chrysalises were named after those, so the saying goes that dead pilots reincarnate into butterflies. If that's true, I sure hope this one isn't my sister. I hope she's gone far, far away from here, somewhere that can't be reached by condemning village elders or nosy gossipers or greedy relatives or scumbag pilots.

A nascent butterfly has been squirming in the chrysalis for a while now, detaching from the surface layer. Now, finally, it's ruptured the membrane. Its head emerges upside-down. Antennae pop out, wiggling. In a grand finale, it wholly unravels from the chrysalis like a blossoming flower.

Butterflies are common in these woods, so this isn't that special a sight.

Except, when this butterfly shakes out its wings, the patterns don't match.

"Whoa." I sit up straighter.

"What is it?" Yizhi looks over his shoulder.

"That butterfly has two different wings!"

Yizhi also makes a noise of surprise, which means this isn't some typical phenomenon I didn't know about because I'm a frontier peasant. He tells me my brows are pretty much done, then raises his tablet to take a magnified video of the butterfly.

Our eyes didn't trick us. One wing is black with a white dot, and the other is white with a black dot—like the yin-yang symbol. These butterflies were named after exactly that, but I've never seen one with both yin and yang wings.

"How did this happen?" I gawk.

Yizhi's smile widens. "You know what to do when you've got questions."

"'Search it up.' Got it." I open the search engine on Yizhi's tablet like he taught me. It's not hard to use—I just have to enter the keywords of my question—but it's surreal and daunting, using just a few taps to access all the knowledge the scholars in the cities have reconstructed from the cryptic manuals the gods drop down whenever we offer enough tribute.

I squint in concentration at the academic writing in the search results. It's way harder to read than Yizhi's class notes, but I'm determined to sort them out on my own. "Apparently having different wings means a butterfly is . . . both male and female." My frown springs loose. I gape at the sentence. "That can happen?"

"Oh, yeah, biological sex has all sorts of variations in nature." Yizhi crawls beside me on the bamboo mat, gathering his robes away from the gray dirt beneath. "There are even creatures that can switch sex depending on their needs."

"But I thought . . ." I blink fast. "I thought females are female because their primordial qi is yin-based, and males are male because their primordial qi is yang-based."

Yin and yang represent the opposing forces that churn the universe into life. Yin is everything cold, dark, slow, passive, and feminine. Yang is everything hot, bright, fast, active, and masculine.

Or so my mother told me.

Yizhi shrugs. "Nothing's ever that rigid, I guess. There's always some yin in yang, and some yang in yin. It's right on the symbol. Now that I think about it, I'm pretty sure there are even cases where humans are born like this butterfly, where you can't really pin down which sex they are."

My eyes widen further. "Which seat would those people take if they became pilots?"

Every Chrysalis has the same seating arrangement. Girls go in the lower yin seat, while boys go in the slightly higher yang seat behind them, wrapping their arms around the girls.

Yizhi taps the bamboo mat. His fine brows knit in thought. "Whichever gender they're closer to?"

"What does that even mean? At what point would a seat stop working for them?" I balk. "What is it about gender that matters so much to the system, anyway? Isn't piloting entirely a mental thing? So why is it always the girls that have to be sacrificed for power?"

"I . . . I don't know."

I try to search for a legitimate answer to this, but I'm met with a red warning box.

WARNING: INSUFFICIENT PERMISSION
RESULTS RESTRICTED

"Oh, you can't search anything related to Chrysalis crafting. They can't have people building rogue units." Yizhi takes over the tablet.

I let him slide it out of my hands. I stare hard at the butterfly with both yin and yang wings.

Female. That label has never done anything for me except dictate what I can or cannot do. No going anywhere without permission. No showing too much skin. No speaking too loudly or unkindly, or at all, if the men are talking. No living my life without being constantly aware of how pleasing I am to the eye. No future except pushing out son after son for a husband, or dying in a Chrysalis to give some boy the power to reach for glory.

It's as if I've got a cocoon shriveled too tightly around my whole being. If I had my way, I'd exist like that butterfly, giving onlookers no easy way to bind me with a simple label.

"Yizhi, do you believe girls are naturally predisposed to sacrificing themselves?" I mutter.

"Well, that can't possibly be true, because you're a girl, and there's no way you would ever do that."

"Hey!" A laugh ruptures out of my gloom.

"What? Where's the lie?" He stamps his hands on his hips, sleeves flopping.

"Okay, fine! There's no lie." I strain back a grin.

Then the curl of my mouth fades.

I wouldn't live and suffer for anyone else, but I would die to avenge my sister.

Yizhi smiles, oblivious. "Honestly, though, there's nothing wrong with cherishing your life. With fighting for what you want. I find it admirable."

"Wow." I snort half-heartedly. "Are my eyebrows really that bewitching now?"

Yizhi laughs. "I'm not brave enough to lie to you, so I'll have to admit—you do look much prettier in the conventional way." His smile softens. His eyes brighten in the patchy shade like night ponds reflecting the stars. "You're still the Zetian I know, though. I think you're the most stunning girl in the world, no matter what you look like."

My heart clenches, cracking.

I can't do this. I can't leave without telling him the truth.

"Yizhi," I say in a voice as dark as smoke.

"Sorry, was I—? Oh, no. Was that too weird?" A chuckle shakes out of him. "On a scale of 'one' to 'middle-aged man asking you to put on a smile for him,' how uncomfortable did that make you?"

"*Yizhi.*" I grab his hands, as if that could brace him for what's coming.

He falls silent, peering in confusion at our clasped hands.

I say it. "I'm enlisting as a concubine-pilot."

His jaw slackens. "For which pilot?"

I open my mouth, but I can't spit out that bastard's name. "For *him.*"

He searches my eyes. "For *Yang Guang?*"

I nod, all warmth gone from my face.

"Zetian, he killed your sister!"

"That's why I'm going." I fling Yizhi's hands away and slide a long wooden hairpin out of my rag-wrapped hair bun. "I'm going to be his beautiful, sultry concubine. And then—" I yank the hairpin apart, revealing the sharp point within, "I'm going to rip his throat open in his sleep."

CHAPTER TWO

LIKE WATER HURLED
OUT THE DOOR

I stagger through the mountain paths with my bamboo cane, alone. A lattice of forest shadows crawls over me, sliced up by blades of scarlet twilight. If I don't get home before the sun drops beyond the western peaks, my family will think this is my latest escape attempt. The whole village will start combing the mountains with flashlights and barking dogs. They can't have their own daughters thinking it's possible to run away.

Soggy leaves turn to mush under my tiny, battered shoes, which Yizhi has offered to replace countless times. But I could never accept his gifts, for fear of my family finding out about him. A lump swells in my throat at the memory of his horrified expression after learning of my self-imposed mission, and the broken way he called my name after I vanished into the woods to abandon the conversation. I shouldn't have told him. There was no way he wouldn't try to stop me.

Now that awful moment is the last we'll have of each other.

I'm not sure if I heard the whir of his hovercycle over the treetops, but I hope he's left the mountains. He can't change anything. He doesn't own me. Nobody does. They may think they do, but no matter how they scold or threaten or beat me, they can't really control what goes on in my head, and I think that frustrates them to no end.

A bloody haze of sunset gapes at the end of the forest path. When the shadows release me, my view opens to the rice terraces I grew up in, whole mountainsides carved like stairways soaring for the skies. Trenches of collected rainwater gleam on each tier, nourishing rice seedlings and mirroring the scorching sky. Fevered clouds drift across every wedge of water as I make my way between them. My cane squelches over platforms of gray mud. Smoke from roasting dinners rises from the clusters of houses nestled in the terraces. The plumes weave into the orange, dusk-tinged mist swirling around the highest summits.

In the skin-cracking winter when I was five, when the cold pressed in so ruthlessly that the rice terraces froze solid, my grandmother forced me to walk over the ice with no shoes. After the cold crystallized deep into my flesh, turning it purple, she shooed all the men out of our house, sat me down on the frosted concrete ground, and soaked my feet in a wooden basin of boiled pig's blood and numbing medicine. Then two of my aunts held me down against the floor as my grandmother broke every bone along the arches of my feet to crush them in half.

The force of the scream that tore out of me still flashes through my memories when I least expect it, always stunning me in the middle of whatever I'm doing.

That's not the case for the pain, though. The pain can't surprise me because it has never left. A lightning strike of it shoots up my legs with every step I take.

Every. Single. Step.

I don't walk. That burning tread over the frozen rice terrace was the last time I walked. Ever since then, my feet have been bound into bulging, misshapen mounds that can only *totter*. Three toes have fallen off from infections that nearly took my life, ruining my balance for good. The other toes wrap around the bottoms of my feet, clutching the other side near the heels, as if trying to squeeze the mess of bones and flesh back up my legs. My soles are smaller than my palms. A pair of perfect lotus feet.

It really boosts my market value.

My family has scolded me endlessly for letting my facial hair grow rampant and having too much fat around my waist, but I face the worst lashings and screamed insults when I rebel against the tightness of my foot bindings. Hairy brows can be plucked, weight can be starved off, but lotus feet stop being lotus feet once they're allowed to grow. And no man from a respectable family would marry a girl without bound feet.

"Without them, we'd be no different from the Rongdi!" my grandmother once yelled while I shrieked and sobbed about going through with the ritual. She was referring to the tribes that largely roam the untamed wilds with a pack-everything-on-horseback-and-run strategy of evading the Hunduns. Some were incorporated into Huaxia when we pushed the Hunduns out of whole chunks of territory; others from further out have been sneaking through the Great Wall in small, persistent trickles. Living on the frontier, we have plenty as neighbors. My family has always cautioned me against being like their women, who "run all over the place with no morals, shame, or decency."

When I was little, I used to buy into this fear of becoming *those women*. But the older I got, the more confused I became about what's so bad about them.

When I pass under a cluster of houses higher on the terraced mountainside, a few men knee-deep in the terraces lurch up from their work and ogle as I waddle by. They wouldn't dare come after me—everyone knows everyone around here—but they never fail to make their desires clear.

See, when every frontier daughter who's remotely decent-looking either enlists as a concubine-pilot or gets sold to richer men in the cities, the frontier men start having serious issues finding wives to bear their sons. The bride prices have soared up to tens of thousands of yuan, impossible for families here to afford . . . unless they enlist their own daughters or sell them to rich city men.

It's a mess of a cycle, and not ending any time soon. No one stays on the frontier unless they have to. Most of us are here only because our original ancestral home, the Zhou province, fell to the Hunduns two hundred and twenty-one years ago.

I throw the men my most hateful glower. The terrace pools blaze like molten copper under the sunset, and I fantasize about real heat building up in them, boiling the men alive.

Then my cane snaps, and I tumble.

Gravity. One of the first scientific concepts I learned from Yizhi. It snatches me toward the mud path and almost into a rice paddy. The heel of my hand scrapes a harsh dent in the mud. Cold density smacks into my nose and cheek.

I push onto both arms. Gray filth plops from my heating face and latches to my tunic. I brace myself for howling laughter.

It doesn't come.

The men are splashing through the terraces instead, hollering excitedly, crowding around someone holding a tablet.

A quiver ripples through my confusion.

A quiver in the terrace waters, specifically.

My breath hitches. Unmistakable vibrations are traveling through the ground, stirring the water.

A Hundun-Chrysalis battle is starting beyond the frontier.

I press my ear to the earth, not caring that it's dirtying me further and dampening the rag tied around my hair. The Great Wall is only a few mountains away. On clear days, we can see the dusty, lifeless peaks that have been sucked dry of qi by the Chrysalises stationed along it.

The men must be watching a livestream and betting on the number of battle points each pilot will achieve. But it's so much more raw and visceral and stunning, sensing the physical force of the Chrysalises through the planet.

What power.

My throat goes dry, yet my mouth waters. I close my eyes, picturing myself taking command of a Chrysalis, towering over buildings and smashing the earth with my colossal limbs or luminous qi blasts. I could crush anyone who's ever tried to crush me. I could free all the girls who'd love to run away.

A whooping cheer from the men fractures my daydream.

I rattle my head. Flecks of dirt fly onto my sleeves. I crawl onto my knees, covered in filth, staring at my broken cane.

I should really stop with the delusions.

I don't know if my father will count me as having reached the house before my curfew. Some last dregs of sun line our fortress of mountains with a ghostly blue halo, silhouetting them into colossal shadows that look eerily like Hunduns.

"Where were you?" My mother breathes through the barred window of the kitchen shack on the side of our house. Her voice is as frail as the steam sighing from the large wok of porridge she's stirring. My grandmother sits on a stool behind her, descaling a *luoyu*, a winged fish, from the terrace waters. Firelight from the hearth flares across their weathered faces, as if they're trapped inside a blazing dungeon.

"Was in the woods." I pass my mother a pouch of herbs and starch roots through the window. Gathering these are why I spend so much time in the forest, and how I first met Yizhi.

"What happened?" My mother puts the pouch on a wooden shelf without looking away from my grimy state. Gray hairs stray out of the faded rag tied over her head, fluttering in the visible ripples of heat.

"Took a tumble. Broke my cane." I resume teetering over the stone walkway that lines the row of houses. I land my feet gingerly, trying not to plummet onto the clay-tiled roof of our neighbors one tier down.

"You're lucky a battle started." My mother darts a look at the main entrance to the house, up ahead. Her eyes glisten orange from the crackling hearth flames. "Go quickly. Don't let your father see you like this."

"Right."

"And scrub those clothes clean tomorrow. You can't look like that when the army comes."

A stab goes through my chest at the casual way she mentions that. She might have no idea about my true intentions, but she must be aware that my enlistment will end in my death, no matter what.

She must remember how it ended for Big Sister.

Or does she? Sometimes, my mother's so good at pretending nothing's wrong that it scares me into suspecting *I'm* the one with the head full of false memories.

"I'm sure they'll give me better clothes." I stare at the bars of light dithering out of the kitchen window.

"But you still have to look presentable."

I stop waddling and turn at the waist to face her dead-on.

There's one big consequence to my assassination plans that I've done my best to ignore: killing an Iron Noble, a pilot with a maximum spirit pressure of over 2000—when the human average is 84—would implicate three generations of my family. My mother, my father, my seventeen-year-old brother Dalang, my grandparents, my aunts, my uncles. They would all be executed along with me. Because pilots like Yang Guang are just too important to the war effort.

Give me one reason to protect you. I gawk at my mother. *Stop me.*

All I need is one sign that they're worth my mercy. One sign that they value my life as much as I'm expected to value theirs.

Since there's no point holding back now, I spew my most burning thought out loud. "Are you honestly more worried about me looking presentable than me going off to war?"

The fire cracks and pops beside my mother. She squints at me through the woodsmoke and fragrant steam. Then a smile blooms across her face like a wildflower in a burning wasteland. "Your brows—you listened. You look beautiful."

I whip my head away and trudge on, no matter that every step is like stomping on a live wire.

It's like she didn't even hear what I said.

Electric lanterns blink on across the village, lighting up windows like the glowing eyes that Chrysalises have but Hunduns don't. A breeze sweeps through the rice terraces, swirling a reedy musk into the roasting scent of humble dinners.

Wheat-colored light spills out of the open main doors of my house. A battle commentator's tinny shouts punch into the falling night, blasting from the tablet granted to our family by the Huaxia government (though, of course, only the males can use it freely). My grandfather, father, and brother have propped it on our grease-blackened dining table. Their eyes bulge at the screen, reflecting the flashing colors of Hunduns and Chrysalises clashing.

I take the chance to step over the house threshold. I hurry toward the room I've been forced to share with my grandparents since my second attempt at sneaking away during the night, years ago.

"—*and here comes the Vermilion Bird!*"

I halt, almost toppling over. My blood runs cold.

Oh, not *that* unit.

Even my Chrysalis-obsessed family, which usually cheers at every big-name unit, remains uncomfortably silent. Nobody wants to acknowledge that the Vermilion Bird is the strongest Chrysalis in Huaxia right now. At over fifty meters tall in its Standard Form, it's the only King class we have. But it's piloted by Li Shimin, the Iron Demon, a half-Rongdi death-row inmate who murdered his own father and both brothers at just sixteen. He's nineteen now. His execution has been indefinitely delayed only because of his freakishly high spirit pressure, the highest in two centuries.

While concubine-pilots are always in danger of dying in battle, only when it comes to him is death so certain.

No one has ever survived a ride with him.

A girl will die soon.

"Hey!"

My father startles me out of my thoughts. I jump, clutching the wooden walls.

His chair screeches back on the concrete floor. He rises, shadows sliding over his frown lines. "Why do you look so dirty?"

Icy sweat beads under the edge of my hair rag. "I fell on the terraces."

Not a lie, for once.

The clashing of spirit metal and qi blasts ring on in the livestream. My grandfather and brother keep watching, as if nothing is wrong. My father steps around them and stalks toward me. His topknot, tragically loose due to his thinning hair, flops against his head.

"You better not have been fooling around with a *boy*."

"Of course not." I back away, shoulder hitting the door of my grandparents' room.

Half a lie. I was breaking one's heart instead.

My father charges closer. His looming figure doubles in my view. "You better be able to pass the maidenhood test when—"

That one jolting word makes me forget how to fear him.

"For the last time, *nothing's ever been up inside me*!" I scream. "Stop being so obsessed!"

He blanks out in shock, but I can feel the utter fury that's coming.

I slip through the bedroom door and slam it in his face.

"What did you just say to me?" His shout shudders through the house, and his fists thunder against the door. The brass handle jangles so hard it sounds like something broke inside.

"Unwrapping my feet!" I jam my back against the door while acting on the threat. Unwrapped feet are more indecent than naked breasts. Not to mention the rotting flesh smell, which is possibly its own class of biological weapon. Girls are supposed to maintain the fantasy of their dainty prettiness by always wearing perfumed, embroidered shoes and never removing the bindings in front of anyone, not even their husbands.

My father's fists leave the door, but his lungs bellow on. *Disrespectful. Ungrateful. Whore.*

The typical.

My mother's mist-frail voice emerges, trying to calm him down. My brother is laughing. My grandfather has turned the livestream to peak volume. A girl is dying in a Chrysalis in the name of mankind.

I don't risk leaving the bedroom for dinner.

My stomach rumbles, bubbling like the porridge it wants, but I stay in the woven wicker chair my grandmother knits in, soaking my feet in the same wooden bucket that prepared them for being crushed.

See, this is why it doesn't matter if you implicate them, the rotten, putrid core of me drawls from deep inside my head.

I uncork the wooden plug on one of the tall thermoses my grandparents keep in the room.

They don't care about you.

I pour another steaming stream into the bucket. Medicinal leaves and roots scramble wildly in the flow, steeping the water maroon, like blood forgotten in a dark corner.

You don't need to care about them.

A lantern buzzes above me. Shadows shift in the room's grimy corners, seeming to creep closer. I set the thermos down and stare blankly at the straw I sleep on, right beside my grandparents' bed. There's a saying in Huaxia: a daughter married off is like water hurled out the door. Unlike my brother Dalang, who will pass on the Wu family name and stay in the house for life to take care of our parents, I was born to have a transient existence in my family's lives, something to set a price on and trade off. They never bothered to give me my own bed.

The clatter of chopsticks on bowls and the babble of Dalang

raving about the battle come muffled through the walls. The Chrysalises won. Of course. If they hadn't, breach sirens would've gone off from the village speakers, and we'd be scrambling east, just like our ancestors did from the Zhou province.

No one else says much. I hope they're thinking of me.

I hope they go to their graves regretting the way they treated me and Big Sister.

People sentenced to familial extermination don't get to have graves.

I wince, shoving away the image of our rotting corpses dangling off the Great Wall.

The door opens. I flinch against the chair, not knowing where to look, hoping my eyes aren't as red and swollen as they feel.

My mother totters to me on her own bound feet, offering me a bowl of porridge. I take the bowl with an awkward nod. My cold fingers wrap around the hot porcelain. A bitterness like tears floods my mouth. My mother sits down beside me, on the foot of my grandparents' bed. Tension coils tight in my belly.

What does she want? part of me snaps, while another part goes, *Stop me.*

"Tian-Tian." She starts with my baby name, picking at some old burns on her hands. "You shouldn't have talked to your father like that."

"He was being weird first." I glare at her, though a stifling shame heats my cheeks. I tip the bowl of porridge to my mouth to hide my face.

Stop me, thumps my heavy heartbeat. *Stop me. Stop me.*

My mother only gives a sad frown. "Must you always make things so difficult?"

I grip the bowl tighter. "Mama, do you honestly feel like your life has been *easy* because you always give in?"

"It's not about having it easy. It's about keeping peace in the family."

I laugh against the bowl, the sound hardening with a dark edge. "Tell him to not worry. I'm only here for two more days. Then he can have all the peace he wants."

My mother sighs. "Tian-Tian, your father just feels emotions very strongly. Deep down, he knows that you've matured after all. That you've understood what really matters. He's proud of you." She smiles. "*I'm* proud of you."

I raise my head stiffly. "You're proud of me for sending myself off to death?"

"You don't know if that'll happen." She evades my eyes. "You've always had a strong mind. Didn't the testing team say your spirit pressure might be over five hundred? Six times the average! And that was four years ago. It must be even higher now. You and Prince-Colonel Yang could turn out to be a Balanced Match. You could be his Iron Princess."

"There are only three Iron Princesses in all of Huaxia!" Tears tumble from my eyes, hazing my view of her. "And their spirit pressures are in the thousands! It's just a low-odds fantasy that gives girls delusions of surviving!"

"Tian-Tian, don't be so loud." My mother darts a panicked glance at the door.

"Is it a fantasy that comforts you, too?" I go on. "Does it help you sleep at night?"

Her eyes glisten. "Why can't you accept that you're doing a good thing? You're going to be a hero. And with the money, Dalang could pay the bride price for a—"

I smash the bowl to the ground. The porcelain shatters, and porridge escapes in a slimy, steaming burst.

"Tian-Tian!" My mother stumbles to her feet. "Your grand-parents sleep here!"

"Yeah? And what are they going to do?" I yell pointedly at the door. "Beat me, so I can turn Yang Guang off with my fresh wounds? Make me sleep in the pigsty, so I can turn him off with my smell? If you all want the money so bad, you can't do anything to me anymore!"

"Tian—"

"Get out!"

You can't speak to her like this, a voice in my head chides, sounding achingly like Big Sister. *She's your mother. The woman who gave you life.*

But a mother who has failed me so thoroughly is no mother of mine.

My chest heaves. I lean forward, hands clutching my knees. My voice squeezes out around a hard sob in my throat. "In the next life, I hope we have nothing to do with each other."

CHAPTER THREE

THE LIFE YOU WANT

The next time anyone in my family willingly utters a word to me, it's them shrieking my name the morning of my enlistment.

I lurch up from my straw bed, where I've been festering with a twisted stomach all night, turning my wooden hairpin over and over and over in my hand like a thick chopstick.

A hovercraft is supposed to take me to the Great Wall. Did they see it in the distance or something?

"Tian-Tian!" My grandmother's voice floats closer to the door. "There's a *boy* here!"

I falter while getting up. My hand brakes against my grandparents' bed frame.

A boy . . .

No. *No*, it can't be—

I totter to the door in a daze. A dangerous anticipation hovers alarm-red in my chest. My thumping heartbeat travels from my palm and into the door as I push it open.

Brightness stings my eyes. Then, when the spots wash away,

there he is. Yizhi. Standing in the blazing sunlight beyond the front entrance, pleading with my family, who cower like cave creatures in the shadows of our house. His white silk robes, embroidered with golden patterns of bamboo shoots and leaves, practically glow like an otherworldly material.

I have never seen him outside the mottled shadows of forest cover. For an instant, I'm disoriented—is it really him? But the gentle tenor of his voice is unmistakable.

"Aunties, uncles, believe me, I can match any price." He shows my family the metal piece of his ID. "So, please. Let me marry your daughter."

My heart chokes like I've missed a step going down the stairs along the rice terraces.

Shock ripples through my family. Jaws drop. Hands fly to their lips. My grandmother, standing closest to me, swings a bewildered look between me and Yizhi. Transaction chimes must be going off like firecrackers in their heads at the sight of his family name and his address in the Huaxia capital, Chang'an.

They might actually forbid me from getting on the hover-craft.

I move without speaking or thinking. I shove through them, snatch Yizhi by the wrist, then tug him into the dimness of the house. His mouth parts in surprise. He almost trips over the threshold. But then his eyes meet mine and light up with an intensity that shoots a pang through my chest.

I drag him into my grandparents' room. Even his shoes don't sound the same when they scuff our dingy concrete floors.

"Don't come in," I warn my family before slamming the door, stirring a flurry of dust.

I turn to Yizhi. The slant of light from the window cuts over him like an ethereal blade, turning his robes lunar-white and his skin translucent.

"This is my house. My home." My voice shakes the silence. The image of him against the greasy wooden walls is so wrong that I'm not sure if I'm dreaming. "You were never, ever supposed to show up here—*how did you even find it?*"

"The official registries." He gulps, thick-lashed eyes wilting. "Zetian, I can take you to Chang'an."

"No, you can't!" I blurt, because my family is definitely eavesdropping. "That's just something you're saying. Your father would never let you marry me!"

"He's got fourteen more sons. He'll get over it."

"Really? Would he? Wouldn't he rather pair you up with the granddaughter of some high-up official? I doubt he became the richest man in Huaxia by missing opportunities!"

"Then we'll make our own opportunities. We can figure it out together. As long as there's life, there's hope." Yizhi lifts my fingers into the spill of window light. His words tremble like winter and fall like snow. "But any life I make will be meaningless without you."

Light shivers in my eyes. His face blurs over.

I know how to be hurt. I know how to take a beating, how to be insulted, how to be ground up and crumpled and thrown around like a piece of trash. But this?

This, I don't know how to handle.

It doesn't feel real.

It can't be real.

I'm not falling for it.

"Give me a break." I snatch my hand away. Hot tears scald from the corners of my eyes. A dry laugh cracks my voice. "Frontier peasant girl marries into the richest family in Huaxia? Can you be even a bit realistic? I'm not some four-year-old child you can swindle."

Yizhi's eyes gloss over. "Zetian . . ."

"Stop pretending like your family would let me be anything but a concubine." I back away with wobbling steps. "And that will never work. There'll be problems when I refuse to kowtow to your disgusting pig of a father. When I refuse to serve the proper wife you'll inevitably get arranged with. When I refuse to bear your son—because I am *never* letting anyone's spawn swell up my body and bind me forever, not even yours. And you will not be able to prevent any of this, because you are barely eighteen years old, and any semblance of money and power you have are based on your father's mercy. Now, you could bravely elope with me, and we could spend our lives as humble migrant workers in some small city, but because I never got to do what I wanted, I will be *miserable*. I'll be constantly thinking about how much more satisfying it would've been if I had *volunteered for my death* instead of going with you. Is that what you want? Is that the life you want, Gao Yizhi?"

My words snap off into an asphyxiating silence.

Yizhi looks at me like a beautiful immortal who's floated down from the Heavenly Court, only to stumble upon the concept of cannibalism.

Then it's not silent anymore.

A rumbling clatter picks up beyond the window. Great winds churn through the mountains, rustling the trees. Our pigs and chickens freak out in our backyard, oinking and clucking in their pens.

Now *that* must be the hovercraft.

I've heard this noise once before, when my sister was taken. I didn't realize it was meant for her until the hovercraft hovered directly over our house, its steel hull gleaming like white fire, and a soldier with a neat topknot and olive-green uniform dropped a rope ladder into our backyard. Everyone had kept it a secret from me. Including her. They'd known they wouldn't be able to predict what I'd do to prevent it if I had found out beforehand.

I couldn't stop anybody then.

Nobody can stop me now.

"Zetian." Yizhi leans closer, whispering, eyes widening. "There has to be a different way to kill Yang Guang. My family has connections in—"

"If there was anything you could do, you would've done it already," I growl under my breath. "You can't touch a pilot that powerful and popular, Yizhi. You just can't!"

"What about his family?" Yizhi's voice sinks lower, deeper. His eyes darken with a menacing fervor I've only glimpsed in him a few times. "*They're* not untouchable. Would it be enough for them to be . . . ?"

"No!" I say on a gasping breath. Yizhi really must be beyond desperate. "They weren't the ones who did what he did! What would be the point?"

"Then just let him die in battle. Even male pilots hardly live past twenty-five."

"You don't get it. It needs to be me. I need to do it. I need to avenge Big Sister by my own hand."

"Why?" His fine brows squeeze up at the middle. "Karma will get him."

"There's no such thing as karma," I say, enunciating every syllable like I want to crush them with my teeth. "Or, if it does exist, it sure doesn't give a shit about people like me. Some of us were born to be used and discarded. We can't afford to simply go along with the flow of life, because nothing in this world has been created, built, or set up in our favor. If we want something, we have to push back against everything around us and take it by force."

Yizhi has nothing to say to that. He just looks at me, weary lines etched around his eyes. Strands of his half-up hair stray across the front of his pristine robes, curling to the side as choppy winds intensify through the window.

"We're all going to die anyway," I say, softer. "Don't you wish you could at least go out doing something you've dreamed of doing?"

"The . . ." Yizhi's mouth opens and closes. His lips have gone pale. I can't stop staring at them. "The thing I dream about most is being with you. No more hiding. No more shame."

My heartstrings pull into knots. "Then you seriously need to dream bigger, Yizhi."

The hovercraft rumbles louder. A buzz goes through the house, vibrating the walls.

"No regrets?" Yizhi leans even closer. "You really won't come with me?"

"It'll be the same fight, just in a city instead of a village," I murmur, focus flicking to his lips over and over. A new kind of tension builds in me. "I'm tired. Just tired."

"But we could—"

I grasp his face and close the gap between us. His plea hushes away between our lips.

Warmth like I've never felt blooms through me. Heat seeps into my blood, and I swear it could've turned luminous. Yizhi's lips are tense with surprise at first, then meld to the shape of mine. His hand lifts up, trembling, grazing my neck like he's afraid to touch me, like he's afraid this isn't real.

When I break the kiss, I thread my fingers through the pulled-back portion of his hair and touch my forehead to his. Warm breaths gust and swirl between our faces.

Maybe, if things were different, I could get used to this. Being cradled in his warmth and light. Being cherished. Being loved.

But I have no faith in love. Love cannot save me.

I choose vengeance.

Gathering my senses, I rip myself away and push him back.

"That's what you were trying to get, right?" I say with no emotion, ignoring his disheveled look, his pained eyes. "You got it. Now let me go. If you somehow retrieve my body, burn it and scatter the ashes in the creek. So I can follow after Big Sister, wherever she is."

Wet lines break from his eyes, glittering in the sunlight.

I can't look anymore. I turn and head for the door.

But before I reach it, I pause.

"One last thing," I say over my shoulder, too quiet for my family to hear over the hovercraft churning. "Don't think I've overlooked that you came to my house and almost foiled my plan, despite knowing how important it is to me. If you tip off the army in even the slightest way, I will kill myself when they lock me up, and then I will haunt you."

I wrench the door open and leave him forever.

CHAPTER FOUR

READY TO SERVE

A dim chamber beneath the Great Wall. A metal platform cluttered with testing equipment. A shining game screen on the ceiling, one I must focus on while being swung up and down on a tilt table.

I swear I'm about to vomit all over my wispy new concubine robes when the tilt table finally jerks to a halt. I clamp a hand over my stomach while lowering the sticky game controller. My senses slosh by inertia. I can see why this test was supposed to be done when we first arrived, but they were having trouble with the machine, so they resorted to prettying us first.

"Six hundred and twenty-four!" Auntie Dou, a senior maidservant, calls out my official spirit pressure value from behind the spectral glow of her screens. The number reverberates off the chamber's metal walls.

Shock pulses through me, and whispers of surprise flutter out of the five other girls on the bench down from the testing platform. So far, their tested values have mostly been in the double digits, with one exception of 118.

When I was fourteen, a mobile testing team came to my village and tested all us children, but I didn't expect their grandiose-seeming estimation of me to be accurate. Spirit pressure is a measure of mental power, of the level of force someone can use to channel their qi. Only some 3 percent of people pass the 500 mark, the minimum required to activate a Chrysalis. I almost laugh at this absurdity.

If I were a boy, I'd be living a dream. I could fight mecha-aliens in my own giant transforming war machine, be loved and praised as a celebrity, and get serviced by a watchtower full of concubines.

But I am not a boy, and this value only means I'd survive a few more battles than most concubine-pilots.

Which is not what I came here to do.

Auntie Dou totters around her screens and comes to me. Her hair is drawn into a high, tight bun. Her shadow grows on the back wall as she approaches. The gold hems and knot buttons on her dark green tunic gleam under the game screen's spotlight.

"Congratulations, Lady Wu," she says while removing the wired probes attached to my head. "You'll be entering Prince-Colonel Yang's service as a full-fledged Consort."

Huh. Even Big Sister was only Concubine rank; my starting salary will be quadruple hers. My family will be ecstatic.

For a few days, at least. Ha.

"Remember, though: this is not an absolute measure." Auntie Dou repeats the same spiel she gave the others. "Things may be different once you get into a Chrysalis, depending on how well you match with Prince-Colonel Yang. You may under-perform due to an inability to empathize with his mind. Or you may undergo metamorphosis, rising closer to his value. My best advice is to understand him, support him, and be there for him no matter how bad the battle gets. Do your part, and you may even turn out to be his Iron Princess."

I barely stop myself from snorting. Even in the face of hard numbers, she's trying to delude us into wobbling toward our deaths with bright smiles, believing we could be that special exception.

I leave the controller and shift my legs off the tilt table's cracked leather padding. Limp by limp, my new embroidered silk shoes clink like pins down the platform's patterned steel steps. Heat scatters from me, robbed by the chilly air. Gooseflesh shudders out of my skin, extra-startling with my pores ripped clean of hair. The bloody taste of rust somehow makes it to my tongue.

The other enlistees huddle on a long bench attached to the wall, hugging their chests. The pale auras of screen lights haunt them from afar. Their shadows skulk on the glistening metal behind them, like predators about to snatch them up.

The next girl to be tested wrings her hands and rises from the bench. We pass each other, the *ruqun* we're wearing ghosting in different directions like pastel vapor, green and yellow and white—Yang Guang's colors. The loose robes are considerably brighter and gauzier than the aunties' garments, flowing like watercolor on our scrubbed, waxed, examined, and perfumed bodies. With the collar as low as our chests, the *ruqun* exposes more skin than I've ever shown in front of others. A smoke-green silk garland wreathes around our arms, dipping at our backs.

Waves of nausea keep twisting me up, but I push through all discomfort. I can't show any sign of not being ready to handle this. I may be starting off as a Consort, but Yang Guang could easily favor and promote another girl. If I don't attract his favor, I could be forgotten among the herd of servant girls in his watchtower.

It'd be way harder to find a chance to slaughter him.

"You are here to provide comfort and companionship to one of the greatest heroes of our times." Auntie Dou's introductory speech replays in my mind, from when we first gathered in a trembling line before her. *"From this day onward, you exist to please him, so*

that he may be in peak physical and mental condition to battle the Hunduns that threaten our borders. His well-being should be the most prominent subject of your thoughts. You will bring him meals when he is hungry, pour him water when he is thirsty, and partake in his hobbies with him with lively enthusiasm. When he speaks, you will give your full attention, without interrupting or arguing. You will not be moody, pessimistic, or indifferent, and—most importantly—you will not react negatively to his touch."

I sit down in the widest gap between the other girls. Cold steel scalds the backs of my thighs. I cross my legs tightly, trying to calm my racing pulse. My mind roils with a storm of thoughts—if Yang Guang might recognize my sister in my face, if he'd really choose me to serve him, if the blade in my hairpin is sharp enough to rupture his jugular.

No one speaks. We haven't spoken much since the maidenhood tests hours earlier by the aunties. One girl didn't pass. She swore in screams and cries that she never did anything with a boy—which made me doubt the accuracy of the checking system—but she was officially disqualified from becoming a concubine-pilot, and then they took her away. To where, I don't know. Hopefully not back to her home. Her family would probably drown her in a pig cage.

I shudder to imagine what might have happened if I somehow hadn't passed their arbitrary standards either. I can't shake the memory of my family assaulting me with questions about Yizhi as I elbowed through them to get to the hovercraft's rope ladder in our backyard.

"I never crossed the line with him," was the only thing I said, my cheeks burning.

I don't know how he handled them after the hovercraft whisked me away. But it doesn't matter when they can't get to me anymore.

It physically aches me to know that, three months ago, Big Sister went through this too. All of this. The whole day of baths, waxing, styling, makeup, rule lectures, and photo shoots for news outlets.

Yizhi will see those photos. And the comments, picking my appearance apart, judging if I'm worthy of being with Yang Guang.

I hope Yizhi gets disgusted enough to forget me.

The awful screeches and booms of the tilt table resound through the chamber again. Bathed a gloomy blue by various equipment, the other enlistees and I watch the girl get seesawed while trying to control a butterfly on the ceiling screen. She has ten minutes to get it as far through a tunnel of obstacles as possible. The game's colors fluctuate on every metal wall. I have no idea why this is considered the best way to test spirit pressures. Maybe it's got something to do with the effort it takes to concentrate while being swung.

I keep a hand on my stomach. Anxiety swishes in my chest like a dog's tail. I don't know if I wish time would speed up or slow down. The thought of actually being done and lined up in front of Yang Guang makes me want to stop existing this instant, but the preparations have also taken long enough. It must be deep into the night by now. Yang Guang is nocturnal—most Hundun attacks happen at night.

I reach absently for my engineering marvel of a hairstyle, consisting of two oiled swirls on top of my head like fox ears, the volume made by fake hair bundles pinned beneath. White crystal lilies serve as the "fur" in the middle of the ears, and silver pins with glittering tassels skewer everything in place. I run a finger over my original hairpin, the only dull thing in the shiny clutter.

"Are you sure that pin goes well with our makeover?" the girl beside me suddenly whispers.

Chills shock through me like I've been thrown into a frozen lake.

Did she notice something? Did the blade part peek out?

I brush the juncture where it would come apart. Still smooth. Thank the skies.

"It's a memento from my mother." I toss out the soft, flat lie that worked on the aunties. My hand drops slowly, casually, though my fingers have gone as cold as the bench beneath us.

"Yeah, but don't you think it seems a little out of place?" she says with her hand on her chin. The white powder covering our blemishes smears onto her palm. Our lips have been rouged and glossed like fresh berries, and our eyes have been lined with feline flicks and shadowed with peach pink.

"Where else am I supposed to put it?" I furrow my brows, probably messing up the scarlet lotus painted between them. "These robes don't have pockets."

"You could leave it with Auntie Dou. I'm sure it means a lot to you, but it doesn't look precious enough to be stolen."

I recall this girl's name—Xiao Shufei. She's the one with the spirit pressure of 118.

"It's fine where it is," I hiss, despite knowing I shouldn't risk stirring trouble. She needs to drop this. "Why do you care?"

"Hey, I'm just trying to look out for you." She straightens, prettied face warping into a scowl.

"Who asked you to? Worry about yourself."

She gapes. "Do you think you're better than us or something? Do you think we're jealous of you?"

The other girls on the bench are gawking at us now, three pairs of paint-lined eyes slick with fear and machine light.

"Well, I do *now*. Or why would you bring it up?" I squint. "What is there to be jealous of? My spirit pressure?"

"Please. No one needs such a *big* pressure to be a good concubine." She sweeps a leer down my figure, which, thanks to the snacks Yizhi brought over, never shrank much, despite my family's best attempts at starving me.

One girl covers her mouth in shock.

But I don't care. I laugh.

This is just sad.

"You think six hundred and twenty-four is big?" My mouth twitches into a stiff grin. "You realize Yang Guang's is over *six thousand*, right? I am nothing. We are all *nothing*."

Xiao Shufei shifts uncomfortably. Her fingers curl over her robes. "Don't call our master by his name."

The term hits me like a punch to the gut. I crush my lips together, blinking stars out of my eyes from a flash flood of fury. A hundred words rush up my throat but get stopped at my teeth. I can't afford to insult him out loud.

I eye Auntie Dou. Still concentrating on running the test. But we'll draw her attention if this goes any further. Releasing a tense breath from my nose, I turn away from Xiao Shufei.

Yet it only cranks up her audaciousness.

"I can't believe your attitude," she says, louder. "We're here to serve a Prince-class pilot. Are you really going to get all cleaned up, only to leave that ugly pin in your hair? Could you be less obvious about being peasant trash?"

"We're all peasant trash!" I snap under my breath, whipping my glare back to her. "Including him! No rich people let their sons be drafted! The noble title, the pretty robes, the fancy jewelry—they're just shiny distractions to make us feel better about dying young. Which we will! Maybe that's even why you're trying to irk me, but let me tell you: you should really be spending your limited time better. Go ahead, feel as classy and dignified as you want." I wiggle my fingers near the silver tassels in her hair. "Because the only reason they gave you all this is because you won't need it for long!"

Frigid silence presses down on us. The beginning of a sob creases Xiao Shufei's forehead and mouth. Guilt squeezes me for an instant.

Then she snatches my pin out of my hair.

Horror almost slams me to the floor. My gaze veers in a panic. I barely dare to look back. Though the pin has, miraculously, held in one piece.

It eases my spiking nerves, but doesn't stop every flux of warmth and adrenaline in me from slowing to cold, dragging shards. I raise my chin. Peer down the slope of my nose at this foolish little girl. She gawks at the pin in her hand as if stunned by her own act. She angles away, evading my eyes.

I smack the bench with a resounding clang.

"I would seriously give that back to her." A chuckling male voice echoes at the doorway. "That girl does *not* seem like one to be messed with."

Our heads turn in sync, but dread breaks over me long before I see him standing there, arms crossed, leaning against the wall.

That voice has a special effect on me, scorched into my mind from the interviews and videos my family watched over and over in awe before forcing Big Sister to enlist for him.

Here he is.

The boy I must kill.

CHAPTER FIVE

FATAL MISTAKE

"**M**aster." We collectively get up from the bench and bow like we were taught.

Even I do it. I say it. I say the word despite how it blisters my mouth like a sizzling ember, because it brings me one breath closer to bathing my hands in his blood.

"Oh, there's no need for—seriously, keep going." Yang Guang waves a gauntleted hand at Auntie Dou, who's rising behind her screens. He's in his spirit armor, a detached fraction of his Chrysalis that he can control without a co-pilot. The amount he's wearing is astounding. Most pilots can only solo-command enough spirit metal to cover the parts they want with a porous mesh. His full, solid suit of bristly pieces glitters with an array of greens, as if chiseled out of minerals. A crown made from the same spirit metal glimmers around his head, rough as if furred, and flaring sharply like fox ears.

Up until two hundred and twenty-one years ago, before the various tribes of the Central Plains unified into Huaxia, pilots were warrior kings. They led and defended the permanent settlements

47

that had popped back up after the Yellow Sovereign and his wife, Leizu, invented Chrysalises some seven centuries ago (supposedly, anyway—Yizhi says historians question if they were real people). Everything noble and regal about pilots nowadays is a remnant of this tradition.

In front of me, Xiao Shufei trembles so hard her silver tassels clink with the sound of a drizzle on glass. She wrings my hairpin in both hands. I scream internally. Instinct charges my body with the urge to snatch it back, but I can't risk it. One wrong tug, one flash of the blade inside while Yang Guang is *right there*, and I'm done for.

"M-master," Xiao Shufei stammers. "We didn't—we weren't expecting you until later."

He breaks into laughter, clear and bright, and it surges through the chamber like spring water into a tin bucket. He pushes off the wall and strides down from the platform in front of the doorway.

His spirit armor clatters, and the long fox fur cape knotted over his shoulder guards whispers above the metal stairs. In the hollow of his green crown, a tall, bronze headpiece adorns his impeccable topknot. If he were a regular boy, he wouldn't be allowed to tie all his hair up until he turns twenty, but the coming-of-age traditions don't apply to pilots. They all wear their hair like grown men. Though he's only nineteen, he's already ranked Colonel, meaning he's served for over five years. But the army will probably give him a big celebration anyway when he turns—

No—what am I talking about? He won't turn twenty, *ever*.

"What can I say?" Dimples curl into his cheeks as he closes in. "I just couldn't wait to find out what lovely new girls are coming into my watchtower. But I hope you weren't using this as a last chance to cause trouble."

"No!" Xiao Shufei jumps. "We were—we were just—"

"There will only be trouble if that hairpin isn't back in this hand in the next three seconds." I hold out a palm. It's too late to put on any of the fake personalities I've been trying on in my head.

She practically jams the pin into my palm. It's slick with her sweat. Ugh.

"Thank you." I slide it back through my fox-ear hairdo, striving to seem much calmer than I really am.

Yang Guang reaches us. Close enough to strangle.

It really gets me, how boyish he looks. Slender jaw, mischievous grin, dazzling eyes. My heart judders seeing the two circlets of his crown, a constant reminder that every pilot is searching for his One True Match. The other girls look transfixed as well, and I know we're all imagining the same thing: him morphing one of the circlets into a second crown and placing it on one of our heads in a lavish Match Crowning. One of my most vivid memories is of swooning in sync with the other village girls as we huddled around the big screen we were temporarily allowed to watch one such broadcast on.

That was when I didn't know any better.

I shake the fantasy from my head.

"So . . ." Yang Guang gazes right into my eyes. "Do you terrorize people often, beautiful?"

"Only if they piss me off first," I say nonchalantly, though my pulse pounds harder, rising through my body.

"This is Consort Wu!" Auntie Dou staggers over, beaming, despite the tilt table still squeaking and thudding the poor girl on the platform.

My gut clenches tighter at her bringing attention to my family name, though it's pretty common in the Sui and Tang provinces. I can't tell if Yang Guang has made a connection to my sister. He wouldn't talk about it if he did. No one talks about dead concubines. I'm counting on him to not even consider the possibility that a girl would doom three generations of her family to take his life.

"Consort?" He blinks and squints at me. His irises light up, neon yellow.

I flinch, despite knowing it's just a sign of his qi conducting through the spirit metal of his armor. Having only glimpsed pilots on screens all my life has made them seem like fantastical beings that aren't quite real, but this . . . this is definitely not computer-generated.

"Yes, I feel it now!" He nods, eyes waving golden light in the dimness. "That's a pretty big spirit pressure. *Huh*." His luminous gaze slides over me like melting honey. "You really are an interesting one."

Auntie Dou glances knowingly between him and me. "So, young master, are you here to choose your companion for your shift?"

"Oh, I think I've found her." He offers his armored hand to me, the golden rings of his irises beaming brighter.

I tense away the tremors in my fingers as I place them in his, bare flesh on warm metal. My insides roil like I'm back on the tilt table.

I'm touching him. Touching the hand that ended Big Sister's life.

I came here with a head full of blade glints and murder, yet he's smiling at me like I'm another plaything ready to please him.

A grin crawls up my face. Xiao Shufei's head is bowed, but I catch her flustered yet fuming expression, and feel a twinge of pity.

He's not worth it, I want to tell her. *I'll show you.*

But my smirk disappears the next second, when the strength of his grip curls around my fingers.

There is no possible way I could overpower him while he's awake. I'll have to wait until he's asleep.

Before I do any throat slitting, I *am* going to have to be his plaything.

In the aerial promo shots I've seen of the Sui-Tang frontier, the watchtowers are built just outside the Great Wall, at the foot of the final mountains before the flat plains of the Hundun wilds. A Chrysalis crouches ahead of each tower. While on active duty, pilots live in the saucer-shaped lofts at the top of their assigned towers, which jut out like rounded cliffs over their Chrysalises.

Yang Guang takes me to his loft by elevator, a thing I thankfully won't have to get used to. It's like a creaking metal casket being wheeled up by demon spirits. He carries me, armored hands bunching my gauzy robes against my shoulder and thighs, arms like heated iron clamps around my body. I couldn't say no when he scooped me up, given the rule against reacting negatively to his touch. When the elevator finally clatters to a halt and groans open, I realize I've been latching on to him too tightly, my forearm digging into the orange-brown fur of his cape. My panting breaths gust right against the fine angle of his jaw. I loosen my grip, cheeks heating painfully.

It's fine, I tell myself while swallowing the hot shame. It adds to my act, and anything that furthers my plan is not a wrong move.

Silver starlight soaks the round loft and splashes over the furniture inside. With the month's new moon not yet reincarnated into the night, the stars flicker like a sea of pinprick flames in the floor-to-ceiling windows. Beneath them, the barren Hundun wilds race all the way to the jagged black hints of mountains on the horizon. A shiver goes through me at the thought of being beyond the Great Wall's protection. But if I went to the window and looked down, I'd be able to see, with my own eyes, the beacon of human resistance that is the Nine-Tailed Fox, and maybe other Chrysalises as well. A buoyant feeling rises in my chest.

Then guilt spears through it.

No. I can't think about the war. It can't matter to me. Not when I'm here to kill one of Huaxia's strongest defenders.

Yang Guang briefly lifts his hand from my shoulders to flip a brass switch. A ring of painted lanterns blinks on around the ceiling, banishing the stars and sending the wilds into darkness.

I can't help but glance around as he carries me over the reed mats on the floor. I've never been anywhere so clean, artful, and pristine. There's a couch of carved red wood and a huge screen in front of the windows. A dining table in the middle of the open space with disks of jade hanging over it. An altar to Chiyou, the god of war, against the rounded brushed steel wall, with incense sticking up in an offering bowl. Silk curtains on a curved railing—

I yank my gaze away, skin flashing hot and cold.

The bed must be behind there.

My eyelids flutter as if I'm drunk, and I catch Yang Guang gazing down at me. Fluorescent lantern light arcs over his soaring bronze headpiece and dances across his mineral-green crown and armor as he walks. He flashes that dimpled smile of his, then sets me down on the cushions of the couch.

Some part of my mind is still crackling like parched wood thrown into a fire, reaching for survival, trying to figure out how I could run away after plunging a blade through his neck. But it's just illogical instinct. What is there to hope for?

Look on the bright side, I tell myself. *After this, I can die. Finally.*

Being alive has been painful, exhausting, and disappointing.

There's a rustling as Yang Guang unfastens his fur cape. He drapes it over the carved back of the couch and sits down beside me. His armored weight crushes the cushion almost to the bottom, making it slope beneath me.

"So you're pretty cynical about this piloting business, huh?" he says.

"And what if I am?" I manage to react in time without stuttering.

"Well . . ." A golden radiance rouses in his eyes again.

A small web of yellow light cracks across his breastplate. With a slight scraping noise, spirit metal spirals and rises from it, forming a rough blossom.

My jaw slackens.

"I get where you're coming from, but it can be pretty magical, don't you think?" He plucks the blossom. It remains connected to his armor, to his control, by a thin tether. He offers it to me with a small, almost embarrassed smile.

I let out a humoring laugh while taking the blossom, but hammer a reminder into my mind that this is not magic. It's just his qi pumping into his armor via hair-thin needles in his spine, stimulating the spirit metal.

Like everything else in the world, qi and spirit metal—which is just qi in pure, crystallized form—are governed by the five subdivisions of yin and yang: Wood, Fire, Earth, Metal, and Water. From most yang to most yin, in that order. They're more metaphorical than literal, and interact with each other in countless combinations. The Nine-Tailed Fox was made from a Wood-type Hundun husk, which doesn't mean it looks anything like lumber, but that it's very conductive and dynamic, like how trees grow on and on and everywhere. When Yang Guang influences his armor with the golden Earth qi dominant in his body—the kind of vital force that provides balance and stability—of course he can churn out constructs easily. It's nothing too impressive.

Despite trying to douse myself in logic, however, I struggle to keep my cool, being this close to him. My every cell hums with not only alarm, but something else. Frantically, I look for distractions from the strange tension tightening around us. My attention snags on a cluster of hotly beaming electronic posters at one end of the windows. On the biggest one, a tiny silhouetted figure stands at the apex of a golden, winding dragon, raising one finger to the heavens.

It's Qin Zheng, the only Emperor-class pilot outside of legend, who had a spirit pressure that was straight-up untestable with the equipment two centuries ago. The authority of his power was what ensured Huaxia's unification. Yet because he suddenly succumbed to flowerpox, a plague going around back then, he left a power vacuum between humans and Hunduns that led to the fall of the Zhou province. That was enough to convince people at last that having pilots as actual rulers was a terrible and outdated idea. So now they're just celebrity soldiers with fancy titles.

"Hey, do you think it's really possible that Emperor-General Qin froze himself in the Yellow Dragon to wait for a cure for his pox?" I ask to change the topic, touching the spirit metal blossom to Yang Guang's breastplate. The blossom wheels back with a surge of yellow light, smoothing out, as if it never existed.

Yang Guang's demeanor turns serious. "Well, they do say his Water qi was so cold he could instantly freeze whole herds of Hunduns without even touching them, so the possibility is definitely there. The problem would be keeping up an endless supply of qi. But there's Mount Zhurong, isn't there? You know, the volcano in the Kunlun Mountains? I've heard strategists theorize that the Yellow Dragon could've been sturdy enough to be dipped into the magma beneath it without melting. That's like soaking right in the qi of the planet then." Yang Guang air-traces the winding body of the Dragon on the poster.

"So he really could be lying at the Zhou frontier, just waiting for someone to wake him up? Have the strategists managed to check?"

"No. Nothing can fly that far out with Hunduns all over the place. But I swear"—Yang Guang leans closer to me, expression darkening—"it won't be long before we take the province back."

"You mean a counterattack is finally happening?" I blink fast, breathing hard to contain the thumping in my chest at his proximity.

"Hopefully. The balance of power is tipping in our favor. Ever since . . . well, ever since Li Shimin showed up."

"Oh," I say, hollow and quiet.

"I know." Yang Guang sucks his teeth. "No one's happy that a family killer like him is the strongest of us. But there are things more important than a single person's issues." His gaze swings back to the poster of Qin Zheng. "There are still some of our own people out there in Zhou, hiding like Rongdi, waiting for salvation. With our current forces, we've never had a better chance of setting them free."

A wave of sickness sweeps through me, crawling under my face.

I push to my feet, unable to sit in place any longer. I stagger toward the poster of Qin Zheng under the guise of paying it more reverence.

A pile of tiny things on the desk nearby catches my eye. They turn out to be pieces of a half-assembled Chrysalis model, made of wood, glass, and metal. A high-end model kit sold by the games division of Yizhi's father's company. Beside the desk, there's a glass cabinet full of these finished figures.

I spin in a panic. I can't look at them. They make me imagine Yang Guang buying the model kits and assembling the pieces with a boyish fervor, and it makes everything *so much more confusing*.

I thought I was sure about the kind of person he is. By the way Yizhi froze stiff when I told him my sister had been whisked into his watchtower reserves. By the black eye she carried during the only video call my family had with her, a bruise she claimed she got from "walking into a drone." By the way she died without any alert of her falling ill.

But this whole time, Yang Guang has shown no sign of being a monster who would murder a concubine outside of battle.

Did I make a mistake?

Have I assumed wrong?

If I've assumed wrong, I'd be dooming not only myself and my family, for no reason, but this hope of taking back the Zhou province.

"I've heard bad things about him." Yizhi's hushed words flit through my head. But, unusually, a second part drifts along. *"Though he did turn down several media contracts with Father's company, so I might be hearing biased opinions."*

"I swear, Tian-Tian, I really did run into a drone." Big Sister's voice further clutters my mind.

Everything's going too fast. I stumble aimlessly, so distraught I forget to avoid my reflection in the windows.

It stops me dead.

This is the first time I've seen myself since Yizhi groomed my brows two days ago.

Oval face pale and flawless with powder, watery eyes looking twice their usual size thanks to black liner and peach shadow, button nose contoured thin and straight, lips painted like lacquered rose petals—I look as beautiful as everyone told me I'd look if I conformed to their standards.

I look as beautiful as Big Sister was.

Yang Guang comes up behind me with a gentle smile. We look as though we could be on a poster too. The charming Iron Prince and his lovely concubine.

Except for the wooden hairpin in my swirling fox ear hairdo.

I touch the crudely carved pin, gifted to me years ago by Big Sister and then secretly modified by me into a weapon. I hate to admit it, but Xiao Shufei was right. It does look horribly out of place.

"Say, what's the story behind this?" Yang Guang lays his fingers over mine, touching the pin as well.

I seize up. Thankfully, the looseness of my robes hides the hint of panic.

Focus, I command myself. He *must* have killed Big Sister—who else could've gotten away with it?

"Is that really what you want to spend all night talking about? Hairpins?" I move my hand to his face, finding his cheek while staring at our reflections in the window.

I can't believe how smooth I sound. I can't believe how heated my gaze can be.

His lips part in surprise. He leans down, almost nuzzling my ear. "You tell everything like it is. I love that."

The heat of his breath on the shell of my ear triggers something visceral in my body. My muscles tighten as if pulled by a string. My breaths shallow and quicken. My blood rushes to startling places, and I have to clench down my surprise.

"Do you now?" I say, a shadow of sound.

His interest travels to our reflections again. "There's something special about you. You see more than most girls. Most of them are so shy, so dodgy about the things in their minds. Not you. You own right up to them."

"You have no idea." I caress his lips, though what I really want to touch is his crown.

I hate the way I've contorted myself into what people think a girl should be, ready to please, ready to serve.

Yet I love the power it's given me, a power that lies in being underestimated, in wearing assumptions as a disguise.

He takes my hand and kisses the pads of my fingers. With a long, weighted sigh, I turn in his arms and cup his face the way I did Yizhi's this morning.

It aches me, how this is not happening with *him* instead, but my body is mine and mine alone. I have chosen to use it for murder and vengeance. And I will succeed by any means necessary.

I draw Yang Guang down into the second kiss of my life. It's less gentle, less timid. Less chaste.

When the hot blade of his tongue parts my lips, I can't help the gasp that rushes out of me. His mouth moves more aggressively than before, scattering my mind. His armored hand runs down my back, making me feel every crease of my robes against my skin. My head lolls as he scoops me into his arms again. His steps rustle over reed mats and toward the silk curtains veiling the bed.

So this is it. This is happening. The thing my family has only ever spoken of as the utmost crime. The surrender of what is supposedly "the most precious gift" I could give to a boy.

At least I'll find out what the big deal is before I kill us both.

All I feel is heat by the time Yang Guang lowers me onto his bed. It's set inside an elaborate carved wood frame, like a tall dresser with a round opening. My hair tassels tinkle against the cool silk sheets. He climbs on after, knees denting the mattress on either side of me. His metallic scent huddles me. I become hyper-aware of how he's still in his spirit armor. I wonder how a pilot takes it off. If he'd have to use his hands, or if it would slip off like a real chrysalis at his mental command.

He kisses a trail down my neck. I reflexively arch my head back. Tingles scurry like electricity through my body, switching on sensations I didn't know I could feel, threatening to undo me. I bite back a whimper. I don't want to lose control.

But if I want him to drop his guard for the night, I'll have to.

I imagine that it's Yizhi touching me, kissing me, and I dare to relax a little, even as my heart pounds against my ribs like it's trying to escape a burning cage. Hazily, I stare at the lantern light glowing through the carved grape vines on the bed frame. I could be diffusing into steam.

Then Yang Guang pulls back, brushes my chin with his knuckle, and looks me in the eyes.

"Are you sure about this, curious girl?" he whispers.

I snap out of my trance.

And out of my resolve, my certainty.

My mouth moves, but nothing comes out.

Are you really the one who killed my sister? is the question I must not ask, yet direly need to find the answer to.

I search his eyes. They need to stop being so sincere. I need to make up my mind. I need to—

An alarm fractures my thoughts, blaring. Red light screams down from the ceiling.

Yang Guang curses, lurching up. "*Hunduns.*"

CHAPTER SIX

LET'S DANCE

No. *No.*

There was just an attack on this stretch of the Wall two days ago. This is not supposed to happen.

Why is this happening?

Yang Guang checks something on a wristlet, its small screen blanching his face. Then he draws me up in the bed.

"It's okay." He rubs my shoulders while I stare at him in a daze. "It's going to be okay. Believe in me. Believe in *us*."

Us.

When called to battle, a pilot must take whichever concubine is closest to him.

I scream, scrambling from the bed.

"No! Calm down!" He wrenches me back.

Pain detonates across my side as I tumble into the bed frame. But I don't stop screaming. I don't stop kicking, thrashing, and biting at him.

With a heavy sigh, he slams me face-first to the mattress and presses his knee into my spine. My shrieks deform into a croak under his weight.

"Sorry about this." He ties my struggling arms with my robe garland.

I gasp and choke, cheek scuffing on a growing patch of tears on the sheets. Makeup rubs off on the stain.

A drawer opens. Rummaging. A slick tearing noise.

His hand comes around and slaps a wide piece of tape over my mouth. No matter how I try to scream, the sound can no longer escape.

In my moment of shock, he hauls me over his shoulder. I wheeze for air through my nose alone. My legs flail uselessly against his armor. Hairpins drop onto the reed mats. My eyes are too flooded to catch if my killer pin is among them. Tears blaze down my cheeks and dampen the top edge of the tape. With me bound and struggling, he runs through the curtains to a pole behind the couch. He grabs the pole, then kicks at a ring of metallic pieces at its base, sliding the ring open. The musk of the wilds whooshes in on a gritty wind. Faint yellow light streams over a gridded steel bridge below. He hooks one leg around the pole, grabs it with one hand, and leaps.

His armored grip scrapes sparks out of the pole as we plummet into the earth-scented night. The concrete of the watchtower rushes behind us. He lands with a concussive force that rings through the whole bridge.

At the other end of the bridge, gleaming like green mineral under the stars, so big it doesn't seem possible, is the back of the Nine-Tailed Fox's head. The rest of it goes on beneath the bridge, perched in Dormant Form, nine tails curling like tulip petals around its body.

I've watched clips of it in battle. I've seen it crush house-sized Hunduns with one claw. I've snarled at promo shots of Yang

Guang posing on its head, braced against an ear as tall as himself. Beneath him, the glowing, slanted slit of one eye has always barely made it into frame.

But none of that has prepared me for this.

Dread carves ever deeper into my gut, yet my squirming and my smothered cries do nothing to stop Yang Guang's momentum. He clanks across the bridge and yanks open a hatch on the back of the Fox's head.

The yin and yang seats are faintly visible in the dark, round cockpit: one low one high, one black one white, arranged like one lover embracing another from behind. The Fox's second suit of spirit armor lies open on the lower yin seat, the pieces wide and slightly curved.

It's not meant to protect me.

It's meant to trap me.

Just like so many girls before.

Another muffled scream strains against my lungs. Yang Guang drops me to my feet, sending a burst of pain up my legs, and tears my robes off. The night chill presses in around my body, naked but for my smallclothes. I try to cover myself, but my arms are still bound, trapping the shredded remnants of my robes.

He tosses the tattered fabric aside and forces me into the yin seat's armor pieces. Cold spirit metal smacks into the back of my thighs.

Terror surging to an animalistic height, I kick and flounder. He drops into the yang seat without letting go of me. His golden Earth qi lights up through his armor and sweeps across the green cockpit walls like autumn decay across foliage.

"Come on, don't make this so difficult," he says through gritted teeth. "There's an invasion coming."

With his heels, he presses my bare legs into the greaves of my set of armor. The pieces snap closed at his mental command, immovable. It frees him to untie my arms and pin them into the gauntlets on the armrests. Those ensnare me as well, and he jerks me back. My spine collides with a column of icy pinpoints—the connection needles, about to bore into me.

Spots rush in from the edges of my vision, brighter than the cockpit. A ringing pitch sharpens through my skull. My stomach convulses uncontrollably. I strain to get enough air through my nose, but I can't.

I can't move. I can't scream. *I can't do anything.*

The rest of the armor pieces crawl and click into place around my body. His legs settle on either side of my seat. His chest presses against its back. His armored fingers lace into mine with unchallengeable firmness.

"Don't be afraid," he whispers in my ear over my shoulder. "Let's dance."

The needles pierce my spine.

CHAPTER SEVEN

INTO THE JUNGLE

M y eyes open to a thick, dripping canopy of leaves. The air is humid with pungent heat. It stuffs up my mind, making it sluggish and slow. When I shift my arms, slimy vines latch to them. Unseen wings bat through the foliage, rustling it. Wet croaks come faintly from the shadows.

What in the skies is this?

Where am I?

I shift harder against the vines. Warm slime gurgles around my limbs. Auntie Dou's voice croons out of my foggy thoughts like a jungle spirit.

"*Sometimes, you may find yourself in a mind realm, a dream-like manifestation of your pilot master's subconscious.*"

Dream? This feels way too real to be one.

My chest grows suffocatingly tight. I can barely breathe the jungle musk. Strange, flesh-colored fruits prod out between oozing bundles of vines. Gooseflesh crawls across my shoulders.

"Help," a child's voice pleads in the overgrown nightmare. "Help me."

I lurch up so violently I finally tear one of the vines. "I'm coming—!"

The reassurance dies on my tongue.

"Follow your instincts to soothe the mind realm."

That's also something Auntie Dou said. Advice probably given to every concubine-pilot.

So it must not be the way to survive.

I have to do the opposite. I have to . . .

My train of thought derails, spinning and crashing. I try to hold on, but some kind of pulling force makes it impossible to concentrate.

I need to . . .

I . . .

Where am I?

What am I doing here?

"Help," a child cries through the dense growth. "Please."

Right. He needs my help!

Twisting and stomping, I wrestle myself out of the tangle of vines. Warm slime sticks to me. I push through the vines to get to the boy, stepping through slick ooze. As his whimpers get close, my hand accidentally brushes a flesh-colored fruit in the thick greenery.

A memory flashes in my head. One of a girl. One second, she's smiling; the next, she's whimpering.

My hand bounces away. I trip and collapse against the vines, yet the confusion makes me come to my senses.

That memory was not mine. I'm in Yang Guang's mind realm. How did I forget that?

The flesh-colored fruit stares back at me like a pupil-less eye in the greenery.

Was that one of his concubines?

My awareness whips across the jungle of other fleshy fruits. I smack my hand on another.

It's a memory of a different girl. When I press my hand harder against the fruit, more memories of her pour toward me like leaves slapping my face as I tumble through a forest.

"*There's something special about you. You see more than most girls.*"

For a second, I think the sound is misplaced, jumbled in from Yang Guang's memory of *me*. But the girl reacts to the words. She blushes, turning away. A hand from the memory's point of view brushes a strand of stray hair behind her ear.

My body goes prickling cold. With tingling fingers, I go for another fruit. I go for all the ones I can reach.

"*It can be pretty magical, don't you think?*"

"*Are you sure about this, curious girl?*"

"*It's going to be okay. Believe in me. Believe in us.*"

The spirit metal flower appears over and over. Same lines, same moves, different girls.

Sickness overwhelms me. But I push further, for a definitive sign that this is far from the worst he's capable of.

When I finally wrench out a memory of him grabbing a girl by her hair and smashing her face against a wall, I get my proof.

My existence goes hollow. I crumple down, huddling my head. My own memories lacerate through me, the moments where I doubted myself because of the warmth he stirred up in me. I double over and retch, though nothing comes out of whatever my body is right now.

"Help me," the child pleads again, suddenly right next to me.

My head snaps up. It's *him*, but much, much younger.

"Help me," he says with vacant, haunted eyes. "I can't get out of here."

His voice is small, but it washes through me like a cleansing tide. It threatens to scatter my rationality again. The memories of the girls float away from me like stray lotus petals heading toward a waterfall.

But I must not let them go. *I must remember them.*

With a howl, I seize the boy's neck and slam him down over the vines.

"This is *your* mind." I crush his throat. "You're the one who trapped yourself!"

He gags and shrieks, but I don't let go. Even when everything screams for me to have mercy and that *I can't kill a child*, I tighten my grip. Every passing second, I force myself to remember how concubine-pilots die: their minds get so absorbed into the male pilot's that the moment the battle link breaks, they can no longer sustain their own heartbeats.

That's what'll happen to me if I show any mercy.

As the light leaves his eyes, the realm destabilizes. Vines disintegrate, rotting to pools of foul muck. Fleshy fruits sink down and disappear.

I scream as I'm flayed apart as well, bones shattering, muscles snapping, skin peeling. My spirit, set free, rushes up and away.

I blink.

In the next instant, I'm standing in a far more abstract realm, face-to-face with Yang Guang at his proper age. There's only black and white around us. Yin and yang. Me on the black yin side, him on the white yang side. Something solid like glass glistens beneath our feet. The sounds of battle, of clashing spirit metal, echo distantly, though I can't see anything in the real world. The phantom sensation of moving in the Nine-Tailed Fox hovers around my mind, but a repressive force prevents me from influencing it.

"What—"Yang Guang gawks around at the realm, then at me. "You actually made it out."

My mouth opens and closes. I gaze down at what seems to be a spirit form of myself, trying to make sense of this.

"But you came here to kill me." His eyes narrow, fuming with black rage.

I bristle.

I went into his mind. Of course he could've also riffled through mine.

Well, then. No need to hide anymore.

"You murdered my sister!" I aim a fist at his face.

He recoils, but chains shoot up from the ground and wrap around my legs, my waist, my arms, my neck. Shock wavers on his face, then he makes a swatting motion with his hand. With a harsh tug, the chains crash me to my knees and curl me over so I'm prostrate before him, right where black meets white.

He breathes heavily, though a grin curls his mouth as I struggle against the chains. Cautiously, he drops to one knee, observing me.

"No wonder you were so eager to be with me." His voice goes soft and low, almost a little sad. He lifts my chin with an armored hand. The chain around my neck jerks straight.

Fury scorches through me. Chain links burn into the back of my neck and strangle my limbs, seeming to get more solid the more I resist. But none of this is real, so how is he binding me?

And why is he wearing spirit armor while I'm not? My physical body is in the same setup, so that must have nothing to do with it. My eyes strain wide, tracing every contour of his spirit armor. If he can create stuff in here, why can't I? As far as I can tell, this is his first time in this realm too.

What exactly is the difference between his mind and mine?

"There really is something different about you," he murmurs, tilting his head. "I wish I could've had you. We would've made such a great pair." He strokes my cheek. "It's too bad you have to die."

Slowly, I meet his eyes. It dawns on me that although this is nowhere close to any of my fantasies, this is the moment I've been waiting for since learning of Big Sister's passing eighty-three days ago. I remember the way I dropped a basket of freshly collected eggs when the world-ending words speared through me, the way all strength left my body. The way my father grabbed my hair and ground my face into the shattered eggs out of his blinding anger over us not being eligible for a war death compensation. For the eighty-three days since then, this confrontation with Yang Guang has consistently occupied a portion of my consciousness, thrumming like a second heartbeat, playing out in ten thousand different ways.

All of that, just to die trapped in his arms, naked and bound and silenced?

Big Sister would not forgive me.

I clench my mind around this spirit form I'm taking. Then, with a scream I've wanted to let out for every smothering second of the past eighty-three days, I summon all the strength I believed I would have in this moment.

The same armor contours as his burst out of my skin.

He staggers back, mouth popping open.

I push off the ground. The chains strain against me, then shatter. The spirit armor flickers on my body—he's trying to vanish it.

This must be a duel of minds, a realm manifested and maintained by both our imaginations across the battle link. All it takes to create anything is willpower.

Luckily for me, he's sidetracked by Hunduns. I'm not.

Roaring a war cry as further distraction, I charge toward him.

"Stay back!" He yelps, hand flashing open. A clear barrier slams against me, stopping me from crossing to the white yang side. A frenzied smile of relief cracks across his face.

But if I can make anything I want . . .

I slap my breastplate, focus, and reach, the way I've seen Chrysalises pull weapons out of their chests, where the bulk of their spirit metal is.

Light fissures under my hand. White light, the color of Metal qi, which represents forces of firmness, persistence, precision, and control. This must be what's dominant inside me. It's perfect for sculpting razor-sharp weapons out of spirit metal. My fingers claw into my breastplate, grabbing hold of a hilt.

I rip a dagger out of my chest in a spray of white sparks.

With a vigorous swing, I drive the dagger into the barrier protecting Yang Guang from me. Cracks spiderweb across it, then it explodes into ten thousand brilliant shards. I dash through the crystalline downpour with a speed and stride I could never manage in real life.

"No! Don't!" He backs away. Vaguely, like reliving a memory of a sensation, I feel the Nine-Tailed Fox stumble in its steps somewhere beyond this realm. "I'm in the middle of battle! You'll kill us both!"

"Good!" I shriek, without losing momentum.

I slam him down by his throat, just like I did his child self. I plunge my dagger into his neck, the way I dreamed so long and so often of doing. His screams gurgle, though there's no blood. Laughing uncontrollably, I keep stabbing. And stabbing. And stabbing.

Warmth fills me, unraveling me again. The sensations of the Nine-Tailed Fox press closer and sharper against me. Yang Guang's mind falters in keeping me from reaching for it—

I'm jarred into a chaotic battlefield under the blazing stars. My senses are all foreign and wrong and different, but I think . . .

I have taken control of the Fox.

CHAPTER EIGHT

WELCOME TO YOUR NIGHTMARE

I cy starlight gleams off a dozen Chrysalises fighting a herd of Hunduns, wrestling and punching and stabbing and firing luminous qi blasts. Shadowy clouds of dust shudder out of the earth under their every booming step.

The view is disorienting, too different from my normal vision. Wider in a freakish way, like someone's ripped my eyelids away. I try to squeeze my eyes shut.

I can't.

Terror singes through me. I can't close my eyes. Can't blink. Can't shut the world out, even for a millisecond.

Sounds bombard me too. Shouts, seeming to erupt right inside my head.

"*Nine-Tailed Fox! Nine-Tailed Fox, respond!*"

"*Colonel Yang! What's wrong?*"

By instinct, I go to cover my ears. But my arms are so heavy, the attempt makes the world gyrate around me. I only get my hands—my *paws*—to my torso level. They each end in three large claws, mineral green and tipped with golden yellow.

I look down. The Fox, collapsed to one knee, has been taken to its bipedal Ascended Form at some point during my stint in Yang Guang's mind realm. The edges of its normally Wood-type spirit metal have been temporarily transmuted to Earth type. It's become lanky and skeletal, as if it's made of filed shards and long stilts. Its waist is tiny compared to its shield-shaped chest. A collar of green and gold spikes has jutted up from its shoulders. I can feel more than I can see nine solid tails shooting up from the base of its back. Waves of Yang Guang's golden Earth qi pump beneath its fur-textured surface, sustaining the transformation. But it's passive. No longer a threat.

He must be lost in whatever my own mind realm is. His qi is mine to control.

If I could figure out how.

"Colonel Yang, are you having connection problems?" a white Chrysalis shouts in front of me, less than half my size.

It's the Moon Rabbit, a Count-class Chrysalis. As a Metal type, it's got clean contours and a porcelain-smooth surface. Its head and hind legs are disproportionately large, and its ears slash up like cleavers. With a pestle-like weapon, it pummels a swarm of Hunduns skittering toward us like humongous beetles. Their qi-filled cores snap like firecrackers as they die.

"Colonel?" the Moon Rabbit cries again over its shoulder, eyes beaming like rubies, small mouth leaking its male pilot's Fire-red qi into the night to make sound.

I don't know how to answer. Literally, I don't know how to speak. When I think hard about the Fox's pointy jaw, I manage to creak it open, but I've got no lungs. No air comes out, and no voice, as if I'm underwater.

The Moon Rabbit isn't killing the Hunduns fast enough. They reach us like rivers of insects. Countless tiny legs scurry up the Fox, mottling its back-lit metal fur, gripping me with crawling pricks of sensation. Tiny sparks of light pop from them as they try to do damage with qi. My—no, *the Fox's* jaw gapes in a soundless scream. I've seen Chrysalises get overwhelmed this way. If they get to the Fox's head, they will burrow into the cockpit and then kill my physical body.

I go to smack them away, but each movement churns my consciousness like a migraine. The Hunduns spread onto the Fox's arms and back. I scramble to claw and swat and pry them off.

"*Colonel Yang, for skies' sake, give a response!*" The voices in my head grow more frenetic. "*What's going on in there?*"

Shut up! I want to scream. It must take qi to form a voice, but I don't know how to channel it, and I can't concentrate with everything that's going on. To make matters worse, flies start to buzz around the Fox's head—

Wait. Not flies.

Camera drones.

Drones that should be as big as a person's torso are whirring around me as swirling black dots.

Something about this makes the current size I'm embodying crash-land into perspective more than anything else. My mind spins with panic.

This is too much. Way too much.

I need to scream. I need to breathe. I need to speak. I need to blink—my eyes are *burning*!

Too late, I realize an actual pressure has built up behind them.

Two beams of cold, Metal-white qi shoot from the Fox's eyes. The rays smash into the ground, continuous, zigzagging in my bewilderment. They blind my vision, though I can hear Hunduns exploding in the sweep.

The voices in my head get louder and noisier, rambling about ineffectiveness and wasting qi, but I ignore them, making myself calm down.

This is a start. I can do this. Control this.

I mentally feel for where the blasts are coming from, locating that precise origin of qi from mine and Yang Guang's bodies, the connection needles in our spines. I retract the flow from the Fox's eyes back there, then shunt a new surge of qi toward the incessant voices.

The blast destroys something. There's a violent popping noise. A buzz, fading.

Sweet silence in my head.

Silent enough to physically hear the metallic Hundun legs scratching at the Fox's shoulders, trying to get past its collar of spikes.

I rush back to whacking and ripping them off.

"Um, Colonel—!" The Moon Rabbit speaks up while continuing to batter Hunduns like it's pounding medicine in a mortar. Its male pilot's Fire qi, the qi of power and destruction, glows within its pestle like an ember behind milky glass, boosting its damage. "The strategists are asking why you just threw out your command speakers!"

Oh. So *that's* what I did.

"Seriously, Colonel, what in the skies is happening with—"

The sea of Hunduns ripples apart. A dark red, rough-textured mass smaller than the Fox but bigger than the Moon Rabbit—a Duke-class Hundun, then—lunges toward us on six insectoid legs. Its own Fire-red glow swells like an evil eye beneath its rough surface.

With a strangled cry, the Moon Rabbit springs up on its hind legs and raises its pestle. The pestle spreads into a curved shield just in time to endure the volcanic blast of red qi. The collision point quivers and expands, frothing wider and brighter. The Moon Rabbit's hind paws sink backward into the earth. Common Hunduns pour up its white surface like giant, multicolored cockroaches on porcelain. I frantically rake them off us both.

"Xing Tian, come help!" the Moon Rabbit screeches. "I think Colonel Yang is stuck!"

The ground shudders with slow, incoming stomps. There's a glint and a massive groan of metal, then a golden ax smashes into the Duke-class Hundun. Its qi blast sputters out, and it lumbers sideways, but it's not dead. The Moon Rabbit falters as well, shield deformed by ugly melted rings.

"What's wrong with Colonel Yang?" the new Chrysalis yells while lifting its ax with another hefty *creeeak*. It's a sluggish and bulky Earth type that sizes up to the Duke-class Hundun. Eyes glowing on its chest, mouth shifting on its belly—it's the Headless Warrior.

The Moon Rabbit morphs its shield back into a pestle. "I don't know, but this is gonna get bad if he doesn't recover! I think I'm gonna have to transform too!"

My spirit quakes in my Chrysalis.

Transforming to a higher form is the most common trigger of concubine-pilot deaths.

Willpower honing to a dagger-sharp point, I crush the Fox's claws around the Moon Rabbit's neck and force it to look at me. Its jaw drops, and its red eyes gleam brighter, flickering. Even without lungs, without air, my voice can't be contained any longer.

"No . . . more . . . killing . . . girls . . ." I growl, a demonic sound that belongs in a nightmare.

"Then—then do something, Colonel!"

Yes. I have to end this battle.

I release the Moon Rabbit and use the same claw to push off the ground, rising to full height. Spirit metal whines, my senses strain and waver and sway, and Hunduns keep crawling over the Fox's every surface, but I tense through it all and take a first step.

It doesn't hurt.

A surreal euphoria courses through me.

Infinite possibilities open to me at once. That's right, I'm no longer human. I've been set free from my broken body, that husk of flesh and bone that has been prepared all its existence to be used for the whims and pleasures of men.

No, I am now the Nine-Tailed Fox, a war machine taller than an eight-story building.

I don't need to blink. Don't need to breathe. A whirlwind could come howling in, and I wouldn't budge. An earthquake could shake the ground, and I wouldn't teeter. I *am* the force that quakes the earth.

Step by thunderous step, I get used to commanding this enormous form. The pesky common Hunduns fall off by themselves when my movements grow vigorous. As I pound toward the Duke-class Hundun, I reach back and pry off one of the Fox's tail lances.

I wish I'd been stronger before this day, strong enough to have watched more of Yang Guang's battle footage so I'd have a better idea now of what to do. The last thing I remember seeing is him taking a running jump and plunging a lance straight through a Hundun core.

That's what I copy when I reach the Duke-class Hundun. My lance whistles through the air and punctures its hull. The spirit metal makes a sound like a thousand windows shattering. Everything shudders. But the lance is less sharp than I would've liked, and I must have missed the core, where its sentience is rooted.

As it pushes back, an overwhelming wave of emotion wracks through me. Grief. Sadness. Anger. I berate myself for the over-reaction, but the moment I stumble back, lance scraping out of the Hundun, the feelings vanish.

It's beyond weird, but I've got no time to dwell on it. A red glow ignites as the Hundun charges another qi blast.

I lurch aside. The red beam chases me, sweeping through the

night. It only cuts off when the Headless Warrior stuns the Hundun with its ax.

All right. This won't work. Something's been off this whole time. The Fox evolved to fit Yang Guang; my qi attributes are completely different.

I have to create my own form.

As the Moon Rabbit joins forces with the Headless Warrior, clobbering the Hundun with its pestle, I reach for the spark of transformation that must exist inside me. Being Wood type, the most conductive of qi, the Fox should be the easiest kind of Chrysalis to propel into higher forms.

In the legends told lovingly to my brother, the word "Hundun" originally referred to a being of primordial chaos. One day, its divine friends took pity on its lack of senses and decided to chisel eyes, ears, nostrils, and a mouth into it. The Hundun ended up dying, yet a new universe poured from its new orifices.

That is exactly what Chrysalises are: Hunduns, transformed with human potential. Which I bet they never saw coming when they came down from the skies to conquer our world.

A firm pressure pulses up to the Fox's jagged surfaces. White radiance cracks across them.

"Oh!" The Moon Rabbit gapes at me while hopping to dodge a pounce by the Duke-class Hundun.

"Heroic Form," the Headless Warrior cries in delight through its belly mouth. "Heroic Form!"

I've only seen Chrysalises go to this form, a third-level trans-formation, when piloted by a Balanced Match. But that's just because the girl can consciously control the spirit metal as well. Me adding to Yang Guang's existing transformation should have the same effect.

In pulses of fissuring light that solidify into smoother spirit metal, the Fox's limbs expand with my qi. White highlights join the yellow ones, forcing the pieces into sleeker shapes, the way timber can be carved and shaped by metal blades.

Heroic Forms are named after how humanoid they tend to be, but they're also more machine-esque, like a person wearing robotic armor. As I imagine what that should look like for the Fox, its stilt legs turn bulky and sturdy. Its three-clawed paws jut into five-clawed hands. Its fox ears thrust farther back and become more sharp and angular, like they belong on a helmet. Its collar of spikes bulges and flares into several layers of shoulder guards. Its overall height keeps stuttering up, up, up, until it's almost a quarter taller. Its nine tails, including the one held in its hand, engorge into something more than lances. Something more like *shotguns*.

The Duke-class Hundun now seems so much punier. After the transformation pressure fades from the Fox, I follow my instincts and aim my detached tail gun. It hums coldly in my hands, then Metal-white qi stammers out like luminous bullets. They pelt into the Hundun, driving it back from my comrades.

Exhilaration washes through me, but I know I can be more precise. Metal qi is all about precision.

Pilots are supposed to be able to sense spirit pressures. Across the distance, I feel out the Hundun's core, that luminous, pulsing seed of life that drives it to terrorize us. I aim again, more patiently this time, building up a single ray of concentrated qi.

I fire.

The ray rips out with a recoil force. It tears clean through the Hundun, taking out its core in a firework of red light.

Cheers for Yang Guang erupt from the other Chrysalises. I'd laugh if I didn't have a battle to win.

I stomp through the herd with much heartier steps than before, rocking the earth, juddering up a burst of dust and a pulse of common Hunduns wherever I land. Brief surges of foreign anguish shoot through me as the Fox crushes the Hunduns, but they become easy to ignore. I fire my tail gun at every big noble-class Hundun I see. Once they're dead, the little common ones will be easy to take care of.

My transformation boosts the morale of the other Chrysalises. They punch harder, strike deeper. Elated howls and shining qi blasts tear through the night air. Sparks fly as Hundun cores fizzle out. Above us, the Silver River arches like a stardust dragon across the cosmos.

After my fifth shot, my deafening steps fall unsteady. My mind wobbles, like when I first emerged into the Fox. Heroic Form can be sustained for only a few minutes. I'm almost drained of qi.

I scan the battlefield with both sight and spirit sense. One last noble Hundun. Huge and imposing, the way only Earth types can be. But that type is too dense to do external qi attacks, so a few smaller Chrysalises are crowding around it at a distance, trying to take it down with radiant blasts.

For a moment, I contemplate letting them handle it. I shouldn't push myself any further; I will actually die if I run out of qi.

But what if this exact moment of laziness causes a concubine-pilot to die?

"Move!" I howl.

The Chrysalises do. I strain out one last shot.

A streaking white ray. A spurt of yellow sparks.

The Hundun staggers on its six tiny legs, then buckles with an earth-shaking force, rocking the surrounding Chrysalises and engulfing them in a storm of dust.

Then I can't hold on to the Fox any longer. It collapses into its bestial Standard Form. My mind plunges backward into darkness.

The pain in my feet is the first human sensation that returns to me, pinching my nerves alive. Muffled, distant cheers swim into my head.

"—that was amazing!"

"I can't believe—"

"—so freakin' boss—"

A flowing white light in the cockpit walls sways into my view. My breathing rustles over the tear-loosened tape on my mouth. My heart beats in my chest like an intrusive object.

But not as intrusive as Yang Guang's fingers, still laced between mine. I flinch. My armored hands, previously fused to my seat, detach at my will like I'm ripping off magnets.

His arms slip from mine and clink to either side of his seat, limp.

A cold calm mutes my emotions. This time, when my eyes burn, it's because I forgot that I have to blink.

Carefully, I detach the whole of my armor from my seat, then pivot to face him.

Yang Guang's eyes are open, but glazed over. His head lolls to one side. Trails of blood, black in the dimness, run from his ears and nostrils.

I feel for a pulse on his neck.

Nothing.

"Yo, Colonel Yang, the strategists are freaking out for some reason!" The Headless Warrior's gravelly voice and thunderous steps boom closer. "Are you okay in there?"

I stare blankly at Yang Guang's face. I imagine slapping it. Punching it. Lacerating his flesh in ribbons off his bones. But he's so puny, compared to the Hunduns.

I just flick him on the cheek.

Nothing feels real. I'm not sure if I'm a human who was piloting a Chrysalis, or a Chrysalis now piloting a human.

The whir of drone rotors intensifies outside the cockpit, buzzing the spirit metal. The Headless Warrior keeps calling for this boy, this corpse that will never hear him again.

I rip the tape from my mouth. It stings, but it's nothing compared to the pain that shoots from my feet when I put weight on them. A pain that is so much worse, now that I've felt what it's like to be free from it. But I have to get out. Show myself. Confess to what I've done. Figure out how it happened at all.

The whole length of my spine feels alive with a cool liquid flow. Vacantly, I examine my gauntleted arms, watching my concentrated Metal qi stream white under the furred texture. Clenching my fists, I propel the qi through the soles of the armor and into the Fox itself. It gives me some basic control over the colossus of spirit metal. I mentally pry open a gash in the cockpit, right between the Fox's eyes.

Lights pour in. A cluster of camera drones whiz outside, now normal-sized. Eager to get the victory shot of the new Iron Prince and Iron Princess.

Instead, I use my armor-boosted strength and steadiness to carry out Yang Guang's lifeless body.

Floodlights from a dozen camera drones pin me, so bright I can't see anything else. Suddenly, like a dam shattering open, emotions crash back through my body. I imagine the audience's reactions to this, and a hysterical laugh bubbles up from my belly. It becomes all I'm capable of.

I drop Yang Guang in front of me and set a tiny lotus foot on his corpse.

What do you know? I really did kill him.

I lift my head, an unhinged grin on my face. The whipping winds from the drones' round rotor wings blow my fox-ear hairdo apart. Black hair hurls back like serpents from my head. Another tide of qi surges from my spine and into my armor. I've seen pilots conducting their qi at full intensity for photo ops, so I know that my eyes and the qi meridians in my face—like a second, more angular set of veins—must be blazing silver-white.

"You've been living a dream for long enough!" I yell at the cameras between bursts of maniacal laughter, raising my arms. "Welcome to your nightmare!"

CHAPTER NINE

STRONGEST OF THEM ALL

O range safety lights rip past me as I'm dragged from a shuttle on top of the Great Wall. A short platform stretching through the air leads to a watchtower much bigger than Yang Guang's. It must be the Kaihuang watchtower, command center of the Sui-Tang frontier. The Sui province is tiny but rich, so it pools its resources with the huge Tang province in matters of defense.

The male pilots of the Moon Rabbit and the Headless Warrior, comrades who protected me selflessly on the battlefield, each twist one of my arms behind my back like they're trying to snap them off. The pressure in my shoulders pushes close to popping. They herd me faster than I can go, making the eternally broken bones in my feet grind like glass shards. Bloodstains bloom on my concubine shoes. The robes Yang Guang tore off me dangle on my body like rotten drapes.

After being forced to ditch my spirit armor, the mangled fabric was the only thing I could use to cover myself. Even so, it hardly does the job, exposing much of my skin to the pilots and four regular soldiers transporting me.

We squeeze into an elevator in the watchtower. At least three guns remain trained on me. Someone's shouting into a headset. I don't know what they're so afraid of. Now that my adrenaline's gone and the exhaustion of using so much of my qi has set in, I'm just a broken little girl who has to be held up to keep from collapsing.

Yet, with my low, weak voice, I force them to think about what happened just now, what I myself have trouble believing.

"It was me, you know," I utter like a curse into the elevator's squeaking, my voice raspy from all my screaming before the battle. "Me who unlocked the Fox's Heroic Form. Me who took out all those Hunduns. Me who was fighting at your side."

They ignore me. It's like I'm nothing but dangerous cargo they must get from one point to another. But I know they're unsettled. They must be.

With a smirk, I relive the utter horror on their faces when they checked Yang Guang's corpse and confirmed that he's deader than dead.

After the doors open, I'm wrestled through concrete corridors and into a white room full of glowing screens. Two men await me on the biggest screen, both wearing blue-gray robes with crisp, wide sleeves. Tall, boxy scholar hats rise from their heads, made of gauze stiffened with black paint.

Yang Guang's comrades shove me to my knees.

"Commanders," says Xing Tian, pilot of the Headless Warrior. A hefty golden crown rests on his brow, double-banded, jutting up at the sides in the shape of axes. His voice shakes with barely contained rage. "This is her. The b—"

"Let her move," says the taller man on the screen, waving a white feather fan. The iconic object makes me realize he's Zhuge Liang, the army's Chief Strategist, basically its top commander. "There's no need to treat her like that."

"She killed—!"

"We are sure of nothing until questioning is done and data is analyzed. Now, please leave the room. All of you."

Hands release me. Boots stomp away. I brace against the cold white tiles, unbound hair spilling haphazardly over my half-naked body. The door slams shut, trapping me with the strategists on the screens.

After Chief Strategist Zhuge introduces himself, as if he's not so famous that everyone in Huaxia basically worships him, the shorter man beside him clasps one hand in front of the other and bows the way pretentious elites do. "Sima Yi, Senior Strategist of the Human Liberation Army," he says, his blue-gray sleeves closing before him like a curtain. He seems to be smirking when he straightens, but he must just have a crooked mouth. He can't possibly be happy. One of his best pilots is dead.

"You can't kill me," I blurt. I didn't plan on living past tonight, but if there's a chance, it'd be silly not to go for it. "I took the Nine-Tailed Fox to a new form. The Hunduns would have definitely sensed it. They're going to attack more often, and with bigger herds," I say, thinking of the sequence of events that led to the fall of the Zhou province. Hunduns get riled up when they sense the power balance tipping. Emperor-General Qin Zheng got so powerful that the Hunduns congregated desperately, risking a whole replication nest to take him down. But he caught the pox before the confrontation. The army couldn't fill the power vacuum in time, so when the attack came, what was supposed to be a fierce battle turned into an easy win for the Hunduns. Thus, they breached the Great Wall and took the whole province. "Plus, I heard you guys are contemplating a counterattack on Zhou. I bet you were counting on Yang Guang. I can replace him. You saw how I piloted the Nine-Tailed Fox."

"Huh." Sima Yi's mouth quirks farther up. "This one knows how to haggle."

Chief Strategist Zhuge shoots him a tired look, then addresses me. "Please remain calm, Consort Wu. We just want to ask you a few questions."

"Like what?" I glare at them through a narrow gap in my hair.

They ask me if I deliberately held back during the spirit pressure exam. If I'm related to any powerful pilots. What I did in Yang Guang's mind realm.

My lips mash together at that last question. It's dangerous, but I won't find out what's going on with me unless I tell the truth.

"I strangled his kid form in his creepy jungle realm and then stabbed his grown form over fifteen times."

Chief Strategist Zhuge's waving feather fan stops against his pristine robes.

A beat.

"And why did you do that, dear?"

Now is the time to lie. It's in my best interests to pretend like I didn't start off with a vengeance plan.

"I saw some of his memories. The horrible things he did to his concubines." My stare hardens. "Things the army honestly should've known."

Sima Yi frowns. "You saw a bunch of memories, so you killed what appeared to be a child? How did you know it was him?"

"What do you mean? It was *his* mind realm. Who else could it have been?"

"Hold on, so even when you were in the mind realm, and had been inside for a while, you were perfectly aware that it wasn't real?"

"I had to keep reminding myself, but yes."

"And then you broke out by *force*? Nothing in the realm guided you?"

"No." I snarl. "I just wanted him to pay."

"Sir." Sima Yi peers at Chief Strategist Zhuge, then back at me from the corners of his eyes. "Iron Widow."

"I know," Chief Strategist Zhuge mutters, face blanching under his black gauze hat.

Chills ice down my back. *Iron Widow.* I can guess the meaning—a girl who sacrifices her male partner to power up Chrysalises, instead of the other way around. If there's a name for this, that implies a precedent. Yet I have never, ever heard of this happening.

I raise my voice. "There are other girls who have done this?"

Sima Yi tilts his head. "Well—"

"Strategist Sima," Chief Strategist Zhuge warns. His eyes flick at me. "Please excuse us for a moment, Consort Wu. We'll have to consult with the Sages."

I bristle. The Sages, the council of old, wrinkly scholar-bureaucrats who spout nothing but "morals," "harmony," and "family values" while governing Huaxia, will have nothing good to say about what I've done.

Chief Strategist Zhuge shakes his sleeve back to tap his wristlet, the same kind of device Yang Guang had. The screen cuts to the army's emblem, a winding and roaring homage to the Yellow Dragon. I flash back to the poster in Yang Guang's loft, how he vowed to take Zhou back, and to find out if Qin Zheng really froze himself into stasis. I can't believe it was . . .

Skies, it couldn't have been more than an hour ago. Hundun-Chrysalis battles don't tend to last more than thirty minutes.

How has everything changed so much since then?

"Hey!" I shout with all my might, though I still can't make much sound. "Tell me about the other girls!"

Silence.

Of course. Who am I kidding? Why would they tell me anything?

The room's ghastly white walls seem to close in on me. My eyes dart left and right. I look at my hands, seeing flashes of them as green fox claws.

Iron Widow. Even if that's not what I really am, even if this is just a fluke, the mere possibility of girls like that sends my heart racing and my head spinning.

But what happened to them? Would the army really rather kill them than use their power?

Do they honestly fear girls more than Hunduns?

Sooner than I expect, the strategists return.

"The Sages have made a decision, Consort Wu," Chief Strategist Zhuge says, looking almost sad. "You will be partnering up with Li Shimin, pilot of the Vermilion Bird."

PART II

WAY OF THE BIRD

There is a kind of bird in the mountain
with only one wing and one eye. To take flight,
it must join with another bird of the same kind.
—*Classic of Mountains and Seas* (山海经)

CHAPTER TEN

IRON DEMON

I lie on the cement floor of a dark, cramped cell. A feeble hint of light seeps through a barred window in the heavy door.

I understand the game now.

It's not that girls are always worse at piloting Chrysalises. It's that whenever there's a girl with a tremendously high spirit pressure, she gets shoved with a boy with an even higher one, so no male will ever be overpowered.

10,000. The number flits around and around in my head like birds on fire. An unimaginable value, one that's supposed to belong only to hyperbole (*"Wow, his spirit pressure must be, like, ten thousand!"*).

Only for one boy in the past two centuries has it been literal.

Li Shimin, the Iron Demon, doesn't have co-pilots. He has *sacrifices.*

My next battle will be my execution.

I curl up tighter in the scratchy, foul-smelling blanket the army tossed me. I rake my nails down my skull and squeeze, as if I could crush the bone and scramble my brains and pop myself

91

out of existence. That would be nice. Better than letting someone else have the satisfaction of doing it.

My laughter flows into the shadows at random intervals. Did I actually think, even for a moment, that what I pulled off in the Nine-Tailed Fox would matter? That they would let me live after I murdered one of their most popular and powerful pilots?

I got what I wanted. I avenged Big Sister. I should've been ready to die . . . thirteen meals ago.

That's my only measure of how long I've been locked in here. It could mean thirteen days. I hope it does. It takes half a moon—two weeks—for exhausted qi to fully recharge. That's how long pilots are rotated off duty after a battle.

I don't know why I ate those meals. I should've flushed them down the toilet and let myself starve to death in protest. Yet when the first plate of stir-fried vegetables and rice came through the hatch near the bottom of the door, it took my grumbling stomach less than thirty seconds to bulldoze my determination. Iron Widow, my ass.

You need to restore your qi, my brain tells itself.

Restore it for what? Going against Li Shimin?

Skies, am I turning into one of those girls who totter to their deaths under the delusion that they could be the one-in-ten-thousand Iron Princess?

That's really what you are, though.

I flinch at the reminder from some deeper part of me.

Yang Guang's spirit pressure was over 6,000. I overpowered him in a Chrysalis.

I am a Princess-class pilot.

It's so weird to think that's true, yet what does it matter? The army would rather send me off to die than risk my partnership with anyone less powerful than Li Shimin.

No wonder we make so little progress in the war.

I can't stop wondering how many people saw what I did. The army is infested with bribes from media companies; there are barely any restrictions on livestreams. Maybe my grandfather caught one. He wakes up a lot during the night. It would've been like I killed Yang Guang right in front of him—a thought that never fails to tug my mouth into an open grin.

But stored videos are a different matter. The Council of Sages and its government full of scholar-bureaucrats have the final say on what stays on the networks. Given that I've never heard of any Iron Widow, there's a good chance they've decreed the scrubbing of all related footage.

Unless the media companies have pushed back.

I'm bound to be hot gossip everywhere; I bet people would pay astronomical amounts to watch what happened. City people would shell out a whole day's salary to unlock a view. Rural people would pool their money and watch it in groups on someone's tablet.

Only sleazy media moguls can salvage my brief legacy now.

Come on, corporate greed.

I snort, then a pang strikes my heart.

Yizhi. His father is the *biggest* sleazy media mogul. There's no way Yizhi wouldn't have access to the footage.

What does he think? Is he as surprised as everyone else? Is he horrified that I really am capable of murder?

Is he proud of me?

I wish I could tell him that Yang Guang never ended up getting what he wanted from my body. It shouldn't matter, yet I can't help wishing Yizhi knew that.

I wish I could've heard his voice one last time.

I lift my hand into the light from the door, which cuts through the cell in slanted shafts. Dust drifts in the dingy fluorescence. I tense my fingers so they make a clawed shadow on the wall.

I've dreamed a lot of being big again. Towering toward the sky, racing over the earth, reaching for the cosmos.

Being free from pain.

I eye my torn robes, which I've thrown into a corner. I couldn't keep them near me after I realized they could be a means of escape, if I had the guts. I could tie one end of the fabric around the toilet piping, the other end around my neck, and then twist until I'm gone.

Thirteen meals now, I've imagined doing this. I swear the fabric is starting to writhe like a bundle of snakes. I *have* heard that the brighter a snake is, the deadlier.

I sit up, ready to—

My bare leg brushes a coarse patch of dried blood on the floor. I jump out of my trance.

Other girls have been locked in this cell. The halos of bloodstains, almost black in the shadows, tell of their miserable stays. It must creep the male guards out to no end, but I'm not scared. I'm a girl; I get it.

I only wonder what those other girls did to land in here. Did they fight back too? Try to escape? Reject orders to pleasure a pilot?

Were any of them also Iron Widows forcibly extinguished from history?

I imagine the struggles that went down in the air around me. The voices that refused to be silenced, the hands that refused to be bound, the spirits that refused to be broken.

Once again, I tear my eyes off the robes and lie down, breathing the chilly phantoms of their fury.

It's hilarious. Men want us so badly for our bodies, yet hate us so much for our minds.

She comes to me in a dream.

"*Jiejie*," I choke out, rushing for Big Sister with no pain in my steps. That's how I always know it's not real.

Yet I can't stop myself from reaching for her, from wanting to stay here forever. Wherever she is, that's where I want to be.

"Don't follow after me, Tian-Tian." She caresses my face, but her fingers crumble into smoke before I can cherish their warmth. "There's nothing here. It's not a solution. Not an escape. I'm not free. I'm just gone."

My knees wobble and give out. I collapse, trying to hold on to her, but my hands pass through her no matter what I do. "I don't care," I sob. "Let me stay with you. Please. He's dead. I killed him. I avenged you."

Her eyelids droop. "And do you really think that changed anything?"

"What do you mean?" I shake my head over and over. "It's one less monster in the world."

"And there are tens of thousands more just like him."

An ache spreads through me, wringing every fiber of my soul. "So what am I supposed to do?"

"Your worst, of course." She smiles. "Don't let them fool you, Tian-Tian. There's more strength in you than you can imagine. Don't run away. Don't let them get what they want."

Her robes turn shapeless, too, like the cloudy mists that drift year-long above the rice terraces we grew up in. The mist we would imagine as different faces, animals, and objects as we huddled together in the backyard, helping each other ignore the echoing shouts in our heads and the fresh welts on our bodies.

Suddenly, her hazy figure morphs into the Nine-Tailed Fox's Heroic Form. Cold metal fingers grasp my face and wrench me to my feet. Burning white eyes glare into mine.

"*Be their nightmare, Wu Zetian.*"

❧ↄ

The screech of Hundun sirens shocks me awake.

I sit up in a cold sweat. The light through the door has turned red.

This isn't the first time the alarms have gone off since I was locked up—triggering new transformations in powerful Chrysalises always provokes more attacks—but it's the first since Li Shimin and the Vermilion Bird have had their full two weeks to recharge. I flash back to the males of my family crowding around the dining table, watching that last battle of his. Funny, how a memory born to be discarded can become so much more significant.

Eyes on the puddle of my robes in the shadows, I rise. Pain shoots through my feet as usual, but the cold has dulled the edges of it and prevented any festering. I pick the fabric up. For a few seconds, I stare at it, kneading it. Then, instead of wrapping it around my neck and yanking, I pull it over my body.

When the door shrieks open to the side, I'm right there, immediately face-to-face with the soldiers. They jerk back.

I offer my hands with no expression. Just a cock of my head.

My compliance seems to unnerve them more than if I'd kicked and screamed. With suspicious eyes, they cuff my arms behind my back and drag me out. Every movement aches after being locked in a frigid cell for so long, and the pain of walking flings stars through my vision, but I don't let it show on my face.

Marching boot steps. Metal corridors. Wailing alarms. Flashing red lights. Jangling elevator.

The doors rattle open to the outside, letting in a flood of pale light and cool humidity.

I wince from the assault on my eyes, but gasp and shudder, taking huge breaths of the fresh air. My eyes take several moments to adjust. Heavy fog has consumed the landscape. Of course. Hunduns never attack without something affecting visibility, because they don't need the visual advantage like we do.

The soldiers march me across a gridded steel docking bridge, like the one that led to the Nine-Tailed Fox. Except this one is set so high that our heads almost brush the watchtower loft above.

My jaw slips open at the sight of the Vermilion Bird. It's so much bigger than the Fox, or even the Headless Warrior. Its Dormant Form looks like a massive ruby bird shielding itself with its wings. Its surface is so Fire-type rough and wild that it actually does look feathered. The docking bridge leads to the back of its slender neck.

I imagine getting in and taking actual flight, wielding the strength of the strongest Chrysalis in Huaxia. Even if I die, it might not be a bad way to go.

The sound of the elevator doors opening again scatters my fantasies.

When I turn, my eyes snag on bright orange. Cold sweat breaks out beneath my pathetic remains of robes.

An olive-green spill of soldiers spreads out ahead of the tallest, most powerfully built guy I have ever seen. His stark orange jumpsuit strains against his physique. Thick manacles bind his arms behind him. A burlap sack obscures his head.

There's also a hefty collar around his neck with a chain leash attached, making me momentarily confused if this is a boy or a beast. The facts jumble in my head—Li Shimin is supposed to be nineteen, only a year older than me.

But, of course, he is also the Iron Demon, murderer of his own family and mind-devourer of every girl he has ridden with. Why wouldn't he look like this?

With both hands, a soldier yanks on Li Shimin's long leash. He stumbles forward, steps booming across the bridge. The soldiers stalk at his side, pointing guns at him. My feet twitch, itching to back away.

When he gets close to the Chrysalis, they yank the sack from his head.

I almost fail to hold back my gasp. I don't know what's more terrifying—the dark steel muzzle clamped around much of his face, the intensity in his char-black eyes, or his short hair.

Hair is considered a precious gift from our parents. We are not allowed to cut it, unless we renounce our family and become a monk or nun. But even those people shave it clean off. To have it short and wild like his is a physical testament to his crime, the worst in the Huaxia penal code: patricide.

I knew this was coming, yet it's my first real sight of someone like this, and it raises my hackles like I've been thrown into a wolf's den.

The soldiers push him toward me.

I try to back away for real now, but my own guards hold me in place. Which makes the ridiculousness of the situation sink in like nothing else—they have really placed me on the same level of heinous as *this guy*.

We stare at each other, the Iron Demon and the Iron Widow, our arms cuffed, a crown of gun barrels around our heads, trapped among soldiers and fog and battle sounds.

Or . . . he's not actually looking at me. His glare hasn't gotten any less intense, but it's piercing *past* me, not at me.

Frowning, I angle myself into his line of sight.

His glower swims elsewhere.

Tension ripples away from me. The corners of my mouth perk up in delirious amusement.

"Hey," I say, because there's a good chance I'm about to die, so why hold back? "At least have the guts to look me in the eye before you kill me."

He ignores me.

I twist to catch his eyes. When his head immediately turns, I do it again. And again. And again.

"Stop!" a soldier shouts, exasperated, after I do a particularly jerky maneuver.

They turn us both to the Vermilion Bird. Spirit metal clashes distantly through the dense fog.

I can't stop looking at Li Shimin. He may be only half Rongdi, but his non-Han blood is really prominent. His face has more depth and dimension than most Han folks' do; his eyes are set deep under strong brows—part of what makes his glare so intense. He wears no pilot crown.

Almost all my fear is gone now, replaced with a giddy fervor. I might as well enjoy this. He's as guarded and bound as I am; what can he do?

"So . . ." I arch a brow. "Killed your whole family, huh?"

He looks farther away from me, his leash rattling.

"Did they deserve it?" I press.

He finally meets my gaze. There's no guilt, no rage, no hesitation in his eyes. Only a resolve so clear it steals my breath away.

He nods.

My lips quiver. I don't know what to say except, "I believe you."

I don't catch his reaction before the soldiers start shouting and pushing us because of some signal they've received. Someone opens a hatch at the base of the Vermilion Bird's head.

While ushering us into the cockpit, the soldiers unzip the back of Li Shimin's jumpsuit. My skin crawls at the patchwork of discolored scars across his back. I swear they look like marks from the electric prods used to subdue livestock.

The soldiers tug me past him to line us up above the yin and yang seats. Keys unlock our cuffs. A new surge of fear crackles through me at the sight, over my shoulder, of Li Shimin shaking his unbound hands. More scars riddle his long fingers.

But why am I freaking out? It's pointless to assume the worst, when the worst would end in my death.

I have to try. I have to fight. If I don't live, he will. And more girls will be sacrificed to him.

The soldiers shove him into the spirit armor pieces on the yang seat. He gives a grunt when the thin but sharp needles enter his spine, then Fire-red qi flashes in his eyes and surges across the network of meridians in his face. The armor pieces snap shut around him.

My flesh goes stiff and cold as the soldiers flip aside the back of my robes and jam me into the yin seat. The familiar tickle of needles dots my spine like ice drops. Armor pieces lock me in. Li Shimin's armored arms come around me. I'm not exactly a small person, yet I feel small now. His heat, even through our armor, stifles me like the worst of summer.

When I turn my head, my temple brushes against the warm metal of his muzzle. It gives me an idea.

"You clearly don't believe in rules, yet you let them put *this* on you," I whisper as the soldiers' boot steps echo out of the cockpit. "Don't you think that's laughable?"

No response.

But—right. Muzzle.

"Come on," I continue. "Do something different once we're in there. Let me take control. It's the only way to free us both."

Someone slams the cockpit shut, plunging us into darkness.

"Let me take control, Li Shimin. Let me—"

Needles thrust into my spine.

CHAPTER ELEVEN

UP THE SWORD MOUNTAIN, DOWN THE FIRE SEA

I'm tumbling down through hot air, hurtling toward a mountain of swords in a sea of fire. My body plunges through a crevasse in the swords, the blades streaking up through my vision. Blistering heat swells toward my back. My hands scramble for something to stop my fall but grasp only blade edges. They slice into my palms in blinding blitzes of pain. I scream through the trench of swords toward a blood-red sky above.

But I push harder against the agony and jam my legs into the blades as well. I know on a visceral level that if I fall into the sea of fire, I will lose myself, and then I will never come out.

Like every other girl who has been here.

My body grates and sputters to a stop, swords gouging into my bones. Hyperventilating, I hang on by only a few fragile points of leverage. Hot blood slips from my mangled, twitching hands. Tongues of fire lick at my back. Sweat drenches my robes and weighs down my hair. My mind lolls in the rippling heat.

The other girls ... why were they here? Why am *I* here? Why can't I remember?

I have to remember. It's important, so important.

Far above the jagged gap through the swords, birds flutter madly through the sky with their wings on fire, their squawks sounding like human screams. Red sky. Red birds. Vermilion Bird. Chrysalis?

What the fuck is a Chrysalis?

My thoughts are melting. Everything is melting. Fire melts Metal. I am Metal, Metal-dominant.

That means something. It can give me power, as long as I'm wearing ...

Yes, somewhere outside of this realm, I'm wearing a suit of armor that can grant me power. I remember what it looks like from so many army promos. The high collar and shoulder guards like flaring feathers. The massive wings. The long, voluminous skirts like phoenix tails.

I hate this armor. Every time it appears, it takes a girl's life. Mine is next.

Unless I win.

Unless I kill *that boy* first.

Whimpers stretching into a howl, I command the armor to emerge from my body. It ruptures out of my flesh, growing from my bones. Red crystals turn inside out from my marrow, spreading on and on. I'm becoming no less than a monster, but that's okay.

It takes a monster to slay a monster.

Harsh crimson wings shudder and sprout out of my back. They curl tight around my chest. Then, with an explosive flap, they smack aside the swords around me. The blades collapse over each other in a tidal circle.

A breath spurts out of me as I plummet, but I grit my teeth and beat the wings again. And again. And again, turning in the air.

In gushes and whirlwinds of heat, the freakish wings carry me up. The swords descend down the sides of my view before giving way to the full scope of the realm. Through the heat-shimmered air, a distorted island floats in the bloody sky, encircled by the flaming, screaming birds. I soar toward it, wings cracking like whips.

The birds come for me.

I jerk to a halt, but it's too late. They crash into a unified stream and course toward me, flapping, thrashing, shrieking as they burn alive. I shield myself with my arms.

A blast of hot air hits me first, then a firestorm of frantic beaks and talons pelts me. They maim and scratch and push me lower, as if killing me is the only way to save themselves. I struggle to keep moving my wings through the flock of them. Flaming feathers swarm me, choke me, roaring like a hundred furnaces.

A chill rattles through me when I glimpse human tongues within the birds' beaks. Violent memories tear through my mind, making something horrifically clear: none of the screams from the birds' throats are figments of imagination.

The muffled cries of a young girl, coming from behind a door I approach with equal parts fear and rage. The shrieks of my own brothers as I smash a cleaver through their bodies over and over. The yowls of fellow boys in bright orange jumpsuits as I bash their faces with scabbed fists. The frustrated shouts from my own mouth as electricity shocks through my body while I lay bricks with bloody, trembling fingers. The desperate, slow-building wail of girls in the grip of soldiers as I'm escorted toward them across a docking bridge.

How could a single person have heard this many breeds of screams?

It's not even all of it. There's more, so much more. Too much to endure. Countless sounds and memories bombard me through the birds, raking into my soul, urging me to dive head first into the sea of fire to put myself out of this misery.

But why should I? These memories aren't mine. They can't be. I would not be sane if this were my life.

I don't have to live with this. As long as I kill *him*, I'll be free.

With a scream of my own, I wrestle through the birds and keep soaring toward the island.

When I finally touch down, he's there. The boy I must kill. Sitting on the edge, wearing a soot-gray robe. I don't remember who he is, but something about his long hair, half tied up with a crimson rag, gives me pause. It doesn't seem right. But I stalk up to him anyway, because it's either him or me. Only one can live.

"I don't know what to do," he says, without looking over his shoulder at me.

His voice, smooth and rumbling from deep in his chest, hits me with a physical force. Waves of grief and tenderness double me over, demanding me to comfort him.

"Do about what?" I say in a soft voice that sounds nothing like my own.

"Everything." Ripples of visible heat lift his long hair above his shoulders, exposing his neck, splashed with horrid scars. "It's all wrong."

"Can't you fix it?"

"I don't know how."

Anger roils through my stupor. This conversation is pointless. *Only one can live.*

"I can't fix anything," he goes on. "I only know how to destroy."

"Then *die*."

I stomp forth and shove him over the edge. Gray robes billow out like smoke. I catch a flash of char-black eyes as he turns in midair.

Unexpectedly, the sea of fire roars up through the whole realm. Flames consume the sky, shattering the floating island with me on it.

My eyes spring open. I come face-to-face with Li Shimin in the yin-yang realm, memories flying back to me. I waste no time.

I wrench a dagger out of my armor and lunge for his throat.

He trips in surprise, and we both topple, crashing hard on the yin-yang border. An unbelievable heat surges from him. I keep stabbing while mentally feeling around for the Vermilion Bird's presence—

The blade melts into a stump.

My heart plummets. A clearer look at him quakes me—his qi is conducting at maximum intensity, igniting his eyes and glowing under his skin like volcanic veins. His armor is lit from within like a crackling ember.

I drop the ruined dagger and wrap my hands around his throat. His hands shoot around my throat as well, and he heaves me to the ground, reversing our positions. His scarlet eyes and the blazing meridians in his face waver above me, horrid and ferocious.

This is a duel of minds, I remind myself.

There's nothing to be scared of. He may be incomparably stronger than me in real life, but that doesn't mean anything here.

I smack my forehead into his, then hurl him over to pin him down again.

He will not kill me. He does not get to make me a *statistic*.

My advantage doesn't last long, but I don't let him gain any either. We grapple along the yin-yang border in a chaotic back and forth, unable to overpower each other. I try to seize control of the Bird the way I did the Fox, but Li Shimin's mind is so strong that

I can't shove it down. Even when part of my consciousness strains into the Bird's colossal presence, gathering some sensations of the real world and flapping one of its wings, I can't divorce myself from the yin-yang realm. It pulls at me, trying to drag my awareness back in. My mind aches like it's being stretched in two directions, two viewpoints, two realities. My control of the Bird feels as flimsy as a drawn breath that could collapse any second.

In my shaky, nauseating view through the Bird's eyes, a Metal-type Hundun pounces out of the fog in a gleam of white. Its body smashes into the stem of the Bird's claws, making us stumble. The world swings. My senses gyrate like I've been thrown into a windstorm, tethered by only a thin thread to the Bird. I hold on desperately, trying to smack the Hundun away with the one wing I can move. But Li Shimin does the same with the other wing, and the discordance makes the Bird flap and stagger aimlessly.

Back down, some traitorous part of me begs. *Let him handle it.*

No! the rest of me screams back.

I cannot give up the control I've gained. I don't care if it kills us both.

As our spirit forms tumble through the yin-yang realm, we simultaneously build up qi blasts in the Bird's beak. It's the only thing we're doing in common, but we have no coordination when releasing the blasts. Streaks of qi sputter disjointly out of the Bird's beak, some as powerful as roars, some as tiny as spurts. It's a miracle when the Hundun actually splatters apart in bright sparks through the dense fog.

"Vermilion Bird, you're out of control!"

We both give nothing but a throttled howl in response. Our frustrations clash and collide, tangling up, choking our minds tighter and tighter. Heat and pressure crest to a peak in the Bird's chest. But it doesn't feel promising, like when the Fox transformed. It just feels like everything's about to explode—

CHAPTER TWELVE

FOR THE FIRST TIME

W arm blood from my nostrils pricks me awake. My mind sways like it's being expelled out of a deep underwater storm. I want to wipe my nose, but can't summon the strength to move my arms.

Two shafts of foggy white light lance through the darkness. Everything smells like metal. Did I fall asleep in the tool shed? Why would I—

A mass shifts behind me. Chains rattle.

My drooping eyes widen. The facts of reality crash back to me, but they don't make sense. My hands lie on the yin seat's armrests, released from the armor. No cold corpse fingers between them.

A zipper purrs closed. Behind me, Li Shimin rises and steps out, knee scuffing my shoulders.

He lived? And so did I?

What?

How?

Did we finish the battle? Wasn't one of us supposed to kill the other?

It hurts to think, so I stop. His heavy steps clang toward the cockpit hatch, accompanied by a rhythmic jangling of his chains. Blood continues to trickle from my nose, pooling between my lips, tasting like iron. Words fight their way out of my throat.

"Hey," I finally manage to murmur. My voice comes out husky, like I've actually been choked.

His next footfall lands with a particularly loud ring.

Silence.

My tattered robes rustle as I pivot to look over my shoulder.

His orange jumpsuit glares through a frail white mist sighing down from two new holes in the cockpit, where the command speakers must've been. Several heartbeats thump by. He's still facing the hatch, not moving. As if afraid to believe what he just heard.

"Hey," I utter again.

Slowly, he turns back, leash swishing over his jumpsuit. His eyes bloom wide over his muzzle and collar, watering, glistening in the lucent vapor, as if he's lived his whole life in black and white and is only now seeing color for the first time.

A laugh tumbles out of me. I wipe the blood from my nose. "Surprise."

He staggers back toward me, steps lighter than before. My smirk fades. The raw tenderness in his gaze transfixes me.

It's heart-stopping, seeing and feeling an emotion that's not some variant of anger from a boy like him. I have to remind myself that those are the same vicious, red-lit eyes that glared at me with bloodlust in the mind link. He is not innocent. Not framed. Not misunderstood. I know that for certain. I have lived through the burning, screaming depths of his mind.

Yet I can't look away.

Without really being sure why I'm doing it, I unfurl my arm over the back of my seat, offering him my hand.

When he takes it, a startling shiver in his bones travels into mine, humming deep into me and taking root.

Our fingers curl together, much gentler than when we were trying to take each other's lives.

CHAPTER THIRTEEN

HUAXIA'S BEST HOPE

"Well," Sima Yi says on the big screen in the white comm room, hands on his hips. "This is an interesting development."

There's a grating click as a soldier in my periphery unlocks Li Shimin's muzzle. It drags off his face, leaving a trace of flushed, dented marks amidst his remarkably dense stubble, denser than anything I've seen Han men grow. A criminal tattoo of the character for "prisoner," 囚, like a person in a cage, becomes uncovered on his cheek. My stomach turns at its raised, unsteady lines, clearly carved by a dull knife—

In a flash of orange, he snatches the soldier by his uniform collar.

I jump. Another soldier yelps a warning, raising his gun. Protests spurt from the strategists on the screen. But Li Shimin just extends his other hand in a demanding gesture. A third soldier rushes a metal flask into his grip. Only then does he release the first soldier with a harsh shove. He unscrews the flask and swigs it like it's the first fresh water he's found after months of drought.

Eyes wide and heart slamming against my ribs, I watch the hypnotic bobble of his throat, the tendons working in his neck, and the shining lines of liquor leaking into his heavy steel collar.

The thrill of survival must've made me delirious in the cockpit—there's really nothing to celebrate about us both making it out alive. It doesn't matter that I've done the unthinkable yet again. It wasn't good enough.

I have failed to kill Li Shimin.

Now, it'll be at least two weeks before I can battle him again in that liberating realm where the only power that matters is in the mind. Two weeks, I'll be confined to this useless mortal body, at the mercy of whatever the army decides to do with me.

Sima Yi sighs from the screen speakers, his crooked mouth making it hard to tell if he's amused or exasperated. "Take it easy there, Shimin."

The flask sloshes as Li Shimin finally lowers it. He catches his breath between hoarse coughs, massaging his stubbled jaw. His chest heaves deeply. The sharp, dreadful, and familiar smell of alcohol stabs up my nostrils. I recoil, shielding my nose with one arm while holding my torn robes together with the other. Memories tear out of the depths of my mind. Memories of bottles smashing into glittering pieces around the house as my grandfather slurs out insults. The crack of his palm against my grandmother's face. My father sitting outside, taking long drags of his pipe, unable to do anything against an elder of the family. The cuts in my sister's, my mother's, and my hands as we're forced to clean up the messes.

Li Shimin's gaze skims mine from the corner of his eyes. He does a double take, and stiffens, as if I've caught him licking a wound. Awkwardly—and pointless to a level I can't understand—he shifts the flask to his side, hiding it from my view.

An eerie glare beside him catches my eye. With a start, I realize the soldiers are united with him in staring at me, faces pale and rigid.

The strategists too. They're watching me. Observing. As if *I'm* a dangerous, volatile creature they've barely managed to corner. I lower my arms, unclench my fists, relax my brows—I'd been glowering.

My awareness shrinks around myself, around my frost-brittle skin and the aching flesh and bone it contains. The pain in my feet tells me this isn't a dream or reverie. I'd been stewing in isolation for so long that I've begun to lose track of the boundaries of possible and impossible, normal and abnormal.

But no. Murdering a Prince-class pilot with my mind is not normal. Surviving Li Shimin, who's got the biggest spirit pressure since Qin Fucking Zheng himself, is not normal.

It's no wonder they're looking at me like this.

That's . . .

Hilarious.

Though my pulse keeps pounding at my temples and jumping in my neck, I pinch back a bout of laughter. Their unease must've transformed me into something more than what I am in their eyes. Even though I'm as powerless as ever outside of a Chrysalis, and they have no reason to fear me in this moment, here they are, with those delicious expressions.

This could actually protect me.

I roll with it. Play it up.

"So, what happened?" I leer at the strategists as if I've known what would unfold since the beginning, and now I'm taunting them. "You got any idea why I'm still alive?"

The strategists exchange a weighted look.

"Pilot Li, did you experience anything different during this battle?" Chief Strategist Zhuge waves his feather fan stiffly.

Wow. Just "Pilot Li." He really doesn't have any fancy titles, even among army folk themselves.

Li Shimin clears his throat, focus darting between me and the strategists. "Her mind was . . . loud," he says, voice rusty from disuse. How strange that I heard his voice in his mind realm before I did in real life. The syllables resonate from the bottom of his chest, raising the hairs that are starting to grow out of my arms again.

He tells of his memories of fighting me within the yin-yang realm. Apparently, he's never been so conscious during a battle. Which is saying something, considering he was trying to kill me the whole time.

Well, I tried to kill him first. But who knows what would've happened if I hadn't?

His eyes keep straying to me while he speaks, narrowing and sharpening like daggers, until he cuts himself off with, "*Who is she?*"

"Were you not told?" Sima Yi speaks up. "She's Wu Zetian, the girl who killed Prince-Colonel Yang."

The tension between Li Shimin's brows snaps loose. "Yang Guang's dead?"

Sima Yi's face screws up. "How did you miss a funeral that big right in your stretch of the Wall? Is that bastard An Lushan keeping you cooped up again?"

My very soul jolts at the mention of Yang Guang's funeral. They didn't tell me anything about it either. I need to find out more—how have the masses reacted to it? Reacted to *me*?

"A funeral?" I say with mock casualness. "Did the attendees know he *died like a girl*?"

A collective look of alarm presses in on me again.

"What in the skies is wrong with you?" Sima Yi cries with a lash of his arm. "Haven't you realized what you've done? You killed a human being! You ended a life! You took someone's son away from them!"

My grin stiffens. Not because I feel a single twinge of regret, but because my rage has boiled over so fast that I have to tense my everything to contain it.

"Yeah," I say with bulging eyes. "I sure did."

"You—" His face strains red.

I could fire back with how people's daughters die in Chrysalises all the time, but I don't want to put any effort into justifying myself. I know his outburst is coming more out of his unease about me than any degree of empathy. He sure wasn't this devastated during our first chat, right after Yang Guang's death. No, he's trying to worm into my mind and shackle me down with morals, so he can feel more comfortable about my existence.

Too bad. I am exactly the kind of ice-blooded, rotten-hearted girl he fears I am. And I am fine with that.

May he stay unsettled.

He looks about to yell at me some more, but Chief Strategist Zhuge silences him with a weary wave of his fan. "Let's not venture too far from the matter at hand, shall we?"

As Sima Yi fumes, Chief Strategist Zhuge goes back to teasing information out of me and Li Shimin. I give my answers begrudgingly.

Neither of us remember the battle climax. After getting nothing but confusion from us at his mention of our "strange transformation," Chief Strategist Zhuge shows us a video.

The footage opens in a corner of the big screen, showing the Vermilion Bird in partial patches through fog. The Bird throws its head back, charging a pink qi blast in its beak—must be a mixture of my Metal white and Li Shimin's Fire red—then spews it at a Hundun. The Hundun stumbles into the fog, missing half its body. But instead of moving on to the next enemy, the Bird wobbles blindly on its claws, wings flapping out of sync. It shakes its head violently. Black specks fly out.

"Those are the speakers, by the way." Sima Yi points down at the video. "Speakers that engineers worked *hard* to wire in."

Before I can pointedly refuse to apologize, white radiance splinters the Bird's feather-like roughness. Spirit metal bursts and expands in lurching spurts, except the Bird doesn't turn more humanoid, like higher forms should be. It fails to achieve any particular shape. Its body bloats like a red boil spewing out Metal-white pus. Some Earth yellow comes out, too, but does nothing to stabilize the transformation. The Bird becomes a diseased-looking creature as formless as a Hundun. Its wings crumble and melt into its lumpy body. Its claws swell to fat stumps.

My hand flies to my mouth.

I was definitely not conscious during this.

"There are clearly two types of transmutative qi at work here." Chief Strategist Zhuge strokes his long, wispy beard with his fan. "However, we are hesitant to call it a proper level-three transformation."

"Yeah, nothing Heroic about it." Sima Yi rolls his eyes. "It's more like a . . . Villainous Form."

"Every male pilot that connects to a Chrysalis is in danger of losing his rationality to it," Chief Strategist Zhuge adds. "The presence of the female pilot is meant to soothe his subconscious and keep him sane. However, you two—you both lost all capacity for rational thought."

"And, gee, do I wonder why!" Sima Yi glares at me.

The video ends with the Bird hurtling right at the camera drone, one eye red and one eye white.

My head lifts with a creaky motion. "So what does this mean? Are we a Balanced Match?"

"No," Chief Strategist Zhuge says. "That is the only thing we know for sure. Judging by the data transmitted from the Vermilion Bird, your hearts did not beat in sync."

"Then how were we both transforming the Bird at the same time?"

"That's the big question, isn't it?" Sima Yi peers at Chief Strategist Zhuge, who waves his fan harder.

"Our tentative hypothesis is that you both have a very, very rare type of hyper-adaptive spirit," Chief Strategist Zhuge says. "You could match each other's spirit pressures no matter how they spiked, but as a result, neither of you could assume dominant command, so your Chrysalis deformed under the equal yet discordant signals."

"Equal—does that mean my spirit pressure hit *ten thousand*?" I gape. Something about putting this into tangible numbers shocks me all over again.

"Try *eighteen thousand*," Sima Yi says, like an accusation. "That's the highest transient reading we got from the two of you."

Shivers sweep up my back and shake my shoulders. The soldiers sneak bewildered looks at each other. Even Li Shimin's head snaps up.

I breathe in and out through my mouth, trying to wrap my mind around the number. It's so big it's almost senseless. 18,000, when the average is *84*.

"How?" I shake my head absently.

Something brightens in Chief Strategist Zhuge's eyes. "Although you were not a Balanced Match, you are truly an extraordinary pair. If you could achieve a stable bond, it could change the dynamics of the entire war. You could indeed have the power to liberate the Zhou province. The Emperor-class Hundun defending the replication nest in the Kunlun Mountains is Metal type. Given that Metal is weak to Fire, a proper Heroic Form in the Vermilion Bird would be Huaxia's best hope for defeating it. It sounds like there is plenty of room for improvement in your synergy, which is excellent. In your next battle, could you perhaps try not being hostile toward each other?"

A cross between a snort and a scoff rips out of me.

Me. Li Shimin. An assassin. A murderer. *Huaxia's best hope. Not hostile.*

"And what would you give me for trying?" I purr. "At least every privilege a non-criminal boy with my spirit pressure would have, right?"

Sima Yi makes a noise of disgust. "Sweetie, you are in no position to make demands. You should be thanking your ancestors that we're keeping you alive at all."

I stare at him for a long moment.

Then I lumber toward the nearest soldier.

"Hey!" The soldier raises his gun.

I don't stop. I don't blink. Not when adrenaline crashes through me and sets off my nerves like Hundun sirens, not when other soldiers lurch into motion, not when his finger meets the trigger.

I push my skull right up against the barrel.

Shouts muffle through the roar of blood in my ears: Sima Yi blurting out curses, Chief Strategist Zhuge shouting, "Don't shoot!"

"Go ahead," I say, cold as the metal circle burning into my forehead. The barrel doubles in my view. My pulse climbs into my throat, thrumming so hard and fast I can hardly hear my own voice. I could die. I could really die with one twitch of the soldier's finger. *Bang*, and then nothing.

But if I don't detach myself from this fear, they will pummel me with it, choke me with it, enslave me with it.

What would be the point of sticking around then?

I actually feel a rush of disappointment when the soldier's finger leaps off the trigger. The instant the cold circle leaves my forehead, a surge of madness makes me seize the gun with both hands and grapple it back. Its sullen metal, chilling my palms, becomes the only constant in my frenzy of thoughts and sensations. The muzzle wobbles in my view, a gaping black hollow that could suck me in and end me.

"You think this scares me?" I say, unbelievably calm for how rabidly I'm fraying apart on the inside. "You think I ever liked being alive? Go ahead. *Do me a favor.*"

The other soldiers wrench me away. After a brief struggle, one clamps my arms firmly behind me. But I think I've made my point. I catch a glimpse of Li Shimin's stupefied expression and hold back a satisfied grin. It feels good, unnerving a boy as powerful as him.

"If you want something from me, you better pay what I'm due!" I yell to the strategists with a cock of my head. The tangled mess of my hair drapes over my cheek and across my throat.

"Consort Wu . . ." Chief Strategist Zhuge says, much more cautious than before. "It's not that we wish to deprive you of anything. It's that the situation is more precarious than you think. Truth be told, there is much division among us strategists on how to handle you."

"Yeah, we're not the ones who want you dead, you unhinged bitch!" Sima Yi says, sounding winded.

"Explain," I demand.

Chief Strategist Zhuge sighs. "To be honest, there have been certain rumors claiming that you are, how should I say this, a fox spirit. The spirit of an actual nine-tailed fox, possessing the body of a beautiful girl in order to devour men."

What?

I nearly burst out laughing. But judging by the tense looks on the strategists' faces, even their educated minds—which should know that spirits only do stuff like that in legends, and that nine-tailed foxes are normal animals—are finding it difficult to entirely dismiss the idea.

"Oh?" I simply say. "What gave them that idea?"

Sima Yi lashes a dirty look onto me. "Do you not remember how you acted when you came out of the Fox?"

I flash back to me dumping Yang Guang's body at my feet and laughing maniacally. "Oh. Did the Sages not order that footage removed?"

"They did, but too many people saw the livestream! Skies know why they were up that early, but by morning, the rumors were everywhere. Trying to remove the footage just made it worse. *Aiya*, why on earth was doing *that* your first impulse after finding a boy dead?"

I shrug. "Sorry, I got caught up in the moment. It happens."

Sima Yi scowls like he wants to tear my arms off. "Listen, not-so-little girl: your existence is making people question the army's integrity. There's something messed up with you in the head, and everyone can see it. The only reason you're still alive is because Chief Strategist Zhuge and I are willing to look at the bigger picture and not give up on your potential. Though I'm really starting to regret it. So if you want any privileges, you'd better prove you can work well with Shimin!"

His tone may be nasty, but my mind hitches on the confirmation that real pilot privileges are a possibility for me. At last, we're getting somewhere.

"And what exactly does all of this entail?" I squint. "What would I need to do before the next battle?"

"Well," Chief Strategist Zhuge says, "we are still negotiating the training arrangements with the Sui-Tang strategists. But at the very least," he beams at Li Shimin, "you'll be gaining a roommate, Pilot Li."

My gut ices over. "I'm—I'm not going back to the prison cell?"

"Of course not. We are hoping that you could become like husband and wife, after all. A responsible husband disciplines his wife when she missteps, and a noble wife guides her husband when he wanders astray. Such is the natural balancing order of the world. Pilot Li, Consort Wu, we believe that, together, you can be something better."

I finally fail to hold back my laughter.

Chief Strategist Zhuge furrows his brows in confusion.

Oh. He's dead serious.

Terror streaks through me. My awareness slashes to Li Shimin, who's taking another swig from the flask.

They want me to live with this murderer. This convicted murderer, who needs to be muzzled, collared, and held at gunpoint to be forced into cooperation while sober.

What in the skies will he be like once the alcohol kicks in?

CHAPTER FOURTEEN

THE LIES BOYS TELL

A concentrated smell of grain liquor smacks me in the face when the soldiers pry open the heavy steel door to Li Shimin's quarters. I stumble back into the underground hallway, dim with only night lights, but a soldier seizes my arm.

Another reaches past the door and flips a switch. A grimy, caged bulb blinks awake on the ceiling, revealing a room like nothing I expected for the most powerful pilot in Huaxia—just a tiny concrete bunker.

I knew it wasn't going to be a lavish loft like Yang Guang's when the elevator went down instead of up, but this is basically a prison cell with some furnishings. Li Shimin staggers in through a narrow space between the bed and concrete wall, one hand braced on the wall, as unsteady as a girl thanks to the liquor in his blood. He's not built for this place; his short, wild hair almost brushes the caged ceiling bulb.

In the corner, on the floor, is a neat formation of flasks identical to the one in his hand, which I've seen the soldiers refill for him at least four times so far. They probably don't trust him and the damage he could do with a glass bottle. Though I have no idea why they would go out of their way to let him drink at all.

Well. For tonight, I know why.

Pain pulses through my arm as the soldier crushes it harder and tosses me into the bunker.

When Li Shimin turns around, another shove heaves into my back, making me stumble forward and collide with his chest. His flask sloshes in his hand. I tense against the stunning solidity of him, cheeks flashing hot, hands curling on the rough fabric of his jumpsuit.

The soldiers burst into laughter, cackling and hooting like children.

Though the blush scorches all the way into my ears, I resist the urge to flounder away from Li Shimin. That's what they *want* to see. Me, flustered and panicked. A state of female being that makes sense to them, that comforts them.

Their jeers muffle beneath the crash of the door. The squeal and jangle of them bolting it from the outside echo like hammer strikes on my rib cage.

I stop breathing.

Li Shimin does not have concubine privileges. Wherever the girls sacrificed to him came from, they were never his to enjoy.

I am the first girl he's seen outside of a battle in two years.

His muscles remain taut under my palm, feverish hot with alcohol. His heart thrashes like something fighting to burst from a prison. My breaths quicken into short spurts that I have to harden my stomach to control.

I have no delusions about being able to fight him off. I won't try. It'd only let him know that my will is powerless against his strength. There's no way to keep my dignity except to act like he is not capable of taking mine away, no matter what he does to me.

And, in the end, isn't that all dignity is? The boundaries and values you decide for yourself? I know what matters most to me, and it has nothing to do with any semblance of "purity." I will not make myself small and crumple into a sad creature of fear that lives to please Li Shimin in hopes of earning his mercy.

Despite the fear wracking through me, I raise my head.

It takes all my discipline not to shudder at the black intensity of his eyes, like spots charred into my vision by staring directly at the sun. The murky light of the caged bulb near his head casts a shadow under every prominent angle of his face. My focus bounces to the ghastly "prisoner" tattoo on his cheek, but I jerk it back to his eyes. I stare coolly into them, conveying a silent threat that he can't watch his back forever.

The caged bulb buzzes above us. His arms shift.

I brace myself.

But his hands don't land on me. Instead, he drops his flask on the bed. Then, slowly, he pivots to sit down. His leash clatters into his lap. Shadows peel away from his face, revealing an expression that's almost awkward.

He raises his hands in defense.

My brows twitch in shock.

"Listen," he says, the edges of his syllables melting from the heat inside him. "I won't—I won't make you do anything you don't want to. I know this," he side-eyes the flasks in the corner, "all of this, looks bad, really bad, and you won't believe me, but I won't hurt you. You have my word." He hiccups, then shields his mouth with the back of his hand. "Sorry."

A wrongness crawls up my skin like common-class Hunduns.

This cannot be the boy with fire and swords for a mind. I was *in there*—he knows it! I'm the first person who's lived to tell of his mind realm! He was there when I described it to the strategists! So who does he think he's fooling?

"I have . . . a spare jumpsuit." He continues to speak as if I've got him at gunpoint, even though he never acted like this while at actual gunpoint. He opens a drawer in the metallic base of the bed while keeping one hand up. He fishes out a heap of neon orange and offers it to me.

The glaring color of the fabric scorches into my eyes, too bright to seem real.

"You can . . . change in the lavatory." He points to a rectangular metal booth beyond the foot of the bed. "There are also some things under the sink. That you could use."

My heart skitters.

A space where I could be somewhat alone. Yes. Please.

I snatch the jumpsuit and blunder for it as fast as I can, hand braced against the wall.

I give my feet a much-needed soak with a tin bucket and a bunch of medicinal herbs I found in the cabinet under the sink. Using the bone-chilling water from the tap is probably doing nothing good for my qi flow, but hot water has become a distant dream. I'm not sure what it feels like anymore, if anything that soothing ever existed.

It's hard keeping a grip on reality after everything that's happened. I watch my cold-numbed hands scrub my feet wrappings through the gap between my knees, slipping in and out of the awareness that I'm the one making the motions happen. Water drops make hypnotizing ripples in the bucket, buoying the herbs. The cloth is filthy with dried blood and suspicious yellow ooze. I planned on tearing my discarded robes into new wrappings while these dried, but, to my surprise, there were also fresh wrappings in the cabinet. And pouches of wood ash, the kind used to soak up monthly bleedings.

I have no idea why Li Shimin would have this stuff when he's never had concubine privileges. Maybe they're left over from a girl who used to be held here.

She must be dead now.

Like I should've been, thirteen days ago.

I scrub until my fingers chafe and blister, yet not even that can fully convince me I'm alive. That I've lived through all that I have. That I'm not still lying in the darkness of my original cell, going finally and utterly mad.

That Li Shimin promised not to hurt me, when the army practically deployed him as a weapon to pin me down and remind me that I was born to please and serve, not to murder and defy.

It makes no sense.

If he were capable of self-control, he wouldn't be a drunkard and a murderer. So why is he acting like this? What game is he trying to play?

I've got half a mind to stay in the lavatory until the Hunduns somehow breach the Wall and crush us all into paste, but eventually a crisp knock startles at the door.

"You . . . okay in there?" comes Li Shimin's muffled voice.

"Fine." I go from clawing my hair to knotting my fingers near my chest.

"Well, um. Lights are going out in ten minutes. Will be dark. Real dark. Would be hard to move around. Thought you should know."

"Okay. Fine."

Looks like I have no choice but to finish up my soak and leave.

When I emerge, my feet newly wrapped, Li Shimin wobbles off the edge of the bed, nursing a flask with both hands.

We gawk at each other across the narrow space.

"You can . . ." He gestures at the bed, gaze sliding around mine. "I'll sleep on the floor."

Discomfort wrings me tight. I can't shake the feeling that this is a trap.

"No, it's fine." I keep my tone flat. "I've never even slept in a proper bed before. I'll take the floor."

His mouth parts in surprise. Then a sternness hardens his expression. "I can't let you do that."

A visceral anger flares from my core. "You do not get to decide things for me."

"No. I'm deciding for myself." He bends to toss every loitering flask into a drawer under the bed, then backs against the wall and sinks to the concrete. He barely fits in the space, his shoulders pressed in by the bed frame and the bunker wall.

I bite the inside of my cheek. I'm tempted to demand he get back on the bed, but the argument surging up my throat gives me pause. *Don't be ridiculous. It's your room*, I nearly said. Except it's not. It's my room now too. So why should I insist on being the uncomfortable one?

"All right. Suit yourself." I crawl onto the mattress. I don't thank him. That would be acknowledging he's doing me some sort of favor. If his agenda is to make me emotionally owe him for something I never asked for, he'll learn his lesson real fast.

His spare jumpsuit overwhelms my body like rich people robes—though I doubt rich people ever land on death row. Now I know how Yizhi feels when trying to do anything in those overblown designer robes of his.

A pang spears my heart at the thought of him. My fingers crimp like spider legs on the bed. Did he watch the battle today? Did he know I was ordered into the Vermilion Bird? The strategists waved off all my attempts at finding out what the masses have been told about me.

As I settle down, folding my legs, I catch Li Shimin staring intently at his flask, eyes shifting. His finger glides along the metal.

I frown. "What are you doing?"

"I'm read . . . ing," he says, face seizing up halfway through, as if realizing how absurd it sounds as he says it.

"But . . ." I lean to get a closer look at the flask. I can't find a single character on it.

"I . . . um . . . used to have the Four Classics," he says. "You know. *Outlaws of the Hundun Wilds. Dream of the Red Watchtower. Romance of the Three Provinces. Journey to the Western Stronghold.* I read them so many times, I memorized them. If I pretend hard enough, I can read them all over again."

Okay. So Li Shimin is absolutely fucking bonkers, I guess.

There's so much to unpack about this that I just bat my eyelids and remark, "You can read full books?"

Han script is made of thousands of complicated characters like individual drawings. Only educated people like Yizhi can read and write things beyond casual postings.

Li Shimin raises his gaze with a weary look. "Yes. I've gone to school. They let you, when the Rongdi blood is from your mother's side, not your father's."

"Was she Tujue or Xianbei or Qiang?" I squint, failing to figure it out by his looks alone.

The heaviness loosens from his eyes. "You actually know the different tribes?"

"I'm a frontier girl." I shrug. "There are lots of Rongdi in my village. They don't like it when you get them mixed up. Usually, I can tell by name or clothing, but . . . well."

He huffs, chin lifting, whole demeanor lightening. "I'm Xianbei. Don't know much about the customs, though, and only speak a bit of the language. Mother passed away when I was little." He examines his scarred, muscular arm. "Wish she could've taught me more."

My mind sways, churned by a dissonance between the invincible, nightmare concept of "Li Shimin, the Iron Demon" and this boy below me, who's awkwardly squeezed between a bed and a wall, talking about his mother.

It's true that the most powerful pilots come from the most unexpected backgrounds. There's no way to predict where the next astonishing spirit pressure will pop up—Qin Zheng himself was the son of a prostitute and grew up in a brothel, with no idea who his father was. But I cannot imagine Li Shimin as a little kid. Did he cry when his mother died? Did his father and brothers try to comfort him, with no idea they would meet their own end at his hand? As they went about their lives as a family day after day, did they ever catch an inkling of what he would be capable of?

Or what were *they* capable of, to make him snap that hard? I want to ask, but the question catches in my throat like a fish bone.

Right. Why should I care?

"So what happened to your books?" I say instead. It would've been nice to have snatched one of them to distract myself, even though I can't read that well.

"Um." He flashes a guilty look. "I made a shiv with the pages and stabbed two soldiers with it."

My mouth hangs open.

"And why did you do that?" I say after a long lapse.

"They were taking me to battle. I didn't want to go." He shakes his flask next to his ear; his eyes are dull and distant, glazed. Then he wedges open the drawer, unscrews a new flask from it, and takes several hard gulps.

"You don't like going into battle?" I say.

He falls still with his mouth over the flask opening. "Do you think that just because I'm a murderer, I *like* sacrificing girls?"

An acrid tide of feeling rolls through me. "I don't know. The other pilots sure seem like they do."

"That's not true. That can't be true." His voice shakes on top of his slurring. "Nobody could enjoy that. We can feel them die, you know. And their last fears. Their memories. Their dreams."

"None of you care about any of that."

"We're led to believe we're not allowed to care. There's a difference." He meets my eyes in a way he refused to do before our battle.

My stomach twists, squeezing bile up my throat.

This is the first time I've heard a male pilot express any hint of guilt for what they do. But instead of feeling better about him, I'm *more* agitated. It disturbs me in a whole new way. Because it makes no sense. How could he, of all people, care about the girls when no one else does?

"I, uh, could ask for the books again." He suddenly changes the topic, seeming to sense the warring emotions in me. "It's been a while. They might grant them to me. I could teach you how to read. If you want."

I flush. "Please. I know how to read too!"

He makes an expression that I assume was my exact one moments earlier. "I thought you said you were a frontier girl."

"Yeah, but I knew a city boy. He taught me."

I smirk at the confusion that furrows Li Shimin's features, until he says, "Where is this boy now?"

My grin wilts.

"Chang'an, I guess." I shrug.

"He didn't care that you were going to enlist?"

"He did." I tense my neck to keep my voice from wobbling. "It just didn't matter, because I chose this for myself."

"Oh. Poor guy."

I swallow the impulse to justify myself. I don't need to. I shouldn't need to. I made my choice and achieved my goal. *That's* the only thing that ever mattered.

Before I have to respond, the electricity goes out.

Darkness and silence plunge down. It wasn't just the ceiling bulb; whatever machinery and wiring are in the walls have stopped operating as well. The utter darkness sends a scribble of fear into me, but I clamp it down. What's the point of being afraid? Worst-case scenario, I'll find out this partnership isn't worth it a lot faster, and then I'll kill us both. Big deal.

"Well, then. Good night." The mattress puffs and groans as I lie down and shut my eyes.

His chains jangle as he does the same.

I release a quivering breath between my lips. My heart thumps into the pitch-black silence. I pray he can't hear it.

But what *I* can hear is his breathing. In, out, in, out, labored with drunkenness. I can almost feel the heat of the air cycling through his burning lungs, intensifying. The harsh scent of liquor and the iron smell of his chain waft closer and closer, right against my cheek—

"Get away!" I scramble against the wall.

"What?" His chains rattle in what sounds like a motion of jolting up.

I gape. His voice is still coming from past the bed. Nowhere near me.

Oh, no.

I am also absolutely fucking bonkers.

"What's wrong?" he presses.

A sour coldness creeps under my skin, like ice crystals melting into acid. My head goes light, spots dancing across my vision. "You—*what's your deal*?"

"Huh?" His voice shrinks.

"Cut the act!" I slap the mattress. "Do you honestly expect me to believe you're some misunderstood, secretly sweet guy? We both know that's not true!"

"I . . . I don't understand why you're suddenly angry."

"Because you're putting on an act, and I'd rather you not," I say, edging close to a growl. "I do not want to deal with you playing games to get what you want. You're a boy. Let's—" My voice catches, but the darkness is making this easier. He can't see my face and the way it's burning. "Let's not pretend like you don't have needs. I don't want you going mad, so I'm willing to get them over with under a few conditions: no surprises, no schemes, no—"

"Stop, stop!" he blurts, then his tone mellows into a dark, low murmur. "I think . . . you've been lied to about what male needs are like. We aren't animals. Yes, our desires get pretty strong, but they're not *overpowering*. There's no such thing as going mad because of them."

A bitter laugh grinds out of me like glass shards. "Tell that to all the girls getting raped as we speak."

"That's not a matter of losing control. Every guy who does something like that knows exactly what he's doing. There is always a moment where he consciously decides that he will ruin someone's life to feel better about his own. Always."

"Speaking from experience?"

"Yes. Because this is why I murdered my brothers."

I go cold from the neck down.

"Back in the building my family lived in, there was this one girl," he slurs on while I'm still reeling from the shift in topic, struggling to get enough air. "She was one of the few people who weren't afraid of me, who'd act halfway decent to me. One day,

I found out some of my Big Brother's friends were blackmailing her, so I beat them up. Soon after, I came home and heard some weird noises in the room I shared with my brothers. Went in and saw them. With her. And . . ."

He fails to finish the sentence, and I'm glad for it. Otherwise, I would've screamed at him to stop talking.

"There's a certain way Big Brother looked back at me," he continues after a pause, slurring hoarser. "He was smirking. Slightly. Just slightly, but enough to make me realize they had a plan. If I'd called the district soldiers, they could've easily blamed me instead, and everybody would've believed it, because Big Brother . . . looked more trustworthy. We weren't born of the same mother. His was Han. The district soldiers would *always* take his word over mine, and he knew it." His voice compresses into a growl. "So I didn't call them."

I lie stiff on the bed, curled around my booming heartbeat, staring into the pitch-black nothing. I don't react. I don't know how to react.

"I guess he didn't realize I had it in me to come for his life." Li Shimin's story keeps haunting the darkness. "And neither did Yuanji, our little brother. I'm still angry he got himself involved. He was old enough to know better. And . . . as for our father . . . well. He came home before I could get out. Saw what I did. Grabbed a cleaver, too, and came for me. I . . . had to defend myself."

"What about the girl?" I say, my lips and tongue numb as frost. "What happened to her? After?"

"Oh. Heard her family drowned her for being dishonored."

I squeeze my eyes shut, sincerely not wanting to open them again and find myself still part of this world. Wet heat pushes at my lash line, dampening it.

"So, no." Li Shimin's voice cracks with pained amusement. "I would never rape anyone. That is something done by cowards of the highest degree. And I am not one of them."

Abruptly, I lurch out of the spiraling blackness inside me. He's accidentally tipped me off—there's an agenda to this tale. He's trying to convince me he's more noble than other boys. And I almost fell for it, just like I did after Yang Guang's spiel. Which came close to costing me everything.

Why should I believe this?

Is this story even real?

Here's what I know for sure about Li Shimin: he has gone into at least a dozen battles. Thus, he has sacrificed at least a dozen girls.

Finally, it comes clear to me, why his show of guilt disturbed me so much. Until today, there was perhaps a part of me that believed boys were physically incapable of sympathizing with girls. He has proved me wrong. They do understand. In his own words, they know exactly what they're doing. That includes him. Him, who, despite knowing what's right and wrong, *went into the cockpit. Every. Single. Time.*

"You're wrong." I break the silence, emotionless. "You're a coward too."

A noise catches in his throat. "What?"

"When you're sent into battle, they get you into your Chrysalis at gunpoint, right?"

"What are you—?"

"So, the big question is, why didn't you just let them shoot you?"

"*What?*"

"You're over here claiming you're better than other guys, but what do you really have to show for it? One life you didn't even manage to save?" I say, through a growing lump in my throat.

Tears tumble from the corners of my eyes. "Those girls had everything to live for. What about you? What do you have left? *What do you even have to live for that was worth their lives?*"

My almost-shout reverberates through the bunker.

His jumpsuit rustles with violent movement. His chains rattle.

Fear and regret rush through me. That was too much. He's going to hit me now. That's how it goes.

I brace for impact, yet relief courses under my adrenaline. I knew this wasn't going to work out. I'll be free much sooner now. After he falls asleep, I could find something to start a fire—

"Man," he mumbles. "Aren't you a charming lady?"

Alarm rises in my chest at how his words wobble with what sounds like a restrained sob, though it could just be his drunkenness.

Whatever it is, he slumps down without the strike I was waiting for, and doesn't say another word.

CHAPTER FIFTEEN

THE SUPPOSED PINNACLE
OF FEMALE EXISTENCE

In the stories about Emperor-General Qin Zheng, they say his spirit pressure was so strong and his mastery of it was so fine that he could integrate the spirit metal of Hunduns right on the battlefield to extend his Chrysalis, the Yellow Dragon, indefinitely. Some say the Yellow Dragon was the inspiration for the Great Wall. So, when I was little, I pictured the Wall exactly like a dragon that straddled mountain peak after mountain peak, huddling us in the safety of its embrace.

In reality, as I've come to discover through my constant shuttle trips, the Wall is more of a road system between watchtowers and army bases. A lot of the middle parts are straight up nothing but rail tracks cutting across the sides of the barren frontier mountains. That imposing monolith of steel and concrete that looks so reassuring in army promos comes in sporadic fragments when it has to plug up valleys and canyons to prevent common Hunduns from pouring into Huaxia.

Our shuttle screeches and skates toward the Tiger Cage training camp, where qi-depleted pilots are meant to make productive use of their recharging periods. The tracks take huge, winding turns to stay on the fringe of the Tang Mountains. A grainy, rushing blur of rock dominates the windows on one whole side, while cloudy gray light steeps in from the side that towers over the Hundun wilds.

My body teeters and rocks with the steel-cold train car. I clench my stomach, still not used to traveling in something so fast. The whiff of motor grease and chemical cleaners clings to my lungs, making me sharply aware of every breath.

Li Shimin and I sit opposite each other as if we're in the yin-yang realm, my black-clad knees almost touching his white-clad ones. We're wearing the uniforms of proper pilots, mine black with white accents, his white with black accents. They consist of a conduction suit that's skintight to make it easy to wear under spirit armor, then a long, sleeveless coat overtop for modesty, drawn in by a wide belt.

Li Shimin has never had the privilege of wearing this, and girls are technically only allowed a uniform if they've been crowned a Balanced Match, but the army has been forced to change their approach to us. Sima Yi, having traveled all the way from the Sanguo province overnight, burst into our bunker at five in the morning and announced two things: first, the army's Central Command Committee has appointed him our official coach; and second, we are to immediately make a media debut as a pair. The panicked rumors and speculation after the Vermilion Bird's monstrous transformation have grown out of hand. Journalists are coming to take some candid shots of me to prove I'm a normal human girl, not a malevolent spirit. A girl with a freakishly strong spirit pressure, but nothing supernatural.

Funny how they didn't have to do this for Li Shimin, the literal murderer.

Sima Yi took us to the watchtower closest to Li Shimin's bunker so the aunties there could clean us up for the cameras. It basically felt like being prepared as a concubine again. Hours of scrubbing and creams and powders have covered up the toll left by my imprisonment and qi exhaustion, while making it seem like I'm not wearing makeup at all. The front half of my hair has been twisted into girlish loops on the sides of my head; the back half is gathered into a tall bun on top. No tassels or jewelry—they're really going for that "ordinary girl" look. I could fool myself into believing I woke up among the ranks of the beautiful and powerful.

I stare down at my white-patterned black uniform, a surreal sight I've spent my whole life believing I would only see on army promos of Balanced Matches. This is it, the supposed pinnacle of female existence. What I've been taught to wish for, what so many little girls dream about. I have been permitted to share a male pilot's glory, instead of merely dying to fuel it. What's more: I am not only the strongest female pilot in Huaxia, I'm tied for the strongest pilot *in general*.

Yet it doesn't take much thinking beyond the surface glory to lose any pride I might've taken in it.

This is not true power. True power is when I stood on the Nine-Tailed Fox with Yang Guang's corpse at my feet, playing by my own rules. Victorious by my own standards. Reliant on no one but myself.

I will never get that feeling back as long as the army is maneuvering me like a shadow puppet.

In fact, I am what the worst kind of hope looks like. The kind that has driven group after group of girls here to be prettied into concubines. Families will point at me—this tamed, airbrushed image of me—to calm down their daughters about being sold to the army.

I want to vomit. I want to tear my hair out and rip this uniform off my body.

But I can't give up the chance to go back into the Vermilion Bird. Worse than being a beacon for false hope is being another female corpse easily erased and forgotten. Only in a Chrysalis can I go out with as much force and defiance as possible.

The shuttle shrieks and swerves onto a new curve, throwing me against the windows.

Li Shimin's hand darts out toward me.

I raise my brows at it, then at him.

Eyelids stammering, he returns to sipping from his flask.

"Don't drink too much," Sima Yi chides in the seat beside him. "You can't be wobbling in front of the cameras!"

I wish we could've gotten the nicer-seeming Chief Strategist Zhuge, but Sima Yi was apparently Li Shimin's first coach, after plucking him out of the death row labor camp. I have no idea why he doesn't just confiscate the liquor.

Li Shimin makes a hum of acknowledgment, then clutches the flask to his chest and turns his attention beyond the windows. Trails of condensation tremble near the bottom of the glass, trying to hold on despite the speed.

Gritting my teeth, I glare at his profile, at the "prisoner" tattoo on his cheek. He has yet to lash back at me for what I said last night. It makes me more anxious than if he had retaliated instantly.

To make matters worse, the aunties have transformed him even more drastically than me. When I first reunited with him outside the dressing rooms, I couldn't believe it was him. His stubble has been shaved clean, making him look like an actual nineteen-year-old. A black head wrapping in the Tang province style, which has a stiff cap inside that's meant to house a topknot, blatantly hides his short, condemning hair.

But what's throwing me off most are the ridiculous glasses he's wearing. He gazes at the elapsing wilderness through lenses thicker than liquor-bottle bottoms, the area around his eyes so distorted it doesn't align with the rest of his face.

I thought it was some try-hard trick to make him look less Rongdi, but, as it turns out, this is his actual prescription. He is basically blind. When the elevator to the top of the Wall first opened, he actually stumbled back from the onslaught of the view.

My eyes bounce between different parts of him. It's like my brain frantically wants to categorize him, to make sense of him, but can't. It's receiving nothing but a jumble of conflicting cues. Han versus Rongdi. Danger versus docility. Drunkard criminal versus invincible pilot. Iron Demon versus human boy.

Abruptly, I pick out another aspect of what's making him so unnervingly different: the distinct lack of scowling.

Skies, was all that scowling just *squinting*?

"How in the world did your eyes get this bad?" I blurt, the first thing I've said to him since last night.

With a start, he turns his attention to me.

"Torched them studying," he mutters, eyes traveling over my face like a shaky touch, as if trying to memorize the details of my features in case he loses the ability to see them again.

Even though I have never cowered from his worst scowling or squinting or whatever, I have to look away from this.

"You need to make sure he doesn't misuse those this time," Sima Yi says, leering at me.

"How do you misuse glasses?" I scoff.

"Well, *supposedly*, you smash the lenses, sharpen the biggest fragment on the floor of your bunker, hide it in your collar, and try to slit a soldier's throat with it." Sima Yi shakes his head at Li Shimin, who turns back to the window with a much duller gaze than before. "Seriously, I will not be able to get them back for you a second ti—" Sima Yi does a double take on me. "Don't look impressed!"

"Wh—I'm not impressed!" My hands flash open. "I'm—why am *I* responsible for *his* behavior, anyway?"

"You're basically his wife now! That's what you're supposed to be."

A crushing exhaustion weighs down on my face, my brain, my bones, my everything. I swear, people cannot make up their minds about who are supposed to be the clueless infants who can't live without supervision: men or women.

"Strategist Sima," Li Shimin grumbles, features twitching with a surprisingly similar exhaustion. "Leave her out of this. She's not responsible for my anything."

"Yeah, does it look like I'm capable of controlling him?" I say.

Sima Yi snorts. "Please. He may be a beast to everyone else, but he's soft to his girl. You should've seen him with his last partner. I could barely stand to watch all that mushiness."

Everything in me screeches to a halt.

"His *what*?"

"Partner" is strictly reserved for Balanced Matches. A concubine-pilot would *not* be referred to as that.

Pain passes Li Shimin's face. "Strategist Sima—"

"Right, this was never public info. Well, there was this girl who we thought—"

"*Sima Yi!*" Li Shimin raises his voice. It booms through his chest and snaps off into the cold, buzzing air.

I shrink against my seat. He has never spoken louder than a murmur, and now I know why. The soldiers guarding us jerk alert in the seats all around, reaching for their guns.

The shuttle lurches over a bump, rattling us all. My blood pulses beneath my cold skin.

Sima Yi's brows have shot high, but he recovers after a second, calming the soldiers with a wave of his hand.

"Don't speak of her," Li Shimin tells him, then addresses me. "She's dead."

Even though questions spark and sizzle in my head—how could he have had a partner if no girl has survived a battle with him before me?—the crushing aura around him chokes my throat shut. His fingers clench around his flask, the skin tightening around the many scars riddling them. I shiver. It's moments like these that give me an uncomfortable hint of the level of fury and violence that he's holding back. At any moment, he could tip over the edge. I'm making a mistake, constantly challenging him, pushing at his buttons.

Two weeks, I remind myself, making my body relax. All I have to do is ride out these two weeks, then I'll have my rematch with him.

Strip away our mortal flesh and pulverize our bones, and whatever still exists for the both of us, exists with the same ferocity.

I will not fail a second time.

CHAPTER SIXTEEN

THE CROWNLESS KING,
THE HEARTLESS QUEEN

"Shimin, put your arm around her," Sima Yi says as the elevator shudders down from the Great Wall. "It's showtime."

When Li Shimin's hand grazes my shoulders, I do my best to swallow my panic. The tight sleeve of his conduction suit, poking out of his pilot coat, glazes every rise and valley of his muscles like thick white paint, contrasting glaringly against my black uniform. The heat and weight of his arm, along with his suffocating proximity, make my every cell shrink against my thudding veins.

But even if I protested, I wouldn't have a choice. A soldier has had to drag me everywhere so I'll keep up with Sima Yi. They won't let me have a cane because . . . I don't know, fox spirit danger or something. Now Li Shimin has to take over the duty because the soldiers are not to appear in frame with us, lest they make us look too dangerous. The collar around his neck is proof that he's under control, while his arm around me is proof that *I'm* under control.

It's a delicate balance.

"With bound feet, you learn the value of the bonds between family."
My grandmother's voice saws through my head like a rusty knife.
"No one can do everything alone. We all must rely on one another."

Yeah. Now I have to let strange men touch me when I want to
go anywhere. Thanks, Grandmother.

I fume, trying to radiate the message that no, I have not been
"tamed," but the instant the elevator doors grind open, revealing a
valley full of buildings and people about to scrutinize my every
move, my blood goes cold. A calming cold that switches on a completely different circuit in my brain: the circuit for slow-brewed
vengeance.

For the sake of pacifying those in the army who want me outright executed, I follow Sima Yi's instructions: I make myself
small and keep my eyes on the paved stone path cutting through
the camp, performing the role of Li Shimin's accessory.

It proves difficult when, after a few moments, it becomes clear
that I'm not the only one who needs support to walk straight. Li
Shimin leans just as heavily against me, steps wobbling dangerously. I'm forced to brace him with a hand on his back.

"He told you not to drink so much!" I hiss, then immediately
hate myself for how Hopeless Wife I sound.

"I'm sorry," he slurs breathily.

"No, you're not! Or you wouldn't have drunk in the first
place!"

He has no response to that. His bleary gaze just floats somewhere much, much farther in the distance.

I focus on matching his rhythm and balance so we don't humiliate ourselves by crash-landing on flat ground. While the black
lines on the white leggings of his conduction suit disappear into
sturdy boots, the white lines on mine extend toward a pair of tiny
shoes that look like a tacked-on joke, with a bunch of deformed
butterflies shoddily embroidered on black canvas.

The tiled roofs of the training buildings on either side of the path flare like claws against the clustering storm clouds. There aren't that many idlers milling about outside—pipe-smoking pilots, mostly—but people alert each other behind windows, and whole clusters of ogling faces rush up against panes of glass. Lit from within by fluorescence brighter than the dreary weather, they point, exclaim, and run their oily stares over every detail of me. I take long, tranquilizing drags of the cool air, crisp with the tension of impending rain. The sound of a shuttle, now as distant and unearthly as a ghost wail, lures my awareness over my shoulder.

This section of the Great Wall is one of those that actually look impressive, silhouetted a heart-jolting height against the somber clouds, filling the valley entrance. The shuttles racing over it now look as small as eels. The Kaihuang watchtower looms outside like a giant spying on humanity, housing the most important strategists and equipment of the Sui-Tang frontier. My eyes linger on it for a moment extra, as if searing a mark, before peeling away.

When Sima Yi pushes through the cafeteria's double doors, sticky heat pours over us, filled with chattering voices and clinking noises. I recoil—I've never seen so many people in the same place at once.

Then the camera flashes come.

Reporters with neat topknots and stunningly clean city robes swarm up to us. Soldiers cry for them to keep their distance, while Sima Yi leads us to the food lineup. Even though I'm freaking out on the inside like a spirit spooked by firecrackers at New Year's, I keep my expression unchanged.

Quick glimpses fly from the tables we pass, but they must've received an announcement to ignore us. Their reactions are a lot more subdued than the ones outside.

There are also a lot more different kinds of personnel here, making me realize the sheer collaborative effort it takes to keep the Wall running. Soldiers in olive green, slurping huge steaming bowls of noodles and porridge as if they have a ten-second deadline to finish. Maintenance workers with neon vests over their tunics, wolfing down even bigger bowls. Strategists and student strategists in blue-gray robes, debating with their tablets out, while their food gets cold.

The pilots are the definite stars, though, with their carelessly loud talking and explosive laughter. Their double-circlet crowns glimmer under the greasy lights: stylized beast horns, fish fins, butterfly wings, and more. Everyone makes way when one of them strides between the tables, especially if it's an Iron Noble powerful enough to command a substantial amount of spirit armor. My belly jumps whenever I recognize one from media promos, but I remind myself that I have no reason to be impressed.

I am now more powerful than them, after all.

Only when we get to the food lineup do I find other women: aunties in stained aprons, hustling in a large kitchen behind steamy windows. They're ladling soy milk, frying dough sticks, stirring porridge, and draining noodles. Grimly, I look back to the tables in search of black uniforms like mine, for the fellow lucky girls allowed out with the boys to fuel the illusion that the world is just and hope exists.

Instead, my attention hitches on a ranking board on the wall. Pilot names and their respective battle points shine in neon against the black screen in two columns, one for Huaxia overall and one for just Sui-Tang. The camera flashes in my face make them hard to read, but I don't need to, to know who's first.

The top rank for both is blank.

My gaze crawls toward Li Shimin. He's staring blankly ahead. It gives me a sick satisfaction to know that the army punishes and taunts him in this way, and ensures the other powerful pilots hate his guts. There's supposed to be an annual King of Pilots award given to the top-scoring pilot, which comes with a huge cash prize to the winner's family. The award has not been given for the two years he's been active.

Instead of a revered champion, he's nothing but a nuisance dragging the others down.

Squinting, I try to decipher who's currently in the unlucky second place. It's usually a tight race between—

The screen suddenly changes to a black-and-white picture and some text.

A picture of Yang Guang.

Oh.

It's his obituary.

Sweat breaks across my back like condensation on steel. Not because I'm struck with guilt, but because the cafeteria chaos noticeably chills and quiets. Only the reporters continue to buzz like wasps.

If anyone was doing a proper job of ignoring me before, they aren't anymore. Glares slice into me like razor edges, glinting with a demand for justice. I swear I even spot Xing Tian, pilot of the Headless Warrior, in the fuming masses across the tables. The phantom pain of his grip, quivering with crushing force as he wrenched me away from Yang Guang's corpse, throbs in my arm. The bruises are still a deep, sickly green.

Despair sinks through me, filling my limbs like the cement of the Wall, numbing me to my fingertips. I shouldn't have been giddy about these army people hating Li Shimin—they must hate me so much more. I don't want to imagine the things they'd do to make me pay for taking their beloved golden boy's life.

How will I possibly convince them to accept me?

The reporters are allowed to capture us for only a brief few minutes before Sima Yi shoos them back to their cities. After a breakfast of tea eggs, soy milk, fried dough sticks, and wonton soup—which is named after how they pronounce "Hundun" in the south, Sima Yi randomly tells us—he introduces me and Li Shimin to a partner exercise called ice dancing. The training camp has an artificial ice rink to simulate the frozen lake surfaces of the Qing province up north, where the exercise originated. For the longest time, Sima Yi explains, strategists used plain old regular dancing to improve the synergy of Balanced Matches, but adding ice to the equation boosted the effectiveness so much that even strategists in provinces with warmer climates now swear by it. The instability of skates forces partners to work together and lean on each other to do basic routines on the rink.

Theoretically, anyway.

After a full morning of stumbling across ice, enduring blazing agony in my feet, yanking each other out of balance, and bruising every substantial surface of our flesh with our endless falls, Sima Yi leads us back to the cafeteria for lunch, his face as sullen as the sky. I don't know what he expected. We're the duo that kicked the Vermilion Bird into an unprecedented monstrous form *yesterday*; how could we do any better in less than twenty-four hours?

"How hard is it to just work with each other?" Sima Yi launches into another rant as we walk with our metal trays of greasy soup and stir-fry toward a cafeteria table. "I swear, you're the worst couple I've ever—!"

A rushing maintenance worker trips into him.

I catch the distinct moment Sima Yi's tray tips, yet I'm unable to stop it. His bowl of egg and tomato soup overturns. Both of them cry out, though Sima Yi's exclamation sharpens into a scream when the hot soup drenches his robes. The bowl smashes on the floor in a steaming puddle.

Insults more creative than I could ever imagine spew from Sima Yi's mouth. The worker apologizes while bowing endlessly, clenching his hands together and shaking them over and over.

"Ugh! You two eat first; I'll go get changed," Sima Yi says to us, then sulks off, soup dripping from his hems. The worker scrambles after him like a startled rat.

I blink blankly at his storm of a departure, but we've still got two soldiers supervising us. They sit down with us at an empty table.

At this point, I don't know if they're guarding the masses from us, or us from the masses.

I focus on my cluttered plate of rice and vegetables, ignoring the assorted death glares jabbing toward me. I especially don't look anywhere near the ranking screen, which, as I discovered during breakfast, shows a rolling memorial of recently deceased pilots every few minutes. I thought about asking Sima Yi to remove Yang Guang from it, but I don't want him to know how terrified I really am. And the noticeable breach in tradition would probably make people angrier.

I'm shoving my food down as fast as I can when a loud argument erupts at a table nearby.

I seize up, but thankfully, it has nothing to do with me. It's one pilot shouting about owed money and another shouting about "not being a good pal."

A wave of whoops and whistles sweeps through the cafeteria.

"Fight!" someone shouts, laughing.

"Fight! Fight! Fight! Fight!" others join in.

The argument spikes in volume like a hot wok splashed by oil.

Our soldiers snap to attention, hands tensing beside their trays. I start swallowing whole mouthfuls without chewing much. I'd like to get out of here before—

The first punch is thrown.

Half the cafeteria springs to their feet, exploding into cheers. Tables squeal aside as people stampede toward the fight. The rumble of boot steps fills the building like a storm on a thick roof. I back toward the end of my bench and against the grease-sticky wall, clutching my chopsticks.

Our soldiers jump up and elbow through the crowd coagulating dangerously near us. A pilot with a partial suit of Earth-yellow armor stumbles back, laughing.

His attention catches on me and Li Shimin. His grin morphs into something more dubious. He glances between us, then at the empty seats beside us.

Don't, I plead in my head.

He sits down next to me, and I almost scream. Much of his spirit armor is stretched as a thin golden mesh over the tightness of his conduction suit sleeves and the cut-off shoulders of his white pilot coat, but his gauntlets and diamond-shaped breastplate are solid. That amount looks about Earl class, the starting rank of Iron Nobles. His spirit pressure should "only" be in the 2000s.

But it doesn't matter how badly Li Shimin and I beat him out in that regard. It means nothing without armor of our own.

"*Wa sai*," the pilot remarks with amused wonder, almost inaudible under the crowd's racket. "Li Shimin, the Iron Demon, here in the flesh."

Li Shimin chews a bite of bean sprouts without reacting.

"I have to say, you look a lot more . . . wild than I imagined." The pilot leans across the table, chuckling. The dog ears of his golden crown perk up, kept under command of his spinal signals by a thin strip of spirit metal along the back of his neck. "Are you sure you won't turn the Vermilion Bird around and crash down the Great Wall to let the rest of the Rongdi in or something?"

I pause with a mouth full of rice and green beans.

A memory rushes out at me, one that isn't mine, but a fragment I glimpsed in Li Shimin's mind realm. Him, laying bricks to reinforce the Great Wall under the constant threat of a zapping electric prod.

Bile rises like lava in my chest.

I shouldn't say anything. I wouldn't need to if Li Shimin would defend himself.

Yet he just lowers his head and keeps chewing.

I swallow my food like a gulp of fire and say, loudly, "Why would you think he'd do that when he's been in more than a dozen battles already? And if you didn't know—he *worked* on the Wall, genius."

The pilot's armor makes a scraping noise as he turns to me. The air chills several degrees, prickling my skin. It's not common for male pilots to have yin-based qi—with Qin Zheng being the notable exception—so it takes me a second to realize I'm not imagining the effect. This pilot's dominant qi must be Water, the most yin type. Its pervasive coldness is conducting through his Earth-type armor. His eyes don't glow; they subtly darken into a deeper, icier black.

"So you're that girl who killed Colonel Yang, huh?" he drawls.

His presence and the noise of the fight press against me like a swarm of flies, burrowing into my ears and cluttering my head. I eye the crowd, hoping the soldiers will come back soon. Or Sima Yi. How long does it take to change a freaking robe?

I fling a large piece of ginger out of my stir-fry. "Not my fault he couldn't handle me."

"Oh? What tricks did you use?"

"That's classified. I don't think you're important enough to know."

A muscle twitches under his eye. "I'm Wang Shicong, Earl-class pilot of the Sky Dog."

"I don't care."

He draws a sharp breath, then laughs it out. He peers at Li Shimin. "She's a feisty one, isn't she?"

Neither of us acknowledge him.

"Are you really a fox spirit?" His breath comes right against my ear.

I whip around, intending to slap him away, but he grabs my wrists. His Earth-type gauntlets give him such inhuman strength I gasp. Pain shoots through my arms.

Li Shimin slams his chopsticks down and rips him off me. The force screeches the table onto an angle.

Wang Shicong braces against the bench, a look of utter scandal on his face.

Partly hunched over the table, Li Shimin stares him down. His leash clatters over his tray.

I see Wang Shicong eyeball it. I see his hand dart out, snake-quick.

I don't see how the colossal crash ends up happening.

Food flies everywhere. Grease splatters onto me. I shudder, but then the sight before me freezes my breath in my lungs: Li Shimin, wringing his leash around Wang Shicong's neck, dragging him kicking and choking away from me.

He's strangling someone with his own chains.

I shouldn't be happy about this. It won't end well. Yet I can only watch in awe, feeling the rising pulsation of a single word inside me: *Finally*.

CHAPTER SEVENTEEN

UTTERLY RELATABLE

I t takes a few moments for the crowd to notice the new spectacle behind them. Then, with a ripple of over-shoulder glances
and slaps to friends' elbows, more and more turn around. Eyes
brighten, and voices holler even louder. Even the original fight
slows down to rubberneck in our direction. Our soldiers cry out,
but their shouts drown under the collective noise. The shifting
crowd seals shut before the soldiers, cutting them off from us.

"Shicong!" Another pilot shoves out of the mob. With partial
Fire-red armor over his shoulders and arms, he charges a qi blast
in his gauntlet palm.

Li Shimin pivots, releasing Wang Shicong. The red blast skims
just in front of Li Shimin's nose and shatters against the wall.
Debris showers across the table. I shriek and shield my eyes from
the dust.

But I'm compelled to keep watching through my fingers.
While Wang Shicong hobbles up from the ground, wheezing,
purple in the face, yellow armor shiny with grease, Li Shimin
dashes to elbow the Fire pilot in the throat. The pilot gags,

floundering. A crack of Li Shimin's hand across his cheek sends him careening in a different direction, then Li Shimin hooks the back of his neck and yanks down. Li Shimin's knee smashes a gush of blood out of the pilot's nose.

As the Fire pilot trips backward, wailing and holding his face, Li Shimin swerves to avoid a punch from Wang Shicong. My gut lurches. There's no danger of a destructive qi blast from Earth-type armor, but a direct hit anywhere guarantees a ruptured bone or organ.

Skies, where are the soldiers? No matter how much experience Li Shimin has had in prison, he can't fight two people in spirit armor!

Yet, as he and Wang Shicong trade blows, I start to unclench. There's a method to his drunk-seeming moves. He constantly swivels behind Wang Shicong while deflecting his strikes, stepping in fluid circles. It's like he's something windblown instead of a boy twice my size. Wang Shicong's gauntlets fail to give him any advantage. He can't get a single hit in, while Li Shimin keeps elbowing and smacking and striking his face. And he does it all while turning. Turning and turning, with a grace he should've had on the ice, dizzying to look at. It seems like an unnecessary flourish, but then Wang Shicong tries to kick him in the middle of a spin.

Li Shimin grabs his leg, yanks him off balance while completing the turn, then stomps on the highest part of his thigh. There's an audible *crack* as his leg juts up to an unnatural angle. Everyone gasps in giddy shock, pierced through by his guttural scream. Even I can't help the cry that leaps from my throat.

Li Shimin adjusts his glasses, a jarring move in this animalistic madness. The bloodlust in his eyes rouses something primal and deep-rooted inside me, something that finds it so . . .

Utterly relatable.

Tension dissolves from me. The bestial cheers and howls get louder, but I no longer fear them. It starts to feel natural, being in this nest of beasts.

As Li Shimin hurls Wang Shicong across the floor, red light gleams in the corner of my eye.

The Fire pilot is charging another qi blast.

I snatch my metal lunch tray and hurl it. It strikes the pilot in the chest, making him stagger and lose focus. It buys enough time for Li Shimin to reach him, twist his arm behind his back, and smash his face against the edge of our table. Then again. And again. And again.

Teeth and blood fly from the pilot's mouth. A crack splits down his lips. For an instant, his bloodshot eyes meet mine.

I regard him coolly, mindful of the still-flaking hole in the wall, a hole that could've been in Li Shimin. I take my chopsticks and slowly chew on another green bean, letting it dangle out of my lips.

The thrill of the fight clearly overpowers any resentment and prejudice against Li Shimin. The mass of spectators chants his name, quickly making it sound less like a name and more like the rhythmic howls of a wolf pack.

While it didn't seem like he'd be able to stop before, sense suddenly returns to his eyes. Discomfort writhes across his face. With a growl of frustration, he slams the Fire pilot against the table one last time, then lets him slump to the floor.

Blood dribbles from the table and from Li Shimin's fingers. A sheen of sweat glistens where his head wrapping meets his forehead. His chest heaves rapidly.

His eyes meet mine.

Oh.

I gulp down my mouthful of green bean.

This is it. He's snapped.

And I'm next. I'm about to pay for all the things I've—

"Thanks for the assist," he says, barely discernible under the realm of noise. "You all right?"

My mouth moves several times without managing sound. I thought I heard him wrong at first, but the mellowing of his gaze makes it undeniable.

"Um." I rub my sore wrists. "I'm fine."

"Okay. Sorry." He peels off his loosened head wrapping and shakes his wild hair free. His eyes glide aside, drooping.

"Sorry? Why?"

He runs a bloody and gashed hand through his hair. "No one will be happy about this. I've probably made things way harder for us."

That's not wrong.

However, when I look within myself for the logical strength to care, all I find is a flat relief, like the calm I felt about death after realizing how much I hated living.

"Let's be real." I let out a cross between a scoff and a sigh. "We were doomed from the beginning. The world will never forgive us for what we've each done, and there will always be those who will love to make us suffer. Not like we would've gained any respect by lying down and letting them do it."

His mouth pops open, then he huffs. "Yeah. That's true."

When he looks me in the eye again, a small smile cracks across his face.

A startling sensation shivers through me, like a hundred butterflies fluttering free in my chest. I tear my gaze from him, lashes batting.

A loud *bang* makes me cringe against the wall. The smell of gun smoke drifts over. A soldier has fired a warning shot into the air. The crowd finally disperses, shouts turning from elated to frightened to annoyed.

Soldiers swarm our table. They snatch Li Shimin by his arms and shoulders and try to slam him to the table, but fail to do so until he unclenches his torso and lays down himself.

"Something doesn't feel right about all this," he utters to me as they cuff him. "Be careful. Don't—!"

They fit the dark steel muzzle over his face and tighten it with a screw at the side. His eyes widen, shining with terror. He launches into a much fiercer struggle, noises squirming in his throat, but someone thrusts a syringe into his neck.

He slumps against the table, gaze clouding over. They drag him away around the moaning and weeping pilots he defeated, being tended to by other soldiers.

It's not until he's out of sight that I realize I'm covering my mouth with both hands and shaking uncontrollably.

CHAPTER EIGHTEEN

SOME OTHER GIRL I WOULD NEVER WANT TO BE

After the last rays of sunlight shrink beneath the Great Wall, Sima Yi and the soldiers escort me back to Li Shimin's cell via shuttle and then shove me in by myself.

"Be ready same time tomorrow morning!" Sima Yi says with no remaining patience before slamming the door. The crash reverberates through the walls, shaking off flakes of debris.

I swear he almost had a stroke when he finally came back to the cafeteria in fresh robes. After yelling his head off about how he was "gone for less than ten minutes!" and how much of a "nightmare couple!" we are, he managed to get Li Shimin's penalty reduced from three days in solitary confinement to just one, citing "special circumstances."

Sighing heavily, I collapse onto the bed. My hand scrunches the cold, coarse sheets. Concrete looms in every direction. As the silence stretches, it creeps in around me, squeezing my heart with a pang of fear.

I immediately get up to find something to do.

This is absurd. I should be relieved to not be locked up with Li Shimin again, not unnerved.

In the lavatory, the girl things under the sink look different now that I know he once had a partner.

During my solo lessons through the afternoon, while Sima Yi filled me in on details about Hunduns, Chrysalises, and qi, I pried for more intel on this girl. All Sima Yi would say was that her name was Wende, and she was powerful enough to have initially activated the Vermilion Bird with Li Shimin out of a rare King-class Hundun husk, but she didn't survive their first real battle.

After scrubbing the layers of makeup off my face, I rummage out the bag of painkilling herbs that belonged to her.

The lavatory door creaks.

My spine whips straight. I glance over my shoulder. The lavatory doorway's emptiness seems to warp, pulling at me.

But I shake off the fright as quickly as it came. If this girl has the ability to haunt the living, I sincerely hope she's not wasting that energy on me.

"Girl, go somewhere else," I say out loud, weary. "Go kill *anyone* else."

Silence.

"Help me," I mutter.

Nothing responds.

Duh. If dead concubine-pilots had any power, the army would be decimated by now.

Or maybe those girls are trying. Maybe they've reincarnated into Hunduns. That's an unsettling thought—

A pounding booms against the bunker door.

My spirit almost scrambles out of my body. I keep still, braced at the sink, heart hammering.

A voice shouts something, but I can't make out the words.

When I don't respond, another bout of knocks comes, increasing in urgency. And so does the voice, but I still can't understand it.

"What?" I call out.

More knocks. More unintelligible shouts.

My zapped nerves coil with frustration. Does this person not know I can't open the door from the inside?

"What is it?" I leave the herbs on the sink and head to the door. "I can't—"

The lock grinds. The door's hurled open.

A hooded man barges in.

As I cry out in shock, he pulls a bag over my head.

I scream and fight back with every bit of strength I can muster, but he smashes my face into the wall. Pain explodes across my cheek. A sharp tone rings through my head.

Still, I bolt for the door. I need to get out and shut it. Then he won't be able to—

A boot stomps on my foot.

Pain seizes me, frying my vision black. I collapse into his arms. He flings me to the bed and straddles me, his weight trapping my hips. His hands come crushing down on my windpipe.

Stars flood my obscured vision. Pressure surges into my head, seeming to compress my blood right against my face. I scratch and claw at his arms, but it does nothing.

"This is for Colonel Yang," comes his muffled, hissing voice.

It's Xing Tian, pilot of the Headless Warrior. He's come to avenge his friend.

I writhe uselessly against him. My legs, dangling off the bed, kick at nothing. Tears burn my eyes. This is not how I want to die. This can't be—!

"Get away from her! Now!"

Every raging stream of my blood stops moving at the voice.

Footsteps storm in. The pressure around my throat loosens, and I draw a huge breath. The moment Xing Tian's weight leaves my hips, I scramble wholly onto the bed. A brawl erupts between him and the newcomer. Shouts rebound through the tiny space. Fingers trembling on an unreal level, I rip the hood from my head.

Xing Tian is scurrying out the door. The person left in the bunker with me, panting, covering one eye, wearing blue-gray robes and the folded black hat of a student strategist, is Yizhi.

CHAPTER NINETEEN

MY POLAR STAR

He can't be real.

He can't be *here*.

Did I black out and dream him up?

"Skies, Zetian—" He rushes beside me on the bed. His hands find my face.

My labored breaths come hysterically fast. I can't tell if I'm hallucinating. A real-seeming ache throbs where my cheek bashed into the wall, but when am I *not* in pain? I trace the delicate angles of his features, shaking so hard I can barely make contact. Redness blooms around the eye he was covering, yet there's no denying the spirit in his thick-lashed gaze, shimmering with love and terror in equal ferocity.

I throw myself against his chest and shatter into hoarse sobs, digging my nails into his robes.

"I'm so sorry." He clutches my back as if I'd vanish if he didn't hold on. "I should've slipped out sooner. I *knew* it was suspicious when Li Shimin got an opening to do something that drastic, and no one stopped him."

As I blubber and cough, my head spins with the implications. I seize Yizhi's hands to secure a hold on reality. The soup spill on Sima Yi . . . the fight . . . the pilots provoking Li Shimin . . .

How much of this was connected? *Deliberate?*

"Everyone wants me dead," I force out of my ruined throat. Nausea rises from my belly. My shoulders refuse to stop shivering, as if my soul has had enough and is trying to worm out of this useless mortal vessel for good.

"I should've petitioned for them to post soldiers at your door." Yizhi unsashes his robe coat and drapes it around me. Our hair stirs in the breeze it creates. The scent of ink, leaves, and springtime spins through the dim bunker, chasing away the wraith of liquor haunting the stony air.

I draw the robe coat tighter around myself and rasp, "How are you even here?"

"I flexed some connections. Slipped into an ongoing strategist class."

"*Why?*" I push him away, though immediately ache for his warmth and solidity. "Look at . . ." I graze the edges of the hot, rapidly swelling skin around his eye.

"I had to come." He brushes away the wetness at my lashes with his thumb. His throat bobs through a difficult gulp. "The moment I saw you coming out of the Nine-Tailed Fox alive, I knew I had to come help you in whatever way I can. I found out you were assigned to Li Shimin, but I had faith that if anyone could survive the impossible, it was you. And you did." He breaks into a wide smile. Tears slip from his eyes, shining in the grimy light from the caged ceiling bulb.

"Why didn't you tell me somehow?"

His smile wavers, though he wrenches it back. "You're Li Shimin's partner now. It wouldn't have been fair to you to let you know I was around."

He's right. How am I ever supposed to think about that murderous drunkard again while Yizhi's here?

"You should go," I mean to say with conviction, yet my hands run down his torso, unable to keep from touching him. "I told you to let go of me. I *denounced* you."

"Nothing wrong with that when I deserved it." He curls his hand around mine and shifts it over his heartbeat. It thrums unabashedly fast. "Sometimes, I find it hard to stop prying for what I want from people. Not you, though. You always keep me in check. You made me realize I did a terrible thing, showing up to your house and putting you on the spot like that. I—I tried to buy you, for skies' sake. I even timed it so I knocked on your door just before the hovercraft came, to catch you with your last-minute regrets. I'm sorry."

I frown a little at how deep his plan went. But he's apologizing now, isn't he? "I'm glad you realize why it was wrong," I mumble with my head low. The front loops of my hair dangle in the sides of my vision.

"Yeah." He runs his knuckles along my cheek. "When you cherish someone for how amazing they are, you don't pluck them from their roots just to watch them wither in your hands. You help them bloom into the incredible thing they're really meant to be. And no, I'm not expecting anything back from you, so don't feel pressured. This is simply what I want to do."

My composure wobbles close to breaking again. "But your dream was to be a doctor."

Yizhi scoffs. "Zetian, I'm young and rich. I could go back to that any time. But, you?" He lifts my chin with the side of one finger. Warmth flutters through me like the air-rippling heat from a fire. "You're not something I could ever come across again."

"Oh, shit." My voice teeters toward an edge, high-pitched and airy. "You really do love me."

Yizhi gapes at me. Then a disbelieving laugh rolls out of him. "All right, let me make this clear: Wu Zetian, you *inspire* me. Whenever I lose hope that the world can change, I remember you. I remember how you fight for what you want, no matter what anyone says, no matter what stands in your way." He draws me into his arms and murmurs into my hair. "You're my polar star. I'll go wherever you guide me."

My heart bursts open. Out spills everything it's been holding back for the past two weeks in various prisons. I crumple against him and descend into another fit of wretched sobs, my tears staining the white fabric of his inner robes.

Eventually, I cry myself exhausted and simply weep with my head in the crook of Yizhi's neck. He strokes my hair gently. I hate that he had to save me; I hate how weak I am outside of a Chrysalis, yet for the first time in a long, long while, some semblance of peace settles inside me.

If it's him, I don't mind surrendering like this. I could spend an eternity here.

"When should I contact Strategist Sima?" His whisper makes a small yet irrevocable tear in the serenity.

My awareness lifts out of the haze it was drifting in. Everything sharpens painfully. Cold tingles numb my face. The pockmarks on the walls stare at me like a hundred accusing eyes.

If the army has any way to find out the exact time Xing Tian attacked me, we'll have to tell someone soon, or the discrepancy will be suspicious.

Then, afterward, I'll have to go back to spending my every waking moment with Li Shimin. The army cannot discover that

Yizhi and I know each other. Who knows how they'll twist it to control me?

Doom pounds in me like a funeral drum, but I straighten myself and steel my nerves. I have to make best use of this time.

I ask Yizhi to fill me in on everything I haven't been allowed to know about my notoriety. How the public has really reacted to me, what exactly they've seen.

He shows me some reactions on the message boards. I've been a consistently trending topic for the past two weeks, despite the Sages' initial efforts to censor mentions of me. It's mostly speculation on *what* I am; people seem determined to believe I'm either possessed or not human at all. They can't fathom the idea that "some random girl" could be so powerful, even though Yang Guang, Li Shimin, and Qin Zheng were all "random boys" before *their* enlistments. The pictures from today are turning the conversation to Li Shimin's and my looks, though. Curiosity makes me scroll to the actual shots, but upon the first glimpse of his arm around me, a surge of discomfort hits me.

I cannot look at these while Yizhi is here.

You know this was fake, right? I want to say, but that would sound too defensive, which would make everything worse.

Instead, I change the topic, asking if he can research whether there have been any other Iron Widows. He says he can try, but the army keeps records of previous pilots on tight lockdown.

No matter what, I refuse to believe there is anything inherently natural about the army's arrangement.

"How could they refuse to let girls have their own Chrysalises?" I say through clenched teeth. "It would be such a help to the war!"

Yizhi's eyes darken. "What family would let their son enlist if there's a realistic possibility that he'd be killed by a girl? I bet Xing Tian didn't try to murder you just because of Yang Guang.

He and the other pilots must also be terrified of you. You could kill any of them by dragging them into a Chrysalis, something that has given them nothing but power up until now. They have no idea how to handle that."

I release a sigh that seems to go on for a thousand years. "I'm so tired of being a girl."

"Yeah. If you were a boy, you'd be ruling the world by now."

"Oh, I don't know if it's that simple. I'd still have to be the right kind of boy. That's probably something you have to watch out for if you're getting a wish granted by some spirit. 'Make me a boy!' Bam. I get turned into a big, buff Rongdi. Everyone's so scared of me that they'd rather chase me to the wilds. I can't get anything done."

"That's not untrue." Yizhi quirks his brows in thought. His eyes slide aside before slowly sliding back. "You're saying that because of Li Shimin, aren't you?"

I stiffen. "I . . ."

"What's he like?" Yizhi's expression stays tame with what I can tell is active effort. "Does he treat you well?"

"I—I don't know. It's only been a day."

"Does he drink a lot?" Yizhi sniffs the air. "It smells like a distillery in here."

I tug open the drawer under the bed. The herd of flasks glimmers into view.

Yizhi's eyes jump wide, then narrow stiffly. "This isn't good. He needs to get sober. He'll never pilot with full control unless he's sober."

"Okay, you go ahead and tell him that." I heave the drawer shut. "Right after he comes out of solitary confinement for beating two armored pilots to a pulp with his bare hands."

"Good plan." Yizhi nods. "Now that you know I'm here, I might as well help you directly."

"Wait, no, I was being sarcastic."

"I know. But it's fine. I *will* need to explain why I happened to be the one who rescued you. And, honestly, I kind of want to meet him."

My mouth opens and closes. "*Why?*"

Yizhi sucks in a sharp breath. "Okay, this is going to sound really weird, but I've spent the past week digging up info on him, and he's not who the media made him out to be. Did he tell you he was enrolled in the Longxi Phoenix High School? That's one of the best in the Tang province!"

"*High school?*" I'd assumed he went to middle school at best. Anything more is overkill for anyone not aiming to be a scholar-bureaucrat under the Sages, and the bureaucrat exams are so rigged that it's virtually impossible to pass unless your family is noble or rich.

"Yeah, and he was top of his class!" With animated gestures, Yizhi tells me about his research journey tracking down people from Li Shimin's life. An old teacher, Wei Zheng, said that Li Shimin would always show up to class with fresh bruises on his hands and face, and he'd sit in the very back and never speak to anyone, but he'd ace every exam and assignment. His grades were so good that they couldn't bear to expel him. He was bringing up the whole class' grade point average.

As to how he, a boy from a family of construction workers, could afford high school, a club bouncer named Yuchi Jingde had the answer. Turns out, Li Shimin fought in this exclusive fight ring where rich people go to watch Rongdi beat each other up. The story from that end is that he would always be studying between matches, no matter how dim the lighting was. His eyes got really, really bad, but he was still one of their best fighters. Everyone found it mystifying.

"It *is* mystifying!" I splutter. "He makes no sense as a person!"

"Oh, wait until you see his art. Especially his calligraphy. I know I make fun of art students a lot, but check this out." Yizhi takes his tablet out of his robes and swipes to a photo of a poem written on paper, something not commonly used nowadays due to the need to preserve forests in Huaxia territory.

I go to remind him that I'm a frontier peasant girl who knows nothing about calligraphy—I can't even read the poem, with how stylized the characters are—but something about Li Shimin's script makes me fall stunned. The strokes and lines exude a layer of abstract meaning, like tone made visual. A tone of grace and power.

I have to pry my eyes away.

"Anyway, it's kind of sad." Yizhi gazes at the poem with heavy-lidded eyes. "I think he was genuinely trying to make a life for himself before . . . you know. And they tried him as an adult, for some reason. Even though he was only sixteen."

My heart clenches. I didn't need to hear this. "Are we exonerating murderers because of their pretty writing now?"

Yizhi lifts his head in alarm. "Since when were you bothered by the murder of non-innocents?"

"The stuff with his family—that's not the murders I'm talking about."

"Oh. Um . . ."

"I just think—okay, the only reason you're giving him these huge concessions is because your opinion of him started at rock bottom. The moment you found out he's not the total monster you expected, you had no choice but to think better of him. Way better than he deserves." I wince, pushing away the reminder of how Yang Guang caught me off guard. "But imagine if you were one of his classmates or neighbors, and you knew about this scholar stuff he did, and *then* you found out he murdered his family and became the Iron Demon. Wouldn't you have the opposite reaction? Wouldn't you stay far, far away from him forever? But it's the same information, just given in a different order."

"I mean . . ." Yizhi grimaces, then sighs. "I should still at least try to talk to him. Think about it: if I could find some opportunity to befriend him, it would be the perfect excuse to stick around you two. Then I could step in and help at any time without looking suspicious."

My jaw falls. Yizhi, *pretending to befriend Li Shimin so he can stay at my side?*

I want to reject this idea immediately—I *should* reject it, because it's begging to go wrong—but after what happened tonight, I can't find it in me to push him away yet again.

"Okay. Fine." I draw his robe coat closer around myself, praying this collision won't end in disaster.

CHAPTER TWENTY

TEN THOUSAND REASONS

L i Shimin looks worse coming out of the solitary cell than he did coming out of the fight. They didn't take his glasses, but behind the thick lenses, his eyes are bleary and bloodshot. Dark circles hang under them, deep as the bruises that have developed on my cheek and neck and around Yizhi's eye.

Guess we've all had a bad night.

"I need a drink" is the first thing Li Shimin rasps after the soldiers unlock his muzzle. A relentless stubble has slashed out of his jaw again. His hands stay in fists, clenching down tremors. His leash is conspicuously shorter.

Only after a long moment does he balk at my battered face and neck.

"I'm going to kill him!" His shout ricochets down the concrete hall after Sima Yi tells him what happened.

"*No.*" Sima Yi has to hold him back, and he gives a pacifying wave to the soldiers. "Leave the investigation to the disciplinary committee. You cannot afford to get into any more trouble. You're testing the limits of the Sages' patience as it is. This is Student

Strategist Gao." He points his thumb at Yizhi. "He happened to be wandering near your bunker and took a black eye to save your girl. Then he stayed outside all night to make sure she was safe, even after I posted soldiers at your door. He's a good kid. Thank him. Don't scheme about punching his other eye."

"Oh." Li Shimin sweeps his vein-laced eyes over Yizhi. "Um . . . thank you."

Yizhi stares up at him, chest rising and falling. I don't think he was mentally prepared for how imposing Li Shimin is in person. He reacts a second late. "It's—it's no problem! I'm a fan, you know. Read a lot about you."

"*Uh* . . ." Li Shimin starts, but doesn't seem to know how to go on.

Yizhi gulps. A blush reddens his ears, and a quizzical feeling stirs inside me.

Sometimes, I've wondered if Yizhi's attractions extend beyond girls. We never dared stray onto topics like this during our forest liaisons for fear of admitting the tension between us, but I've wondered, because of the way he would talk about certain male celebrities. Things like this are a common topic of gossip back in my village, but honestly, I've been transfixed by pictures of women myself. The notion that men and women must be with only each other tires me as much as the pilot system.

But Yizhi only spends another moment looking winded by Li Shimin's presence before he toughens his demeanor and launches into his spiel. Claiming to have been looking into Li Shimin because of the rumors of us having the power to take back the Zhou province, he offers to help him detox from alcohol with the best resources money can buy. Yizhi did discuss this with Sima Yi on our way here, and Sima Yi grudgingly agreed that we'd have much more of a fighting chance if Li Shimin piloted sober.

Li Shimin is not receptive to the idea, though. His expression snaps flat and emotionless. He starts walking away.

"No, listen." Yizhi blocks him. It takes all my discipline not to cry for him to be careful. "I don't know how things got this way, but I have faith in you. They say spirit pressure is really a measure of willpower. That means you have *ten thousand reasons* to at least try to beat this."

A tender, conflicted pain squeezes around Li Shimin's eyes. There's a second where it seems he might say yes, but then he tries to slip away again. "Leave me alone."

"*No.*" Yizhi snatches Li Shimin's leash and pulls him to his eye level. The chain rattles. Both Sima Yi and I gasp out loud.

"Let go. Now." Fury charges Li Shimin's eyes, like someone switched his soul back on. The soldiers grasp their guns. His hands clench and unclench, but stay near his legs.

Yizhi holds on, his grip quavering yet his gaze chilling into that ice-cold, single-minded vacancy that never fails to surprise me when it overcomes him. The air crackles between him and Li Shimin. I forget how to breathe.

"If you don't sober up, you'll waste both your and Pilot Wu's power," Yizhi enunciates, sounding like a completely different person. No more blushing. "That is not fair to her."

Li Shimin's scowl twitches. "What does that matter to you?"

A tiny crack splits through Yizhi's composure. I tense up, hoping only I know him well enough to have caught it.

He releases Li Shimin's leash slowly, one finger at a time. "What does this matter to *you*? You must've been waiting a long time for a girl like Pilot Wu, haven't you? There's not a single pilot who doesn't secretly long for his One True Match. You must've thought you would never find yours. Yet here she is." Yizhi's eyes drift toward me, gaining a wet sheen. "The girl who, against all odds, has made it to you."

My body goes stiff as stone.

Look away, I silently plead. *You're being too obvious.*

Yet when he does, it rips along a little piece of my heart.

"This isn't just about you anymore," Yizhi says to Li Shimin. "Look at her. Look at this girl. Are you really going to drag her down with you, even though you have ten thousand reasons to try to be better?"

Li Shimin stays silent for a long spell, but then closes his eyes and sighs through his nose. "It's eighteen thousand reasons now, actually."

"Good." Yizhi's voice shakes with loosening tension. "You will quit your vices, and you will be the best partner a girl could have. And I will be there to help you, in whatever way I can."

I don't know whether to laugh or cry.

Oh, this won't be weird at all.

CHAPTER TWENTY-ONE

NOT WEIRD AT ALL

"The army is not responsible for anything that happens to you, okay, Rich Boy?" Sima Yi unlocks the door to Yizhi's—*our* new quarters.

Yizhi has not wasted time. While Li Shimin and I spent the afternoon failing to ice dance again—made harder by his worsening alcohol withdrawal—Yizhi bought a multi-room suite right in the Kaihuang watchtower.

Okay, he didn't *buy* it. You can't buy property along the Great Wall. But he made a "generous donation" to the army, and they let him "borrow" a spare suite reserved for a high-level strategist and his family when they visit from their home city.

So the three of us are moving in together.

What I have learned through this madness is that you can absolutely solve your problems by throwing money at them. If you can't, you probably don't have enough money for that particular problem.

Since Li Shimin is supposed to be confined at all times, the lock on the front door has been replaced with one from a prison cell. We have to call Sima Yi if we want to leave. Which is fine, because his own suite is just three floors up. He warns us not to annoy him too much with door-opening requests, then shuts it behind him, penning us in for the night.

As the echoes of the door's impact fade out, a numb relief settles through me. I breathe in, breathe out, look around the suite. It's compact, practical. Not big or flourished, like a pilot's loft, but still paradise compared to Li Shimin's bunker.

Yet another reason to thank Yizhi. I could not have slept soundly there ever again.

An orange-red haze of sunset slants through a slender kitchen and across a wooden dining table. I slide open the glass doors that take me into the kitchen and lean through an open window. Barren plains spread to infinity under the setting sun, bringing the scent of earth and wild things. Here in the northwest of Huaxia, the soil is gray with deposits of Metal-white and Water-black spirit metals. These crystallized granules of qi are what Hunduns came to our planet to harvest. They need it to heal and replicate. But what *I'm* looking for is—

The White Tiger crouches in its Dormant Form beside the window, mind-bogglingly huge, ready to pounce. At the watchtower's thirteenth floor, our suite is level with its soap-smooth yet powerful neck. It looks naked, not being striped with the green and black lines bestowed by its legendary pilot pair, but an intense thrill roils through me nonetheless. It's like I'm a kid again, back when I could relish the tales of Chrysalises and pilots without thinking about the implications.

"Yizhi!" I squeal and grab his arm as he comes beside me. "That's the White Tiger! The White Tiger! Right there!"

"What's the deal?" He laughs. The blazing sky flushes his face and ignites his eyes. The wild winds skim a stray hair across his cheek. "You pilot the Vermilion Bird!"

I sigh, guilt and cold reality draining my excitement. Even though the White Tiger is piloted by a Balanced Match and is safe to root for, it's still part of this terrible piloting system. I cannot buy into the fantasy of power and heroism that hides the true horrors. "Right." I tuck the stray strand of hair behind Yizhi's ear, then peer at the ceiling. "Dugu Qieluo and Yang Jian live in the loft, right? Wonder if we'll run into them."

Yizhi shies at my touch, but smiles wryly. "I heard it's best never to cross paths with Dugu Qieluo."

"Oh, please. You know they exaggerate any stories about a girl with an attitude. Besides, isn't Yang Jian the one I should be worrying about?" I drop my voice. "He *is* distantly related to Yang Guang, right?"

"I heard they didn't get along." Yizhi shrugs. "Plus, he's a freaking Prince-General. He wouldn't do something as impulsive as Xing Tian."

"Hope you're right. I don't want to worry about another—"

Li Shimin's looming figure catches the corner of my eyes. He's standing outside the kitchen, the fiery sunset gleaming off his glasses.

My hand springs from Yizhi's arm as if scalded.

"Uh, I'll start brewing the medicine." Yizhi manages a smile, lifting the paper-wrapped package of herbs that the army doctors recommended for Li Shimin. They prescribed some expensive lab medicine, too, but traditional herbal remedies are better for qi flow in the long run.

As Yizhi sets up a clay pot, I leave the kitchen. Li Shimin doesn't get out of my way, even when my face nearly skims his chest. My ribs cringe against my lungs, but I click the glass doors shut behind me, shoulder past him, and sit down at the table, acting nonchalant. The weight of his gaze follows me, clings to me, presses down on me.

Footsteps. Wood screeches against tiles as he pulls a chair out and sits down as well.

A prickle travels up my spine and over my scalp. My throat goes dry. I eye the bulky metal front door that's preventing me from escaping. The memory of him smashing the Fire pilot's face against our cafeteria table shudders through my mind. I keep my eyes on the table's sticky vinyl surface, heart pounding out a prayer for him to not ask questions about me and Yizhi.

Then I snap out of it.

Countless times, I watched my father turn my mother into a nervous wreck by simply transforming himself into a dark cloud of a presence. He wouldn't use any curses or shouts, but he'd set his bowl down a little too loudly, or slam doors a little too harshly. She'd step cautiously around him as if he were a bomb, worrying about her every move for fear of setting him off. Without uttering a single word, he'd teach her to twist herself into knots to prioritize his needs and wants, in some strangling hope of quelling the pressure in the house and returning things to normal.

I was never willing to learn my father's lessons. My default solution was always to push him until he exploded. A few moments of pain were better than days and nights of fear.

"Do you have a problem?" I hiss under my breath, jerking my head up.

Li Shimin's gaze bounces away from mine, but his shoulders keep quivering with strain. The dark circles under his eyes look dented into his bones. His lips press into a tight, flat line, as if holding back a shout—or a cry of pain. His body is a war zone of conflicting things. I can't tell what's a symptom and what's an emotion.

Water boils and whistles from the clay pot, muffled through the kitchen doors. Steam fogs up the glass, lit a volcanic orange by the falling sun.

"Don't *sulk*." My fingers retract like claws across the tabletop. "I *hate* guys who sulk."

Shock flashes across Li Shimin's face. Then, between ragged breaths, he starts speaking. "I . . . I just didn't know you were capable of looking that happy."

"And that bothers you?"

"You're hiding something."

"Believe whatever you want. We're not a real couple. I owe you *nothing*."

A muscle works in his jaw. He adjusts the wristlet Yizhi gave him to keep track of his bio-stats. "This isn't about that. This is about us having to be honest with each other. Whatever it is, I could find out in our battle link, and it could ruin our synchronization if it's shocking enough. So . . . what really happened last night?"

I grunt. Fine. Better to come clean early than to let his suspicions brew. The important thing is that the army stays ignorant, and I doubt he'll blab to them when Yizhi is doing so much to help us.

I lean over the table while beckoning for Li Shimin to come closer. He does. Our faces pass each other. His stubble almost grazes my cheek.

"Remember that city boy I told you about? The one who taught me to read?" I whisper near his ear, my eyes sliding toward the orange-misted kitchen doors. Yizhi's flowing-robed figure shifts like smoke behind them. "That's him. Right there."

Li Shimin's chest hitches. He pulls back slightly. "He came here for you."

"Yes. He did."

A soft breath shudders out of his mouth, the heat ghosting past my cheek. To my surprise, his eyes moisten. Or maybe it's just his glasses reflecting the orange light.

"And do you love him?" he whispers, without malice, without accusation.

My everything comes to a standstill.

I've never admitted it out loud, but when I look deep inside myself, the answer is clear. Undeniable.

"I do." My voice trembles as hard as Li Shimin's hands. "He's the most amazing boy to ever walk this planet."

His brows squeeze upward. "And yet you chose enlistment over him?"

I fall back against my seat. How is Li Shimin sounding like a naive romantic?

"Yes, because love doesn't solve problems," I say. "Solving problems solves problems."

"Poor guy." Li Shimin gazes at the kitchen doors, then back at me, shaking his head slightly. "Don't you ever let that boy go again."

"Too bad." I pick at the edge of the table. "You're the one I'm stuck with."

Yet after the night deepens, after failing to control my whirlwind of thoughts, it's Yizhi's door I knock on.

"Zetian?" He blinks sleepily while opening the door. "What are you—?"

I grab his face and pull him into a kiss.

His words muffle against my lips, dispersing into hot, brilliant tingles that tide through me. They streak across my nerves, jolting lower, lower, awakening the parts of me I've been taught to hide and ignore my whole life, because although they are part of me, they were never for my free use. They hold my family's honor, they're property that must not be damaged before delivery, they're meant to be saved for my eventual husband. For Yang

Guang. For Li Shimin. To pleasure him, to extend his bloodline.

Well, fuck that.

I push Yizhi farther into the room. A nudge of my hand closes the door behind us. Our frantic breathing and the soft sounds of our mingling mouths crowd around my head, making the world shrink down to just the two of us. This is a different kind of desperation than our first kiss, right before I left him to come here. Feather-soft heat buoys through my body and stretches a tender, aching tension in me to the point of snapping. I hate that I'm not immune from this want, this *need*.

But if it's him, it just might be okay.

He steps back, carried by my momentum, but then stumbles. He pries himself from the kiss.

"Zetian . . . we shouldn't . . ." he says, light and airy. His hair is completely down—the first time I've seen it so. It frames his elegant face, making him look so vulnerable, so beautiful. Moonlight strains through a thin curtain, caressing his features as if it adores him too.

"Yizhi, we're finally alone," I whisper, peering up at him through my lashes. "Truly alone. And I know you want me." I take his hands and guide them over the curves of my body, emboldened by the anxiety that something ever more terrible might happen at any time and cost us the chance to do this. "You've wanted me since the first time we met. Isn't that right?"

Three years ago, when we were both fifteen, I found him meditating near one of my favorite herb bushes. I had never seen anyone with skin that clear, hair that glossy, or clothes that clean and white. It was unnatural.

So I snapped a branch off the nearest tree and attacked him.

I have no idea why he ended up promising to come back. But whatever it is about me, it made him keep that promise, again and again, at the end of every month.

It spellbinds him still, intoxicating him, clouding over his eyes. He bites his lip.

"I want it to be you." I gently trace the bruise around his eye. The bruise he took to save my life, the only flaw I've ever seen on his face. "I'll have no regrets if it's you."

He tenses twice. First at my words, then again, tighter, when I skim my lips down the pulse at his neck. His chest lifts with a shaky, almost inaudible gasp. His blood throbs faster and faster near the tip of my tongue. His fingers crumple the sides of the proper night robes he got for me. Finally, he pulls my head back with a slight tug on my hair and joins his mouth to mine with an unleashed hunger.

An electric storm crackles through me like Wood-type qi, wild and lively, the kind of force that drives the rampant growth of all things during springtime. My lips pull into a grin under the onslaught of his. A growl of relief crawls through his throat.

So this is what he was holding back while smiling innocently at me and teaching me a world of knowledge I'm not supposed to know.

Good. Because this is what I fantasized about as well while acting cool and collected and making wry comments about his class notes.

For a sudden, still moment in the madness, like passing the eye of the storm, our eyes meet. His sly, mine challenging. The same dark energy hums between us. It's like seeing each other unmasked for the first time.

Then we're back to kissing fervidly, longingly. Our hands claw, knead, and swim over each other's bodies, touching one another in all the ways we could not have in the woods. In all the ways we still shouldn't.

I urge him forward again, on an angle, until the bed collides with the back of his knees. He slumps onto the silk sheets, the mattress gasping under his weight. His hair flattens out around him. I flip my own over one shoulder while climbing over him, watching the drags of his breaths, running my knuckles along his delicate jawline. He lets out a long exhale, baring the pale column of his neck. I trace the ridges, the valleys. His pulse palpitates against my fingertips. I feel every bit like the fox spirit people believe me to be, here to seduce him and then eat him alive.

My fingers slither down, twirl around his robe sash, and pull it loose.

"Wait—" Sudden clarity surges into his eyes.

Too late.

His robes fall open with a small gust of heat. The sight beneath dazes me.

His torso is covered in tattoos. Colorful blossoms outlined by thin gold, entwined in a forest of vines and leaves. Roses. Lilies. Poppies.

He sits up, gaze unreadable. I scoot back in his lap to accommodate the motion.

"Do you know what these mean?" he mumbles huskily, touching a poppy on his chest.

"No?" I shake my head while taking in more details. Dragonflies, butterflies, moths. And the vines aren't just vines—some of them are *snakes*.

"They mean I'm part of the family." His jaw tightens. "My father's family."

"He makes you and your siblings get tattoos?"

The lean muscles in his body slacken. His expression turns both sad and amused. "Some of us."

Chills crawl up my scalp. There's something he's not elaborating on. "Is this good or bad?"

"Depends on your perspective." He caresses my cheek, smile softening. Then he lies back while guiding me down again.

"Someday I'll explain it better," he whispers in my ear while shrugging off his robe top. I move to kiss him again, hair swishing over his.

But something's not the same. Deep in my mind, something has cooled off.

My awareness lingers on his tattoos. They meander over his shoulders and down to his elbows. I've seen his floppy luxury-brand sleeves slump near there so many times, yet never have I suspected that all of this could be lurking just beyond the perfect pale skin of his forearms. My mind reels back, farther and farther from where it should be, splintering. Cold logic worms into the cracks.

I've always known Yizhi wasn't a "good" person. The only utterly good people in the world are either naive or delusional. I could never associate with someone like that. There was always an element of danger, an edge of a thrill, to our meet-ups. I could've died if someone had caught us together. He knew this. No one truly pure would've continued subjecting me to that kind of pressure.

But how far does the darkness in him go? How well can I really know someone after seeing them a mere once per month for three years?

What do I actually know about doing *this*?

A growing anxiety simmers in me. I kiss him harder, drawing a sweet thread of blood, yet it just feels more wrong. Images shred through the mess in my head. Me not resisting as Yang Guang hovers over me, his armored weight trapping my body, his mouth kissing me just like this. Me not being able to resist as Xing Tian straddles and strangles me.

Me not wanting to resist as Li Shimin leans over a puddle of fresh blood on our cafeteria table, flashing a rare, precious smile.

I jolt up in a burst of horror.

The trance clears from Yizhi's eyes. "What's wrong?"

"It's—it's nothing." I rattle my head, leaning down again.

Beep. Beep. Beep.

Our eyes whip toward the wristlet on the nightstand. Yizhi gives a reassuring pat to my shoulder, then maneuvers out from beneath me to go check it. The screen illuminates his face.

His features twist with shock.

He grabs his robe top and dashes from the bed.

"It's Shimin," he gasps, ripping his door open while dressing. "His heart rate is spiking out of control."

CHAPTER TWENTY-TWO

MESS

We find Li Shimin collapsed on the floor of his room, clutching the woven mats in agony.

"Shimin?" Yizhi drops down beside him, taking his hand, feeling around his wrist to diagnose his pulse. A slight hoarseness in Yizhi's voice is the only indicator of what we were doing. "What are you feeling right now?"

"Wende?" Li Shimin looks at Yizhi with an expression so raw and tender it stops me dead in the doorway, my moon-cut shadow looming over the pair of them. He cups Yizhi's face with a scarred, shaking hand.

Then terror kindles in his eyes, and he pushes at Yizhi. "Don't ... no ... get away from me, Wende ... don't go into the cockpit ..."

"What in the skies is wrong with him?" I make myself totter in and crouch down. The smell of acid and herbs gags me. He must've retched up all the medicine Yizhi barely managed to coax into him.

"He's hallucinating and delirious." Yizhi grimaces with his fingers on Li Shimin's pulse, then brushes Li Shimin's short hair out of the way and puts his forehead to his. "And he's burning up. Skies."

"All this, just from not drinking alcohol?"

"That's exactly how bad withdrawal can get, Zetian. Stay with him. I'll go call Sima Yi and the doctors. Outside." Yizhi pushes off the woven mats. "I think I'm confusing him."

"Wende . . ." Li Shimin latches to Yizhi's robes. "Don't go into the cockpit . . . don't go . . ."

A startling feeling clamps around my heart. Shaking it away, I wrench Li Shimin's face toward me. "That's not your dead partner!"

"Zetian," Yizhi gently berates over his shoulder as he shuffles out of the room. "No need to make it harder on him."

I huff, but catch Li Shimin's lolling head. His scalp heats my palm through his chopped hair. Sweat beads at their roots. A tremor comes over me, almost matching his.

I gnash my teeth together. Why does my body keep reacting to him in ways I don't want it to? Is my subconsciousness *that* determined to serve the male master the world appoints for me?

"I hate you." My voice squeezes high and unsteady. "You're messing me up."

His gaze swims in and out of focus. "Sorry."

"And stop apologizing!"

"Sorry." His eyelids fall shut, yet continue to quiver.

"*Aiyah*, I didn't know it had gotten this bad," Sima Yi grumbles, rocking on a stool in the medical bay. His hair is tied in a hasty topknot, and his strategist coat is draped over his night robe like a cloak. "I cannot believe the incompetent fools at Sui-Tang let it get to this point."

"Central Command wasn't aware of his condition?" Yizhi sits on another stool beside Li Shimin's bed, holding his hand while he shakes uncontrollably.

"No. He wasn't like this when *I* trained him. I even left them with a detailed training plan, yet here we are." Sima Yi draws his robe coat tighter and turns away. "Though it's true that I didn't leave him in the best mental state, after what happened with Wende. They likely got tired of dealing with his emotions and just enabled him."

I sit near the other side of the bed, pressing down on Li Shimin's quivering arm. The tremors are so bad the army doctors have left us for now, saying they can't do acupuncture until the lab medicine injected into his bloodstream calms his nerves.

Medicine like that makes me nervous. It's not natural to mess with your qi flow that drastically. But I guess that was exactly what he was doing with the alcohol, long term.

The doctors say Li Shimin's primordial qi—the qi that breathed life into him, that runs out over a lifetime with no possibility of being replenished—has been severely damaged, and his liver is hanging on by a thread. We can't call the detoxing off. If he relapses, the next withdrawal will be worse. And no one knows if he'll survive that.

No one knows if he'll survive *this*.

A thin pitch sharpens between my ears. The world crumbles away, closing in on Li Shimin's trembling arm in my grip.

Wouldn't it be perfect if he died now? If I kill him in the Vermilion Bird, the Hunduns will sense his death and be pacified into backing off a little, so the army will feel less pressure to keep me around. But if he dies of natural causes, not only will the army have no crime to execute me for, the Hunduns will keep coming at their current intensity. The power vacuum might make the army desperate enough to let me inherit the Bird in my own right.

"—especially when he lost half his liver in prison." Yizhi's words rupture my reverie.

"Wait, what?" I blink, raising my head.

"Half a liver and one kidney." Yizhi's eyes flick up at me. "That's what they take from every healthy death row inmate. For anyone who needs a transplant."

My blood crawls into slush. The kidneys are the most important vessels for primordial qi. By losing one, Li Shimin's healthy lifespan has essentially been slashed in half.

"Could you not buy him replacements from another murderer?" Sima Yi asks.

"I could," Yizhi says. "But a surgery that big would leave him unable to pilot for months, way longer than this. Would the army sign off on that?"

Sima Yi's mouth goes tight. "Not until after we take back Zhou."

"Always comes back to that, doesn't it?" Yizhi sighs, clasping Li Shimin's hand tighter.

I can't stop staring at their joined hands. A slender one meant for sorting medicinal herbs and pipetting solutions in a lab, entwined with a brutalized one meant for beating enemies half to death.

Or for conjuring poems in stunning calligraphy, apparently.

My awareness strays to Li Shimin's face, then darts away from the anguish contorting his features.

No, never mind, he can't die like this. Yizhi would be held responsible for making him detox.

"Power through this, Iron Demon." I squeeze his arm.

He coughs, dry and raspy. He tries to get up.

"Don't move." Yizhi rushes to cradle his head.

"Don't go," Li Shimin murmurs, nuzzling against Yizhi's hand. "I won't."

My gut twists. This level of caring for someone else is beyond me. I shouldn't rely on Yizhi, shouldn't drag him into my mess, yet I could never support Li Shimin through this.

Yizhi helps him to a mug of water. Li Shimin takes a shaky sip, then immediately retches over the side of the bed. I suck in a sharp breath when blood dribbles out of his mouth in addition to acid.

Then *everything* goes red.

An alarm bleats through the watchtower's concrete hollows. A large, round bulb on the ceiling floods the room with a warning light.

"Um . . ." I sit straighter.

Sima Yi rises from his stool, mouth moving absently and inaudibly over the sirens before he raises his voice. "This is very soon for another Hundun attack!"

"Does it concern us?" I shout.

"No, ignore it!" Sima Yi waves his hand, sitting back down. "You aren't on active duty!"

"Right!" I say, but can't wrestle down the urge to do something. It feels different, now that I know there's such war-changing power within me. Like every girl that dies after this would be partly my fault.

A massive crash outside quakes the walls. Then another. Then another. Then another, growing in speed.

I stagger up from my stool and toward the buzzing window. I throw the curtain aside.

The White Tiger has awakened. It races away from the watchtower on all fours. Its pale limbs, striped by green and black, blur into spectral streaks, smearing into the night. The thundering impacts of its motions swiftly fade out. Metal-type Chrysalises may not be good at conducting qi into outward blasts, but they can harness their internal properties. The lively Wood qi humming through its body makes it run astoundingly fast, while the adaptive Water qi keeps its movements fluid and easy.

"Wow," I breathe, relaxing a little. "Look!" I turn to Yizhi.

He's paying no attention. Instead, he's wiping the blood from Li Shimin's mouth with a wad of gauze, saying something I can't hear over the sirens. Li Shimin nods, though he keeps shivering like it's the dead of winter.

An absurd feeling of being left out throbs within me.

But it's not like this room needs two Yizhis. I have my own strengths in other things.

The sirens fade after a minute, giving way to the tinny noises from a livestream Sima Yi opened on his wristlet. I limp over to him, kneading along the bed frame for balance.

With a burst of green light on the screen and a roar that crackles the speakers, the White Tiger rises on its hind paws while transforming. Legs lengthening, shoulders growing, paws extending into clawed hands. Its jaw gapes wide, and a human face morphs out inside it, so it ends up looking like a warrior wearing a tiger helmet. Its torso becomes like armor sculpted from milky glass. Solid green and black highlights transmute around every piece.

A Heroic Form, achieved in less than three seconds. Even though Metal-type Chrysalises are the second hardest to transform, right after Earth types.

"How do they work together so well?" I shake my head. "What's the secret?"

"They know they're supposed to be a team." Sima Yi angles an unamused, condemning look at me. A strange shame sears through me. "They do the parts they're good at, then pull back when it's necessary. They don't fight each other for control. They trust each other."

The White Tiger slaps its breastplate and begins wrenching a long dagger-ax—its signature weapon—out of its chest. Its eyes dim from Wood green to Water black, from most yang to most yin. Which makes sense, because while Wood qi is best for triggering transformations, it's Water qi that's best for shaping spirit metal. A black-hazed dent sinks around the dagger-ax as it emerges. The moment the end snaps free, the breastplate morphs back to its original look.

Twirling the dagger-ax, the Tiger takes a springing leap into battle. Its eyes change color: one green and one black, two qis surging in sync, two hearts beating as one. It vaults, stabs, and sweeps through a glinting swarm of Hunduns.

I peer at Li Shimin over the top edge of the screen. My teeth dig into my lip.

"Hey, what's that noise?" Yizhi's head perks up.

"The ba—" I start. But then I hear it too.

A storm of boot steps grows steadily louder in the hall outside. Shouts surge from the soldiers at the door. I look to Sima Yi.

Before anything helpful makes it out of his mouth, the door bursts open, revealing a strategist with a huge potbelly. He must be An Lushan, Chief Strategist of the Sui-Tang frontier. Sima Yi cracked a few jokes about him during my solo lessons.

"Here you are." He breathes deeply, then points at Li Shimin. "You. Into battle. *Now.*"

CHAPTER TWENTY-THREE

UTTER AND MUTUAL MISERY

"No!" Yizhi, Sima Yi, and I exclaim at once.

"This is an order." An Lushan keeps scowling at Li Shimin. "Get on a shuttle and head for the Vermilion Bird. Immediately."

Soldiers pour into the room like clots of blood in the red light, but not all of them point their guns at us. The ones who came with Sima Yi turn around, guarding him. The two sides hold each other at gunpoint, but confusion and uncertainty flicker across the soldiers' faces and stances.

"Pilot Li is in no condition to battle!" Sima Yi hops off his stool and marches in front of the bed. He would look a lot more assertive if he weren't dressed like he's on a midnight trip to the lavatory.

"He was certainly well enough to beat up two of my pilots yesterday." An Lushan approaches, steps shockingly light and nimble. My body screams with the urge to back away, toward Yizhi, toward some semblance of safety. But I cannot betray that level of weakness. I stay rooted in place, bracing myself with Sima Yi's stool to keep from falling over.

"He's going through alcohol withdrawal now." Yizhi pushes to his feet, stool screeching back. His fingers linger on Li Shimin's shoulder.

"Oh, I know." An Lushan's eyes crinkle. "But this is an urgent situation. A pilot must always be ready to give their all for the sake of Huaxia."

"It's been only two days since their last battle!" Sima Yi says in his bone-jolting commander voice. His personality makes it easy to forget his true stature in the army sometimes, but this tone never fails to slam in a reminder. "Two. Days. Strategist An, are you mad, trying to send them in again?"

An Lushan shakes his head slowly. "Strategist Sima, the fact of the matter is, the unnatural transformations of the Nine-Tailed Fox and the Vermilion Bird have agitated the Hunduns beyond our normal defense capacities." His scrutiny slicks past me, leaving my skin crawling. "A *compromise* must be made."

"*No.*" Sima Yi's eyes slash into daggers. "No, you are not *tributing* him!"

"Well, we, the Senior Strategists of Sui-Tang, who actually know the intricacies of this frontier, have just reached a majority agreement that this would be for the best. Pilot Li has been impossible to control. Every time he's summoned for battle, it's like trying to take a bull to slaughter—when it's not even his life that's at risk! We cannot factor him properly into our tactics at all!"

"Highest spirit pressure since Emperor-General Qin himself, and you want to *tribute him*? In the name of Central Command, I will not allow this!"

"When under direct and active threat, local strategists reserve the right to deploy any pilot as deemed necessary." An Lushan's nostrils flare. "And we have deemed this necessary to protect our troops and our people!"

Sima Yi is not winning this argument.

An Lushan and his soldiers seem to close in like figures in a blood-tinged nightmare, even though their boots haven't budged. My knees wobble, and I try to gulp down breaths to calm myself. But urgency froths over in me, and I have to do *something*.

"Hey." I jut my chin. "Does tributing a pilot mean what I think it means?"

An Lushan's glare slices into me. "Shut your mouth. The men are talking."

Rage charges my body, scattering my fear, setting every muscle on edge. I scan the soldiers and their guns, wondering if it'd be worth getting shot to break An Lushan's nose.

"Tributing is the ultimate coward's way out, is what it is!" Sima Yi responds without taking his eyes off An Lushan.

"With all due respect, Strategist Sima, we don't have time for this. Huaxia's safety is at stake." An Lushan tilts his head, an eerie scarlet glint dancing in his eyes. He makes a gesture at a soldier beside him.

The soldier brings a full bottle of grain liquor out from behind his back.

Wheezing out a gasp, Li Shimin lunges for it.

Exclamations erupt from Yizhi and Sima Yi as they hold him back. I falter against Sima Yi's stool, head spinning, pulse quickening with explosive force.

Why do they have that bottle ready?

An Lushan takes it from the soldier and dangles it by its neck. He shoots Li Shimin a pitying look. "You want this, don't you? You know the deal. Go battle like a good boy, and this is yours."

Bile scorches up my throat.

This has happened before. This is why the Sui-Tang frontier

has enabled Li Shimin's drinking: they've gotten him to go into his Chrysalis and sacrifice girls by using liquor as bait.

I stomp through the pain in my feet and smack the bottle from An Lushan's pinching fingers. It smashes on the floor in an eruption of glass, fluid, and noxious fumes.

He gapes at me. Then his arm jerks.

The slap collides with my already-bruised cheek, flinging me against the foot of the bed. Heat and pain shatter through my face. A ringing drawls through my skull.

"Zetian!" Yizhi rushes to my side.

"Rich Boy, get her! Go, go, go!" Sima Yi drags Li Shimin off the bed and charges for the door.

There's only a brief flash of bewilderment in Yizhi's eyes before he scoops me up.

"You can't shoot me; I'm from Central Command!" Sima Yi shouts, ramming through the soldier standoff.

"You can't shoot me; I'm rich!" Yizhi slips through the opening created.

They haul me and Li Shimin into the hallway, bathed a darker red than the room. Boot steps clatter after us, but they remain slow and hesitant. The soldiers must be confused by this power struggle between Central Command and the local strategists. An Lushan bellows curses over our heads. The mighty sounds bounce around the walls.

I dip and sway in Yizhi's arms, my weight curling him over. Li Shimin staggers on with Sima Yi's help.

Our eyes meet in a moment of utter and mutual misery.

Maybe it'd be better to throw our lives away in the Vermilion Bird after all, just to stop being so helpless.

But then I'm furious. I'm this way because my family crushed my feet in half when I was five—how did *he* end up like this?

Sima Yi scans his wristlet at an elevator.

Beep.

He shoves Li Shimin through the opening doors. Yizhi carries me in, then collapses to the ground, gasping for breath. Sima Yi jabs a button repeatedly. The doors start gliding shut as the soldiers approach.

Close! Close! Close! I scream in my head.

The doors slide past their faces, but someone's hand darts through the final gap.

Just as I'm about to tear my hair out, Yizhi stabs it with a syringe from his robe pocket. The hand slithers out like a startled snake.

The elevator rumbles, then scrapes downward.

Heavy breathing. Buzzing metal.

"*You!*" I stagger upright and shove Li Shimin on the chest. He's so weak he crashes against a wall, rocking the whole elevator, and slumps to the ground. I ignore the protests from Yizhi and Sima Yi. "You've let him manipulate you into battle with that trick before, haven't you?"

With labored effort, Li Shimin sits up against the wall. He wrings his shaking hands together and presses them to his forehead. No answer.

Yizhi reaches for my shoulder. "Ze—"

"You sacrifice girls like they tell you to so you can drink again when it's all over, don't you?" I scream louder, batting Yizhi's hand away.

"That's never the whole reason!" Li Shimin chokes out, chin snapping up, smeared with vomited blood as if he just devoured a freshly extracted heart.

"Stop it!" Sima Yi barges between us, barring my chest with his arm.

"It seems to me like it's a pretty strong factor!" I keep yelling. "You knew that a girl would die every time you activated a Chrysalis! You knew that, and yet you decided that your *liquor* was worth more than their lives!"

"Zetian!" Yizhi raises his voice.

I flinch. He has never spoken to me like this.

His eyes soften immediately. "Zetian, he's legitimately ill. The brain is just another organ, and his is sick. He can't will his mind to stop wanting alcohol any more than someone with a cold can will their lungs to stop aching. It makes him not himself. Please try harder to understand."

"No . . . she's right . . ." Li Shimin rises on his knees, glaring at me from under his wild hair. "This is exactly who I am. But . . . it was never the alcohol that I decided was worth more than those girls. It was *me*. I let them die to save myself. Every. Single. Time. That's the truth you want me to admit, isn't it?" He coughs. Blood splatters out of his mouth, which he shields with his wrist. "Well, there it is! Happy?"

He lashes his bloody arm to the side. His hoarse voice rings into oblivion. The elevator grinds deeper and deeper, swaying.

The trails of tears shining down to his jaw are too much to look at. Eyes wedging shut, I thump backward against the wall. My heart throbs, a small and lonesome thing in the hollow of my chest.

"Are you two done?" Sima Yi says, sullen.

"Where are we going?" I mumble, cupping my head with both hands.

"The concubine quarters. Prince-General Yang Jian doesn't keep any, so they're empty. We can hide there until the battle ends, then An Lushan won't be able to do anything anymore. But I don't think you two understand how important it is to get over whatever qualms you have with each other." He vibrates with barely contained rage. "He was right about one thing: for the Hunduns to attack again this soon, they're reacting as if you've managed a real level-three transformation in the Vermilion Bird. They, too, can sense that we now have the potential to take out their nest in Zhou. They'll attack and attack until we either lose enough Chrysalises to lose our advantage or actually gamble everything on a counterattack. But until you two get your act together, your potential won't translate into substance! Chief Strategist Zhuge and I will be powerless to stop you from getting tributed when things get worse! *Do you hear me?*"

"*Is* being tributed exactly what it sounds like?" Yizhi repeats my question from earlier, and I'm grateful. Because I can't find the strength to shape any words.

Sima Yi massages the bridge of his nose. "Yes, it's when pilots are deliberately and abruptly pushed into battle in subpar circumstances. So the Hunduns can feel their deaths happen and be appeased. Obviously, it's not talked about openly, but it happens. Especially to pilots deemed too difficult, or too uncooperative, or getting too old."

My stomach pulses against my lungs. Twenty-five. That's the age the brain stops developing, stops being malleable enough to command a Chrysalis well. The age pilots almost never pass. Even twenty is hard enough.

This information chills deep into my core, yet when I think about how things are, how quickly pilots spin in and out of media coverage and popularity, it's not that surprising.

Yizhi rakes his hands through his hair, messing up his half-do. "Can't—can't you get the Sages to order Strategist An to leave them alone?"

Sima Yi shakes his lowered head. "Not all the Sages believe in the idea of launching a counterattack. Not even all of Central Command. If it doesn't go right, the Hunduns would decimate our forces, breach the Wall, and we'd almost certainly lose Tang. Just like we did Zhou."

Blood drains in a tingling tide out of my face. When he puts it that way, I get it.

"It's our lives against everyone's." My knees buckle. I slump to the ground, just like Li Shimin. "Everyone in Sui and Tang."

"But that's the coward's way of thinking!" Sima Yi says with surprising force. "How will we ever win the war if we don't gamble on powerful pilots? You both have astronomically rare spirit types, and you've come together. There won't be another chance like this in hundreds of years. I am not giving up on you two!"

The elevator clatters. Once again, my eyes and Li Shimin's find each other in misery.

I can't kill him. Not even in a Chrysalis. Clearly, a good portion of the army would rather tribute the pilots they don't like than use their power, no matter how rare and incredible it is.

Maybe he and I are truly like two wing-sharing birds, those pitiful creatures that hobble around the forest floor with one wing and one eye, who can only take flight if they find a mate to lean on.

I let out a growl of frustration, digging the heels of my hands against my temples. This is wrong. All wrong. He and I are the two most powerful pilots in Huaxia, by a gigantic margin.

He should be the Iron King, and I should be the Iron Queen.

Yet Iron Demon and Iron Widow is all they'll let us be.

This will not do. I will not let this power go.

But if there's one thing I've learned so far, it's that brute strength means nothing on its own. It just makes everyone else want to strike you down.

I need friends. Allies. Someone actually from the Sui-Tang frontier, instead of Sima Yi and Chief Strategist Zhuge, who are no doubt pissing off the Sui-Tang strategists harder by overruling from above. I need someone who can convince these strategists to reverse their emergency vote to tribute us.

I need help from someone like Dugu Qieluo.

When Sima Yi turns on his livestream again, I watch the White Tiger intently. I think, of all people, Qieluo would understand me best. She was the most powerful female pilot before I came along, after all. And she must've gotten familiar enough with the Sui-Tang strategists in her seven years of service to potentially change their minds.

It's about time I paid her a visit.

CHAPTER TWENTY-FOUR

THE TIGRESS

An Lushan is of course livid at the stunt we pulled. But with Chief Strategist Zhuge Liang on our side, he couldn't do much against us after the battle ended.

We can't coast on that forever, though. The various frontiers and their local strategists may technically be under the authority of Central Command, but Central Command answers to the Sages, and can't claim to know the intricacies of each region. If every single senior Sui-Tang strategist insists it's a better idea to tribute us than to risk our continued existence, the Sages will take their word, even if Central Command is an all-star team of the best and most experienced strategists from across Huaxia.

We need to start changing attitudes fast.

Even though the Kaihuang watchtower is right in front of the Tiger Cage training camp, some rigid rule forces Qieluo and Yang Jiang to relocate from their luxury loft to a camp bunker all the same once they're qi-exhausted and off-duty, so there's an opportunity to catch Qieluo at the communal showers. With a jade necklace as incentive (courtesy of Yizhi, after we waited out the battle), the auntie who manages the showers alerts me the next time Qieluo shows up.

When I push through the showers' translucent vinyl curtains, naked, I find half a dozen women and a few children in the steam. Mostly servant aunties, I'm assuming—and Dugu Qieluo.

She's impossible to miss. She's sitting on a short wooden stool away from everyone else, shampooing her hair. The Metal-white spinal brace from her White Tiger armor runs like a strip of porcelain down her back. With that on, and its connection needles constantly in her spine, she'd only have to lean against the rest of her armor to reconnect with it. This saves pilots from having to endure the jab of the needles over and over. The needles are thin enough that they don't impact the regular mobility of pilots.

I stand rooted to the tiled floor for a few moments, gripping my basket of small glass toiletry bottles. Despite the whole baffling list of things I've been through, Qieluo's presence makes me feel like a simple frontier peasant again, unworthy of gazing upon a Princess-General, the highest status a girl could achieve.

Until you, I remind myself.

I grab a stool and totter over to her.

Her shampooing hands halt when I clank my stool down beside her. A caged heat lamp seethes in a crevasse in the wall, infusing the steam with the taste of wet metal. Slowly, she turns to me, features stiff with offense. But upon catching sight of my face, she abruptly slackens with surprise. Her irises sizzle with her Wood-green qi—a spinal brace still works to conduct it.

I struggle not to make the same expression, because, *oh skies, Dugu Qieluo is looking right at me.*

"Uh, hi." I clear my throat, carefully sitting down on my stool. "I'm Wu Zetian. I'm new."

She narrows her eyes, which are even more deep-set and blade-like than Li Shimin's, given her full Rongdi heritage. "Yes. *You.*"

My mouth dries up. I catch sight of her feet, unbound in wooden slippers. We Han folk scoff at the Rongdi for being "barbarians who let their women run around everywhere," yet right now, it's me who wants to tuck my deformed, "civilized" feet out of sight.

"Um . . ." I sputter out, "I just thought we should meet, Miss. Ma'am. Lady Dugu."

She juts her sharp chin. "It's *Princess-General* Dugu."

Heat whooshes to my head. "Right. Princess-General."

She turns on her shower with a shrill *squeak*. "What's wrong with your face?"

"Oh." I touch the monstrous bruise on my cheek. "I got attacked. Twice."

She rinses her hair aggressively. "And you think I care?"

I bite my lip to stop myself from pointing out that she was the one who asked. "No, I'm not expecting you to."

"Then why are you here? Trying to get on my good side to get favors from me?"

My flush deepens. That's not untrue. "I just wanted to meet—"

"Let me tell you something, fox girl." Her gaze slashes into mine, crackling a brighter electric green. "I know your type. So it's best that you stay away from me, and especially away from my partner."

"*What?*"

"Stay. Away. From my partner."

"What—I—*how is that relevant?*"

"You think you're the hottest new shit? You think you're special? The Iron Widow of the Nine-Tailed Fox?"

"If you're talking about the stuff in the media, that's completely beyond my control! I was locked up for almost two weeks with no knowledge of it whatsoever!"

She wrings a towel on her lap. "You know what I saw in my battle link yesterday? *You*. You, in my partner's head."

Fury, blackened by disappointment, rushes through me like toxic smoke. "And—and that's *my* fault? Are you kidding me? I'm here, trying to talk to you girl to girl, yet you—are you *incapable* of using your brain for anything but a man?"

Her arm moves too fast.

My head crashes into the tiled wall. Pain bursts through my skull. My stool skids, tangling in my legs. I slip and collapse to the slimy floor, winded by agony.

"Stay away from my partner, you man-killing whore," Qieluo snaps, towering over me.

She leaves me in a puddle of cold, clammy water, her unbound feet slapping assuredly over porcelain, the way mine never can.

CHAPTER TWENTY-FIVE

PREY

My head swivels and pulses in a hot haze of pain. I clutch it for a solid minute before I'm able to move again. Shivering, I sweep my gaze across the sprinkling showers and drifting steam, gauging if everyone else is as shocked as I am.

A child cries. Another laughs. I catch a few bewildered glances from the other women, but they flit away quickly. Hair gets rinsed with frantic movements. Towels get wrung. Showers get turned off. Glass toiletry bottles get thrown in baskets. Legs hurry to leave.

I can't believe this.

I clank my stool onto its legs again and drag myself back up, pressing my palms to my eyes. They ache with the pressure of surging tears, which pool in my hands and leak down my wrists. I grit my teeth. My chest hitches and shudders.

Solid footsteps patter my way.

I whip around, tensing, thinking Qieluo is back for more, maybe with a harsher weapon.

But it's a different woman.

"Are you all right?" She bends low, hair gathered into a bun at her neck, mostly dry but collecting beads of moisture. She's got soft, creaseless eyes, a low nose bridge, and a broad face. She could not look more typically Han if she tried.

However, her feet are unbound as well.

I realize a second later that I'm ogling them, and I try to pass it off like I'm taking in all of her, but she flashes a dimpled, knowing smile, puts her palms together, and gives a little bow. "Ma Xiuying, yin pilot of the Black Tortoise."

"Oh!" My brows fly up. "Of course!"

One of the other two Iron Princesses, not counting myself. I should've recognized her—the lack of makeup and hairstyling threw me off. Her plain appearance and upbringing are in astounding contrast to her rank. She was a farm girl who never gave a thought to becoming a concubine, or even a wife to a decent family, before a spirit pressure testing team caught her incredible value.

She chuckles. "Yes, they call me Big-Footed Ma."

I hurry to return the bow. "Aren't you supposed to be in the Ming province?"

"Yuanzhang and I transferred overnight. Central Command says there's been some severe Hundun agitation here."

That makes sense. The Black Tortoise is Water-type; those are the easiest units to maneuver across vast landscapes, thanks to their flexibility.

"Yeah, that would be partially my fault." I massage around the hot, swelling bump on my head. "I'm glad they had the good sense to send you in. You're definitely more pleasant than *her*." I glare toward the foggy vinyl curtains sealing the doorway.

Xiuying laughs, covering her mouth with her hand. "To be honest, I came here to get a look at her too. Guess it was good that I missed the chance to start a conversation."

I roll my eyes so hard it shoots another spike of pain through my skull. "I can't believe her."

"Well, you know how those Rongdi girls are. They're fire-crackers." Xiuying leans closer, whispering giddily. She speaks with a heavy northern accent, emphasizing her *r*'s. "I heard she held her hunting knife to Prince-General Yang's throat on the night of their Match Crowning and made him vow never to bed another woman. And *that's* why he never took any concubines."

I recoil a little at the way Xiuying is saying this, but I *have* heard that Han-Rongdi tensions are higher in the Ming province. "I actually have no problem with that, but blaming *me* because he might have thought about me briefly? That's just ridiculous!"

Xiuying quirks a gently curved brow. "Sometimes, it's the betrayal of the mind that hurts more. Way more than the betrayal of the body."

"Okay, it *is* weird that I'm on his mind at all, but still . . ."

Xiuying shrugs. "It's not a surprise that men find you intriguing. Especially pilots. If I looked hard during my battle link with Yuanzhang, I'd probably see traces of you too."

"Seriously?"

"Men are always enticed by the fresh and new, even if they don't admit it. Anyway, if you want to keep talking, shall we . . . ?" She gestures to a wooden tub on the other side of the showers. Her two toddler sons are there, giggling and splashing each other.

Not wanting to be rude, I force out a smile and wobble over with my stool and basket. But I can't shake the knowledge that Zhu Yuanzhang's concubines filled in for Xiuying during the late stages of her pregnancies. Deaths happened when they didn't need to. I don't understand why she had children at all in such a high-risk environment. She's twenty-three, pushing the limits of pilot longevity. Zhu Yuanzhang is even older, at twenty-four. In about a year, the army just might tribute them.

Though maybe the children were the army's idea to begin with, and I shouldn't be so quick to judge. When a woman gets pregnant, her body is suddenly everybody's business. Endless restrictions could be clamped onto her "for the good of the baby." There's no better tool of control.

If Li Shimin and I live through these two weeks, I can see them forcing him to impregnate me.

My stomach ices over at the thought. I grasp my gut, my *womb*, thoughts tearing in a hundred dreadful directions. I blink hard to squeeze the images away.

"Biao'*er*, Di'*er*, say hi to Big Sister Wu!" Xiuying strides much more steadily than me on her natural feet. Her black spinal brace slithers down her back like a dark snake. I don't think it's a coincidence that two out of the three Iron Princesses have unbound feet. But when it comes to motherhood, I doubt she had a choice.

"*Wu-jiejie hao,*" the boys mumble, suddenly shy.

I nod at them, ignoring the gaping doom in my chest, and turn on the shower beside Xiuying's. After a rusty squeak, hot water splinters out, washing away the film of slime on me from hitting the floor.

By now, every other woman has hurried out. Xiuying sits down on a stool and scrubs her children with a towel, but raises her head, expression more somber than before.

"So, listen," she says. "I know I might be stepping out of line, but if there's ever anything you want to talk to someone about, I'm here. I know you're new and must not have access to much. I can lend you anything you need. Such as . . . cover powder. Do you have any of your own?"

"Cover powder?" I tilt my head.

"You know, for your . . ." She points around her cheek, then her neck.

My hand sails near my bruises. "Oh, these? Thanks, but I won't bother. I've got no one to please."

"Just know that I understand." Light dances in her sad eyes. "I know men can get carried away. Especially a Rongdi like Pilot Li."

My lashes stutter as if they're glitching. "*Oh*. Oh, no—these aren't from—Li Shimin didn't do this! Skies, I'd literally kill him if he did!"

"Oh. My apologies. I just assumed—"

"Why do *you* have cover powder on hand?" I scan her on abrupt alert, though I don't see any bruises, which the water would've revealed.

Her gaze hardens again. "For the girls who need it, of course."

"Why cover any of that up? The men who do these things should be judged and killed, not endured!"

Her mouth parts in surprise, then closes into a weak smile. "I can see why they call you the Iron Widow now."

"I just see no point in tolerating stuff like that." I face the wall, fists curling. Shower water runs in sheets over my vision. Big Sister's ghost smiles in my mind. Smiling and smiling and smiling, because skies forbid she be anything but the perfect, obedient daughter. "You endure and endure, and for what? As long as you keep appeasing them, keep letting them get their way, why would they ever get better? Violence gets them everything they want. And then what is there in the end but death?"

"But you have to realize that most concubine pilots can't just make a scene," Xiuying says, weary and hollow. "The safety and livelihood of their families are on the line. The best we can do is to support each other. Promise me you'll contact me if you need to talk anything out, okay?"

Something wound tight inside me slowly gives out. She's right. I should try harder to understand. Everyone's in a different situation.

"Okay. Thank you," I say, because she's just looking out for me, and it's honestly nice after what Qieluo did.

In hindsight, I was such a fool to have assumed Qieluo would stand by me just because she's also female.

It was my grandmother who crushed my feet in half.

It was my mother who encouraged me and Big Sister to offer ourselves up as concubines so our brother could afford a future bride.

It was always the village aunties who'd sit around gossiping about which girl hadn't been married off yet, despite complaining nonstop about their own husbands. And then they'd congratulate new mothers for being "blessed" to have a boy, despite being female themselves.

How do you take the fight out of half the population and render them willing slaves? You tell them they're meant to do nothing but serve from the minute they're born. You tell them they're weak. You tell them they're prey.

You tell them over and over, until it's the only truth they're capable of living.

Back in the suite, in the bathroom, I stare at myself in the mirror. Murky yellow light filters through the frosted-glass window. Noises from the never-ending construction projects on the Wall clink, patter, and echo outside. Yizhi is in Li Shimin's room, staying by him at all times to keep him from slipping through death's gates.

I should be sleeping, according to our new nocturnal schedule. Hunduns attack more often at night, so it's better to be awake then and prepared to deal with An Lushan, in case another battle happens before we're recharged.

Yet how could I rest? I might've gained an ally in Xiuying, but she can't help with our most urgent problems when she has no connections in Sui-Tang. Her words, and Qieluo's, keep cycling through my head.

"It's not a surprise that men find you intriguing."

"Let me tell you something, fox girl. I know your type."

My type? What exact type is that?

Do I come off as some boy-playing, life-ruining vixen *that* much?

I think of the comments Yizhi has shown me, from people trying to figure out what I am, discussing if the army should use me or execute me. I can imagine why Yang Jian was thinking of me. The freaky new girl who even he, a Prince-General, wouldn't survive. I shudder to think about what Qieluo really saw in his mind, but she shouldn't have felt threatened. I doubt it was fueled by anything close to love or respect.

But maybe this magnet for attention is a power I'm not tapping into.

My blood pumps faster through my veins. I lean closer to the mirror, examining my bruised features. My eyes are haunted, bloodshot, ringed by dark circles. My lips are cracked. My complexion is deathly. But the base is still there; I've got good bone structure.

I watch myself pull back from the mirror, a dark fire igniting in my eyes. People love to ogle pretty girls, but they love to hate them even more. There's no one the masses are more obsessed with railing at than the women who dare to stray from the docile ideal of wives and mothers. *Too vain*, people like my father curse at those women. Too self-obsessed. Too devious, getting everything they want by draining men dry.

This is the type of girl Qieluo thinks I am. And by virtue of what I've done and how I've acted, nothing I say or do can distance me from it.

But there is money to be made in being hated this much, and being a source of money means power and protection. Media traffic doesn't care about right or wrong. Every click on a scandalous headline brings profit; every view of a condemning picture generates revenue. If you're a big enough cash cow, the media companies will lobby and bribe every government connection they have to keep from losing you. I know this because Pan Jinlian, a close friend of Yizhi's family, is constantly in the headlines for being frivolous and outrageous. By all means, the Sages should've banned her from the media long ago for "corrupting social values," but as long as people can't stop talking about her, the media companies will always support her from the shadows. Yizhi says she knows exactly what she's doing. She laughs at the hateful comments while watching her fortune tick higher and higher.

I could go the same route. If I sign a true exclusive contract with a media company, I would make them a lot richer, thus compelling them to support me.

I could compel *Yizhi's father* to support me.

A restless momentum spirals to the top of my skull. My hands curl on the sink counter. I've overlooked Gao Qiu all this time because I have no faith in his capacity to be moved by Yizhi's love for me, and I've heard too many stories about his shady business tactics. But the influence of media companies is the only thing I've seen that has changed a pilot's fate. The biggest example is Sun Wukong, ex-pilot of the Monkey King. He helped a distinguished monk cross the Hundun wilds and complete a legendary mission to retrieve academic manuscripts and tech diagrams from another human stronghold, Indu, which Huaxia lost communication with after losing Zhou. After his *Journey to the Western Stronghold* memoir and its adaptations, he exploded to such popularity that his media engagements saved him from going into serious battle for the rest of his Chrysalis-capable years. He then retired to become an actor and comedian, and is still super popular. My brother watches his videos daily.

Gao Enterprises is the company that manages him.

This means Gao Qiu is capable of stopping a pilot from being tributed. If I start making him an absurd amount of money, I bet he has all sorts of ways to force the Sui-Tang strategists to change their positions.

I hurry out of the lavatory. This time, when I seek out Yizhi, it is not to kiss him.

CHAPTER TWENTY-SIX

DESPITE ALL THAT

D ealing with Gao Qiu is exactly as grating as I imagined. He will work in earnest with me only if I prove I can survive Li Shimin again.

"The Sages aren't happy with her, so I'd have to grease a lot of palms to make them look the other way about me promoting her for real," he tells Yizhi over a voice message, because he won't even speak directly to me. "No point doing that if she's just going to die two seconds later."

So everything still depends on how well Li Shimin and I balance in our next battle.

My head clears. I stop pushing him away, no matter the things he's done, no matter my mess of feelings about him. After he survives the worst of the withdrawal with Yizhi's help, I do every partner exercise Sima Yi suggests without complaining. Ice dancing, regular dancing, trust falls, balancing on an elevated beam while holding hands, whatever. I don't question his methods.

Not even when he tells us to jump off the Great Wall together.

As the moon soaks through the clouds above in a luminous smear, Li Shimin wraps his arms around me as if attempting another dance. Thanks to the cascading disasters, Sima Yi got enough support from his fellow Central Command strategists to grant us spirit armor privileges—partly to help with training, partly to deter further attacks from other pilots.

The weight of the Vermilion Bird armor's expansive scarlet wings, each longer than we are tall, teeters us on the concrete edge we're on. The weather-stained and lichen-coated side of the Wall plunges down through the night, the ground so distant it's nothing but beckoning oblivion. I would've liked to learn to fly from solid ground, but Sima Yi says I could accidentally waste a lot of qi trying to figure it out, so he's only letting me have one try, under his strict terms.

A night wind keens across the Hundun wilds like a dead concubine crying out from the beyond, stirring Li Shimin's chopped hair, chilling me down to the marrow. His tremors haven't completely stopped, and his features remain lifeless and impassive, weighed down by heavy shadows.

If it was strange to see the most powerful pilot in Huaxia without a crown before, it looks even weirder now that he's armored. I mean, the armor is so grandiose, with its wings and long phoenix-like skirts and metal feathers flaring over his shoulders, and then there's just his head. Something is clearly missing.

I'm wondering what his crown would look like when Sima Yi gives the official order to "Jump!"

For the first time in the flesh, I witness the spectacle of Li Shimin, the Iron Demon, conducting his qi.

Fire-red radiance scorches like rivers of lava under his skin and courses into his armor. Heat rushes against my body, pressed to his. His irises singe as bright as embers. His wings spread against the night, ablaze.

Since the maximum force with which someone can channel their qi is directly proportional to their spirit pressure, this really is the most intense that anyone in Huaxia can look right now.

By a sonic crack of his wings, he springs off the Wall with me in his arms. I cling to his hot armor, biting back a scream at the sudden weightlessness. Wind whooshes in my ears. The world loses its edges, its logic. The qi-heated gusts of his wingbeats churn around us. I have no idea if it means we're dying or not, and I can't bear to open my eyes to confirm.

However, as oxygen shudders in and out of my lungs, frustration sizzles inside me.

Is this who I want to be? A girl who has to stay attached to a boy?

With a deep breath, I channel my Metal-white qi outward from the meridians in my body. A cool sensation floods through my spine and into my armor. I untangle from Li Shimin, pushing off his chest for good measure.

My terror spikes when I immediately pitch down, but I flap my wings again and again, pouring my qi into them, relentless. Pale radiance puffs along the edges of my view. The gusts chill the sweat drenching me.

And just like that, I'm flying.

My vast wings buoy me on the wind, defying gravity, defying death. Exhilaration buzzes through every cell in my body, as twinkling and unearthly as starlight. Slowly, I soar higher while turning in a circle, taking in the world with new eyes. A far bigger world, filled with so much more space and sound and freedom. It's a vantage point only Chrysalises should have, yet here I am, a human bobbling through the air as if it were as wide and cradling as the Hundun-filled ocean at the very east of Huaxia. The squares of light from the watchtowers outside the Great Wall make a serpent constellation from horizon to horizon.

I look at my arms. My very own Metal qi, cold and calm and silver-white, flows beneath the feather texture of my armor.

So many emotions spill free inside me that I have no idea how to handle it, to control it, to keep it from overflowing from my eyes as windblown tears. Sobs wrack my weightless body so hard that I whirl off balance, one wing higher than the other. Li Shimin pulses up after me and catches me by the waist. My cold wingbeats mingle with his hot ones like shared breath.

I'm so overwhelmed that I make no move to shove him away.

"Even *walking* was a luxury for me," I croak, hammering my fist on his feathery breastplate. Then I outright lean against it. The heat of his qi warms my cheek.

He says nothing. Just holds me, bobbing in midair, in the unthinkable distance between heaven and earth that humans are not supposed to reach.

Despite all that, and Sima Yi looking quite pleased after we returned to the Wall, our synergy doesn't improve.

"You're just yielding to him, not cooperating with him!" Sima Yi yells at me after Li Shimin drags me through yet another clumsy routine on the ice rink. "It is not the same thing!"

Easy for him to yap about. *He* should try cooperating on slick ice with someone whose mind is constantly straying in a hundred directions, to wherever the nearest bottle of liquor is.

By our fifth day of training, a constant anxiety quivers inside me, chipping at my hope that we can pull ourselves together in time. As if mirroring my mood, a thunderstorm beats against the rink building, rumbling through the concrete and tinkling down the windows.

"Hey." Sima Yi beckons me from the edge of the rink when Li Shimin sulks off to a lavatory break. "I need to talk to you."

"About what?" I skate toward him hesitantly, shifting my wings behind me for balance. Having armor has at least stopped us from falling all over the ice and kept my feet from hurting too much.

Sima Yi clenches the low glass barrier surrounding the rink. "You'd better not be tangled up in a love triangle."

My tiny skates screech to a stop. I open my mouth to splutter a denial.

"Don't try." Sima Yi flashes his palm. "I've seen the way you and Rich Boy look at each other. But you'd better not be doing anything out of line with him." He hunches lower, voice dropping low. "Shimin is the one who's supposed to be your partner, your One True Match. Remember that. And especially stick to it in public. Popular opinion in the army is already against you. You cannot afford to be labeled a *cheater* as well."

Regaining my composure, I roll my eyes. "Quit worrying. I know my priorities." Not a lie. I haven't kissed Yizhi since that mess of a night. "Besides, don't you know basic geometry, Strategist Sima?" I make a triangle with my fingers and look through it. "A triangle is the strongest shape."

"I'm being serious," he snaps. "You and Shimin are so unnaturally uncomfortable around each other. What's going on? Are you not doing your chamber duties properly?"

When I realize what he means by "chamber duties," heat blazes from my neck to my ears. "No! That's none of your—*we've never done it at all*!"

Sima Yi smacks both hands over his face. "Oh, that explains *so* much. No wonder you're making no progress!"

"What does *that* have anything to do with our training?"

"Are you joking? It's the ultimate partner bonding activity! Why haven't you done it?" Sima Yi demands, as if asking why I didn't turn off the stove before leaving the suite.

I glide back on my skates, waving my wings to stay steady. "I . . . I just don't want to!"

"This isn't about what you want," Sima Yi says through clenched teeth, and my gut chills with how utterly stern he is about this ridiculous subject. "If you could do it with Prince-Colonel Yang, you can do it with Shimin. I understand if you're terrified about being with a Rongdi, but—"

"I didn't do it with Yang Guang either!" I practically scream to shut that sentence out of my ears.

Sima Yi gapes for a long moment. "You're still a *maiden*?"

"Does it matter?" My cheeks have gone so hot that I'm sure I've turned fluorescent red.

"Yes!" He slaps the rink barrier. "Listen, you cannot pilot properly with Shimin if you have this mental blockade against him, so you need to get over it. I will literally let you and Shimin go and get it done right now. This is urgent. It is not the time for you to be such a little girl about it!"

"Too bad—I *am* a girl!" Tears prick my eyes, welling to the dangerous brink of spilling over. "All my life, I've been told this is the worst and filthiest thing I could do! Do you know how many times my family has threatened to shove me in a pig cage and drown me because they *suspected* me of getting close with a boy? And now you want me to spontaneously sleep with a guy I *hate*?"

My voice snaps off the concrete walls in cavernous echoes. Sima Yi opens his mouth to argue back, but does a double take to the side.

My attention whips that way as well.

Li Shimin stands halfway back from the lavatories, gawking at us. We failed to hear the clattering of his armor over the rain beating down the walls. Thunder rolls above the building, booming.

Regret breaks through me. I almost go to cover my mouth.

But it's not like I ever hid my disdain for him, so what does this matter?

I keep my hands in fists at my sides.

"Oh, whatever." Sima Yi rattles his head. "Might as well—Shimin! Get over here! I need to talk to you about consummating your partnership with Pilot Wu!"

Li Shimin's brows twist in an emotion I can't decipher. He pivots on his heels and storms back toward the lavatories, the long skirts of his armor clinking against his greaves. "I am not having this conversation."

Sima Yi chokes on thin air. "What's the matter with you? She may be a little chubby, but she's still decent-looking!"

Li Shimin lashes a look over his shoulder with the kind of fury he unleashed in the cafeteria fight. "I am not an animal, Strategist Sima." His eyes flick toward me, mellowing. "*We* are not animals."

"No, but you're pilots!" Sima Yi insists. "And your very lives depend on your next battle. Look how awkward you two are around each other—you need to fix this!"

Li Shimin keeps walking away. I shut my eyes, breathing slow and deep.

Are we messing this up for ourselves? Maybe it really is part of our problem.

I force myself to stay logical: if we don't resolve this now, it will hang between us, making us stumble even harder than before. And we don't have the time or luxury for more stumbling.

Face searing with another flare of heat, I draw a deep breath. "Li—!"

Red lights flick on in the ceiling. Hundun sirens bellow through the building, resounding.

Li Shimin whirls around.

Panic flashes across Sima Yi's face, but he tames it within a second and starts shouting legitimate, non-absurd commands.

Survival instinct erases all jagged edges of our conflict. Li Shimin runs toward me. I wrap my wings around my torso to make it easier for him to carry me. He scoops me up, because it'll be faster than my attempts at walking. We can't fly. We'd become huge glowing targets against the night, and any soldier could shoot us down with the excuse that they were preventing our desertion.

But we don't make it more than ten steps out of the building before soldiers crowd around us anyway, boots splashing in the storm. I flare my spirit sense by conducting my qi through my armor at a special intensity. Like a third eye opening, my body gains a new layer of awareness, picking up on the spirit pressures scattered through the camp. More signals are approaching from every direction.

Did every soldier in the camp receive a command to corner us?

"Oh, you won't be dodging battle this time," An Lushan's voice hisses out of a tablet speaker. A soldier holds up a livefeed of his face, while another angles an umbrella over the screen.

Sima Yi lashes his sleeve, already drenched. "I have orders from Central Comm—!"

"Orders overridden." An Lushan holds up his own tablet, displaying a document. "By sagely decree from Chairman Kong himself."

CHAPTER TWENTY-SEVEN

WITH A BANG

My face goes colder than the rain streaming down it.

Chairman Kong is the leader of the Sages. And he has essentially declared that he's giving up on us and the chance of the counterattack.

My eyes swing toward Sima Yi, but there's only dread on his face, lit faintly by the rain-hazed lanterns across the camp. With the next flash of lightning, I realize how much of a toll these few days have taken on him as well. Water trickles down the sunken lines of his face and drips from his soaked beard.

He doesn't meet my gaze. Just closes his eyes and says, "Understood."

My heart plunges like a stone into a never-ending abyss.

An Lushan grins wider on the screen. He tips his chin. "Get them to the Vermilion Bird."

Soldiers close in. One of them holds up a muzzle. Rain slicks across dark steel.

"Don't put that on me!" Li Shimin shouts, the deep timbre of his voice rumbling through our armor. It actually jars the soldiers to a stop. He grips me tighter in his arms. "I'll go. I won't resist this time. I have *her*, now."

A belated realization, or maybe more of a reminder, stirs in me. I'm not the only one supposedly being "tamed" by this arrangement.

But none of that is real. We're not functional partners. We can barely look at each other. Our qi has been recharging for only six days.

This isn't going to work.

Li Shimin starts following the soldiers, raindrops cluttering his glasses. Sima Yi does, too, but gets held back.

"Strategist Sima, there's no need for you to accompany them," An Lushan says with a smile and a wave of his hand, as if doing him a favor.

Sima Yi bares his teeth, but has no choice but to remain behind gunpoint.

"Remember, you can still try rapid-charging the Vermilion Bird itself!" he calls at us through the downpour. "Glean as much qi as you can from other Chrysalises, and it might be okay!"

No, it won't! Who'll lend qi to *us*? Xiuying might have, but she's recharging as well. She won't be part of this battle.

I want to push out of Li Shimin's arms and run, but what use is there? I'm physically incapable of running. I can't ever—!

Wait. Armor.

Maybe I can make a break for it.

I twist my body to unfurl my wings. They scrape across Li Shimin's breastplate with a *shing*, then I go to flap them—

Bang.

A blinding white force throws me against him. A second later, pain detonates across my back. Spots flood my vision. My mouth opens, stretching, every muscle too taut to release a sound. Shouts drift in and out of my ears like I've plunged into ice water.

"—*are you kidding me*—"

"—*how is she supposed to*—"

The smell of gunpowder drifts on the damp air. Li Shimin is screaming my name—has he ever called it before?—and he's cradling me, shaking me, yet I can't focus. Pain devours all of my senses, gripping my every cell.

The world shifts.

We're still being ushered onward. Faintly, through my shattering agony, I sense the detail of my drooping wings chafing across the flooded concrete path.

There is no escape.

My consciousness stutters and flickers through the journey to the top of the Great Wall. Dingy elevator lights. Creaking noises. Gleaming guns. Hoarse moaning coming out of my own throat. Rain colliding in a layer of mist on concrete structures and steel tracks.

Then we're in a shuttle, speeding toward the Zhen'guan watchtower, where the Vermilion Bird is parked. Raindrops rake across the windows like luminous claws in the dark of night.

"Th-they actually shot me," I wheeze, coiled stiff across Li Shimin's lap, facing him. I might have said these words several times already. I can't tell. Chilly sweat wobbles down my forehead.

"Stay with me." He holds me by my shoulders, huddling me closer. "Stay until we link to the Bird. Then you won't feel it anymore."

My teeth chatter. I can't stop shivering. Is this how he felt on that first night of detox? Under my armor, my wet conduction suit clings like ice to my skin.

Red light smolders under the metal feathers of his armor. Heat surges around me, rippling through the air. I take a trembling gasp.

"No . . ." I palm his breastplate. "Don't—don't waste qi . . ."

"It doesn't matter at this point," he mutters, irises sizzling red. The beads of moisture on his glasses evaporate rapidly. He rubs my armored hands to warm them up. His ashen features, however drained and tortured by withdrawal, tense in concentration. The storm whistles outside and pounds down on the metal around us like a thousand invading heartbeats. The shuttle jangles over drenched tracks. Rain shadows streak across his face. I stare up at him, slack-jawed.

"Why are you so nice to me?" I choke out through a thickening constriction in my throat. "When I'm terrible to you?"

His eyelids droop, so dissonantly tender over the demonic red of his irises. He laces his fingers between mine. "You're the miracle I've been waiting for all this time, going into these battles, praying that something would be different. I can't bear the thought of losing you."

My shivers travel down to the core of me. Warmth stings my eyes; my vision quivers. I turn toward his legs so he can't see the evidence.

"I don't hate you." My voice pinches to its highest, flimsiest register. "Not that much. Not anymore. You just confuse me."

"I'm sorry," he whispers, hands slipping out of entanglement with mine.

I grasp them in place.

"I heard you write things real prettily." I brush my thumb over his, my thoughts sloshing like the water outside. I don't know what I'm saying anymore. "You should do that again."

A dry laugh breezes out of him. He flexes his fingers between mine. They twitch. "My hands . . . all the labor they made me do . . . I don't think I can ever hold an ink brush properly again."

My heart clenches. I clasp his hands to my chest, delirious. "You have to try. You have to try again."

The shuttle screeches to a stop, rattling me against him. I cry out in pain. His hands break from mine to brace me. Soldiers rise around us, cocking their guns.

He tucks his arms under my body. "We have to go now. I'm going to pick you up."

I nod, wincing.

Still, I'm not prepared for the anguish that lacerates through me with the large movement. Static froths through my eyes. I tense back a scream as I steady my head against his shoulder.

Maybe it wouldn't be terrible to go into battle. At least I'd be free from *this*.

However, after we're herded into the elevator that leads down to the docking platform, a fresh edge of fear slices through me, sharpened by the resignation on Li Shimin's face.

Is he giving up?

"Li Shimin," I plead. "*Shimin*."

He turns a sad yet mellow gaze to me. The most mellow I've seen him look since I met him, since he walked out to me from this exact elevator, a prisoner jumpsuit on his body, a muzzle on his face, and fury in his eyes.

This won't do.

I pull myself up by his neck and press my lips to his.

A sharp breath lances up his nose. He trips a step back. His armor gleams like a fanned ember, heaving warmth through the elevator. Sensation races in a circuit between us, bright above my pain like a lightning flash. It startles me just as much as him.

"Fight," I breathe, mouth parting a little way from his. My heart hurls itself against our connected breastplates like a mad, freed monster. "Fight, no matter how much it hurts." I drag my fingers across the back of his neck. "Because this is not how we deserve to die."

He cradles me tighter, fingers digging into my armor.

The elevator doors open to the raging, howling, whirling wetness outside. The spill of light catches the Vermilion Bird's long, arched neck at the end of the docking bridge. The soldiers file out, boots clanging on gridded metal. They line up on either side of the platform, pointing their guns because they hate us, yet getting out of our way because they need us.

Shimin marches between them to the Vermilion Bird, carrying me. The storm hisses off his armor in a halo of steam. Through my fever of pain, I glare down every single one of these cowards.

Just when I wonder how they're supposed to force us into battle when we both don't want to go, two soldiers hop into the cockpit after us. After we sit down in the yin and yang seats, they strap themselves into two side seats I haven't noticed before.

Then they point their guns to our heads.

CHAPTER TWENTY-EIGHT

THE STRONGEST SHAPE

Rage chars through me as my mind ascends into the Vermilion Bird. Burning, roaring rage.

I don't land in Shimin's horrific mind realm this time. My wrath collides directly with his, like oil smashing into fire, and a scream scours out of the Bird's beak, luminous into the night. Rain clinks down over us like a thousand needles per second, lit ahead by the glow of the Bird's eyes—one Metal-white, one Fire-red.

"*Move out, Vermilion Bird, or you will be terminated for disobedience!*" An Lushan's voice grates through the new speakers they must've installed.

I—or maybe both of us—scream again through the Bird's throat. The only solace is that I've been freed from my pain-filled body. The boundaries of my existence scatter out like mist, reaching into the Bird's gargantuan wings. I fan them to life. I want to turn around and smash down the Great Wall itself, but there's no doubt that the soldiers will splatter my brains across the cockpit the second I make a wrong move.

As Shimin and I pilot the Bird in clumsy sync, a haze of black and white persists in my consciousness like another layer to my mind. When I force it into focus, it sharpens into the yin-yang realm. Shimin's spirit form kneels before mine, our knees touching at the border of black and white. I take his face in my hands. "Let's throw the soldiers out like we did the speakers last time."

He flinches, seeming shocked to see me, to be conscious of this realm. It occurs to me that this is the first time we've acted normally in here. No bloodlust on his part. That's a good sign.

His eyes dart around before slowing down, searching mine. "Throw them out, and then what?"

My mouth hangs agape.

Yes, and then what? Deactivate the Bird and sit until the battle's over, only to return to a death sentence anyway? Refuse to leave the cockpit, and die from my bullet wound? Try to escape into the Hundun wilds with the Bird, where they'll swarm a Chrysalis our size anywhere we go?

As if. As if. *As if.*

Resist, get executed. Fight the Hunduns, possibly prove ourselves and live.

Impassiveness settles over Shimin's face, and I reach a sudden clarity about his resignation earlier. He's been trapped in far more of these battles than I have.

When I feel him making the Bird claw forward over the dark, riotous puddles littering the Hundun wilds, I fail to find the strength to counteract his momentum.

False hope. I swear the army is sustained on it.

However, our weariness, our half-charged qi, immediately take their toll. The Bird's movements are sluggish, weighted, like a real bird blundering through a storm with drenched feathers. Camera drones whiz around us like taunting flies, red-eyed with hunger. I imagine Gao Qiu, the Sages, and strategists from both the Sui-Tang frontier and Central Command observing us through different drones, making judgments. Lightning streaks through the thick black clouds overhead, illuminating the plains in flashes.

The first Hunduns roil in from the horizon in less than five minutes, an unnervingly close battle distance to the Wall. First their tiny gleams of qi diffuse through rain and darkness, then their silhouetted bodies appear.

"Wow, the scouting drones are doing a terrible job!" I yelp in the yin-yang realm.

"Or they've told the others to deliberately not hold back the Hunduns that come for us." Shimin's fists clench over his knees. With our spirit forms both sitting in place, it feels like I'm looking at a comm screen of him in my head.

"Oh, they *would*."

Hunduns aim to destroy Chrysalises, not the Wall itself. Whole streams must be breaking from the main battle to come after us, like insects to a sweetly rotting peach.

As our collision with the first wave becomes imminent, Shimin hurls back the Bird's wings and snaps them forward. The gale force blows the common Hunduns off balance. Water mists and sprays everywhere. Three noble-class Hunduns, looking no bigger than cats but definitely larger in reality, charge through the wind and pounce at us.

I swing a claw toward one of them.

"No! Don't!"

Shimin's mental resistance slows the claw, but it's too late. The talons skewer through the Hundun's round body.

Instead of a satisfying killing crunch, it feels like I've stabbed chopsticks through rice. The Hundun's spirit metal ripples around the talons, then binds them. I shake the claw but can't get it off.

"Oh, of course! No visible glow—Water type!" I berate myself. The other two noble Hunduns ram into the claw we have on the ground, trying to make us topple.

"*They know they're supposed to be a team.*" Sima Yi's words about Qieluo and Yang Jian's battle prowess echo through my mind. "*They do the parts they're good at, then pull back when it's necessary.*"

Feeling no danger of losing my control of the Bird altogether if I yield, I momentarily stop trying to command it, trusting Shimin to handle this. With a few wet wing beats, he lurches the Bird off the ground. He charges a qi blast in its beak while flicking off the Hundun on its claw with the other claw. The Hundun tumbles to the ground, legs flailing like an overturned bug, the kind that would explode in a gush of guts if stepped on.

Shimin throws the Bird's head back before releasing the qi blast in a wide stream at the herd, razing the flooded landscape. Hunduns crackle and pop under the Fire-red assault. I jump in, adding my own qi, turning the stream pink. The blast propels us farther into the air for a few seconds, then we can't sustain it anymore. We sputter out and crash into the Hunduns' smoking remains. The Bird's wings flop down and go dim.

"What class were those nobles?" I say, winded. "I can't tell. The perspective is messing with me."

"Earl class. Maybe low Count class?"

A wave of terror and nausea and *exhilaration* sweeps through me at this reminder of the size we currently embody. Earl-class Hunduns are ten to fifteen meters tall, the size of three- or four-story buildings, yet they look no bigger than the average stray cat to us.

But none of this power means anything as long as I'm being held at gunpoint in the cockpit. I can *feel* the two soldiers shifting in their seats, recovering from our slump. It takes all my restraint to do nothing as they right themselves.

Shimin drags the Bird onto its claws again and keeps trampling across the muddy plains, toward the color-speckled mass of the next wave of Hunduns. Rain darts both white and red through our view. The Bird flounders even more than before.

"We shouldn't use any more qi attacks," I say, anxiety sprouting through my mind like mold.

"Too bad," Shimin grunts. "The Bird doesn't do anything better. It's not a melee unit."

"Then let's go to a higher form. Channel my Metal qi to at least make our blasts more focused. How is that done?"

"I don't know. I've never consciously triggered a transformation."

"Right. You're Fire on Fire."

Spirit metal can't be transformed with the same type of qi—which is why Hunduns can't transform, since they're always a single type. Pilots like Shimin would have to put in the extra effort of using the second most dominant qi in their bodies. In his case, Earth.

"It's a miracle I'm this lucid during a battle at all." Shimin wrings his spirit hands together. "And I have no idea if that's making things better or worse."

The next line of Hunduns storms close. We have no choice but to spew more qi blasts at them while advancing. I do my best to go along with Shimin's momentum. Controlling one body with two minds is a delicate art. There's no room for pride; I *am* the less experienced pilot.

Ahead, hints of the main battle become visible at last. Chrysalises and Hunduns struggle against each other as massive silhouettes, movements loud as the thunder in the background. Radiant qi lines burn through the sheets of wind-blown rain.

I can barely tell Hundun from Chrysalis, especially the Chrysalises with less-dramatic shapes. Now it's clear how the army has been able to tribute pilots without the masses questioning it. It would be so easy for us to be killed by anything—*anyone*—in this pandemonium.

"How do you usually feel when you're piloting?" I ask Shimin more frantically.

"Out of control." His eyes pinch shut as the Bird battles on in the physical world. "Like there's nothing left to my mind except the instinct to kill every Hundun I can sense. The strategists don't even typically talk to me in the speakers. They know I won't hear."

"Can you channel that state now? I'll shut up."

"No, no point. Your mind is always there. Too loud. Even when you're not speaking."

I let out an exasperated cry. "Okay, then let's try—"

Lightning flashes, revealing the Chrysalises tangled in the battle.

I freeze.

The Headless Warrior is among them.

"Oh, no. No, no, no, no." I grasp my head in the yin-yang realm.

"What's wrong?" Shimin grazes my shoulder.

There's no need for air, yet I'm hyperventilating. Outside, thunder rumbles across the world. I flash back to the crushing weight of Xing Tian's body over my hips and the grip of his hands around my neck.

There's no way he'll let me leave this battle alive. He'll find some way to kill us, tributing us and avenging Yang Guang at the same time. We have no hope of surviving after all.

Then what's the point of obeying orders?

Every restraint inside me snaps. I spring from my knees and throw my spiritual weight into Shimin, slamming him to the yin-yang ground and straddling him. My hands go around his throat, just like last time. His hands dart for mine, as well, but stop midway.

"Fight me, and we'll both die a pointless death," I breathe, thumbs on his throat but not pressing down. "Let me go, and it'll at least mean something."

He stares at me, stunned. There's no actual pulse in my grasp; I don't really know how our mutual strangulation worked last time when breathing is not an issue here. I guess it's more about the violence of the act and how it tilts the balance of our mental strengths.

There's no such struggle this time. Shimin simply closes his eyes.

I flood my control into every metal granule of the Bird. Shimin's mind throbs in shock, but eases off.

I deliberately take a fall from the next noble Hundun that charges at the Bird. As our supervising soldiers sway in their seats, I ambush them with the metal of the cockpit itself. I wrap it around them and shunt them out like two rats, swallowed in red aluminum, out of a storm drain.

They might die from the fall or get crushed by the battle.

I don't care.

Attention fixed on the Headless Warrior's distinct shape, its glowing nipple eyes and belly mouth, I stomp the Bird through the battle chaos. The storm howls so wildly all around that no one realizes my intent until it's too late. I slap Xing Tian off balance with a crack of the Bird's wing. It's so easy. He's just half our size. Still, he crashes with seismic impact. As the strategists start yelling in my speakers, I raise a claw.

Just when I'm about to impale him through the cockpit, a chilling reminder pierces me. This isn't just Xing Tian. It's the Headless Warrior. There's an innocent concubine in the cockpit with him, trapped in his arms.

I can't kill him without killing her.

My split second of hesitation gives him the chance to push off the ground. With the Warrior's bulky hand, he grabs the stem of the Bird's raised claw. I bat him away, my thoughts racing and tangling into a single trembling speck. Such frustration fills me that I shriek toward the sky yet again.

Realization flashes across Shimin's face. He sits up, forcing my spirit form back. My hands slip from his neck. "Wait, is this the guy who tried to kill you?"

"Yes." I claw at my head. "It's *him*."

Shimin's expression blanks out. At once, his eyes and meridians gleam into blazing scarlet life.

The Bird makes another lunge at the Warrior.

"Wait—!" I try to stop it, but Shimin's fury is so overpowering, it's like being blown back by the flock of screaming birds in his mind realm.

He throws his arms around me and crushes me against himself. Even in this imaginary realm, his heat is overwhelming. My heart skitters, and there's a moment where I consider melting against him and letting him kill as he wishes.

But I can't.

I can't.

"Stop!" I gasp over his shoulder.

He makes the Bird leap, wings spreading like looming fire, claws angled at the Warrior.

"Stop!" I scream louder, shaking him. "*Haven't you killed enough girls?*"

The Bird's wings hitch and flicker. It collapses over the Warrior, talons shredding across its front but not puncturing through.

Shimin's rage churns into a deadlocked frustration that matches mine, but with a grief that I don't carry. Like boiling water with nowhere to go, a pressure expands to the Bird's surface. A familiar pressure.

New growths pop and protrude from the Bird. I can feel the lumpy, diseased look it's taking. Villainous Form.

And so be it.

I can't kill Xing Tian, but I can make him suffer. And not only that, I will *use* him.

I clench one deforming claw around the Warrior's hip and the other around its leg. Then I tug with all my strength.

The leg lacerates from its body. Xing Tian's shining qi pours from the breakage. While I glean his qi into the Vermilion Bird, yellow light rippling under red metal feathers, Xing Tian screams from the Warrior's belly mouth.

Sima Yi has warned me about taking sudden and brutal damage in a Chrysalis. Which is how I know it must hurt like someone has torn Xing Tian's leg off in real life.

Another Chrysalis comes to his rescue, but I smack it aside with the Bird's wing and rip off the Warrior's other leg as well. Xing Tian's scream sharpens in agony, then gurgles into silence. His qi fades out. The Warrior's nipple eyes dim.

I hurl its leg onto its torso face.

This Chrysalis will never be used again. Common Hunduns scurry around it to go after other Chrysalises, pacified by the faux death.

Shimin is still holding me in our mind link, but his arms are slackened, defeated. I know he won't object to what I'm doing next.

I turn the Bird around and flap it into the air, burning the small reserve of Xing Tian's qi that I gleaned. Being the last resort that it is, it feels like pushing a foreign, dead liquid through the Bird, though it works to sustain the basic motions of flight. A few Chrysalises chase after us, but none of them can fly—it takes a very high spirit pressure to fly—so we lose them quickly.

The Great Wall reels into view. I fly along the Wall toward the Kaihuang watchtower. Strategists shriek and scream, but I don't chuck the speakers out.

I love hearing them panic.

I make the Bird soar on an upward arc when I approach the watchtower, then lurch down, beak pointed directly at it. So many of the people inside have either put me in this position or refused to help me. Since they want me gone so badly, I'll go.

But they're all coming with me.

I fold the Bird's wings against its sides. It accelerates.

"Zetian! Shimin!"

Everything screeches to a halt inside me at that voice. *Yizhi.* I fan the Bird's wings, ripping it out of its momentum. After the roaring gust, eerie silence falls. Rain patters off the Bird, echoing into the cockpit.

"Calm down," Yizhi goes on through the speakers. "Please calm down."

Guilt overwhelms me. I didn't even think about the possibility that he might be in the watchtower.

"You came back for qi, right?" he says. "Wait for me."

I touch the Bird down as gently as possible. It still rattles the watchtower's windows, shattering a few. My line of sight settles over the Great Wall. The buildings of the training camp behind it look like toy models sold by Gao Enterprises.

There's a lull, then elevator doors open at the back of the watchtower, spilling light over the short bridge that connects it to the Wall. A tiny figure hurries over the bridge. A figure that can't be anyone but Yizhi.

Only he would be brave enough to face us now.

I look away, suddenly unable to bear the thought of him seeing me in this grotesque form.

"Zetian!" he shouts through the storm on top of the Wall, so faint, so tiny, so human.

Shimin makes the Bird turn back while I'm wallowing. Our vision zooms in on Yizhi, which surprises me; it must be an advanced technique I didn't know about.

The rain plasters Yizhi's half-up hair against his pale neck. His blue-gray robes become so quickly and utterly soaked that they look black as ink. The sight squeezes at my heart. I swing the Bird's wings over him. It doesn't shield him completely from the rain. I want to warm him up the way Shimin did for me in the shuttle, but that's not what my qi does. Metal qi can only be cold.

I wouldn't have enough to do it, anyway. I'm barely hanging on to the Bird.

"Take my qi!" Yizhi flashes a hand, points to it, then reaches toward us.

I'm not sure what he's getting at, but Shimin and I make the simultaneous decision to bend toward him. Yizhi's palm meets the Bird's beak. A tiny point of contact, like a star in the night sky.

"You're my polar star." Yizhi's voice echoes in my memories. *"I'll go wherever you guide me."*

The Bird's wings shiver. How did Yizhi not realize it's actually the inverse that is true?

Suddenly, like the bellowing wind, certain diagrams from his class notes come back to me, diagrams of qi meridians throughout the body and the enormous concentration of acupuncture points on the hands. And I know what to do before he explains further.

With my Metal precision, I concentrate on the tiny dot of his hand, then gently pierce it full of needles.

A yellow radiance switches on in his eyes, beaming through the stormy darkness. His meridians ignite like a network of molten gold across his skin.

Qi courses into the Bird. Earth yellow, streaked by a few electric-hot crackles of Wood green, far more alive than the stolen, detached surge from Xing Tian. A soothing force spreads and expands through the Bird. Yizhi is here with us. Not in mind, but in spirit.

In the yin-yang realm, ethereal tendrils like colored mist swirl around me and Shimin. We've both stood up at some point. We turn to each other. The golden swirls of qi wrap around our arms and lift them until our fingers touch. Shimin's heartbeat pulsates against mine through our fingertips, both calming to a slower rhythm. A small white butterfly with dots of black on its wings breaks from his knuckles. A black one with dots of white quivers out of mine. I don't know what's making it happen: him, me, or something intrinsic in the Vermilion Bird. Maybe it doesn't matter.

Instead of freaking out, I trust it, like I trust the currents of Yizhi's qi. Outside, Yizhi touches his forehead to the Bird's beak. My heart slows further. More and more butterflies flutter out of me and Shimin.

Then both our spirit forms utterly shatter into black and white and flood into each other. Our minds soar like never before. There's no longer a separation, no longer a yin-yang realm.

We are wholly the Vermilion Bird, commanding it in sync.

Our form shifts, becoming more humanoid. Claws stretch into legs. Arms detach from our wings, which flare even wider. Our torso lengthens, tightening. The lower half of a human face morphs out beneath our beak, so the beak becomes the tip of a bird mask. Everything grows closer to how our spirit armor looks. Metal-white and Earth-yellow highlights etch onto our native Fire red.

The storm rages on around Yizhi, tossing his hair and billowing his wet robes, but when lightning flashes again, his smile is brighter than ever.

We pick him up, cupping him in one hand. He stumbles against our beak mask, laughing. We curl the spirit metal around his palm into a sort of glove so he can move his arm while staying connected by a thin tether. Then we peel open a gap between our eyes, right into the cockpit. He clambers in.

"Yizhi . . ." My consciousness sways down to my mortal body. I think I spoke, but it might be just in my head. Dreamily, I see him approach through my flesh-and-blood eyes, swathed by the waves of red, white, and yellow gliding through the feathery cockpit walls.

"Zetian." He takes my face into his hands. The white aura of my qi meridians lights him like a screen. "I'm here. I'll see what I can do about your wound. Go fight."

"Okay . . ."

My awareness ascends back into the Vermilion Bird before the pain catches up with me. Shimin and I roll the Bird upright. Metal skirts like long, wide feathers drape around our legs. The Great Wall only comes up to our breastplate.

When we turn around, a semicircle of Chrysalises is right behind us, stances unsure.

"Let's go kill some Hunduns!" we shout, charging through them, giving them no time to question us.

On the way, we press a hand against our breastplate, feeling for a weapon we now have the hands to use. Our fingers sink into spirit metal, wrapping around a handle. We pull.

With a glimmer of sparks and the scrape of metal on metal, a longbow morphs out of our chest.

We crouch down, then spring into the air. Rainy wind whistles faster and louder across our wings. Once we approach the main battle again, we pull the glowing bowstring. An arrow of focused qi dithers to life against it, radiant. We aim at the biggest Hundun in the field before loosening it. In a clean, piercing shot, we silence the Hundun's spark. The husk collapses, intact enough to stand a good chance of being salvaged.

No matter how the army will reprimand us for our actions in this battle, they cannot say no to salvageable husks of this size.

From the air, we take out any noble Hunduns in sight with our humongous bow. The other Chrysalises look up in alarm but don't stop battling. Whenever a Wood- or Fire-type Hundun tries to direct a powerful qi blast our way, someone slashes it with a melee weapon.

After we strike down the final noble Hundun, it doesn't take long for peace to descend over the field of misting metal husks. Finally, I'm sure of the potential Chief Strategist Zhuge and Strategist Sima saw in us.

Told you the triangle is the strongest shape, Strategist Sima, I want to say, knowing he would hear through the camera drones flitting around us.

But I can't move the Bird's jaw.

I can't move anything anymore.

My mind hangs in suspension, growing fuzzy at the edges. As much as I hate pain, it's important. It lets you know something is wrong. It makes you panic when you need to.

Not like now. When something is clearly wrong, yet all I can do is watch blankly as my Metal-white qi drains from the Bird's body.

Multiple voices are calling my name, but it's like I'm being carried off on a wave, into darkness.

It's peaceful, at least. Just cold.

So cold . . .

PART III

WAY OF THE SNAKE

The Ba snake can swallow even an elephant,
but it will take three years to spit out the bones.
—*Classic of Mountains and Seas (山海经)*

CHAPTER TWENTY-NINE

CITY OF EVERLASTING PEACE

I swim between many, many dreams.

Go, I tell a shaking, sobbing girl while blood soaks my clothes and dribbles from the cleaver in my hand. My voice rasps like I've swallowed ash. Only when she's out of sight do I collapse in the red puddle between the bodies and start to shake and sob myself. The cleaver clatters onto the red-drenched tiles.

But I'll be needing it again soon.

I resist the inevitability. I don't want to see it happen. Yet no matter where I try to escape, I find only other nightmares.

Brawls behind steel bars. Mangled fingers in labor trenches. Lying on my back, hands shuddering over fresh stitches on my torso, dumbfounded with the shock of being robbed of my very organs. Lying on my stomach, wheezing and feverish, fresh burns searing my back.

Then there's a rosy-cheeked girl, stepping in circles with me over a field of scintillating snow, teaching me a fighting form as graceful as the calligraphy I used to write. Our arms and open palms gently deflect each other's moves. Our legs sweep up mists of ice crystals. Spirals of footprints trail after us. She flashes a sweet smile that belies her lethality.

But she will not win in the end, and this is anything but a reprieve.

Panic sharpens through me. Everything in me screams for this to stop, for her to vanish at once, before I can see what this will lead to.

—*get away! get away!*—

—*don't go into the*—

—*please*—

"*What do you even have to live for that was worth their lives?*"

I jolt at my own voice, slicing through a memory that's not mine. My eyes stutter open to reality.

The scent of iodine and sterile chemicals invades my nostrils like sharp winter air. My hands grasp scratchy white sheets. I look around in a frenzy.

The sight at my bedside halts me. It makes me wonder if I'm still dreaming.

Yizhi and Shimin are asleep on stools backed against the wall, leaning on each other. Yizhi lies in the groove of Shimin's shoulder, while Shimin rests his head over Yizhi's.

Their hands are laced together, clasping where their legs are touching.

"Uh . . ." I start, but can't bring enough substance to my voice to continue. Everything feels fuzzy and drifting—since when could I inhabit my mortal body without pain?

Their eyes flutter open in sync.

"Zetian!" Yizhi bolts up, untangling his fingers from Shimin's to take mine.

Shimin almost leaves his stool as well, mouth open to say something, but ends up staying put. His eyes dart between me and Yizhi, as if unable to decide which one of us to look at.

Terror comes crashing back to me as I stare at him.

My dreams weren't dreams. They were his *memories*. Through our battle link, more of them have spilled over into my head.

Now I can no longer meet his eyes.

"So," I wheeze to Yizhi to distract myself, brows squeezing from the effort of speaking. "What happened?"

I've been dragged back from death's gates with three fractured ribs and a lacerated kidney. The Vermilion Bird's Fire-type armor may be the worst type for protection, but it at least prevented the bullet from puncturing me all the way. The doctors extracted it after other Chrysalises hauled the Vermilion Bird in from the battlefield, and I've been recovering in the Kaihuang watchtower's med bay for the two days since. My respite from pain is due to the painkillers they gave me. It feels so amazing that I dread going back to an existence without it, but Yizhi suggests, in a dark whisper, to refuse any further doses. If I get hooked, the army will be able to control me the way they control Shimin with liquor.

I take Yizhi's advice.

Our final battle damage: two dead soldiers, one mutilated Duke-class Chrysalis, one traumatized Xing Tian (whose concubine-pilot probably woke up to quite a shock).

Our final battle achievements: twelve noble Hundun husks in ideal condition to be converted into Chrysalises or offered to the gods as workable spirit metal, and definitive proof that Shimin and I can sustain a stable Heroic Form.

If the strategists were conflicted on what to do with us before, I can't imagine what their conference calls are like now.

The only thing I regret is trying to destroy the Kaihuang watchtower. Sima Yi, however, has helped us vehemently deny that mass murder was our intention when we flew back to the Great Wall. He was the one who let Yizhi into the war room and onto our speakers. He claimed that he'd once told us about the possibility of using a third person as a qi battery, and recommended we try it if we got desperate. The concept is not without precedent, though it's historically had a very low rate of success. Usually, the addition of a third person's qi just causes further dissonance between the main pilot pair. No one's sure why it worked out for us.

And, of course, I doubt the other strategists buy this story. But it doesn't matter.

What matters is that we flew too fast for the camera drones to keep up, and they only caught the part after Yizhi reached us on the Wall.

What matters is that Gao Qiu is thrilled about this development. He has now greased the palms he needed to and received clearance from the Sages to officially invite us to Chang'an, the capital of Huaxia, to discuss a media deal with him. As long as I'm still recovering and we're both waiting for our qi to replenish, An Lushan has no excuse to stop us from leaving the frontier.

When the lights of Chang'an glimmer in from the distance, it's disorienting, because they sparkle brighter than the stars. For an instant, my brain panics over the possibility that the hovercraft has swung upside-down while I was dozing, and we're actually plummeting to our deaths. I flinch against the crossed straps of my seat and squeeze Shimin's hand for dear life.

Then I lock eyes with Yizhi, who's strapped into a seat opposite us.

"Zetian, I think you're hurting him," he says with an awkward smile over the rapid *whump whump whump* of the rotor blades, his voice broadcasting through our headsets.

"I'm fine," Shimin wheezes.

"Sorry." I let him go, flushing.

Wind wails around the small private hovercraft Gao Qiu sent for us. Clouds skim its windows, pale like Metal qi against the night. I turn to the view, despite my lingering anxiety, so I don't have to face either of them. My lips tingle with the phantom of my kiss with Shimin before the battle.

I haven't told Yizhi about it.

Should I?

I have no obligation to. Yizhi knew from the moment he touched down at the Great Wall that he would have to deal with me being tied to Shimin forever.

Yet I can't ignore the lost way he watches me and Shimin when he thinks I'm not looking. And I don't know if telling him would make things better or worse.

Ugh.

I lose myself in the sight of the city.

Pretty quickly, the mess in my head gives way to wonder.

This isn't like my hovercraft trip to the Great Wall. That was nothing more than a dark, bleak tenure in a metal cage that happened to be really loud and wobbly.

This is transcendence on par with piloting a Chrysalis.

Tall buildings cluttered with neon signs soon fill all visible space below, a forest of metal and concrete bathed in lights and holograms. Specks of people and vehicles stream within it like blood cells. There's so much to take in that I find myself pressing against the window.

So this is what a city looks like.

Ads shift across whole sides of buildings. The Wei River slithers like a dark serpent through the city, glittering with sickles of reflected light. Human achievement floods through every breath of space between the two mountain ranges that separate Chang'an from the Han, Jin, Sui, and Tang provinces. As the heart of Huaxia, it is its own administrative division.

I'm so dazed by everything that I have to make myself remember Yizhi's tales of how the dazzling lights are only a surface glamor, like the perfumed silk shoes that girls wear on their bound, festering feet. Most Chang'aners struggle to get by. Apartments can be divided into literal cages stacked on top of each other, each just big enough for one person to sleep in, and still sell for astronomical prices. There could be twelve people sharing the kitchen and washroom in a suite the size of ours at the Wall.

Such is the competition that comes with wanting to live in the safest place in Huaxia—a competition involving more than six million people, almost a fifth of Huaxia's population. It's not named the City of Everlasting Peace for no reason. Chang'aners may struggle to pay rent, but they're the last people who have to worry about Hunduns.

My amazement curdles. I'm abruptly reminded that this *isn't* the most humanity has achieved, only the most we've recovered. My gut twists as I try to imagine the human world before the invasion two millennia ago. The buildings that must've soared so much higher than these. The technology lost even to the gods. The thousands and thousands of years of history we will never get back.

It makes me all the more furious that Shimin and I were thrown to the Hunduns like trash.

Yizhi points out the Palace of Sages when it comes into view. It's a complex of flared-roofed manors and temples built against the mountains, lording over the city, housing the Huaxia government. I fume at it, wishing I could go down there and demand a direct audience with Chairman Kong. But his new decree is clear: he and the Sages will approve the counterattack only if *all* senior Sui-Tang strategists agree it's a safe gamble.

While that doesn't sound unreasonable, given the risks, the likes of An Lushan prove that not every person with power works with the greater good in mind.

Fine. Then they leave us no choice but to use questionable forces as well.

Shimin and I have had enough of begging for forgiveness for being what we are.

The hovercraft lands on a launchpad in the Gao estate, which is another mountain complex, built suspiciously like a copycat of the Palace of Sages. Though I bet the Sages don't have music pumping and strobe lights flickering everywhere.

As soon as the hovercraft hatch skates aside, the party frenzy floats in on my first ever breath of city air, shockingly smoky. Distant voices and laughter pepper the murky electronic beat pounding like a heart through the mountain. According to Yizhi, everyone noteworthy in Chang'an has come tonight to ogle us.

A line of maidservants scuttles onto the launchpad, colorful silk robes snapping in the waning rotor winds. "*Wushaoye*," they acknowledge in unison, shivering. *Fifth Young Master*.

Removing his headset, Yizhi bows back with a meek smile. His mother was one such maidservant, knocked up and forgotten by Gao Qiu. Until the day he ordered her flogged to death for not smiling with enough enthusiasm at a banquet he held for the Sages.

Nausea overwhelms me at the proof all around of his untouchable power. This is the kind of man I must rely on to get what I want.

These are the kinds of men that run the world.

One of the maidservants pushes a wheelchair toward us. With my injuries, it's too dangerous to be on my feet. Shimin's offering hands hover around my body, and I'm forced to accept his help. Yizhi hops from the hovercraft to take the wheelchair from the maidservants.

Frustration coils inside me. I know they don't do things like this out of some malicious intent to get something out of me or to bind me more tightly to them, so I don't resist or say anything, but I hate that the world keeps stripping me of my ability to do things for myself. I hate that I have to have Yizhi and Shimin in my life, even though I love one of them, and the other is a necessary partner. Can I really call myself a strong girl if I'm relying on two boys?

But what else am I supposed to do? Distance myself from them and tumble stubbornly to my death? It would not be noble or respectable just because I did it alone.

After I settle in the wheelchair and figure out how to move it with its control stick, the maidservants lead us to a courtyard huddled by multi-story buildings. I've seen pictures of the Gao estate, but I'm still aghast. It looks more like a small town than a family home.

A breeze blows across my face, carrying an algae scent that reminds me of the rice terraces. There's a lily pond ahead, lit from within by shifting colors and bisected like the yin-yang symbol by a winding stone walkway. The partygoers are, thankfully, not right up against us, but cluttered on the wraparound balconies of the buildings. Crimson pillars on every floor hold up flared, tiled roofs. Strings of traditional red lanterns dangle from the edges, but pulsing neon sweeps through paper windows and open doors, backlighting the mingling crowds in flashes. Music thumps into the square of starry sky above the courtyard.

To my shock, some partygoers are wearing pieces and meshes of spirit armor over their shoulders, arms, and, sometimes, chests.

I thought only pilots were allowed to wield spirit metal, and with heavy restrictions. Shimin and I were banned from taking our armor on this trip. But I guess rich people scoff in the face of laws, and it's not dangerous when their spirit pressures are so low. They can't seem to do anything other than faintly strobing their qi in time with the music.

As we get close, their voices drain of life. Cameras keep flashing, yet the previously lively party congeals to a standstill.

Everyone stares at us. Neon rays of light swing over hesitant male faces and half-veiled female ones.

I stop, too, not knowing what to do. Another wind sweeps over us, bringing the sharp tang of alcohol.

Shimin clutches my shoulder. I let him.

"Welcome!" a husky voice booms through speakers.

I search for the source, and find him on the third and highest level of a building across the courtyard.

"Welcome, my guests of honor—Li Shimin, the Iron Demon, and Wu Zetian, the Iron Widow!" Gao Qiu raises his arms at his sides, mostly a silhouette in the radiance of the open double doors behind him. The bronze headpiece over his topknot shoots as tall as his head. His sleeves drape in crisp angles from his arms. Lines of maidservants stand like docile dolls on either side of him, heads bent, hair fastened into twin loops like little girls.

Disgust eats at my innards as cheers erupt from the partygoers.

"Father." Yizhi wraps his hands together and bows, reminding me to do the same.

"Gao-*zong*," Shimin and I call out, meaning Big Boss Gao. Though there's so much noise I doubt he can hear us.

"Thank you for your service, pilots!" he says.

"Thank you for your service!" the partygoers slur in remarkable sync, becoming suddenly welcoming of us because Gao Qiu has said it's okay to do so. Half-shadowed figures in fine robes lean on each other or the balcony railings, raising bronze goblets. Noblewomen, who I've heard can't show their faces in public, sip their liquor by poking metal straws under their gauzy veils, which are hooked ear to ear on intricate bronze frames.

"And my son—the hero! The *Baofeng Shaoye!*"

"*Baofeng Shaoye!*"

Young Master of the Storm. Sounds like Yizhi will never be just *Wushaoye*, Fifth Young Master, again. His eyes widen in the flowing pond glow, and he kneads the edges of his sleeves.

Gao Qiu has not missed Yizhi's star potential after what he did. There's one breathtaking shot of him that's gone viral. Taken mid–lightning flash, it captured him with his hand on the Vermilion Bird's beak, hair wild in the storm, wet sleeve blowing past his elbow, eyes and meridians lit up like a glorious golden circuit. A brave human boy standing on top of Huaxia's strongest bastion, giving strength to a gargantuan beast of metal that is Huaxia's brightest hope.

Gao Qiu outed him as a son of his own in no time. He even mailed Yizhi civilian robes with golden lightning bolts on them in place of the bamboo patterns he usually likes.

"My guests will be released to you after just a short meeting between them and me," Gao Qiu announces. "Until then, enjoy the finest food and drink in Huaxia!"

More throat-shredding cheers surge into the night. Someone lights a string of firecrackers. They pop against my eardrums and fill the courtyard with smoke. Fireworks whistle into the night, exploding like Hundun cores against the stars.

The maidservants lead the way across the pond's winding bridge. I activate the wheelchair again, but Yizhi grasps the back of it.

He doesn't dare say anything, but I can read the urgency in his eyes: *Be careful of my father.*

CHAPTER THIRTY

THE DEAL

I had no delusions about Gao Qiu being motivated to help us out of a burning sense of righteousness, like the Central Command strategists. He's only considering lobbying for our lives to profit from our fame. I'm guessing he already spent quite a lot getting us out of the frontier, though, because he tells us that, from now on, he'll use only the profits we generate to nudge the army and Sages toward approving the counterattack. He won't sink another yuan of his existing fortune into further bribes.

There are some key players, like An Lushan, who likely can't be bought to our side with any amount of money, but it's no secret that Gao Qiu's connections extend into the criminal realm. I trust that he has more pointed methods of persuasion.

He must have a personal price in mind to justify using them, though. Some kind of threshold where Shimin and I become worth the trouble of activating his shadiest connections. We will have to prove ourselves as assets to him. Which means giving him absolute freedom over the remaking of our images to make as much money as possible.

"I do see tremendous star power in you two." He twirls his long chopsticks, decorated at the ends with gold. He sits across from us at a round table full of colorful, steaming food, most of which I don't recognize. Honey-soft light flows from the private room's carved wood crevasses, immersing his features.

A tension pulls at my spine at the hints of Yizhi all over him. The same inflections in his voice, just deeper with age. The same slender shape to his face, just coarsened with a salt-and-pepper beard. It takes no effort to imagine Yizhi becoming him, or him having once been kind and gentle like Yizhi. Which is the most terrifying part of looking at him.

This world can make monsters out of anyone.

"Li Shimin." Gao Qiu plants his elbow on the golden table-cloth and points at Shimin, designer black robes gleaming with a leather shine. "We barely have to do any rebranding for you. You're the baddest of bad boys. The ultimate alpha male. You live by your own rules, not giving a fuck about what other people think, and that's exactly what makes you so alluring. Men want to be you; women want to be protected by you."

"Um," Shimin says. "Okay."

He's not looking at me, Gao Qiu, or even the tentative contract on a tablet propped in front of us. He's eyeing the glittering crystal liquor bottle on the glass turntable holding the food. Beneath the table, his arm quivers in my grip.

A humorless laugh dies without leaving my chest. But I can see people buying all this about him. Paying attention to only the superficial glamor of his strength.

Gao Qiu swivels his finger to me. "Wu Zetian." He pronounces my name like an intriguing new taste. "Oh, Wu Zetian. Exploding out of nowhere like a firecracker, offing that brat Yang Guang while at it. Fantastic debut, by the way. I can't get that moment out of my head. '*Welcome to your nightmare*'," he mimics in a growl.

Aiyah. Now it feels weirdly embarrassing that I ever shouted that at a dozen camera drones. "Was it not too much?"

"Oh, Pilot Wu, people *love* too much. Pilots are supposed to be larger than life—that's what makes them such effective celebrities! In fact, I'd like to take this fox spirit rumor and run with it. You can be the mysterious vixen. The femme fatale." Gao Qiu's eyes, which hold a stunning feline beauty, pierce me with a knowing edge. Shadows slide over his features, cast by three gold-dusted lanterns above the table. "Women will hate you for carrying yourself with the kind of domineering confidence they wish they had; men will hate you for scrambling their minds and luring their thoughts toward places they know they shouldn't go. But their hate will scorch so hotly under their skin that they won't be able to look away or stop talking about you. Together with Shimin, you will be Huaxia's premier power couple. You're not good, but you're bad in the best way." He fans his hands, as if offering us something invisible. "How about it?"

It's unnerving, how similar his thoughts are to mine.

Shimin puts his finger to his lips in a pondering gesture, but cuts a panicked glance at me. He shifts his arm out of my grasp to clench my hand under the table. Tendons work along his neck from an active and dire effort to keep his eyes off the liquor bottle.

I get the message. He can't think clearly right now. He'll go with whatever I decide.

"We're in," I say.

"Perfect." Gao Qiu's mouth stretches into a grin, dimpling one cheek the exact way Yizhi's does, chilling me again.

Shimin and I sign the contract with our fingerprints. My hand shakes as hard as his, but this document is really just a formality. Gao Qiu is too powerful, and our status is too unique. If we become unhappy with him, or he becomes unhappy with us, this legal jargon won't matter a single bit.

258

"And the deal is sealed!" Gao Qiu claps his hands. "Let's drink to celebrate, shall we?"

Shimin and I seize up. A maidservant spins the turntable and stops it at the bottle of liquor. She unplugs its crystal cork.

I straighten in my wheelchair, switching on an apologetic smile. "Oh, we would love to, but—" I look to Shimin. "Dearest, didn't the doctors say your qi flow would get messed up if you did any more drinking?"

Knowing what happened to Yizhi's mother, I have to perform the kind of femininity Gao Qiu tolerates. It's not enough to be subservient; I have to seem *happy* while doing it.

"Nonsense!" Gao Qiu grasps his bronze goblet as the maidservant fills it. "It's just one drink. What harm could it do?"

Shimin starts to say something, but then the maidservant waddles toward us with the bottle. Lantern light whirls through the chiseled crystal.

"One drink can be a tipping point." I lash my attention between Shimin and Gao Qiu, forcing my smile to stick. "I'm just not sure if this is a good idea."

The maidservant pours a sparkling, gurgling stream into the goblet in front of Shimin. The liquor smell hits my face, making me gag. But what it does to Shimin is infinitely worse.

Something snaps loose behind his eyes. The tension goes out of his face. "No, it's fine. It's just one drink."

My fingers dig like talons into the tight sleeve of his pilot uniform. "But the doctors—"

He wrenches his arm away without looking at me. "It's just one drink."

The maidservant fills my goblet as well.

"Perfect!" Gao Qiu rises, chair screeching over the polished wood floor. He raises his goblet. "Let's toast to our collaboration!"

Shimin mirrors him.

While doing the same, I bump hard into his elbow. Liquor flies out of his goblet and splatters over the golden tablecloth. I gasp in both real and imagined pain. "Sorry, dear. My wounds . . ."

"It's okay, Pilot Wu," Gao Qiu says, though his voice slows like slush, and his whole demeanor darkens. "No need to get up."

He glares at the maidservant and gestures at the mess. I bite my lip as she hurries to bring a few towels over.

"I think this is an omen from the universe, dear." I give Shimin's arm another squeeze. "You should take care of your qi flow. It'd be unfortunate if we had hiccups in our next battle because of it. Gao-*zong*, I'd be glad to drink for us both."

"Well." Gao Qiu gives a slow blink. "If the *universe* says so."

Oh, skies. I've displeased him.

Hopefully, the money I make him will push this out of his memories.

I snatch the half-empty goblet from Shimin's hands so it doesn't possess him anymore. I top it up myself, then raise it toward Gao Qiu like an offering. "It's a pleasure doing business with you, Gao-*zong*."

I tip the goblet between my lips. It's my first taste of alcohol, and it scorches like liquid fire down my throat, as intense as it smells. I cough, but make myself down the whole thing in several rapid gulps.

"Yes. A real pleasure." Gao Qiu does the same.

Shimin sits down awkwardly. I grab my own goblet, hold my breath, and guzzle it as well.

I have no idea how he drank flasks upon flasks of this every day. No wonder he's so Fire dominant.

"The business is done for you then, Pilot Li." Gao Qiu points to his wristlet. "I've gotten quite a few nudges from my other guests about your whereabouts. You should get to the party. They're growing tired of waiting."

Shimin swings a questioning look between me and Gao Qiu, though his eyes remain unfocused.

"Pilot Wu and I still need to discuss a few things. I have some possible lodging options in Chang'an if she wishes to relocate her *family*." Gao Qiu enunciates the word like a taunt. "I don't believe you would find a topic like that relatable, would you?"

Shimin's eyes go huge, and so do mine.

"Please, go enjoy yourself." Gao Qiu flashes a too-bright smile.

My dread spikes. I stare at Shimin like my gaze alone could hold him back, but Gao Qiu doesn't seem to be leaving us any options. If we want his support, we'll have to do things his way.

I lower my eyes.

"Thank you, Gao-*zong*," Shimin mutters after a smothering pause. He gets up again and gives a small bow, then his steps fade out over the floorboards.

Not ready to face Gao Qiu alone, I follow Shimin with my eyes. My head throbs. My chest burns. Even the breaths that spurt out of me smell flammable. I wish this limbo of a moment could stretch forever, but the door soon closes after Shimin, and I'm forced to turn back.

Gao Qiu's cold stare seizes me at once.

"You're a dangerous girl for real, Pilot Wu," he drawls, sounding completely different. "More dangerous than I thought. Catering to your man's ego while making all the decisions in reality? How sly of you."

"I only wish to support my partner," I say in a rush. "He is my heaven and earth."

"Oh?" Gao Qiu's head tilts ever so slightly. "And what about my hero of a son? What is *he* to you?"

A spasm shocks through me. Words tumble out of my mouth. "Student Strategist Gao was greatly helpful when my partner—"

"Stop pretending." Gao Qiu's voice lashes across the table like a whip. "I know about you and my son. In the mountains."

I forget how to breathe.

His stare goes even colder, darker. "I'm not as inattentive a father as you think, Pilot Wu. My fifth son is not the type to fall in love. What kind of spell have you put on him, I wonder."

"He and I never did anything we shouldn't have," I somehow manage to say. How much does he know? Was there a hidden microphone on Yizhi or something? Since when?

"But this is quite the history of tugging boys along like pets, isn't it?"

What, *two boys*?

But I can't defend myself like that. Two boys is two too many for people like him.

"I—I'm still a maiden," I stammer the only other defense I can think of. "Honestly. Ask an auntie to check."

Surprise ripples across Gao Qiu's face. I'm hopeful that he might back off and let me go, but then his features tighten into an even harsher scowl.

He rises from the table again, chair scratching out an ear-splitting noise. I wish I could wheel away this instant and never look back, but Gao Qiu has already sunk all that money into getting me and Shimin away from the Great Wall. If I don't do what he wants, I have no doubt he'll turn against me instead. And I cannot afford to have him as yet another enemy.

In slow strides, he comes to my side of the table. His hand snags my shoulder. He leans toward my ear. "If you're not lying through your teeth, then that makes it *so much worse*."

"Why?" I cry out. Too freaked out to face him, all I hear is Yizhi. A distorted Yizhi from the depths of the eighteen hells.

"Why? You don't get it? You don't understand the concept of

giving back when you take? That would be highly problematic, Pilot Wu."

"They didn't want it." My body shudders with every breath. His touch burns through my pilot uniform, making me want to chop off this shoulder and run.

"All. Boys. Want it." The liquor-tinged heat of his voice worms into my ear. "I see the way they rush to your whims. If you truly have no intent to put out, then they must not realize they're being deceived."

Is he talking about the way Yizhi and Shimin helped me out of the hovercraft? Is that what brought this on?

Don't speak for them, I come close to shouting. *They're not like you.*

Then horror flashes through me—why did he really keep me behind?

I raise a terrified look to the maidservant. She stands between two painted scrolls hanging on the dimly lit wall, gaze on the ground. Her presence is the only thing keeping this situation ambiguous.

But she can't do a thing to stop Gao Qiu if he decides to—

My mind freezes over. I can't think. I can't speak.

Help me! I scream in my head to no one in particular. Shimin? Yizhi? I don't know. *I don't know.*

"See, Pilot Wu, business is based on equivalent exchange, on giving out a proper amount whenever you take something. It's a very important principle. I need to know you understand it, and don't think you're too clever to abide by it." Gao Qiu pivots behind my wheelchair and clutches my shoulders. "So, to make sure we can trust each other, I would like you to strip off your clothes and read our contract on camera. In the nude."

The bottom drops out of my world. I could be falling forever into an endless abyss. My hands flex, wishing for the power of my spirit armor. But there's nothing. I have nothing.

"I—I can't read very well," I say in a voice so small. So powerless.

"I can read it for you, and you can repeat it after me."

Tears burn my eyes like acid. My throat swells near shut. I tense up, but it only intensifies the grip of his hands on my shoulders.

"Gao-*zong* . . . why do you hate women this much?"

There's a small pause, then he bursts into startling laughter. The sound pounds against the back of my skull like drumbeats and vibrates through my wheelchair. "Hate women? Don't be ridiculous! The world wouldn't function without women! Who would bear our children, make our meals, sew our clothes, warm our beds, and so, so, *so* much more? Please." He leans into my periphery, feline eyes narrowing into slashes. "Nobody in this world hates women in general. They just hate the ones who *won't listen*. Who think they can break the rules and get away with it. So, Pilot Wu, are you one of them?"

"My body . . ." I keep trying. "I was shot. It's not a pleasant sight right now."

"I'm not here to ogle you," he says, flatly.

Chilled sweat drenches my skin beneath my uniform. This is about control. Nothing but control.

"It's your choice, though, of course," he adds, releasing my shoulders and backing toward his side of the table. His fingers graze the tablecloth.

Bull. *Shit*.

Choice? As if there's a real choice! If I refused, he would use his money and resources to discredit me and Shimin instead. He's just trying to further humiliate me. Bind me with the shame of having chosen this myself.

Shame.

My mind catches on the word.

Is this really such a shameful thing to do? He'll have a video of me . . . what, naked? Wow, the horror! As if I wasn't naked when I was born.

My thoughts clear. I wrestle myself out of the pit of endless shame that my family has beaten me into all my life, and this scenario suddenly becomes hilarious.

This silly man is trying to shame me with my own body.

Well, guess what? I have a fine body. He can get it from any angle he wants, but the video will have no real leverage over me. I don't give a shit if he might release it to the public.

Shame and humiliation are self-imposed emotions, and from here on out, I choose not to feel them.

Make no mistake, though. He is *dead*. As soon as Shimin and I take Zhou back and receive credit for it, I will come here and slaughter Gao Qiu in the worst possible way. He doesn't understand how far I'm willing to go to get what I want, and this is how I'll gain the advantage over him.

This isn't his victory. This is my temporary mercy.

With a head full of fantasies of how I'll flay him alive after he outlives his use, I unzip my pilot coat.

CHAPTER THIRTY-ONE

BAD EXAMPLES
FOR THE CHILDREN

Shimin and I get put through our first studio photo shoot the next morning. The shots are released in time for the network traffic spike at dinner.

Out of morbid curiosity, we bend our heads together and check them out on the tablet Gao Qiu gifted to us, which carries our copy of the contract. The first chill of nightfall sweeps through the gazebo we're in, stirring the willow branches draped over its pointed roof. A pond ripples around its base, isolating it from the other buildings of the Gao estate. The setting sun melts in an orange-gold path over the water.

While I don't blame Shimin for what happened during the meeting, I'm not happy about it. But at least he didn't mess anything up once we got in front of the cameras.

It's a whole new level of weird, seeing professional renditions of ourselves. Gao Qiu really played up the controversy. The production crew wound my hair into the same fox ear hairdo I killed Yang Guang in, complete with the silver hairpins and crystal lilies. And as if regular concubine robes weren't suggestive enough, they fitted me into a more outrageous getup: a short, low-cut robe with fur hems that framed my cleavage and flashed ample swaths of my thighs. Nine huge, fluffy tails trailed from the small of my back.

Shimin, on the other hand, they dressed in a long leather robe with tight sleeves. Ember-colored feathers fluttered over his shoulders and down a deep groove at his chest, which exposed a sliver of his scarred skin. Besides having to ditch his glasses, there was one big difference from his normal look: while he still wore a collar with the army's Yellow Dragon insignia, he didn't have a leash anymore.

I did.

The first photo is of me sitting on the ground, legs curled languidly in front of an elaborate brass chair. The background is pure black. Shimin is lounging on the chair, tugging my chain, expression nonchalant, as if I'm a pet of his. Yet I'm eyeing the camera with a qi-charged sizzle in my gaze, as if this is all part of my wicked plan.

"You will look like a slave to him on the surface, but the audience won't be able to help wondering—who's really in charge?" is what Gao Qiu said while directing this photo.

Watching how I handled the meeting last night must've inspired him. I tell myself I'm over what he made me do, but rage roils all the same inside me, a constant simmer.

I can't deny that he knows how to snag attention, though. Each picture hits with breathtaking impact. I remember what the shooting was like—the awkwardness, the blinding lights, the pain as assistants posed my body—but the finished products seem to hail from a different world, capturing two unearthly, untouchable pariahs taunting Huaxia with carnal intrigue.

"Sorry," Shimin blurts when we get to a particularly racy shot involving him standing behind me and pulling my leash taut.

I was so disgusted during this shoot that I barely managed the sultry expression Gao Qiu demanded. However, looking at it now, it's so dissonant from the reality between me and Shimin that I just want to laugh.

"Don't be." I point at his cool expression in the photo. In it, his qi-lit eyes glare even more intensely than usual thanks to the smoky powder defining them. "Look at you. You're killing the part."

Discomfort twitches over his face. "Are you honestly fine with doing pictures like this?"

"I get it now." I release a heavy breath, then smirk. "This isn't us. It's two characters we're playing. Isn't it funny, knowing we're convincing people to believe a totally fabricated version of the truth?"

"You mean, we're lying to them."

"I prefer to think of it as *storytelling*, my dearest." I cradle his face with one hand, switching on my best vixen vibe. "A story of the Iron Widow and the Iron Demon, taming each other. Redeeming themselves in a battle over a lost province. Transforming from villains to heroes. What is this if not the first page?"

Several heartbeats pass. He stares at me, tensing back an expression I can't read.

My facade starts to slip, and reality shivers in, like the water-cooled breeze blowing past us.

I take my hand off his face and return to scrolling. "Oh boy, now let's see the reactions."

The outcry has exploded immediately. Our revealing clothing. Our provocative poses. Our killer statuses. Our shameless confidence despite it all.

We are bad examples for the children.

However, stunned awe has welled up with equal force, and the conflicting opinions have only drawn more attention and cashed in more picture views. Everyone has to see the spectacle for themselves. On the message boards, debates heat up over whether our Hundun kills make up for our human ones, and whether we can truly liberate Zhou. The mere possibility of it, the *hope*, burns like a supernova shining in rival to the sun, yet it infuriates many that it's up to *us* to do it.

The argumentative posts look spontaneous and casual, but some of them must be staged by Gao Qiu's lackeys, designed to hog as much space for us in the casual reader's mind as possible. It's impossible to tell how many conversations are legitimate, and how many are wolves herding the sheep in secret.

Even Yizhi becomes a part of it. After Shimin and I move to a private room for dinner, I prop up the tablet to catch the live variety show Yizhi was invited to go on.

His unassuming charm is naturally endearing on camera. A rich *shaoye* brave enough to confront a King-class Chrysalis in a thunderstorm, yet painfully polite in real life, even a bit shy.

There's a moment when he's deep into answering a question about transitioning from life in Chang'an to life at the Great Wall, and a person in a Hundun costume stalks up behind him. He makes a hilarious noise when suddenly tapped on the shoulder. It gets a laugh out of everyone at the studio, including himself, and he noticeably opens up more. You'd never guess that he's in on a scheme to make the counterattack happen, basically risking two provinces to save my life and Shimin's.

"And what do you think about the *pilots* of the Vermilion Bird?" The host finally drops the bomb. Probably paid by Gao Qiu to do so. The audience "Ooooohh"s in anticipation.

"I think the thing that matters most is whether they have the power to win against the Hunduns," Yizhi says after a moment of fake pondering. He looks straight into the camera. "And they do. If they're willing to risk their lives for humanity, then I don't care about who they are, what they are, or what they've done in the past. I'll gladly supply my qi again, whenever they need it."

As the audience breaks into cheers, I imagine the invisible flow of money and power slowly creeping up against everyone who's trying to kill me and Shimin.

"Has this been enough?" I ask Gao Qiu in a voice message, via my new wristlet.

Seconds later, his response arrives with a *boop* of a noise. When I tap it to listen, his bellowing laughter bursts from the speakers.

"Not even close, Pilot Wu!"

Ugh. That's not good. These racy photos may have caused a stir, but things like this won't be so shocking a second time. We'll drop from the headlines if we don't do something more. Something bigger.

Think, I command myself, clawing the tablecloth. What could get much, much more attention than this in the shortest time?

A vivid memory hits me.

A memory of me, Big Sister, and every other girl in our village watching a Match Crowning on the biggest screen we were temporarily granted. It was Dugu Qieluo and Yang Jian's Crowning, actually, seven years ago, when they were thirteen and fourteen respectively. The fact that they were the first Iron Prince and Princess to debut as an existing Match—Yang Jian has *never* had concubines—made it extra special. Everyone obsessed about it for weeks prior, speculating on what the White Tiger crown and armor would look like, and how that armor would be bedazzled in Qieluo's crowning look.

When the broadcast finally came, we gasped in sync as she marched onto the stage with trains of flowing, translucent silk perfectly integrated with her lithe white armor. Crystals practically dripped from her on a whole-body net of silver string.

But what eleven-year-old me remembered most was the pure, dark satisfaction in her eyes as Yang Jian placed the pearl-smooth diadem on her head. Instead of having just stylized tiger ears, as expected, her crown was bottomed with a row of sharp teeth, as well. The long fangs slashed down near her temples.

"Hey, Shimin." I raise my attention to him. "How would you like to outdo Dugu Qieluo and Yang Jian's Match Crowning?"

CHAPTER THIRTY-TWO

DESPITE THEIR BEST EFFORTS

After getting an ecstatic response from Gao Qiu to the Match Crowning idea, I voice-call Sima Yi about convincing Central Command to let it happen, arguing that it'd be contradictory to keep depriving us of honors while at the same time saying we should be trusted to risk the counterattack. Sima Yi promises to do his best to arrange it.

Relieved by the sense that things are finally moving away from certain doom, I wait in Yizhi's chambers for him to come back.

Motor beeps, human clamor, and smoky air drift up the mountain and through the balcony from the valley of earthbound stars that is Chang'an. Pale lanterns with dark wood frames dangle above an absurdly large bed. Yizhi's room is bigger than our entire suite at the Wall. I first explored it while drunk out of my mind from Gao Qiu's liquor the night before. There's a whole side room dedicated to luxury silk robes that I could not stop rubbing against my burning face. A dedicated skin-care fridge that I made fun of for at least ten minutes. A glittering washroom that blew my mind with its carved crystal tub and hot water that could run at any hour. Another side room is filled with glass shelves lined with Chrysalis figures, which Yizhi sheepishly admitted he never told me about out of a fear of offending me.

He shouldn't have worried. I have nothing against Chrysalises themselves. It's not like I *wouldn't* want humans to annihilate the Hunduns and end this nightmare at the root. What I hate is the pilot system that insists girls are an unavoidable sacrifice in the process.

My wandering gaze lingers on an ink brush painting that spans the wall behind the bed, depicting Chrysalises and Hunduns charging at each other. In the clouds above them, gods with robes like colored mist are plucking *guqin* lutes.

A scene that could exist only in fantasy. In reality, no one knows what the gods look like, and no one's been physically helped by them in battle. We know they're up there; Big Sister and I used to watch for the twinkling speck of the Heavenly Court as it orbited over our skies every few months. And we've all heard some of their legends: Nüwa the Snake Goddess molding the first humans out of clay, Chiyou the God of War commanding ghosts and demons into battle, Zhurong the God of Fire fighting Gonggong the God of Water, and so on. But if the stories are true, it begs the eternal question—why don't they use their incredible powers to help us against the Hunduns? No matter how sincerely we pray to them, they're as aloof as cats, and don't seem to care too much about us. All they do is drop cryptic schematics of technology and knowledge for our scholars to figure out, once we offer enough tribute—mostly spirit metal. It's so strange and ironic that only the spirit metal from Hundun husks can be crafted into sturdy constructions. Whenever we try making anything from the raw granules from the ground, they always tarnish within days. They're only good for being burnt as fuel for trains and hovercraft. And judging by the gods' incredible demand of Hundun husks, even they can't mimic how Hunduns stabilize these granules when they replicate. Funny that this isn't even the Hunduns' world, yet they can use this resource in a way we can't.

No one knows what the gods are doing with so much spirit metal, but we know better than to ask questions. We just keep hauling Hundun husks to designated offering sites a little way outside the Great Wall, along with lumber, soil, seeds, various animals, and girls. Girls left in chains and then never heard from again, a fate eerier than becoming a concubine-pilot, since the gods never appear when we can see them, or even when there's a single camera drone in range.

Gao Qiu was right about one thing: there's not a stratum of the world that doesn't need girls. Maybe we're devalued precisely because we're so valuable. The world is too afraid of not being able to obtain and control us to respect our true worth.

The door to Yizhi's chambers unlocks.

I glance over my shoulder. Yizhi steps into the moonlit room, eyes brightening at the sight of me.

Anticipation rising, I drive my wheelchair to him. When I stayed with him last night, we traded kisses again, the first time we've done so since I became determined to improve my partnership with Shimin. Yizhi insisted that I was too drunk to do anything beyond that, though.

Well. I'm not drunk tonight.

When the distance between us closes, I pull Yizhi into a soft kiss. His mouth moves naturally against mine, a comforting familiarity by now.

"You know, I had a dream like this once," he says against my lips, fingers grazing my neck.

"A dream?" I inhale his scent, clean and warm like something grown on a sunny plain.

"Well, more like an ongoing fantasy." He lets out a small laugh. He curls a lock of my hair, his gaze mellow, wistful. "I wish I could come home to you every night and wake up beside you every morning. Not here, though. Somewhere quieter, like a cabin in the untamed mountains. With no one to bother us."

The image is so painfully wonderful that the tenderness inside me arches to a peak. Then it shatters, plunging me into the coldness of reality.

"There would always be people who'd come hunting us down." I pull away from him, hair unraveling from his fingers. My voice wavers on the verge of cracking. "We can't just run. Your father would—"

"I know," Yizhi cuts me off gently. "That's why it's just a fantasy."

The warmth between us wanes, chilled by a new tension. Guilt weighs down on me like frost, but we don't have time for fantasies. Especially fantasies of *simplicity*.

That's a quality our lives will never have again.

"Listen, Yizhi, you know I can't promise you anything," I say in a quiet but firm tone. "Shimin and I are Chrysalis partners. I don't know what we'll have to do to pilot well together, and I can't have any reservations when so much is on the line. So, be honest: does it hurt you, seeing me and him together?"

A flash of conflicting emotions passes over Yizhi's face, but pacifies quickly. With a soft sigh, he sits down on the pale silk sheets of his massive bed. "Instinctively, yes. I wish I was him. I wish I was your Chrysalis partner. I wish I had his strength to protect you."

My stomach twists into a knot. "Then I think it's better that we don't—"

"*But then* I remind myself that there's no real reason to be jealous." Yizhi's gaze brightens again, clear as truth. The distant lights of Chang'an glimmer in his eyes. "Where does jealousy come from, if not an insecurity that I'll lose you because of him? But that's not how it works, no matter how many people believe it so. You're not something to be kept or taken, and love isn't some scarce resource to battle over. Love can be *infinite*, as much as your heart can open. I mean, when you think about it, love is fueled mostly by compatibility. Whether two people make each other happy by being close. So it'd be pointless of me to resent Shimin. However compatible you are with him, it doesn't have anything to do with how compatible you are with me."

I turn his words over in my head. "It's just . . . compatibility?"

"That's what I believe, at least. True love comes from synergy and trust, not merely chemistry." He gulps, the groove of his throat bobbing in the moonlight pouring between us. "Growing up around here, I've seen too many people try desperately to control others to hold on to them. I never saw strength or dominance in it. Just a sad, sad insecurity."

"Yeah," I grunt, thinking of my father's muffled screams through the walls, accusing my mother of glancing too often at Old Wang next door. I finger the layers of collars in Yizhi's robes, revealing a peek of his tattoos. "That's not what I'm worried about with you, though. I know you'll never get that way. I just don't want to trap you in pain."

"No, don't worry. I don't consider my instincts logical, so I don't want to be defined by them." He touches his forehead to mine, thumb stroking my cheek. "Zetian, every time you choose to look at me, I know for certain that there's a place for me in your heart."

My eyes widen, vision splintering with tears. My mouth slackens in wonder.

Yes, there is. There will always be a place for him. And this is why. This is why.

"*My fifth son is not the type to fall in love.*" Gao Qiu's words intrude into my thoughts, but I scatter them like dust. Yizhi met me when I was a powerless frontier girl. What ulterior motive could he have possibly carried for this long?

I have never been ashamed of loving him, even when my family would've drowned me for it, and I'm not about to start.

We don't turn the lights on.

Yizhi doesn't have Shimin's strength to carry me effortlessly, but that's okay. He helps me climb onto the bed, gentle as ever. Even the pain of cracked ribs is bearable with his hands on my smashed-up body, keeping me whole. I kiss him like only the air that has cycled through his lungs is safe to breathe. An automatic wave of nagging, terrorizing voices spikes in my head, shouting insults—*whore, slut, cheater*—but they melt in the heat building inside me.

I'm rising, rising above that collective bullshit. So many attempts to stop me from existing comfortably in my own skin, yet here I am, doing what I want with a boy nobody appointed to me. And it's not dirtying me. It will not ruin me. It is not obscene, filthy, or shameful.

Shame. That was their favorite tool. A tool to corrode me from the inside until I believed I could only accept whatever lot they threw at my bound feet.

It didn't work.

Despite their best efforts, I find myself worthy of happiness.

Everything they've used to bind me, I will turn against them. My looks are an illusion to snag their attention. My decadence is a bait to stir their outrage. My perfect partnership is a lie to keep them obsessing.

The very force of their judgment and hatred will make me unstoppable.

CHAPTER THIRTY-THREE

UNSPEAKABLE

A metallic chill in the air. The taste of rust on my tongue.

A dirty light. Shadowed corners. A heavy steel chair; leather straps, binding my arms to it. The flesh and blood of a failed struggle under my fingernails.

"It really didn't have to come to this, kid." A figure looms toward me, holding a bottle of liquor. *An Lushan*. "But if you're going to be this big of a pain in the ass, you should have a drink to calm down."

Soldiers wrench my mouth open, keep it open with metal plates. Razor-sharp, wedging between my teeth. Blood floods under my tongue. A rubber tube comes jamming down my throat. All the way through. I choke on it, scream against it, try to bite through it, try to spit it out, but it won't budge. There are only more gushes of blood.

An Lushan tugs my leash stiff. His grisly hand tips, pouring the bottle of liquor into a funnel. *Glug glug glug*, ceaseless. Scalding heat courses through my body. I can't even beg him to stop. I'd gladly repent. I wish he'd have the mercy to kill me.

I'd do anything to make it end. But it burns and burns and burns and—

‿‿‿‿‿‿‿

I shudder and wheeze as I tear myself from the dream. Sights, sounds, and scents take several seconds to slam into place.

Moon-drenched sheets. The warmth of Yizhi around me. City lights far beyond the balcony. No An Lushan, no steel chair. I touch my throat, work my jaw, look at my hands, swallow huge gulps of air.

"What's wrong?" Yizhi murmurs, blinking awake, shifting onto his elbow.

"Just a—" My tongue parches. A cold horror trickles along my veins, which seemed to be scorching with liquor a moment ago.

Just a nightmare?

Or . . .

I throw off the silk covers and maneuver into my wheelchair, clenching against the pain from my bullet wound but too frantic to slow down. Yizhi follows me, helps me, breathing out more questions, but I can't give him any answers until I get them myself.

A short glide down the hall takes me to Shimin's room. I rattle the brass handle. Locked.

I pound the door until light flicks on through the crack beneath it, and heavy footsteps approach.

Click.

Amber light blasts over me, making me wince. Shimin appears in it, eyes bleary, short hair sticking up at all angles.

The question I need to ask jerks up my throat, yet hitches. I can't get it out. I can't make it real.

"What's going on?" Shimin strains to keep his eyes open.

"I had—I had a dream," I say, hoping he'll just roll his eyes and close the door in my face. "I was strapped to this steel chair. They forced my mouth open with razors. Stuck a rubber tube down my throat. An Lushan poured—"

A wild panic surges into Shimin's eyes. "*Stop.*"

I go cold below the neck.

"He *gave you* the addiction," I say in vacant horror.

Beside me, Yizhi's fingers fly over his mouth.

Some kind of barrier ruptures in my mind. Phantom memories flood out. The number of times Shimin went through *that* to be messed up for good. The way it twisted his will, made him claw for the bottles himself. The hot, agonizing blur of days and nights spent on the cold floor of a prison cell.

An acrid feeling pulses in my face, too hot and too cold at once.

Shimin stares through me, like his mind is somewhere else. Then he flinches and starts to shut the door.

I catch it with both hands.

"*Why didn't you tell us?*" I cry.

"Does it matter?" he snaps with startling force, half blocked by the door.

"Yes! This means you fought harder against the army than I ever gave you credit for!"

More images flash through my head, images I once dismissed. The shiv made of book pages. The shard sharpened from his own glasses.

"Your credit," he says on a brittle laugh. "Your credit can't bring them back."

Them. The girls.

My stomach churns, coming close to heaving.

"I'm sorry." Sobs bloat my voice. "I'm so sorry. All those times I railed on you . . ."

His grip tightens on the door frame. "It's fine. It's . . . whatever." He pushes the door again.

"Wait—" I brace harder against it.

"What more do you want? I said it's fine. Let go!"

"Shimin," Yizhi breathes.

The resistance eases off. The door opens wider, revealing the whole of Shimin once more.

It's astonishing, what Yizhi can do with a soft utterance that all of my strength can't.

They behold each other. Yizhi touches Shimin's elbow. There's a mild twitch, but Shimin allows the contact.

"Shimin, please remember that you've protected a lot of lives in your battles." The light from the room dances like gold flakes in Yizhi's eyes. "Not just those behind the Great Wall, but other Chrysalises too. You took out entire herds single-handedly. That wasn't meaningless."

Shimin stares at the ground, shoulders curling in, barely holding something back.

"We're here for you," Yizhi continues. "We believe in you. We can liberate Zhou and save so many more lives. Together."

Hesitantly, Shimin lifts his head.

Then his attention whips between me and Yizhi, sharpening with a new clarity.

I realize I've grasped Yizhi's other hand at some point. And I become acutely aware of how it must look—how it *is*. Me and him, arriving together in the middle of the night.

"Yes. I know." Shimin's expression goes cold and stony. "You don't need to have this pity party for me. Go . . . go be happy!"

He slams the door in our faces.

CHAPTER THIRTY-FOUR

EVER-GROWING HIT LIST

W hen Shimin places his armored hand against the Vermilion Bird's beak, red qi tides through it. At his mental command, the beak yawns open. He swings in from the outside and braces himself at the top with one hand, like the mythical giant Pangu separating the heaven and earth.

I haven't known how to talk to him since finding out the truth, but I have to force myself to collaborate with him on these photo shoots. Just like he must've had to force himself to dwell in the murky layers of truth and deception that I dragged him into. Me, just another person in a long line of people who've used him like a tool.

I don't know how to fix it. I don't know how to take it back. It's not like my apologies would be of any use when I've done what I've done, said what I've said, and we're *this* deep into it all.

Aside from a few white smears of clouds over the Hundun wilds ahead, the sky is blue and bright enough to ring my vision with a faint gold aura. Our photographer is taking this shot with a whirring camera drone. Following his instructions through an earpiece, I flap my own wings to pivot in the air and sit down on the edge of the Bird's beak. Even the best medicine in Huaxia hasn't healed my bullet wound completely, but moving around isn't so painful with my armor on.

When city people get married, they rent some nice clothes and take a bunch of nice pictures to make a commemorative album. Match Crownings are basically pilot weddings, so it's been the perfect excuse to keep us in the headlines. We've spent much of the past two weeks in photo shoots.

Sima Yi has kept us updated about the four Hundun attacks since we left for Chang'an—an exhausting frequency for such a short time. The sunny weather has concentrated them at night, though. Hunduns never come when our scouting drones can spot them from far away, so there shouldn't be an attack while we get a few photos with the Bird, which will be a sure hit. We had to come fetch our armor for the Match Crowning anyway. To prevent theft, pilots usually leave their armor melded with the cockpit seats, so only we could loosen them.

"Oh, pull one knee up and hug it, Pilot Wu!" my earpiece buzzes.

Resisting the urge to roll my eyes, I do so. The camera drone whirs in front of us against the gray wilds. The photographer adjusts me a dozen more times while Shimin holds his one-handed lifting pose. It's always easier to pose him: go for whatever makes him look the most domineering. Me? It's a persistent struggle for photographers to strike a balance between making me look either aggressive or subservient.

Female starlets have usually not been allowed to be presented as brazenly as I've been. In media, they're the brightly smiling dream girls, loving wives, or caring mothers of the male protagonists. They're there to be his reward for defeating the villain, to comfort him when he's lost, or to motivate him by being killed. If there's an aggressive female, she has to be among the antagonists. Not even the main antagonist, but the villain's own source of support and comfort, who fawns over his twisted intelligence and is always willing to die for his cause. I think that vibe is what they're trying to go for with me and Shimin, but it doesn't quite work. I have my own legacy, separate from Shimin's. I am equally difficult to look away from. It messes with the photographers' instincts, and they keep trying to squeeze me into smaller poses and meeker expressions, only to remember they have to stay on our provocative brand. It takes them forever to figure out what to do with me. Especially now that Gao Qiu doesn't leer over the shoots anymore.

He's been busy having "chats" with the Sui-Tang strategists, including An Lushan. But whether or not An Lushan caves to the pressure, I've decided something: I will slaughter him for what he did to Shimin. He has shot to the top of my ever-growing hit list.

It's the least I can do.

By the time we pack up the shoot and get to our hovercraft, Qieluo, Xiuying, and their partners are waiting on the launchpad on the Wall. Since they're all off duty, recharging from recent battles, Gao Qiu has asked them to attend my Match Crowning in two days. Though he's so stingy that he's making them hitch the same ride as us and our production crew.

The four of them seize up when we approach. Only Xiuying flashes a smile at me, but it wavers as her eyes stray to Shimin. She shrinks back, a small gasp tripping out of her mouth.

It's bizarre. A Princess-class pilot, showing fear. Her partner, Zhu Yuanzhang, a burly former warrior monk with a shaved head, raises a protective arm in front of her. A miniature tortoise shell hangs over their foreheads from their thick black crowns.

I roll toward them in my wheelchair, meaning to say something pleasant to make things less awkward, but one quick glance at Qieluo, and the memory of her slamming me against the shower walls heaves fresh anger through me. It accidentally activates my armor, my spirit sense—

And makes me notice something strange.

"Um . . ." I scan them all, then gesture between Xiuying and Qieluo. "Why do your spirit pressures both feel stronger than your partners'?"

Surprise does not ripple through the group.

"Oh, female pressures can be felt more acutely." Xiuying shrugs, then laughs. "Kind of like how we have higher pain tolerance! In basically all Balanced Matches, the girl seems stronger by spirit sense alone."

"Really?" My frown loosens. "That's a thing?"

"Yup. You and . . ." She whips a look at Shimin, eyes subtly darkening with Water qi. But then her lashes stutter, color creeps into her cheeks, and she returns focus to me. "You feel the same way too!"

"But your actual value *is* lower than his, right?" I eye Zhu Yuanzhang, who's glowering at Shimin with his arms crossed in front of his broad chest. Shimin scowls slightly, but doesn't look away.

"Yup," Xiuying says. "I'm fifty-one hundred, and he's fifty-eight hundred. But that's just his stable base. He can fluctuate a lot higher in battle."

Okay. That explains it. The army would never let Xiuying ride with him if her spirit pressure could exceed his.

"All right, enough of this awkward small talk." Qieluo flashes her palm at me. Blinding sunlight ricochets off her fanged tiger crown. "Let me make something clear: I am only coming on this trip because I never miss a chance to go to Chang'an. This has nothing to do with you or your creepy partnership with a literal murderer." She swivels the palm to Shimin. "Full offense."

Shimin's eyes narrow further. He responds with something I don't catch.

But Qieluo reacts with a start. She spouts out something incomprehensible as well, gruff and throaty.

Oh—they're speaking their mother tongue. They're both of the Xianbei tribe.

Zhu Yuanzhang suddenly throws Xiuying behind him. "Enough of this!" he bellows. "I am not getting on a hovercraft with two *barbarians*!"

My jaw drops. Shock stuns Shimin and Qieluo.

Then her partner, Yang Jian, has to hold her back as she spews curses at Zhu Yuanzhang, who simply stomps away, white pilot coat flapping behind him.

"Sorry, so sorry." Xiuying waves her hands, looking caught between staying to explain and going after him. "He lost his family to a Rongdi raid."

I scoff. As heated as the Han-Rongdi conflict in the Ming province is—so much so that their temples train their monks in martial arts more than meditation—this is just ridiculous.

"But in Ming, those Rongdi would've been Menggu tribe, wouldn't they?" I say. "These two are Xianbei!"

Xiuying manages a weak smile that suggests the distinction doesn't matter to him. She excuses herself, then runs after Zhu Yuanzhang, calling his name. Envy curls in me at how fast she can go on her unbound feet.

Grunting, Qieluo shakes free of Yang Jian's restraint. She fixes her pilot uniform. Shimin stares after Zhu Yuanzhang, looking even more lost than usual.

Unexpectedly, Qieluo taps Shimin's elbow.

"Chin up, *Khan*," she mutters, softer and milder than before.

Shimin's face lights up with surprise.

Before he can respond, she loops her arm through Yang Jian's and struts off to the hovercraft.

"*Khan?*" I blink at Shimin.

He lets out a small huff. "It means King."

I let go of my wheelchair armrests, which I didn't realize I was clenching so hard.

Well. I don't know if this means Qieluo will be less hostile toward us, but this trip will be weird no matter what. Because before we get to Chang'an, we have to make a detour. We have another photo shoot today, scheduled for the beautiful, bloody lighting that comes with the setting sun.

A shoot in the rice terraces of my home.

CHAPTER THIRTY-FIVE

SPECIAL LEVEL OF HELL

I f my family tried to contact me during the month since I went off, the army didn't let me know. Probably as a means of punishing me, thinking it'd make me anxious.

In reality, I've done a pretty good job of pushing their existence to the back of my mind. The only update I've gotten was from Yizhi, who said that he told them the truth about us—that we met in the woods, that we never did anything out of line—and offered to sponsor an electronics-repairing apprenticeship for my brother in the nearest city, on the condition that they never speak of our relationship again, not even to me. I'm thankful for his foresight. Although questions burn behind my family's eyes the minute we're lowered by the hovercraft's rope ladder, at least that topic is strictly forbidden.

But it doesn't stop this reunion from becoming an utter disaster.

As the production crew goes to scout out a good place in the terraces for the shoot, and the other pilots get swarmed by my starstruck neighbors, my family pulls me aside, into my grandparents' room.

My father wastes no time in yelling at me about what they've experienced for the past month: absolute torment from the other villagers for my "murder" of Yang Guang. Everyone has been talking both behind their backs and to their faces. They've been dumping filth in front of our house, writing "mankiller" on our walls. He demands to know how much I'm making from the media, and why I haven't sent them a single message or made a single attempt to get them out of this miserable village.

When I stammer out that my earnings are all going toward making the Zhou counterattack happen, he practically explodes with anger.

"We birthed you and raised you, clothed you and fed you, and this is how you repay us?" His voice shakes the grimy walls. "By refusing to get your own family out of a special level of hell that *you* made? But I guess you've always been an ungrateful brat, haven't you? I bet you would love it if we rotted here in this frontier slum! If we were first to be crushed when the Hunduns break through the Wall!"

Tremors come over me. I know what will happen, what has *always happened* if I don't rush out the lie he wants to hear.

But why should I? He's not wrong.

"*Yes, and what of it?*" I lash my arm.

My father's face goes bright red, but he jars to a stop when qi courses through my meridians, silver-white through my armor and cold in my eyes and skin. The rest of my family staggers back, eyes widening in the light I'm generating.

"Don't pretend like any of you saw me as anything but a tool!" I go on. "You were all fine with selling me as a concubine to Yang Guang, who *really did murder Big Sister, by the way*. I shared a mental link with him—I confirmed it! None of this would've happened if you had just cherished us, so the consequences are yours to deal with!"

My mother slaps her hands over her mouth. She shudders with restrained sobs, afraid to even cry with too much noise. Her eyes moisten in the slope of dusty sunlight from the window, where Yizhi stood a month ago as I left him, left this family.

The sight wrenches my heart, but I have nothing more to say to her.

I swerve around in my wheelchair and storm out.

I roll into the backyard, stirring my armor wings behind me, and settle near the pigsty. Our pig oinks, rolling in filth. May the smell keep me undisturbed until the crew is ready to shoot.

Before long, however, footsteps scuff up behind me.

It sounds like a man's at first, setting me on edge, but to my surprise, it's Xiuying. I peer past her. Zhu Yuanzhang, who really did take the equipment hovercraft rather than fly with Qieluo and Shimin, isn't with her.

"Hey." She leans toward me, eyes soft. "I came in to use your latrine, and your mother wanted me to give this to you."

She holds out a doll. A baby-blessing doll, the kind of thing mothers in our parts of the mountains make for their daughters before sending them off in marriage. It's sewn from the daughter's baby blanket and stuffed with earth from her maiden family's yard. Blessings for motherhood.

Xiuying presses the doll into my hands. "She says she doesn't know exactly how a pilot marriage works, but she hopes you'll get to have your own children soon."

I gawk at the faded, puffed-up fabric that once kept me warm in infancy, at the awkward smile hand-stitched with yarn.

It is so, so wrong. Bearing a child is the last thing I want to do. My mother doesn't understand that. She doesn't understand *me*.

Yet a hot pressure loosens behind my eyes. My vision shivers and blurs. I clutch the doll, furiously holding back my tears so they won't streak through my makeup as evidence for all to see.

I blow out a sigh to fake nonchalance. "Why did she give it to *you* to give to me?"

"I think she's a little afraid of you."

My chest hitches, as if clamped between two heavy weights.

Biting her lip, Xiuying peers at the ground, then into my eyes. "Listen, I overheard what happened, and if I were you, I'd move your family to Chang'an."

"Why?" I snap, though my voice wavers. "They don't deserve it."

"But it's true that they must be suffering here. Even disregarding how the other villagers have been treating them because of you, does anyone deserve to live on the frontier?" Xiuying gestures around. "Where do you think your family's misery comes from, Zetian? Don't you think they'd become different people if you could get them out of this place and give them all the food and security they've lacked in their lives?"

"Appeasing them would only make it worse." I crush the blessing doll. Its stitched smile bloats up. "It has only *ever* made things worse. My mother and grandmother have been appeasing my father and grandfather for a lifetime. They haven't changed one bit. *You cannot appease someone into loving or respecting you.*"

"But those appeasements didn't work because they never solved the root of the problem. You know what they say, 'Poor mountains and vile waters make foul people'."

"That's not an excuse! There are plenty of families here that don't function by hurting each other!"

"But this is the only true family *you'll* have." A cloudy shine glistens in Xiuying's eyes. "Do you really want to give up on them without taking a chance this big to help them change?"

Shaking my head, I cradle my face with my fingertips, careful not to smear my makeup. How embarrassing, fighting with my family within earshot of a pilot like Xiuying. I mentally curse Gao Qiu for being so cheap that he made them tag along on this trip instead of sending them their own hovercrafts. I assume the fear of qi blasts is the only thing preventing my father from storming out to make this uglier. Thank the skies I'm wearing armor—

A chill runs through me. My attention snaps back to the house.

What misery is my father going to unleash once we leave?

"My mother and grandmother—" I gasp, steering my wheelchair into motion. "They definitely need to come with us. Or my father will take it out on them the minute we're gone."

Xiuying whips around with me, hair bun wobbling above her pilot crown. "You really think they'd be willing to leave on their own?"

I pause, imagining how that conversation would go.

I can't just leave.

This is my home. My family.

He's my husband.

I knead the blessing doll in my lap. This is all they've ever known. Marry the husband picked out for them, obey him, bear and raise his children. A lifetime of having their sense of self hammered down until they can only take shape when fitted against a man. They wouldn't be able to detach without crumbling.

I won't be able to talk them out of it. I know this, because Yizhi never talked *me* into leaving.

I never believed it would work out. I couldn't physically imagine any life but the one I had. On a visceral, gripping level, I was afraid the change would make everything worse, tip me into an even lower level of hell. There just wasn't enough solid context in my mind to make me feel secure about letting everything go.

I turned him down out of fear, and he never called me weak for it.

Xiuying crouches in front of my wheelchair, speaking in hushed tones. "It's true that there are some irredeemable people out there whose hearts are carved from something different than the rest of us, but most of us are the way we are because of something beyond our control. Even those who hurt others on a regular basis or have *killed*."

A sharp pain lances through my heart. I look away from the house, trying to banish the images of Shimin's suffering from my head.

Xiuying keeps pinning me with a piercing look. "Some people have learned the unfortunate lesson that causing pain to others alleviates their own. But maybe they truly haven't been taught anything else. Maybe they can change, if given the opportunity. A little compassion goes a long way."

"Yeah. Maybe." I watch our pig wade through the sty. It must think the world is nothing but filthy muck, having never left the pen.

"Sorry, I'm being nosy again, aren't I?" Xiuying gets up, scratching her brow.

"No, no, it's fine." I wave a hand, smiling.

"Oh, good." She laughs, but her eyes remain glossy, sincere. "I just didn't want to see a family get broken up when there's a chance at redemption. Family is worth fighting for."

"I hope so." I trace the crooked smile on my blessing doll.

I once mentally relinquished my family, when I decided to kill Yang Guang, but this is different. It would hardly take any effort to convince Gao Qiu to let my family stay in his estate for a while. There's plenty of room, and he'd love having more perceived leverage over me.

If I were to leave my family with nothing now, I'd be dooming my mother and grandmother out of sheer pettiness.

Maybe I'm not bad enough to do that. Maybe I don't know everything I think I do.

Everyone lives in a different world. So much of the time, people make decisions they don't want to. It takes more than *just get out* or *just stop drinking*.

I've misjudged Shimin so badly. Maybe my family will surprise me, too, when they're no longer suffering from a hard life.

Big Sister died for this family. She would not want me to give up on them.

"You're pathetic, by the way," Qieluo scoffs later that night in the dim halls of the Gao estate, after we've landed back in Chang'an.

"Huh?" I stop my wheelchair in a feathery halo of lantern light. My hair, still wet from an intensive wash the maidservants gave me to cleanse away my makeup, soaks through a towel around my neck.

She leans against the wall, which is painted with abstract clouds and dragons. "I overheard the way your family speaks to you. And then the way you caved."

Oh, not *her* too.

"Um . . ." The syllable drags out of my mouth, unable to string along anything else.

She crosses her arms. Lantern light seeps over half her face, leaving the other half in shadow. "You should never grant your forgiveness so easily."

A dry laugh spurts from my mouth. "Oh, yeah? If that's true, then why aren't we tearing each other's faces off right now?"

"This is not forgiveness on either of our parts." Qieluo's deep-set eyes slash down toward mine. "This is tolerance out of convenience.

Don't you try to stab me when I'm not looking, and I won't make you pay for trying to take out my watchtower. Got it?"

I'm instinctively outraged at her self-righteousness, but then I smell a whiff of fear in the temperature-controlled air. She's realized what she did to me in the showers is worth a stab in revenge. She should be livid about the watchtower incident, yet she isn't taking measures against me.

She can sense that she can't push me around anymore.

"Fine." I leer up at her. "Compromise accepted."

She rolls her eyes before continuing. "But your family wanted something from you that they did nothing to earn. And you just gave it to them."

It hits a sore spot, but I keep my tone casual. "Whatever. I didn't have to do anything but send a message to Gao Qiu. Literally a few keystrokes of effort."

"That's how they get you. Framing you as the selfish bad guy if you don't dish out *this one thing, just one thing* for them. It's bullshit. Listen up: just because you have the capacity to do something for someone, it doesn't mean you have the obligation to, especially when they won't even appreciate you for doing it."

"Why does it sound like you're projecting on my life?"

"Because I am. Duh."

Well. At least she's honest about it.

"Let's just say I have countless relatives who suddenly warmed up to me after I got rich and famous," she goes on. "I admit, it was nice, being showered with praise at so many family gatherings, outshining all of my siblings and cousins. When some aunts or uncles couldn't make rent, or were being chased by debt-hunters, or needed 'just' a few more thousand yuan to get their kid into a better school, well, it was natural to look out for family. So I did. But the next thing I knew, I was supporting at least four houses for jobless people, three boys getting terrible grades in expensive schools they didn't care about, and five gambling habits. Those were the worst. They always swore the debt-hunters would *literally cut off their fingers* this time and they'd never do it again. But then what did they do? It. Again."

"Oh, wow."

"Yup. Took me a good year and a half to realize most people should be left to solve their own problems." Qieluo tips her head against the wall. "And guess what they did after I finally cut them off? Called me all sorts of names. Spread all sorts of rumors about me. Many of the people I gave the most to ended up respecting me the least. So, I no longer care about how many fingers my uncles have lost. They shouldn't have kept putting their hands under the fucking cleaver."

I take a deep breath, then sigh it through my nose. "My case isn't like that, though. It's different."

"Sure. It always is."

"Seriously! I—"

"You know, there's a kind of predator that disguises itself as prey. That's the most dangerous kind to people like us."

I pause. I swear my towel grows colder against my neck. "People like us?"

"People who refuse to break under any number of harsh strikes and any amount of loud words, but crumple as soon as someone touches us gently or speaks to us softly."

My spirit quivers in my body, as if I've been stripped naked in the middle of the hallway.

"You should've taken your own advice." Her stare pierces through me. "Never appease. No one's ever been respected for appeasing. The only thing you did was let them know there are no consequences to treating you like trash."

My hands clench and unclench on my wheelchair's armrests. "Why do you even care?"

"The entitled assholes of the world are sustained by girls who forgive too easily. And there's nothing I'd like to rid the world of more than entitled assholes. Except Hunduns, of course."

"Well, ridding my family of assholes is exactly what I'm trying to do. It's just that the more innocent half of my family needs a stronger push to break free."

"If you say so. But mark my words: one day, this will come back to bite you in the ass."

Another rebuttal shoots up my throat, but Qieluo strides away before I can let it out.

CHAPTER THIRTY-SIX

THE CROWN

The day of my Match Crowning, I wake before sunrise, untangling myself from Yizhi's warmth.

It's strange, knowing I'm heading off to be paired for life to someone who's not him. I don't plan on stopping our relationship, even after we go back to the Great Wall, yet I kiss him with a doomed urgency, running my hands all over the inked skin I've gotten so used to.

I'm late when I get to the dressing rooms.

My mother is there. As I expected, Gao Qiu happily flew my family in. A little too happily, but who else could I have turned to?

After the production crew helps me bathe, my mother insists on sitting me down in front of an open window and conducting a pre-wedding hair combing ceremony, because she still thinks this is a wedding. I can't help but smile as she raves about the wonderful city things she's experienced in just two days.

However, more than anything, she's overjoyed about my "marriage." I haven't seen her this happy ... ever. I don't know if it's more sad or harrowing that she's been crushed into dust by marriage, yet is ecstatic to see the same hammer swing toward me.

As my mother runs a sandalwood comb through my hair several times, a blessing for a long life and long marriage, Xiuying's and Qieluo's differing words clash inside my head. But when I think about how they are as people, it comes clear to me: I don't want to be bitter and broken like Qieluo. I want to be at least halfway happy, like Xiuying.

And I want my mother and grandmother to be that way too.

What's holding them back is that they don't believe there's any way for a woman to live a meaningful life other than by rearing a family. I'll show them; I'll prove to them that it's not true. We can live for more. We can live for justice. Change. Vengeance. Power.

The Match Crowning itself happens in the banquet hall of the most luxurious hotel in Chang'an: the Golden Lotus. To no one's surprise, Gao Qiu owns it.

He slithered past the moral ambiguity of throwing two killers such a lavish ceremony by staging it as an army fundraiser. Seats were auctioned off in the name of the war effort. Chief Strategist Zhuge Liang himself flew in from the Great Wall to officiate at the event. I convinced Central Command to belatedly grant Shimin the King of Pilots title that he's been deprived of for the past two years. It's the perfect excuse to finally give him a pilot crown. He has to relinquish the cash prizes meant for the winner's family, but we'll be earning way more money for Gao Qiu from livestreams of this ceremony anyway.

During Chief Strategist Zhuge's opening speech about my and Shimin's power and potential, Shimin stands behind a secondary stage curtain, ready to be revealed first. Yizhi, Sima Yi, and I wait in the dim wings. With how elaborate my crowning look is, I'm barely managing to sit in a chair, clutching the heavy cloak I'm wearing to hide everything until the reveal. Yizhi carries the crown on a gold-embroidered cushion; a cut of red silk covers it. Sima Yi . . . Sima Yi just wanted to be here.

When the curtains open, and honey-golden lights break over Shimin, an uproar of cheers surges from Huaxia's richest. Dressed in expensive designer robes, they rise around the eighty-eight tables scattered around the glistening marble banquet hall. Red tablecloths and paper fans surround every plate, looking like an autumn carnage of fallen leaves. This is a noticeably warmer reception than the one we got when we first arrived in Chang'an. We may still be controversial, but we're stars now. These people don't care about Yang Guang or Shimin's murdered family; they care about being able to brag forever about getting a seat at this event.

As for the viewers at home . . . well, even if they're checking this out to further hate on us, they're boosting our profits.

The applause drowns out the clinking of Shimin's armor as he marches up to Chief Strategist Zhuge. A gauzy, gold-dusted red sash wreathes around his neck to cheekily hide his army collar, trailing down between his wings. Two more sashes stream from the poofy metal feathers of his shoulder guards, whispering over the polished stage.

"Li Shimin," Chief Strategist Zhuge says. "For your unrivaled contributions to the war effort, the Human Liberation Army shall now recognize you as the King of Pilots of the years 219 and 220 of unified Huaxia!"

Yizhi and I exchange a quick smile. Yizhi strides into the light with the crown cushion, drawing another wave of hoots and applause. He flicks off the red silk covering while crossing the stage, revealing the crown. A low murmur goes through the audience. They're underwhelmed. Two weeks of hype, just for a standard double circlet with some feathers at the front?

I smirk.

Just you wait.

On cue, Shimin makes an offended face and raises an armored finger. Yizhi sputters to a stop.

Peering down in theatrical disgust, Shimin touches his finger to the crown. He closes his kohl-lined eyes. Red qi sweeps from the spinal brace of his armor and into the crown.

The feathers flutter alive.

Spirit metal from Shimin's armor streams into the crown in the form of new feathers, pushing them along like a conveyor belt. Wings wiggle and flare out of the crown, as if a bird shaking off a downpour. The banquet attendees gasp in glee.

The wings flap larger and wider, four of them at the sides of the crown, gigantic and epic in a way only a King-class pilot could handle. The double circlets morph into a twisting and winding flame pattern. Crimson spikes jut up like crystals across the top of the crown, between the wings.

The audience lives for it. Gags for it. An already intoxicated Yang Jian at a table full of famous pilots snaps his fingers through the air while screaming "*Yeeeeees!*" Qieluo glares at him in the next seat over, but doesn't stop him.

Chief Strategist Zhuge picks up the crown, fingers straining at the weight. Spirit metal is heavier than lead if you're not connected to it.

"Welcome to the Hall of Fame, my King." He smiles while placing the crown on Shimin's head. Shimin has to bend quite low to let it happen.

When Shimin straightens again and opens his eyes, he lights up with not only Fire qi, but his secondary Earth qi as well. Meridians like passages of lava and gold pattern the skin on his face and neck. His irises beam with both colors, a ring of shining yellow around a ring of vicious red. Radiant gusts of qi stir into his armor and crown, making them look alive with fire.

At last, he looks complete. Like a true pilot.

I hear a sniffle beside me.

I gape. "Strategist Sima, are you . . . crying?"

To my surprise, he doesn't deny it.

"I still remember when we fetched him out of that prison camp. It took six days to get him to speak a word." Sima Yi wipes his eyes with his knuckles, then swats my shoulder. "Anyway, go."

Giving a half-hearted grunt, I rise from the chair with his help. My armor gives me the strength to stand in spite of my healing wound. Cautiously, I shuffle onto the stage behind yet another expanse of curtains. My heartbeat picks up when I settle at center stage, behind Chief Strategist Zhuge's silhouette. He talks about how Balanced Matches can help each other grow, planting the first seed of a redemption arc for me and Shimin.

"There's nothing that rocks people to the soul more than a genuinely good redemption story," Gao Qiu said to us a few days ago. *"After you return victorious, preferably with a self-sacrificing move in the climactic battle, even your worst critics won't know if they have the moral high ground to keep hating you. The ambiguity of your characters will spark conversations for years to come."*

The blood thrumming in my ears almost makes me miss my introduction.

"And now, the girl who has done the impossible—Wu Zetian!"

The curtains wheel apart. Lights stab my eyes. I decide last-second to close my eyelids altogether. Only after several seconds of the cheering do I open them, slowly, tauntingly.

Yizhi and Chief Strategist Zhuge back away into the wings. I step up beside Shimin without looking at him, heavy cloak dragging over the stage. The banquet attendees lean forward in their seats, squinting, as if trying to X-ray what I'm wearing beneath.

I milk the moment, sweeping a cool gaze over them.

Then I unfasten my cloak from the inside and throw it off with a hurl of my armor wings.

The audience explodes with delight. Yang Jian forgets he's holding a goblet and spills half his drink over Qieluo while pumping his arms.

I like him a lot better than his distant cousin who I killed.

My crowning look is honestly not that complex, but it is *grand*. Red, gauzy silk billows under the phoenix-like tails of my armor skirts, so voluminous that I'm now nearly as wide as I am tall. I'll have to crush all this down in a second for Shimin to reach my head. A storm of golden feathers spirals out of the red gauze near the bottom. Rubies on gold string dribble over the rest of my armor. The same gold-dusted sashes as Shimin's dangle from my shoulder guards.

As I turn and look up at him, I try not to sway under the weight of my elaborate hairstyle, made possible by wrapping my hair around several wig bundles. Bejeweled gold pins stick up around it like sun rays. The style barely leaves enough room around my forehead for the crown.

"Wu Zetian." Shimin speaks, the sound conducted through the banquet hall by a hidden microphone. I can practically feel the audience hold a collective breath, because this is the first time they're hearing his low, rumbling voice. "May our hearts beat in sync, and may our Chrysalis vanquish the Hunduns."

Carefully, he lifts the top circlet of his crown off his brow. Two of the four wings come with it.

My composure almost cracks as I meet his pained gaze. He must be the only pilot to crown a Match who doesn't belong to him.

Then again, I don't *belong* to anybody, and I never will.

I peer past him to Yizhi in the shadows of the stage wings, who smiles and flashes a thumbs-up.

Releasing a slow breath from my nose, I bow my head.

There's only the slightest shake in Shimin's voice as he continues. "Under witness of Heaven, Earth, and our ancestors, I hereby declare you my One True Match."

He places the magnificent crown on my head. In the same instant, I mentally slither a line of spirit metal up the back of my neck to connect with it. Its boggling weight vanishes at once, becoming part of me.

Air shudders out from my rouged lips. Emotions war inside me when I think of the little girls who must be swooning across Huaxia right now, learning all the wrong lessons, wrong aspirations, and wrong dreams from this. Such is the price we're paying for survival: allowing this terrible system to use us as bait.

My real redemption can only come from overhauling the pilot system before those girls get old enough to enlist. I don't know how yet, but I will surely have power I can leverage after coming back glorious from the counterattack.

I lift my head with the same dramatic blaze of qi through my irises, meridians, and armor as Shimin. They shine Metal white first, then Fire red joins in with a slight delay. When I first began pilot training, my secondary qi fluctuated between Water and Fire. Sima Yi said it was really weird, because people usually lean one way or the other, but he has since taught me how to coax out Fire over Water. That's the type best for defeating the Metal-type Emperor dwelling in Zhou.

Hand in hand, Shimin and I bat our wings and lift off the stage. The winds of our wingbeats lash around us. The audience bursts into screams and applause yet again. Their chairs screech back in unison, echoing through the hall, as they rise to their feet.

We turn to them in sync, the King and Queen of Pilots peering down at these wealthy, sheltered weaklings who must rely on our strength. In the days before Qin Zheng's death, they would've dropped to the floor and kowtowed to us. Now, we're only transient entertainment. We stay in character to keep their interest, looking not much more than bored (him) or smug (me).

Until my attention snags on a particular table in the back.

As if hunted beasts herded into a gilded pen, a few Sui-Tang strategists are here. An Lushan is among them, begrudgingly clapping along.

I squeeze Shimin's hand tighter. It takes all my restraint not to break character. My body twitches with the urge to fly over and stab a hairpin into An Lushan's jugular.

Yet a flood of awe surges under the blinding red in my mind. Gao Qiu has done it. He has not only pacified our most pressing enemy, but made him one of our *party guests*.

I glance at Gao Qiu's table through the corner of my eyes. He stares straight back, smirk at the ready, as if awaiting this exact moment.

Hate boils alongside my awe, but I swallow them both down. This is not the time to fixate on him. I have to focus on pulling off the counterattack that's definitely happening now. Or I'll be dooming two whole provinces.

CHAPTER THIRTY-SEVEN

INFINITE

The banquet ends deep into the night. After our guests ride off in their luxury electric carriages, drunk out of their minds, Shimin and I are escorted to one of the hotel's penthouse suites.

He lets me bathe first to free myself of the layers of makeup and neck-aching hairstyle. The moment I emerge from the washroom, he breezes past me in the sigh of released steam, then shuts a door between us again.

His intention must be for me to fall asleep first, so we can ignore the issue of consummating our Match.

Instead, I slump down on an intricate wooden chair under the sitting room's red lanterns and wait. Anticipation swoops up and down through me. This tension between us has gone on for far too long. Tonight, it's about time I resolved it.

When he comes out, red night robe loose on his body, he puts his glasses back on after a long day of suffering contact lenses.

He recoils at the sight of me.

"I couldn't manage the walk to the bedroom," I say as casually as I can, though I can't stop my ears from going hot, especially at the glimpse of skin down his chest. "Could you carry me? Please?"

"Um. Okay." He sashes his robe tighter before coming for me.

If he meant to make this less intimate, it doesn't work. The heat of our bodies presses through our thin layers of steam-dampened silk, practically skin on skin. I can feel every curve and contour of his muscles as they tense up to carry my weight. They daze me, making my blood flow go haywire.

Until he came into my life, I never realized how mesmerizing this kind of masculinity can be. A steady, controlled power used to protect and defend, not terrorize and take. In his arms, I feel safe being vulnerable. I don't have to force myself to be the cold, guarded, lonesome Iron Widow all the time.

I press my ear to his chest. His heart beats fast.

As fast as mine.

Good.

A burning fragrance stirs out of the bedroom when I push the door open. Low red light bleeds through a wooden lattice on the ceiling. On a mahogany dresser, two maroon candles flicker in bronze candlesticks, making the room's ambiance palpitate like a heart chamber. Even our skin gets dyed a pulsing red. I turn my hand in the light, transfixed.

The bed is the same fancy style as the one in Yang Guang's loft. It's boxed inside a tall, carved frame with a round opening, and beckons in the ebbing light.

Shimin lowers me onto the silk sheets. Crossing the bed frame feels like crossing a threshold to a new world. A denser, more compact one where every sense comes sharper and deeper. For a second, he hovers over me, the hard angles of his face sculpted by red light and velvety shadows and a dithering arc of candle glow. The gap between us seems compelled to close.

But then it doesn't.

His cloud of heat leaves me, chased by a cold rush. He turns to the door.

I seize the back of his robe.

"Where are you going?" I say.

"I'll sleep on the couch," he says, without facing me. "It's fine."

"I don't want you to sleep there."

Slowly, he turns around, a glistening wonder blooming in his eyes. Just like after our first battle, when he discovered I'd survived.

"The bed is big enough for the both of us," I add in a spill of words, in case he's intent on misunderstanding me. I let go of his robe. My body feels charged up to the brink of endurance, ready to snap or shatter.

The cautious wonder vanishes into him. His expression darkens. "There's no need to act anymore, you know."

"I'm not acting." I scowl, throat drying, heartbeat accelerating. "I'm really not."

His brows furrow. "Then what are you doing?"

I snort out a laugh. "Seducing you, I guess."

Surprise flashes across his face.

I hold his gaze, untangling my fingers when I notice them clasped together. Letting him know how serious I am, how sure.

It takes him a while to find his words. He ends up repeating the same ones, but in a different tone. A more tortured one.

"What are you *doing*?" He shakes his head. "You have Yizhi."

It sends a shot straight through my heart, but I maintain my poise. "I do. Does that bother you?"

"No, he's perfect for you." All hardness wilts from Shimin's eyes. "He's kind, he's brave, he's reliable, he . . ." Shimin blinks rapidly. "His skin is so smooth. It's like porcelain."

I blink. Sometimes, I wonder if Shimin's range of attraction extends just as far as Yizhi's.

I don't know if Shimin would be comfortable expressing it, though. In my village, it would mark him as a target for heated gossip for sure. When Yizhi and I were chatting in bed about this a few nights ago, he said city folk don't care as much, but he's rich and from the capital. He has it a lot easier than most people.

Anyway, that's for Shimin and Yizhi to figure out. This is between Shimin and *me*.

Shimin staggers back. "Yizhi's the one you should choose."

I lean forward with a growl, digging my nails into the edge of the bed. "Choose? Why do I have to *choose* only one of you?"

"You can't . . . cheat . . . on him."

"Cheating is deception. He and I have talked about this. He's secure enough to know it's not a competition. That any feelings I have for you don't cancel out the ones I have for him. He's okay with however close you and I get."

"He's just saying that."

"No. There's something he told me: love can be infinite, as much as your heart can open. And my heart is open to you, Shimin."

His face goes blank. He just stares at me.

I don't know what it means.

A sudden shyness rushes through me, bowing my chin. Maybe I shouldn't have crossed this line. "If it's too weird, that's fine. We can stay—"

Shimin steps close again. My head swings up.

Our eyes meet. His vulnerable, mine tender. The opposite of what we're supposed to be. Even hunched over, his shadow eclipses me. He seems to become aware of this, and sinks to one knee to regard me at eye level.

"Is this really what you want?" he whispers huskily. "If Sima

Yi, or whatever, got to you, don't. You really don't owe me any-thing. And you especially don't have to . . . pity me." His eyes glide aside, and the rest of his head starts to follow.

I cup his face with both hands to make him look at me.

"I don't pity you, you dork," I say with a small laugh. "I cherish you." I skim my hands to his collarbones, feeling his rapid heart-beat at the bottom of my palms. "I cherish who you've managed to be, despite the world telling you over and over that you're wrong. You may have some undeniably monstrous parts inside you, but that's okay. I have them too. No matter what anyone says, I'm proud to call you my co-pilot, Iron Demon."

His brows slacken. A boyish shine enters his eyes. The youngest I've seen him look. Our warm breaths quicken, swirl-ing together. His mouth moves as if to say something back.

But then he just lifts my chin and kisses me.

His gentleness is a startling thing. It takes effort for a boy like him to be gentle, yet that's what he abides by around me.

Our mouths move against each other's with the ghost of soft, slow murmurs. When we run out of air, he sits back on his knees, lifts my hand, and presses a kiss to my knuckles. The gesture scatters any last semblance of my defenses into vapor.

"And I'm proud to be *your* partner, Iron Widow." He looks up at me through his glasses, a hint of red qi sizzling in his eyes from his spinal brace. Simultaneously demonic yet sweet.

"You know, that's not a very auspicious title," I say, though I can't control my grin.

"Charming Lady, then." He runs his thumb over my fingers. "*Mei-Niang*."

"Fine. I do enjoy ironic nicknames." I hook a finger in his robe collar and pull him into another kiss. More aggressive this time. More urgent.

The temperature shifts in the room. He lets me guide him onto the bed and overtop of myself. His knees settle on either side of me, making the mattress rise against my hips. Only with him could I feel so comfortable being pinned down by someone so strong and imposing. His mouth comes down to meet mine. My mind overflows under the sensations of his solid flesh, his crushing weight, his intoxicating heat.

I reach for his robe sash.

His hand flies near my wrist, but then mellows.

"What's wrong?" I whisper against his lips. What is it with boys and hesitating to show me their chests?

"I've got a lot of scars," he mumbles in the lowest register of his voice, the sound dizzying me, making me writhe beneath him.

"I'm not scared," I say on a fast, airy breath.

He drops his hand, but he doesn't kiss me again. He hovers, chest heaving slowly and deeply.

I pull the sash loose.

Whenever I open the last layer of Yizhi's robes, a calm gladness fills me like moonlight.

Shimin's skin makes me feel anything but calm.

I gape in awe at the landscape of muscles and scars across his torso. I wish I had his power, I wish I *was* him, yet I hate that he went through any of this. I can read his life story, the things he's bested and survived, as if I were blind.

I can't help but compare. The sterile ache of Yizhi's tattoos versus the raw agony of Shimin's scars, born from different forms of pain.

There's a reason Shimin has been the most powerful pilot in Huaxia for two years. And it has nothing to do with how easily he can carry me without breaking a sweat.

To have kept choosing to wake up every day and face what life has dealt him, he is the strongest person I can imagine.

Despite the endless horrors that we've both been through, I really am grateful that we survived to meet each other.

CHAPTER THIRTY-EIGHT

FORGET HER NOT

When the girl kisses me on the forehead in the cramped bunker we call home, a cold current of dread and panic cuts beneath the blooming warmth I'm meant to feel, because I know this does not have a happy ending.

—get away! get away! get away! get away!—

She takes my hand and presses her lips to my knuckles. The gesture makes my heart shudder off a layer of grime, and soothing words flow from her mouth, yet the rising screams in my head drown them out.

—run! run! run!—

I don't want to experience another second of this, but I'm powerless to stop the scenes from carrying me on like a tide.

It's like watching a rabbit stumble into a wolf's den. Except she is no rabbit. Despite her tiny size and sweet face, her spirit pressure is a beast of its own. Together, we activated one of the heaviest Hundun husks ever to be salvaged. It took on the shape of a *zhuque*, a vermilion bird. Our hearts were beating in sync as we did it.

They say she is my One True Match.

—*lieslieslieslieslies*—

Strategist Sima trains us. He teaches us to dance on ice. She teaches me to dance in fight. *Bagua Zhang*, the martial art of spins, wind, and evasion. Our steps leave spirals and coils of footprints in the snow. Our time together passes in circular motions, with neither of us knowing how quickly it's running out.

—*don't go into the*—

We think we are ready for battle. I think I can do anything, as long as she is at my side.

—*don't go*—

But the Hunduns push back, push back hard. The battle demands more and more power from us. It's all I can think about. It's all I can claw for.

I don't realize it when I consume her mind.

—*don't*—

—*go*—

I feel every nuance of her last emotions like a silk cord slipping through my hand, the end coming rapidly in sight, yet I can't hold on. She is terrified. Of me. She regrets everything that led her to this moment. She wants nothing more than to get away from me forever.

She gets her wish.

～⟋⟋⟋⟍⟍⟍

I wake up drenched in tears, racked with sobs. Shimin is already holding me up, caressing my back, careful not to touch my bullet wound. It's still night. A sprinkle of city glamor glimmers through the wooden window screen, tracing the harsh ends of his chopped hair in neon pink and blue.

"I hate this!" I scream into the dimness, clawing at my scalp. "Get this out of my head!"

"I'm sorry," he says. "Was it one of my memories?"

I fall dazed.

I should not be the one being comforted. That was *his* memory. Not some grotesque nightmare, not something he can scream away, but something he lived through.

"I dream about walking on daggers every night, you know," he murmurs tenderly. "It feels like a nightmare, but I think it's just your life."

It sounds about right, but doesn't make me feel any better.

"I dreamed about *her*," I croak.

It hits him like a bullet. His hand drops from my back and makes a small thud on the mattress.

"Wende?" he asks on a lost ghost of a voice.

I nod, grimacing.

A long sigh leaves him. His eyes press shut.

I rub his hand, warming it. It's coarse in some spots but stunningly soft in others. An artist's hand, drowned by scars and calluses. "That was the most horrible thing I've ever felt. I'm sorry."

"I'm sorry it got passed on to you. I wouldn't wish it on—no, that's a lie." He clenches my hand. "I wish it on plenty of people."

Not knowing what else to say, I draw him closer and lean my forehead against his shoulder, right next to the sharply scented steel of his army collar. He wraps his arms around me, stroking my hair absently.

There's something fundamentally different about the kind of pain I endure and the kind of pain *he* does. My pain is solely due to being born a girl. I know it for sure, I know it's ridiculous, and I can hate and rebel to my heart's content.

But for him, it's complicated. Wrapped up in fault, in *guilt*. A tangle of impossible choices, each of which has bound him into a deeper mess. Even when he did what he believed was right, the universe only punished him for it.

"I don't understand karma." A tremor comes over him. "Wende was the one who was kind, innocent, and believed in better things. Yet I was the one who lived. And lived for so long, despite knowing I was doing nothing but killing a girl every time I battled."

I shake my head while lifting it from his shoulder. I take his face in my hands, my thumb skimming the "prisoner" tattoo on his cheek. "You didn't do nothing. You were still fighting for Huaxia. And it's not wrong to want to live, in any circumstance. Sorry that I ever . . . implied otherwise. I didn't value my own life back then."

Since the day I was born, the world has told me I must accept whatever worth men assign me. And maybe, despite my nonstop rebellion, I did. They told me to choose between accepting their doctrine or dying, and I did. I chose death. It was the surrender that made me fearless.

Tiny chips of city light quaver in Shimin's eyes. "It's okay. It's a messy issue with me."

I clench my jaw. What would Yizhi say? I try my best to channel him. "You have to remember that pilots are tools. Weapons. None of us have any real agency. It's the strategists and army higher-ups who are controlling everything in the shadows. And they were the ones who decided to keep sending girls your way. Any choice they gave you was nothing but an illusion meant to make you bear the weight of the guilt, so they didn't have to." My voice charges with fresh anger. "Don't let them get away with it. That would mean accepting things as they are, and we shouldn't."

He raises his eyes but doesn't look any less lost. "What are we supposed to do about it?"

Something hits me: this is our last night in Gao Qiu's territory. In the morning, a hovercraft will take us back to the Great Wall. Anything I want to say against the army, I have to say now.

It'll be much more dangerous to bring it up after I'm back in their grasp.

"If the counterattack succeeds, we'll have a lot of influence among the army," I whisper, gripping Shimin's hands. "We could push for some changes to the pilot system. Right now, girls are only being paired with male pilots that have way higher spirit pressures, even if their own values are Chrysalis-capable. This can't be the best way to do things."

"I'm not saying it is, but girls are naturally weaker in spirit than boys," Shimin says, soft and sad. "How would we justify an overhaul?"

I suck my teeth. "Is that factoid even true, or do things just *seem* that way? There's probably a girl with a higher spirit pressure than me in this city right now. But her family will never let her be tested, because they know—"

My words, my whole train of thought derails as two pieces of a puzzle slam together in my head. I lurch onto my knees, facing Shimin straight on. "Wait a minute—girls have lower spirit pressures, yet those pressures can be sensed more acutely?"

"Yeah?" He frowns.

"Why? How? What makes a girl's spirit pressure fundamentally different from a boy's?" I flash back to the butterfly Yizhi and I saw our last time in the woods, the one with both yin and yang wings. The casual proof that male and female are not concrete, unbreakable categories. "Something—there's *something* not right here!" I scour my fingers through my hair. "Take Wende—she was supposed to be your equal. Why did she die?"

Shimin's posture crumples. "I wish I knew. Believe me."

I feel terrible about bringing her up again, but my mind is spinning so quickly toward something game-changing, something world-shattering, that I can't help but push further. "Do you think the pilot system is rigged against girls in some *technical* way? Beyond only pairing us with stronger boys?"

Shimin's eyes widen with slow-dawning horror. "They . . . why would they rig the Chrysalises themselves? It would lower the number of Balanced Matches. They *need* those. One Balanced Match is as powerful as at least five unbalanced matches."

"But would it honestly surprise you?"

Shimin's mouth wavers several times before he says, "No."

I scrunch a fistful of our red silk sheets. "Then we need to investigate if it's possible. If it's true."

"How? If this is really how the system is, it must be classified beyond classified. We'd never get access to proof."

My thoughts continue to race. My eyes dart side to side, then snap up. "The strategists, the highest-ranking of them—they must know, right?"

"They would never admit it to us."

"Unless we make them." A dark energy pumps through my blood, faster, hotter, harder. "The night before the counterattack, we'll be invincible. We'll be able to do anything, and they won't be able to punish us, even if they find out." I gulp. *"Anything."*

I don't speak in more than the most careful of whispers, yet it's like I've fired a gun in the dim silence.

"What are you saying?" Shimin's brows pull tight.

"Do you know how karma really works, Shimin?" I snarl. "It's not something that can be prayed into existence or counted on to fall from the sky. It has to be hand-delivered. A certain senior strategist has made us suffer very much. I'm saying we make him suffer too. So badly that he'll tell us the truth to beg us to stop."

CHAPTER THIRTY-NINE

THAT KIND OF GUY,
THAT KIND OF GIRL

Shortly after we get back to the Great Wall, the counterattack is announced, to considerable commotion across Sui and Tang. Not every reaction is positive. To quell the remaining doubts, we deploy into one last defensive battle to prove we can start the Vermilion Bird off in a stable form.

With Yizhi in the cockpit with us, strapped into a side seat, the battle is so effortless that, when it's over, I'm winded by disbelief as I look around the field of Hundun husks. Victories have come so sparingly for us that it doesn't feel real for one to happen so easily.

But it did, and afterward, the Hunduns stop attacking.

The peace is suspicious. The strategists theorize that the Hunduns have realized a total clash is inevitable, and now they're holding back to have a bigger advantage on their own turf.

The Sui-Tang frontier borrows whatever Chrysalises the other provinces can spare. The recharging they need from their journeys across Huaxia's rivers and mountains gives us a final two weeks before the counterattack is launched.

Shimin has told me more about *Bagua Zhang*, the martial art Wende taught him. It's a beautiful style, but not a noble one. You're constantly swiveling behind your enemy, stepping into their weak spots and tricking them into making moves that hand you control of the fight. It's the style of those who can't win with brute force.

It's how we spin our plan to trap An Lushan. Superficially, we obey orders and do every training exercise the strategists demand. But in the shadows, we move like snakes, coiling and winding around our prey and his daily habits.

Then, the night before the counterattack, as most soldiers are distracted by the drunk pilots partying on top of the Great Wall, we strike.

With a surge of his qi, Shimin heats a tin bucket of water past boiling, then splashes it over An Lushan.

An Lushan jolts awake with a shredding scream. He seizes against the chains and straps binding him to a tilt table—the kind I was tested in to become Yang Guang's concubine. It looks hilariously small under his massive frame. The scalding water dribbles off his prominent brows and nose, mats his beard, and soaks his strategist robes. He was naked when Shimin dragged his unconscious body out of bed, but we took time to dress him, gather his hair into a topknot, and pin his boxy strategist hat in place.

It's very important that he be immediately recognizable as himself.

Shimin drops the steaming bucket. It ricochets off the metal platform we're on with several resounding clangs. We say nothing, letting An Lushan take in the situation for himself. The frigid, rust-clotted testing chamber he's woken up in. The bonds he has no hope of escaping.

The camera between us, glaring a red eye at him.

"*What is this?*" he bellows, breath and wet robes misting in the icy air. Chains rattle as he writhes some more, but they just draw more cries out of him. His every movement must be *blistering*.

An instinctive horror shocks through me, urging me to stop this suffering of a fellow human. But then I feel Shimin's presence beside me, remember the way he suffered with a muzzle on his face and his veins full of liquor, and everything in me goes as cold and hard as the chamber's metal plating.

An Lushan didn't treat us like humans, so why should we treat *him* like one?

It was easy to knock him out with heavy-duty sleeping pills once we'd figured out his routine. Every day, he has freshly made steamed buns delivered to him from the training camp cafeteria. Hours ago, Yizhi bumped into the delivery boy hard enough to knock the steamer out of his hands, apologized profusely while offering to buy him a fresh batch, then poured the dissolved pills over the new buns before handing them back.

"We have a few questions," I coo, caressing a towel in my lap like a cat as I sit in my wheelchair. "About the piloting system, specifically. Tell us—in what exact ways is it rigged against girls?"

"Are you two out of your minds?" An Lushan's face strains red.

"Well, you made us this way." A grin stretches across my cheeks. "So, talk. Talk fast. Or we'll do much, much worse."

"Release me! Now!"

I sigh, whipping the towel open. "Shimin."

He fetches a bottle of liquor from a cluster of tools Yizhi planted behind the tilt table.

An Lushan's eyes go huge.

If he's assuming that we plan on following his example of force-feeding it to him, he would be wrong.

We are not that uncreative.

Shimin shoves the tilt table so that An Lushan's head swings near the ground. I press the towel over his squirming face.

I thought Shimin would look happier to get revenge, but when he uncaps the bottle and crouches down, his expression is chillingly vacant. He upturns the bottle. Liquor pours out in a rhythmic *glug glug glug* over An Lushan's smothered nose and mouth.

A wet, animalistic shrieking gurgles against the towel. The sharp scent of alcohol bursts through the chamber. Shimin grips the bottle tighter. The slightest hint of strain crosses his face.

I remove the towel. Shimin heaves the tilt table upright. An Lushan wails harder and sharper as the alcohol crawls down his body covered with burns. His pain seems to electrify the very air.

Too bad neither Shimin nor I have a high Wood aptitude. Wood qi conducting out of Fire-type spirit metal is an outright spectacle. If we'd been allowed to craft Yizhi a suit of armor, he could've shot green lightning out of it—his secondary qi was tested to be Wood type. It would've been a great addition to this mix of horrors.

"*Talk.*" I wheel out of the camera's sight. "We know the system is rigged against girls. Give us the specifics. And don't even think about lying. Sima Yi is going through the same thing as we speak. If your answers are different, we'll *know*."

Sima Yi is actually safe and snoring in his bed, but it's believable.

"Girls—girls are naturally weaker pilots!" An Lushan wheezes. "That's just the way it is!"

"I don't buy that. Shimin, let's continue."

Table swing. Streaming liquor. Wet screaming and choking.

"How is the piloting system rigged against girls?" I say, impossibly calm.

An Lushan curses rabidly, starting to slur. Alcohol works fast when it goes right through the nostrils. Which was part of our plan.

"You know, we knew you'd be tough to crack." I cock my head. "But you should consider something: is keeping the army's secrets worth losing your bloodline?"

He jerks still against the tilt table. "What?"

Shimin hands me a tablet from the tool pile. I hold it up, showing a picture of a boy strapped to a chair in a dark concrete room. A boy the age and build of An Lushan's son.

It's actually an image doctored by Yizhi's company contacts, but I make no explanations. No attempt at verbal bluffing. An Lushan can trap himself with his own racing thoughts.

He shakes his head wildly. "That's not—that can't be—you *didn't*."

"You have five minutes to tell the truth," is all I say. I open a timer on the tablet and prop it in my lap.

"He's just a kid!" His hoarse voice breaks like glass. "A kid!"

"How is the piloting system rigged against girls?" I repeat. No justifications. No room for negotiation.

"Please . . ." He actually *weeps*.

I motion to Shimin. He goes to flip the tilt table again.

"The yin seat—!" An Lushan cries.

Shimin falls still, hand on a corner of the tilt table.

"What was that?" I lean in.

An Lushan breathes in shallow spurts, squeezing his eyes shut. "The yin seat has less active input, more passive input."

Every muscle in me tightens, quivering. The resignation in his voice is unmistakable.

This is, at last, the truth.

"What do active input and passive input mean?" I grip the armrests of my wheelchair with slick hands. "Explain."

"Active input is spirit pressure and neural signals from the spine." He keeps his eyes shut. "Passive input is just qi flow."

Cold tingles sweep up my cheeks. So, it's like the difference between Shimin and I commanding the Vermilion Bird versus Yizhi simply supplying it with his qi.

Glass shatters on metal, startling me.

Shimin has dropped the bottle of liquor.

"Are you saying . . ." He breathes deeply. "A girl's spirit pressure is actively *dampened* in a Chrysalis?"

Oh. He's thinking of Wende. Wende, who should've been his Match, yet caved under his spirit pressure. It wasn't because she was weaker after all.

It was because the pilot system didn't physically let her pilot at full potential.

"Girls supply more qi," An Lushan says, as if that's supposed to calm us down. As if that doesn't simply mean the boy is set up to drain the girl like a battery.

Shimin storms away, armored steps echoing like gunshots. He braces himself against the steel-plated wall at the back of the platform. His fists tighten and loosen on the glistening metal.

My whole body pulsates with the same realizations that must be crashing down on him: all Balanced Matches are not really *balanced* matches. A girl would have to overcome this artificial dampener to truly balance with a boy.

The girl would have to be stronger.

Which explains why the female pilot in Matches always seems to have a bigger spirit pressure than her partner. In reality, we do. We must.

And those true Matches, Matches like Shimin and Wende, that might've worked out if the inputs had been equal?

All were lost to the artificial imbalance.

"I've told the truth," An Lushan chokes through his pain. "Now let my son—"

"Why?" I cry out, my voice clanging off the chamber walls. "Why would the army do this? Why wouldn't you just make it equal? Wouldn't you get so many more Matches?"

"Spirit pressures . . . too unpredictable. This is . . . only way. To be sure who comes back."

"The *boys*," I say, tongue and lips going numb. "To be sure the *boys* will come back."

"Can't get eager pilots . . . if they're afraid of their partners . . . every battle."

"You don't think girls are afraid?"

"Girls . . . know how to sacrifice."

Nausea overwhelms me. I want to join Shimin at the wall. I want to smash my head against it until my skull shatters into blood and brains.

"Let my son go," An Lushan has the gall to keep pleading.

"You disgust me." My words warp out around a sob. "You all *disgust* me."

"Don't take this out . . . on my son." Horror blanches his features. "The girls knew. They knew they were more likely to die. They chose it!"

"No!" I scream. "Their families chose *for* them! And they didn't fight it, because they believed in that tiny fantasy chance that they'd end up in a Balanced Match!"

"That has nothing to do with my son!" He rattles against his bonds. "Let him go!"

I shake my head over and over. "Your son lives in a world that wastes the potential of half its population. All while the Hunduns are waiting just outside the Great Wall, waiting to pulverize us. We're heading toward our own destruction, and you think it has nothing to do with him?"

"Let him go! You promised!"

"We made no such promise." Shimin's voice booms through the chamber like a tangible thing, so loud it makes me flinch in my wheelchair. He turns around, qi meridians igniting at full intensity, red interlaced with gold.

I'm stunned. Then an ice-clear laugh escapes my mouth. Yes, let's cause An Lushan as much pain as possible.

"That's right." I stare into his eyes and hurl out a lie like a dagger. "Our people killed him hours ago."

A transformation passes over An Lushan. One second, a suffering and tortured man. The next, a wailing and thrashing beast that curses me with every name that can be spewed to degrade a woman.

Shimin stomps back and flips the tilt table with a violent motion. An Lushan's curses hitch.

"Don't speak to my partner like that." Shimin glares down at him.

"You won't get away with this!" An Lushan roars, upside-down. "They'll find evidence! You'll *pay*!"

Shimin laughs, a deep, unnatural sound that pierces me with a twinge of concern. He grasps the heavy steel collar the army has clamped around his throat for two years. Light flushes bright red in his grip. Heat ripples near his hands, warping the metal.

He snaps the collar off his neck and hurls it to the ground with the force of a thunderclap.

Shivers race over my skin as the impact reverberates through the chamber. It's been so long since I've felt any kind of fear around him that I've forgotten how terrifying he can be. Something has awakened inside him. Something not necessarily for the better.

What have I done? My thoughts tangle up. *What have I unleashed?*

But I catch myself the next second, because it's not me who has wronged him. It's everyone else.

That kind of guy, they called him.

That kind of girl, they called me.

Well. Here we are. Meeting expectations.

"Whatever happens, you won't find out." Shimin fetches a fresh bottle of liquor. He speaks like he's finally embodying the Iron Demon he never liked being. He crouches in front of An Lushan, brandishing the bottle. It reflects the glow of Shimin's meridians, which have dimmed to a fuming red. "I'm going to drown you with this, and I'm going to enjoy every second of it."

"It's such a tragedy," I join in with mock grief, lifting the dripping towel. "Senior Strategist An has gone missing overnight. Oh, well. There's no time to comb every crevasse in the Wall for him. The counterattack can go on without him. Chief Strategist Zhuge is helming the battle anyway. And he's way more likable."

An Lushan seems bewildered for a moment, then bursts into hysterical laughter. "You think being heroes will protect you? Good luck! The moment you win is the moment you're free to be slaughtered!"

"Oh, no." I touch my chest. "We have much bigger plans for that moment. And your confession will make it possible."

"You won't be able to change a thing." A wild leer puppets An Lushan's face. "Real women know their place. It won't matter if they learn the truth!"

"You know what I think?" I say. "I think this whole concept of women being docile and obedient is nothing but wishful thinking. Or why would you put so much effort into lying to us? Into crippling our bodies? Into coercing us with made-up morals you claim are sacred? You insecure men, you're *afraid*. You can force us into compliance, but, deep down, you know you can't force us to truly love and respect you. And without love and respect, there will always be a seed of hatred and resistance. Growing. Festering. Waiting." I dig my nails into An Lushan's upside-down head like roots pressing at pavement. "Before you die, let me confirm something for you: girls like me are everywhere, barely putting up the facade of wives and daughters and concubines. And I don't think they'll be very happy about the army's lies."

An Lushan opens his mouth to spew something else, but I silence him with the towel, like he tried so hard to silence *me*. Shimin unleashes a nonstop deluge of the liquor once used to break his mind.

An Lushan's last words drown in wet, choking misery.

When we return to our suite, Yizhi rushes to the door in a flour-caked apron and a pair of floral-patterned sleeve protectors usually worn by kitchen aunties.

"Hey, was the party fun?" he asks, his intense stare at odds with his fake-cheery tone. "Come help me with dinner! I'm just about to fry some buns."

Yizhi has used every anti-surveillance device he could get his hands on to prevent our suite from being bugged, but still, we take no chances. Shimin and I wrap our armor wings around ourselves to squeeze into the kitchen with him. My wheelchair barely fits. Yizhi turns on the exhaust hood and pours a lake of oil into a huge wok. Beside him, the counters are covered with foil trays full of handmade buns. A clay pot of Shimin's herbal medicine simmers on the stove, providing not only noise but visual cover as well; steam mists the windows in shifting, ephemeral clouds, blocking the view of any potential scouting drones.

If this were any other occasion, I'd be laughing. Perks of refusing to play by the rules: you don't have to choose between the boy who'd torture a man to death with you and the boy who'd welcome you back with pastries after.

But the camera sits in my lap like a bomb. I can't gather the strength to even begin explaining what we've learned.

After Yizhi drops the first buns into the oil, filling the steamy air with explosive crackles and hisses, I hold up the camera.

"Look for yourself," I say through my teeth. "Just look for yourself."

Scowling, Yizhi takes the camera and leans against the counter. Shimin grabs a pair of chopsticks and takes over the bun frying, turning them in the oil. A heavenly scent soon fills the kitchen, making my mouth water despite the tension coiled inside me.

Beyond the hazed-up windows, the drunken war songs of the partying pilots muffle through the glass. A grimy glow shifts over Yizhi's face as he plays back the footage, holding the camera so close to his ear that he's watching with a single eye. For the first time in a long while, self-consciousnesses rises in me. He's watching me and Shimin at our worst. Normal people would be horrified that we could do this to another human and then stroll out with no regrets.

When An Lushan's screams pierce through the camera speakers, however, Yizhi's gaze remains cool. He doesn't even blink. Only when the confessions burst out do his delicate features twitch in shock.

He gapes at us, as if questioning whether we somehow doctored this footage. I return a stony stare, a silent "*Sorry. This is exactly how the world is.*"

Honestly, after the initial shock, the information makes perfect sense. I'm livid at myself for not realizing it sooner.

"*Girls are naturally weaker in spirit than boys.*"

How did I not ask that crucial *Wait, why?* for so long? How many aspects of the piloting system—and the world in general—are based on sterile facts, and how many are just illusions? Illusions that reinforce themselves generation after generation, because people don't question the convenient boxes they're penned into, the arbitrary rules they live by?

When the footage ends, a sharp *crack* startles me. Shimin stands in the pale smoke of the snapping and sputtering wok, eyes shut, pressing an armored fist to his mouth. In his other hand, his chopsticks are now broken. His whole body is stiff with an effort not to tremble, as if he's detoxing all over again.

"Shimin . . ." Yizhi breathes, reaching for him.

"Sorry, I . . ." Shimin falls still. His eyes peel wide, irises kindling scarlet. "No, I'm not sorry!" He whips around. The chopstick fragments clatter to the greasy floor. Tears flow freely down his face from his demonic red eyes. "None of this is my fault!"

"It really isn't," Yizhi says in a dark tone, with a somber look to match.

Shimin lets out a bone-dry laugh, shaking his head. He slaps the window. The foggy glass splinters under his armored hand. The glow of his eyes reflect as fuzzy red spots. "All this time . . . all those girls . . ."

I wheel closer and take his other hand. "I told you. You were being used."

Yizhi leaves the camera on the counter and removes his sleeve protectors. With the clean hems of his student strategist robes, he wipes Shimin's tears away. "And, remember—even if the circumstances were all wrong, those battles weren't meaningless."

Shimin glances between me and Yizhi, eyes dimming black again.

However, a different red glow appears in the window.

I seize up, thinking it's a drone, but then Yizhi clears the glass with his hand—

It's a paper prayer lantern, coasting above the Hundun wilds like a blazing, flickering star, soaring toward the real twinkles that fill the night. A few more trail after it, but are quickly hazed into blurs by the steam and smoke around us. The three of us look to each other, then silently and unanimously decide to open the window.

The dusty scent of the wild courses in on a fluttering wind, entwining with the burning smell from the wok. I fetch another pair of chopsticks and fish out the charring buns. The last thing we need is for the fire alarms to go off.

A noise of amazement from Yizhi turns my head. A line of more lanterns has drifted out, mirroring the Great Wall, making a luminous orange dragon against the sparkling cosmos.

"*For vengeance!*" the partying pilots shout from the stretch of Wall behind this watchtower.

"*For freedom!*"

"*For humanity!*"

"You pilots . . ." Yizhi says without taking his eyes off the lanterns, half-up hair lifting in the night wind. "You do something important."

"But we can do *better*," I say.

"Yeah," Shimin says. He's not looking at the lanterns. He's looking at Yizhi. "We can."

His armored thumb strays over Yizhi's graceful jawline, brushing away a streak of flour.

Yizhi's eyes widen.

"Sorry—" Shimin's hand bounces away.

Yizhi looks at a loss for words for a few seconds, then schools his expression. "Don't be, handsome."

He winks.

I have to bite my lip not to laugh at the look on Shimin's face.

"Really, don't be," Yizhi says again, more serious. More breathless. His fingertips skim the newly exposed skin at Shimin's neck, mottled with red welts and scratchy scars from the abandoned collar.

Shimin takes a shaky breath through his lips. Yizhi peers at them for a long, languid moment, then into Shimin's eyes. Steam and night air billow between them, countercurrents of hot and cold. The distant lanterns hang above their heads like a radiant bridge. My face warms, and my pulse pounds against my eardrums.

Is this really happening?

Is it *finally* happening?

Shimin's gaze pours over Yizhi's features, but jumps to me with a flash of guilt.

I roll my eyes, make a triangle with my fingers, and nod.

A chuckle startles out of him.

Yizhi laughs as well. "There aren't nearly enough nice feelings in the world, so why deprive ourselves?" he says in a near whisper, yet his stare pins Shimin in place with a different intensity.

Shimin gulps. "The last thing I needed was another reason for the world to hate me. Though, now . . ."

"Now?" Yizhi's voice goes as airy as the steam wreathing around them.

"Now, I see—" Shimin grabs Yizhi's chin. "It's all fucking bullshit."

He slams the window shut with his other arm, then leans down and takes Yizhi's lips with his own.

My heart stutters, drawing my chest tight. But I'm at peace with this. Instead of a betrayal of any form, it feels like a completion. My killer boy, my sweet boy. The final line in this triangular formation we've been dancing in, making us stronger than ever.

This is unconventional, yet another implicit rule we're breaking, but you know what? It works for us. And I think the three of us are done with letting this world tell us what's okay and what isn't.

When Yizhi and Shimin break from the kiss, they reach out in sync and pull me closer. Together, they turn to me. My heartbeat soars ever higher, into my throat.

"Well, now that we've gotten that settled . . ." My laugh turns into a sigh. My eyes harden. "Let's change the world."

There's still one last thing to do: trim the video to leave nothing but the confessions.

We weren't bluffing to An Lushan about having a bigger plan. Right after we win back the Zhou province, in that precise moment of victory when all camera drones are focused on us, I will leave the cockpit, raise a tablet, and broadcast the truth to the whole of Huaxia.

PART IV

WAY OF THE
DRAGON

There is a deity in the mountain, with six legs
and four wings, and no discernible features among its
hundun chaos. Yet, it knows how to sing and dance.
It is, in truth, the River Emperor.

—*Classic of Mountains and Seas (山海经)*

CHAPTER FORTY

SCOURGE OF THE UNIVERSE

All three hundred and twenty-nine active Chrysalises that have gathered at the Sui-Tang frontier set off while the stars still glitter above. We race in a spaced-out line across the Hundun wilds, quaking the earth and juddering up gray clouds of dust.

As predicted, there was a freak-out over An Lushan going missing, but they couldn't delay the deployment hour. Daylight is too important. We'd be at a huge visual disadvantage if the battle dragged past sundown.

We hid An Lushan's body in the lavatory of a random bunker. If they find it, I doubt we'll know. They wouldn't compromise morale by announcing something like that.

Shimin and I barrel forth in the Vermilion Bird's Standard Form, claws smashing the ground, splitting it here and there. Wind slices over our wings and tail of long feathers. The White Tiger and the Black Tortoise keep pace on either side of us, still within sight though we're a considerable distance apart. The formation has stretched as widely across the plains as possible so we don't leave any significant gaps for the Hunduns.

Countless armored trucks storm a safe distance behind us, looking as tiny as beetles, ramming through the dust clouds we stir up. They're carrying radio wave transmitters that extend the range of scouting drones and Chrysalis speakers. Whenever they approach a new range limit, a line of them stays behind.

If we destroy the closest line, it will blind the army from our further actions and prevent them from feeding commands to the other pilots. That's how we plan on surviving after broadcasting An Lushan's confession.

I shouldn't even call them "the army" anymore. The strategists are just a bunch of senile string-pullers who have never risked their lives on the battlefield, and the soldiers only deal with regular people across Huaxia, not the terror of the Hunduns. The real army is *with* us. Shimin's reaction to the truth gives me hope that other male pilots might feel the same fury. They can't all be heartless monsters, fine with feeling concubine after concubine die. If we're convincing enough, this unstoppable legion of giant transforming war machines could soon be *ours* instead of *theirs*.

Then the strategists and the Sages will have no choice but to bow.

I catch myself drifting off into outlandish fantasies of the Sages pleading on their knees and pilot-concubines cheering on the Great Wall.

Focus, I berate myself.

We're not in human territory anymore. A Hundun herd could charge out of the horizon at any time. If they somehow got past our line of Chrysalises, it'd mean disaster, since the Sui-Tang frontier is basically undefended. It's also why we can't broadcast the truth before taking down the Hundun nest, no matter how much I want to scream it at the world every passing moment. The chaos it'd cause could mess with the battle too much. We do need to actually win against the Hunduns to guarantee our collective survival.

Keeping our spirit senses active the whole way would be a huge drain of qi, so we're forced to trust the strategists and their scouting drones to alert us to any enemy activity. The Zhou province is so flat, it's like striding over a repeating glitch in the universe. Perfect for farming and herding; terrible for defending against Hunduns. Hence the terrifyingly fast loss of the whole thing when they broke through over two hundred years ago, and probably why they stuck to the Kunlun Mountains to make their replication nest. Even though it's all the way at the other end of the province, the mountain range remains faintly visible on the horizon, like a row of crooked teeth. There are no major natural bastions inland.

I initially fume about how, for two centuries, the Hunduns have sucked these lands dry. Lands that are barren desert now would've been covered in verdant squares of crops and clusters of villages—one of them being my own, my true hometown, the place my ancestors toiled, labored, laughed, and sang for generation after generation.

But then, after about thirty minutes, a lush forest rolls in from the distance. And shows no sign of ending.

Keeping contact with us via the speakers, Sima Yi explains that this is just how it is beyond the battle-intensive zone. The Hunduns have freedom of movement, so they never exhaust any single area of qi, and vegetation can actually grow.

Huh. For so long, I've imagined the whole province as a wasteland.

The trees are at least not an issue to trudge through. The Vermilion Bird's Standard Form is fifty meters tall, more than three times the height of most of them. However, an alarming wrongness squirms inside me as two-century-old trunks and canopies snap and swish and collapse under our prancing claws. It's a disturbing cacophony of death and destruction. The noises rise across the forest as other Chrysalises bulldoze through it as well. Birds constantly startle out, black against the brightening dawn, like a fluttering layer being ejected farther and farther west.

And who knows what creatures are failing to get out of our way?

It's baffling, how neat and undisturbed the forest looks, when Hunduns of all sizes have supposedly roamed it for two centuries. The closest answer to how they've gotten around without squashing everything is a pattern of round gaps in the trees. Each is big enough to fit the leg of a noble-class Hundun. But the holes are so clean-cut, the only explanation is that they meticulously reuse the same stepping spots. That idea is simultaneously absurd yet disheartening. How can they be better at treating this world than *us*?

I find myself looking for evidence that my ancestors even lived here. The sun, climbing steadily behind us and shortening the Bird's shadow over the forest, glints off only the occasional flash of what might be metal or concrete. Sure, the cities and towns back then were smaller, but to see so few signs . . .

Dread hollows through me. We spend so much effort living these lives, yet every trace of their substance and meaning can be erased so quickly. So easily.

For hours, no Hunduns appear, even though scouting drones are usually shot down by them after less than twenty minutes out in the wilds. It's not a good thing. It means the Hunduns have collectively retreated to the Kunlun Mountains, and they are ready for us. The Hunduns seem like such mindless mechanical beasts most of the time that there's something unshakably eerie about the concept of them thinking, making calculated decisions. It *would* be best to face us near the end, after the journey exhausts a good portion of our qi.

There's a volcano at the heart of the Hundun nest, Mount Zhurong, that acts like a portal straight to the hyper-concentrated qi in the planet itself. We might be able to recharge there, but it's also where all the replicating Hundun larvae are. They'll give their everything to prevent us from reaching it.

When the terrain inclines upward, approaching the mountains at last, the newest intel from the scouting drones sets me on edge. It's about to get increasingly misty. We won't have much of a visibility advantage after all.

The Kunlun Mountains are a bad battleground to begin with. Many of them are shaped like chiseled stone pillars soaring toward the heavens, as if skyscrapers carved by nature. Fluffy trees spill over their rough tops and flood the many canyons between them. The Hunduns will have plenty of hiding spots, while our army will be forced to divide like rivulets to deal with them.

Just when the first canyons rise into view, made by sharp peaks that slice straight up like walls, a column of dark smoke rises from one of the possible Hundun stepping holes in the last of the forest.

"*Skies, is that man-made?*" Yizhi says through a microphone connected to the cockpit speakers, something he installed "to better communicate" with us, but which is actually meant to make the An Lushan broadcast audible to the camera drones when the time comes. We also made him an open grid in the cockpit for ventilation and a view of something other than my and Shimin's unconscious bodies.

Shimin and I both startle, causing a hitch in the Bird's steps. The White Tiger and Black Tortoise slow down in the distance as well, but we're closer to the smoke than either of them. We run even faster through the trees, squashing trunks like straw while zooming the Bird's vision in on the source of the smoke.

A *person* dressed in furs trots on a horse inside the hole, steadying the reins with one hand while frantically waving the other. The smoke signal is coming from something behind the horse.

My cry of surprise spurts out loud through the Bird's beak.

A nomad. An actual nomad.

Of course I know there'll always be nomadic tribes persevering in the wild, but this is the first solid evidence of life beyond the Great Wall that I've seen with my own eyes. His courage shakes me. What makes him dare to stray this close to a Hundun nest?

"H-hello?" Shimin speaks through the Bird as we slow to a stop before the hole, overshadowing it. Despite his heritage, he sounds as dazed as I am.

The nomad shouts something I can't make out, so desperately that his face goes red. He pulls a weathered scroll of parchment out of his furs. He lets go of the reins to hold it open, unveiling a line of bold writing.

My spirit quakes when I realize I can read it. It's Han script. That means he's likely not Rongdi, but a descendant of *my* people, those who didn't make it out when Zhou fell.

Can you cure the Emperor? the scroll says.

"*Okay.*" Sima Yi speaks up before questions pour out of us. "*Truth be told, a few other Chrysalises have come across these people as well. We're having trouble understanding their dialect, but they seem to be referring to Emperor-General Qin Zheng.*"

Now I can read the nomad's lips. *Huang di*, over and over. Emperor.

"So he's really here, then?" I exclaim. "Frozen and waiting for a cure for flowerpox?"

"*We'll have to look into it after the battle. But speaking of flowerpox, close your vent and don't lean too close! He could be carrying a latent strain that our vaccines don't work against. Rich Boy, if you see any boils on any of you, inject the antivirals immediately!*"

"*Got it!*" Yizhi says.

"*Also—shit, shit! Go! Pretty sure we just spotted signs of Hunduns!*"

We swing our Bird vision up, zooming out. The chorus of

dying trees amplifies as other Chrysalises kick up in speed and advance into the maze of canyons and pillar peaks.

As much as I wish I could stay to figure things out with the nomad, Sima Yi is right. This has to wait until we finish off our own enemy Emperor. We can't prod around the mountains with Hunduns around.

"Sorry!" I say to the nomad before launching the Bird into motion again, convulsing the ground and startling his horse. He almost falls off.

He gathers the reins and keeps yelling, but he's inaudible under the symphony of Chrysalis movements.

Our frontal assault squad gathers, consisting of the strongest Chrysalises in our army. They'll help us take down the Emperor Hundun, while the others will provide peripheral support in a tightening semicircle, preventing the smaller Hunduns from pestering us too much.

We charge into the canyons, the White Tiger and the Black Tortoise pouncing behind us. It's a little unnerving, having to trust Qieluo and Zhu Yuanzhang, but whatever grievances they have against me and Shimin—and each other—I trust that they'll set them aside for humanity's sake.

The gap between the first two pillar peaks barely accommodates the Bird's wings, and the ones after vary greatly in width. Most peaks are over twice our height—jarring, after we've towered over everything for so long. They splice up our view of the rest of the army as we move. Most other Chrysalises appear in only brief flashes between rock.

Anxiety builds in me. I've never felt small and vulnerable in a Chrysalis, and it's somehow worse than feeling it as a human. I give in to the temptation to flare my spirit sense and scan the area for myself.

It's a terrible idea.

A massive spirit pressure crashes down on me like a torrent of ice water, drowning out all else. My vision flickers black. The Bird stumbles. Shimin has to brace one wing against a pillar to stop us from buckling.

"*Mei-Niang?*" He steadies me in the yin-yang realm.

I gasp, clutching his spirit form, winded.

"Are you guys all right?" The Black Tortoise crawls up behind us, graceful as mercury, speaking with Xiuying's voice. Even though it's a Prince class, the top of its gleaming shell barely comes up to half our height. Water types are the smallest of Chrysalises. Xiuying is Water-dominant herself, so the Tortoise's eyes don't light up visibly as she speaks, but it gives off a faint black aura all over with her increased qi conduction, thanks to Water types' leaky nature.

"Yeah, it's just . . ." I say through the Bird with a strangled, disbelieving laugh. "There is definitely an Emperor class here."

"*Hey!*" Sima Yi chides. "*Stop wasting qi!*"

I keep my spirit sense off as we move on. The misty calm in the air now feels like a massive delusion.

When we finally spot the Hunduns, which appear as a dark clutter inside the trees between pillar peaks, something's not right. The herd is perfectly still. Waiting.

Hunduns are never still. They're supposed to be swarming onto us like bugs.

It's weird, but at Sima Yi's urging, we crack the Bird's wings and stomp toward them.

The herd scurries away from us, shifting under the trees.

Now we're really freaked out. The whole assault squad hesitates to keep going.

There's a long pause before Chief Strategist Zhuge comes onto all of our speakers. His grave voice fills every cockpit, creating an eerie echo through the canyon. He assures us that the strategists realize this is abnormal Hundun behavior, but the herd is likely just baiting us into using qi attacks to exhaust ourselves more. As long as we don't fall for it, we should be fine.

We're still not that eager to follow the herd, but we have no other sensible choice. It's going in the same direction as the volcano.

The fog thickens as we chase them. The narrow gaps between the pillar peaks make it so we have to constantly swerve the Bird's colossal body or fold its wings. We gain on the Hunduns only when the mountains shift from pillar-like to more normal slopes. The temperature plunges from spring to winter as the elevation scales up. The bristly coatings of trees on the mountains become dusted in frost. With the thick fog also present, the world is swallowed up in so much whiteness that when Sima Yi screams for us to stop, that the Emperor is *right there*, it takes me a second to see it.

I mistook it for a mountain.

Chills wrack through me. I grip Shimin's arm in the yin-yang realm. It's dumbfounding, processing something that huge as alive. I cannot imagine encountering it in my human form.

With a slow, shrill creaking, it creeps toward us. I can now see the six unusually long legs on the sides of it, jointed like a spider's and just as thin-looking, a sharpness only Metal types can achieve. It has to walk on the mountainsides to fit in the valley. Every movement of its huge body pushes a tide of chilled fog toward us. The common Hunduns scamper beneath its belly, as if children ducking behind a mother. A frozen black lake gleams past it in the foggy valley.

The White Tiger's eyes shine green as Qieluo speaks up. "Let's—!"

A sudden pressure in the fog tightens around us.

Something compresses the Bird's wings against its body. We panic and thrash, but the pressure refuses to ease off, and we topple against a mountainside with a colossal boom, shaking off an avalanche of frost.

Cries spurt out all around us. It's happening to the others as well. As strategists yell questions through our speakers, I glance around madly, trying to figure out what's going on.

There's a white residue over every Chrysalis. It's as if the fog is condensing into strings—

No. Oh, no. It's not the fog. It's *spirit metal*.

I gawk at the Emperor. It has spun its spirit metal, its own body, so finely that the threads can make webs. They must've been spread across the valley before we got here, disguised by the fog and frost. No matter how we fight, the webs just yield to our movements like mist, impossible to shake off.

The strategists come to the same realization and order us to calm down, but their wavering voices betray how they had no idea a Hundun could be capable of this.

The Emperor crawls backward on its spider-like legs. The webs shrink and drag us along. The threads slice into the Bird's spirit metal, seizing me with my first ever flash of Chrysalis pain. It's different from human pain, less a physical response and more of a mental trauma of being damaged.

An overwhelming wave of emotion courses through me. Grief, sadness, anger. However, the feeling is so abrupt and distinct that I realize it's not natural. Sima Yi has warned me that Hundun emotions can bleed through to pilots via certain kinds of contact. This must be what's happening.

Just when I pray to the gods to never feel this again, a horrible song slices through my head.

"*Humans . . . scourge of the universe . . .*" A voice scrapes out of the dissonant melody like a nail scratching the inside of my skull. "*Get out! Leave us alone!*"

A stupefied silence hushes the valley.

Then a fresh chorus of screams fills it, qi light pouring from the mouth of every web-snagged Chrysalis. I'm a part of it. Fear crushes down on me so intensely that I can't overcome it, can't reason my way out. I have no idea what this voice is. It's unlike anything I've heard before.

The strategists can't hear it. They have no idea what we're shrieking about.

The world seems about to end when a thunderous roar rumbles through the valley, puncturing through the screams. The White Tiger rises against the web it's caught in, green and black light split out from its smooth surface. It simultaneously transforms into Heroic Mode while ripping its signature dagger-ax out of its chest. It swings the weapon against the web.

I come to my senses. Why am I acting like I'm helpless? Taking down the Emperor is the reason we're here. *Fire melts Metal.*

On my call, Yizhi, Shimin, and I surge out our qis. A transformative tension builds in the Bird, then it bursts toward Heroic Form. In the yin-yang realm, Shimin and I shatter into butterflies. Our minds swirl and spiral into one.

We rise, claws extending into legs, arms morphing out from our wings, body turning humanoid like an armored warrior with a bird mask. We stretch and grow as tall as the Emperor. The web around us balloons out, but noticeably forces the Emperor to spin out more thread, like a silk cocoon.

More Chrysalises calm down and follow our example. Lights dazzle through the valley, as if it has stranded a constellation. The Emperor rapidly diminishes in volume. It keeps backing away.

"*Leave us alone!*" the voice growls again. "*Leave us! Leave us! Leave us!*"

We gape at it. Is it this *Emperor-class Hundun* that's speaking to us?

Panic pushes close to overwhelming us again, but we can't afford to think about anything except winning. Crying out, we grasp the web around us and heat our hands with qi. The threads break off and slither away.

No matter how much control the Emperor has over its spirit metal, it's all still part of its body. It must still feel pain through every thread.

We morph a long bow out of our breastplate and flood it with qi so the web can't go near it. Our combined qi shines so brightly, a gold-tinged pink, that it flickers in our vision. We take aim.

"*Die!*" the voice screeches again.

The Emperor leaps on its spider legs and lands with a seismic impact through the valley. Frost shudders off the trees, triggering another cloud of ice crystals. We stagger off balance.

The black lake behind the Emperor shifts. It seems at first to be a trick played on our shaky vision, but then the frozen-looking water floods through the valley, around the Emperor, around *us*. A steel-cracking coldness accompanies it.

Behind us, the water begins to rise. Higher and higher, ink-black and glistening, rounding out, almost like a—

"*Oh, fuck!*" Sima Yi shouts through our speakers. "*That's another Hundun! Another Emperor class!*"

Our minds quake, almost splitting apart. How is this possible? Sure, Water-type Hunduns can change shape slightly, but it shouldn't be able to go to *this* extreme.

Somehow, the Emperor Hunduns' abilities have evolved beyond our understanding. What's more: Fire is weakest against Water.

"*Kill the Metal one!*" Sima Yi keeps screaming. "*Now, now, now!*" Our first instinct is to run.

With a sonic crack of our wings that echoes through the valley, we blast into the air. Web strings cut into us, blinding us with pain. We frantically gush our qi across our whole body. Fog hisses away. The web expands away from the heat but hovers in place, ready to snag us the moment we stop beaming. It's like setting ourselves on fire to stay warm. This cannot last long.

Everything we want to do, want to accomplish, want to *change* flashes through our minds. How have things gone wrong so quickly? This was supposed to be the easy part!

"*Vermilion Bird, where are you going?*" Chief Strategist Zhuge yells hoarsely. "*Do something! Please!*"

"We have to recharge!" We search for the volcano, which should be nearby, but do a double take on the valley.

Our comrades crowd around the still-shifting Water Emperor, desperately blasting and stabbing and striking it, even as they're trapped in the Metal Emperor's webs.

If we fly off to recharge, we'll be risking them all. Especially the concubine-pilots, who are disproportionately bearing the qi burden—while these Chrysalises are fighting at unusually low levels to begin with, thanks to the journey across Zhou.

Clarity surges into our minds. The direst enemy should've always, *always* been these alien invaders who have robbed us of our world. Not our fellow humans. Nothing will matter if everyone dies.

We have no time to set up and risk a ranged shot, so we drop like a meteor.

We crash-land against the Metal Emperor. It doesn't expect this, and collapses on its underbelly, rocking the valley yet again.

"Tell the others to take us to the volcano after!" we roar for the strategists, then press a hand right where we can feel the

Emperor's core. We pour our qi toward it. It blasts out like water hitting a spoon, pushing us up, but we furiously flap our wings and keep the stream going.

"*Die! Die! Die!*" the voice screams in our head.

What feels like a thousand swords slice through us, shaved out from the Emperor's body. But we were ready for it. One does not engage a Metal-type Hundun in melee battle without expecting this.

We flash out our qi from every surface like a dying star. Our spirit metal turns molten from the inside out, every particle slick and mobile with qi, keeping cohesion even when pierced. A war cry bellows from our throat. Frost and fog evaporate around us, revealing a carnage of crushed trees. They erupt into real flames under our extreme heat. We seal our cockpit shut like a tight core of iron to protect our human bodies.

The Emperor writhes under our shining onslaught. Its legs push against the mountainsides, making our grip slide—

A black shape flashes in our periphery.

We panic that it's the Water Emperor, but it's the Black Tortoise in its Heroic Form, like a brawny warrior with a sleek black helmet and muscle-like armor. Shields like tortoise shells are braced against its forearms, ringed in Earth yellow. It prowls across the burning mountainside, then loops its massive, bulky arms around two of the Metal Emperor's spider legs, clamping them in place.

With the support, we push ourselves toward the limit that will automatically disconnect us if we exhaust too much qi. We incinerate the mechanism and keep going.

For vengeance.
For freedom.
For humanity.

The Emperor's core explodes. White sparks fly out with the force of a blizzard, throwing us back. We collapse into Standard Form as we fall.

The Tortoise catches us, supporting us. We hang on to our connection. We have to make sure they take us to the volcano.

We open our beak, but a biting coldness floods into us. The Tortoise's spirit metal worms around us like slush.

"Hey—" we start.

And never get a chance to finish.

With a snaking grip around us and a violent tug, the Tortoise rips one of our wings straight off.

CHAPTER FORTY-ONE

WHAT HE LIVES FOR

O ur minds shear apart, dumping us in the yin-yang realm screaming, reeling, clutching our shoulders.

My every instinct shrieks at me to disconnect, to free myself from this soul-scorching pain, but I can't. It would doom us both. Under my horrific shock and rage, I can still feel the Black Tortoise's cold, slithering grip, groping for the Bird's head.

If we stop fighting, it will crush our cockpit at once.

We swing the Bird's long neck, flail its remaining wing, kick its claws, anything to shake the Tortoise off. Yet it clings on, seeping a crippling chill into us, slowing our already exhausted qi flows and weakening the Bird's spirit metal. Fire types are the most brittle to begin with. Our every movement grates and grinds dangerously, as if rusted metal pushed to the brink of crumbling.

"Xiuying, stop him!" I try to plead through the Bird. This must be Zhu Yuanzhang's doing. But the agony is so intense that it has drowned my mind in blinding sparks. I have no idea whether I got a single sound out.

"Hey!" the White Tiger roars in my faint view through the Bird. Dagger-ax in hand, it charges toward us through the scorching valley. Rippling heat and smoke distort its glassy white Heroic Form.

I cry out in relief, reaching for it—

A black tendril from the Water Emperor snaps around the Tiger's legs. It trips and smashes to the ground, sending a shock wave through the forest flames. It gets dragged back to the battle chaos, clawed hands scraping through smashed-up trees.

My cresting hope bursts into dust.

There's way too much going on.

No one's going to save us in time.

Shimin, crumpled down with me in the yin-yang realm, squeezes me into his arms.

"*Mei-Niang*," he says in my ear, voice breaking. "Catch Yizhi."

"*What—*?"

He seizes total control of the Bird.

My senses shatter into ten thousand pieces, gyrating. Colors whirl. Sounds wail. Winds whistle.

My own flailing arms are the first things that come into focus again. Human arms.

I've been ejected from the cockpit.

CHAPTER FORTY-TWO

ONE WING AND ONE EYE

A warping scream and a flapping of robes lacerate through the stunned haze in my mind. Yizhi plummets near me in a pale blur.

My own scream gathers into a determined howl. I lash my wings against the tunneling pull of air and gravity, turning toward him, hand grasping through the wind. My fingers graze his billowing sleeve, then snatch hold of his elbow. I tug him in. Our weights collide. It sends us both tumbling toward the smoke and fire below. My lungs wheeze flat as we spiral and spiral. I whip my wings relentlessly, seizing control of our momentum.

Finally, in jerks and bobbles, we slow down. I orient upright, buoyed by wing beats. The sea of fire roars up at us like a furnace, drenching me in sweat, filling the valley with smoke. It stings my eyes and chokes my lungs. Yizhi coughs violently in my arms. I hold him tighter while pumping my wings to get out of the smog.

Where's Shimin? He must have ejected himself too, right? He *must have*.

Why would he stay?

I look for him, but the change in perspective is so extreme that I can hardly stand to open my eyes. The burning trees, once insubstantial as straw, now waver several times taller than me. Wildfire whooshes and howls behind them, the flashing yellow and roiling orange shading them into silhouettes, as if monsters grown large to condemn me for their plight. Temperatures ripple around us in visible currents, some gusts singeing hot and others freezing cold.

All thanks to the Black Tortoise.

When I raise my head and get my first good look at it, fear paralyzes me. In its biggest Heroic Form, it shifts like a living mountain, blotting out half the sky. Sun rays backlight it, scattering around its contour. The Bird slumps in its colossal arm.

But what shakes me to the core are the Tortoise's eyes—one glows yellow with Zhu Yuanzhang's Earth qi, and the other is black with Xiuying's Water qi.

She is perfectly aware and in control of what they're doing.

I forget how to move my armor wings. Yizhi and I pitch and fall. Fresh terror tears from our throats.

The misstep turns out to save our lives as the Tortoise's free arm comes swinging by, missing us by a hairsbreadth. A torrential coldness shoves us toward the mountainside, curving the smoke blooming from it. I barely recover in time to avoid the firestorm.

But maybe it would've been better to let ourselves burn. Both smoke and tears prick at my eyes. The world makes no sense—why is Xiuying trying to kill us too? What did we ever do to her?

I flap away from the Tortoise with all my might and urgency, yet my qi is so depleted that even my heart pounds sluggishly.

Another blow comes. I feel the air churn before the impact. I thrash my armor wings so hard that spots flood my vision and blood dribbles from my nose, yet nothing I do is enough. We can't avoid it. We're *just too small*. It's going to smash us into paste against the mountainside—

A low growl resonates through the valley. Creaking like a rusted machine, the Vermilion Bird flaps its one remaining wing and sinks its claws into the Tortoise, shredding it, dragging it back. One of the Bird's eyes beams solid red again.

Looking over my shoulder, my jaw drops. Shimin is still in there.

He's piloting the Bird *alone*.

This is not possible. You can't pilot a Chrysalis alone! Even a full suit of spirit armor is considered a stretch for a single mind!

"Oh!" Yizhi gasps at his wristlet.

Shimin's profile beams on it, a stern ID photo accompanied by live bio-stats measured by his own wristlet. The red, beeping digits of his heart rate stab through my wobbling vision.

380.

A sickening dread fills me.

"We need to help him!" Yizhi cries.

How? *How?*

This is too much. Too much for a heart to beat, too much for one person to take.

Shimin's going to die. He's going to die, and I'm going to break forever, and . . .

No! No, no, no, no, no!

I start charging a qi blast in my palm, but it's so pathetic that I don't have the heart to finish.

Gnashing my teeth, I burn the qi on winging toward the battle down the valley instead. Useless tears fly from my eyes as the metallic scraping and crashing of the Bird and Tortoise echo behind us. My chest clenches, close to exploding, as I imagine what it would take to keep piloting a Chrysalis in Shimin's state. What is he even burning? His primordial qi? That can't be replenished once it's gone. And he's already out half of it from having one of his kidneys harvested.

Horror teeters in me, as if I'm looking down a cliff edge.

Hang on, I beg every force of fate that's out there.

We reach the main battle. The wildfire has spread here, and so has a herd of noble Hunduns. Everywhere I look, colossal forms clash, quaking the smoky air. Yizhi and I are nothing but a tiny speck whizzing through the flame-licked pandemonium.

I spot the White Tiger, which is using its dagger-ax to slash at the Water-black tendril curled around its legs.

"Help!" I lunge to it and slam my hand over and over on its head. Yizhi latches tighter to my shoulders. "Help us! *Please!*"

The Tiger jerks around. I swing back so it can see me. It looks between me and the wrestling Bird and Tortoise in the distance. "What the—how are you—?" It speaks with a blend of Qieluo and Yang Jian's voices, its eyes a mismatched green and black.

"Shimin's piloting it alone!" I sob.

"*What?* That's not po—"

"I know it's not possible! But it's happening, and you have to help him!"

"We're . . . okay, just get in!"

A crudely carved hole flaps open beneath me and Yizhi. We stumble in.

The moment we hit solidity, spirit metal handles jut out beneath our hands. We grab them to secure ourselves. My eyes take several seconds to adjust to the dimness.

Qieluo and Yang Jian's bodies lie in their pilot seats, faces and armor lit up with their respective Wood and Water qis. Instead of clamping his hands over hers on her armrests, he's wrapping his arms around her, and she's clutching his hands to her chest, shockingly tender—and in stark contrast to how ferociously they're yelling with the Tiger's mouth, demanding answers from the strategists.

"*White Tiger, please focus on the battle,*" Chief Strategist Zhuge says, alarmingly calm compared to how he was begging us a minute ago.

"Are you kidding me? You want us to ignore how the Black Tortoise is *murdering the Vermilion Bird*?"

"*Just focus on the battle!*" Sima Yi cuts in. "*Other things are not your concern right now!*"

Blood drains from my face.

"*I am not giving up on you two!*" Sima Yi once said.

Until you've outlived your use, he failed to specify.

The strategists never intended to let us leave Zhou alive.

"Screw this!" The White Tiger's shout booms through the cockpit.

Everything lurches. Yizhi and I have to tighten our grip on the handles made for us.

The Tiger calls for the others to give it cover. Then, at last, it breaks into a free run. Heart fluttering, I check Yizhi's wristlet.

And catch the exact moment it happens. The drop in Shimin's heart rate.

372.

268.

I shriek, but I can't stop it.

92.

43.

0.

CHAPTER FORTY-THREE

ZERO

0.

The digit glares back at me, cold and merciless.

0.

0.

0.

More things are being shouted, conducted through the rattling cockpit, but I can't process them. Can't comprehend them.

Yizhi stares at the digit as well, unmoving.

The ground thunders with the force of something massive collapsing ahead. It snaps me out of it.

"White Tiger, open a grid for us!" I yell, scratching the cockpit walls, my voice shredded down to its last tatters. Maybe that huge sound was another Chrysalis, maybe it was a Hundun, maybe my ears heard wrong. Because it can't be—

A few gashes peel open before me like claw marks. Thin streams of smoke breach through them. I cough on the particulate.

Then the air stops dead in my lungs.

The Bird slumps in a rising cloud of dust and smoke, extinguished of all light. The Tortoise crawls over it, grasping its neck with one hand.

With the other, it smashes down on the Bird's head. Frozen spirit metal shatters like red glass under its palm.

The Tiger jangles to a halt, letting out a strangled cry.

"*White Tiger, there's no point anymore!*" Chief Strategist Zhuge's voice drifts through the static flatlining in my mind. "*Focus on the battle!*"

No point. His words echo around and around. *No point. No point. No point.*

In the first lesson Sima Yi gave me, he told me that humans are the most qi-dense beings on the planet. It's how we can pilot Chrysalises despite being a tiny fraction of their size.

Finally, I see what he means. This body of mine is not big enough to contain the scale of emotion coursing through me. How could I feel a rage like this, and not be able to tear the sky open and scorch the earth? I clutch the gashes I'm looking through, shaking uncontrollably, a weak white light surging in my armor, yet I can't even dent the spirit metal.

"*Why don't you just let them kill you?*" My own words swing out of time to slam me down and grate me alive. "*What do you even have to live for?*"

A tiny noise trips out of my throat, far too meek and small for the storm spiraling inside me. My chest caves in, and my shoulders curl, as if I've been starved for weeks and months and years. A jagged, splintered pain radiates beneath my rib cage, sharpening with my every attempt at getting air. I can't breathe. I can't stop shaking. Flashes of hot and cold loop through me like the jumbling air outside, confused and mismatched. Acid wells up my throat and sours my tongue.

Why did I say those things?

Why didn't I eject him first?

"Zetian . . ." Yizhi utters, sounding far, far away, touching my arm. His face is as pale as death. His bottom lip quivers nonstop.

"I did this." I drag my quavering fingers down my face. "I guilted him into—"

No.

Shimin would not want me to feel this way.

This is the one thing he would never, ever want me to think.

The Tiger charges back into the main battle. Its frustrated curses whirl through my head several seconds too late, already a distant memory.

My thoughts race in circles. For a moment, I seriously consider ripping Qieluo from her seat and draining Yang Jian dry in a rampage. But the White Tiger isn't powerful enough to win against both the Water Emperor and the Black Tortoise. Nothing left in this army can. There's no way out—

One possibility strikes like an electric shock, sending my hand darting to my conduction suit pocket, just under the long skirts of my armor. I fumble for the kit of emergency flowerpox medicine the army made us all carry.

I don't say anything out loud because I don't want the strategists to know my next move, but Yizhi's dazed eyes follow my movements and widen with understanding.

Cure the Emperor.

If the legend is true, if Qin Zheng really froze himself with the chilling powers of Water qi, then wherever he is, the Yellow Dragon is.

That Chrysalis would, indeed, be powerful enough.

CHAPTER FORTY-FOUR

THE EMPEROR'S MAUSOLEUM

With some qi gleaned into my armor from the White Tiger, I fly off under cover of the ruthless inferno, alone. I push myself past the gnawing, all-consuming grief chasing at the back of my mind. The moment I slow down or hesitate, it will catch up, and it will rip me apart.

It doesn't prove hard to find another nomad. They've been waiting for this for two centuries—of course they'd do anything to get our attention. Once I fly high enough to glance beyond the pillar peaks, I spot their columns of signal smoke.

It shouldn't matter which one I approach if they have a unanimous message to deliver regarding Qin Zheng. I go for the nearest one and flap down into the Hundun hole he—*she's* in. Awe cuts through the blank white in my mind at the sight of this elderly woman on a buff stallion, her silver hair braided behind her, no softness or submission in her gaze.

Breathing hard, I show her the syringe and vial in the antiviral kit. She almost leaps off her horse with a cry of utter elation.

We can't understand each other's words well, but my urgency

must be bleeding through my tone. She gestures for me to follow her, then rides off into the forest. Luckily, the trees are very spaced out on a human scale, enough to accommodate common Hunduns, and definitely enough for me to fly through them.

A short journey takes us to a trapdoor that she hauls open from beneath leaves and mud. It leads into a dark labyrinth of underground tunnels. These aren't wide enough for flight, so I get on the horse with her, doing my best to lift myself with my wings so my armored weight doesn't crush it. She rides through the tunnels after lighting a whooshing and fluttering torch. Every minute or so, she cups her free hand around her mouth and makes a signaling cry.

The shimmering blaze of other torches and the galloping of other hooves dash out of the shadows. Other nomads join us, speaking ecstatically in their incomprehensible dialect. Firelight dances in their wide eyes.

The tunnels angle lower and lower, the air chilling steadily. I hold on to the nomad woman's solid waist, pressing against her furs for warmth. It's mind-boggling to think that she and my grandmother descended from the same people, that beliefs and culture can diverge so drastically. Not for the first time, I question if being born inside Huaxia was as lucky as everyone claimed it was. If I'd been born to these left-behind Zhou folk instead, I could've been raised by this stunning, unbound woman. How different would I be as a person?

When we stop at last in a cavernous chamber, it's so cold that my tongue might crack in two if I opened my mouth.

Rows upon rows of unnerving clay statues stand guard, facing us. They look like the guardian figurines that would go into the mausoleum of someone rich and powerful, except they're life-sized. Even the Sages don't get life-sized ones. Their clay features look uncannily realistic. Dusty furs and cloth drape over their bodies.

Just when I'm trying to imagine how they were made, a dull glimmer behind them catches my eye.

The entire back wall is golden.

Is that . . . part of the Yellow Dragon?

My teeth chatter, and I hyperventilate as this begins to feel a little more real, a little more *possible*. Is the rest of the Dragon buried beneath our feet? I imagine it coiled deep underground, ready to spring out at any moment.

Please. Let it be true.

The nomads dismount from their horses. They weave through the ranks of statues with a respectful shuffling motion, backs bent and heads bowed. Despite the terror-laced astonishment weighing down my legs, I make myself follow their example.

Once we get closer to the golden wall, I notice that it's slightly curved, like a forehead. There's a thick wool quilt hanging on it. The silver-haired woman parts it by a slit in the middle.

A tide of even colder air gushes out.

I blink in surprise, then fall stunned yet again.

The vast chamber inside is completely golden. Shadows seem to crawl through the dimly glittering innards. It might have broken my sanity for good, but I spot the dual-chair system in the middle.

This is a cockpit. The Yellow Dragon's cockpit.

A boy is sitting in the yang seat, dressed in full golden armor built like hundreds of little squares linked together. A crown with a long flat top and bead veils in the front and back rests on his head, shading half his face. Dragon antlers shoot out from the crown's sides like mighty, gilded branches. The yin seat awaits in front of him, empty.

For a good few seconds, I can't do anything but stare through the quilt slit.

The nomads file in with utmost reverence, each kneeling to the ground and kowtowing before stepping past the quilt. I stagger after them, disbelief ballooning in my chest. I flare my spirit sense to be sure of what—no, *who* I'm looking at, and get a confirmation as overpowering as the Emperor-class pressure earlier.

This really is Qin Fucking Zheng in the flesh.

And he really is still alive. Black meridians of Water qi sprawl through the cadaver-pale skin of his face.

But so does flowerpox. The telltale blossom-like infection marks riddle his skin between the meridians.

I flash back to my conversation with Yang Guang, how he suggested Qin Zheng could have pulled this off by drawing on qi from the magma under Mount Zhurong. Is that where the other end of the Dragon is?

A hand lands on my shoulder, making me jump. The silver-haired woman gestures to where I'm keeping the antiviral kit. Getting the message, I open the kit and draw the contents of the vial into the syringe.

At once, the nomads begin chanting something I don't understand. They gather in a semicircle around Qin Zheng, dragging me along. One of them calls something out while waving a small torch. She lights it by touching it to a bigger one held by someone else. Then, with a cresting cry, she shoves the fire into her mouth.

To my amazement, the torch simply extinguishes. She passes it to someone else, then rips off one of her fur gloves and presses her bare hand against Qin Zheng's, which are lying, palms up, on his armrests. At the last second, I catch that his golden gauntlets are covered in thin needles.

Blood bursts under the woman's palm like a punctured fruit. A grunt of pain squeezes up her throat. The black of Qin Zheng's meridians crawls up her arm, rapidly reaching her grimacing face. And I get what the fire swallowing was for—she was trying to boost her Fire qi. Which is what's needed to warm Qin Zheng up.

I can help her.

Clutching the syringe, I dash toward Qin Zheng. I morph my gauntlet to expose one hand, then press it down on the needles of his other palm.

Water qi shocks into me, chilling me down to the marrow, blackening my meridians as well. But my training has given me some experience wrenching my secondary qi from Water to Fire. Screaming, I seize hold of my qi flow and force it to heat from yin to yang. My Metal qi lights up on a second circuit from the sheer effort.

Gradually, like trails of coal dust set ablaze, my blackened meridians beam red. Through our joined palms, the change travels into Qin Zheng.

A breath rasps into him, like a fresh wind scraping into a long-abandoned, dust-cluttered room. His eyes peel open in the striped shadows of his crown's bead veil and flit around at us, widening.

"*Where's the cure?*" he wheezes.

Shockingly, though his pronunciation is strange, I can understand him.

Or—no, it's not shocking. Not when my dialect and the nomads' diverged from this same ancestral one.

It rattles me all over again. I'm looking at—I'm *speaking to*—someone who should've died two hundred and twenty-one years ago.

"*Where's the cure?*" he repeats, breathing faster and harder.

Frantic shouts rise among the nomads. I snap out of it and direct the syringe toward his wrist. But his armor stops me from finding a vein.

"Open up!" I raise my head.

Half his face is melting.

I shriek, and so does he. With no more time to dally, I plunge the syringe straight into his neck. He shakes his hand free of the fire-swallowing nomad's, then clasps his blood-coated gauntlet over his slumping features. The spirit metal oozes and shifts onto his face, spreading like mercury, a speed and fluidity I've never seen in Earth-type spirit metal.

But a lot of impossibilities have been shattered today.

"Can you pilot?" I ask the dire question while yanking the emptied syringe from his neck. I press down on the needle mark to stop his blood from leaking. I have no idea if the medicine will work, but the rage and grief I'm barely keeping down pulse against my skin, driving me mad with the need for vengeance. "I need your power, your Chrysalis. *Now*."

To my surprise, though he keeps breathing laboredly, a chuckle chafes out of him. He drops his hand.

The melted half of his face has been covered with spirit metal, looking like a partial golden skull.

I shudder.

His Water qi returns on a second circuit of meridians, black beside red. Then Earth yellow comes in on a third. Metal white on a fourth. Wood green on a fifth.

From behind the shimmering golden veil of his crown, he sweeps a taunting gaze over me, eyes and skin patterned with all five qi types. "You . . . wouldn't last . . . five minutes . . . with me."

He is absolutely right.

He's on a whole different level. Not only is his spirit pressure unrivaled, he can freely wield any qi type he wants. Even if he can pilot again right away, I have no idea how I'm supposed to survive—

No. Actually, I *do* have an idea.

I stare down at the yin and yang seats. They don't look too different from modern ones. If the basic setup hasn't changed . . . if the army's lies have been sustained all this time . . .

My deep-rooted notion of the pilot system rises to resist the idea—*boys go in the yang seat, girls go in the yin seat*—but why does that have to be the way things work? Why would the army have felt compelled to install an artificial difference to the seats if there were any inherent ones?

It's all an illusion. Another arbitrary, made-up illusion.

A deathly calm flattens through me.

Before I slipped out of the White Tiger's cockpit, Yizhi gave me his antiviral kit as well. I take it out of my conduction suit and flick it open to reveal the vial and syringe. Qin Zheng will need some incentive to do what I say.

"Your pox can only be controlled, not cured," I say, which isn't a lie. "If you want to keep getting this medication, *move to the yin seat*."

Qin Zheng's brows pull together. "Excuse . . . me?"

"I know you can understand me," I enunciate. I point down at the yin seat with the medicine kit. "Switch seats. Now."

His chest heaves. "I'm . . . not getting . . . into the *woman's*—"

"Do you want to live or die?" I yell, rattling his arm by our joined hands. "It's a simple question!"

He grits his teeth. "You wouldn't let me—"

"Qin Zheng, I know two hundred and twenty-one more years of what's going on than you do, and I have no time to explain!" I roar in his face. "Do you know Zhou fell because you weren't there to protect it? Do you know your precious Yellow Dragon has been buried near a Hundun nest, and this is the first time anyone from Huaxia has seen it in over two centuries? Get in the yin seat, or you will have survived this long for *nothing*!"

"Two hundred—" Utter shock and dread bloom over his face.

I don't think he expected to wait *this* long for salvation.

His mouth snaps shut. Shakily, he rises from the yang seat, the bead veils of his crown clinking crisply.

In another astonishing move, the suit of armor on the yin seat melts into the ground, then re-emerges from the yang seat. I detach my hand from his gauntlet needles and help him switch over.

The nomads quickly catch on to what's happening and shuffle out of the cockpit. I exchange an extra glance with the silver-haired woman. There are so many questions I wish could've been communicated between us. I hope, somehow, I can live to see her again.

After the quilt flaps closed behind them, I loosen my Vermilion Bird armor from my body.

"Wait for me," I whisper, clutching a red gauntlet to my chest. Tears patter over it.

Even though my crown, the beautiful winged crown that Shimin made, is nothing but dead weight without a connection to my spine, I keep it on. I place the rest of the armor pieces in a neat pile before climbing into the yang seat.

As I do, Qin Zheng speaks up again. "Zhou . . . fell?"

"Yes." My voice wobbles. "It was where my ancestors were from. They were counting on you. You don't have to be sorry, it wasn't your fault you got sick, but the Hunduns who took it are still here. You need to kill them."

He stiffens under my arms, then slowly relaxes. "Always."

I free a shivering breath between his crown antlers, then place my hands over his. A surreal feeling washes over me as I do.

It's just a change of seat, yet everything feels different. For a moment, I feel distinctly *male*, or what it's supposed to mean to be male. But it doesn't matter. Male, female, it doesn't matter when piloting. There's still no guarantee that I'll survive this, but I've come too far to let fear stop me.

I lean back.

The moment the needles pierce my spine, an onslaught descends on my senses. I scream. Resisting is like trying to hold a door shut against a gale-force wind.

A flash of gold is the last thing I see with my flesh-and-blood eyes.

CHAPTER FORTY-FIVE

WHO AM I?

When I open my eyes, salt water singes them. A freezing coldness crushes down to my bones. I try to scream, but water instantly floods my lungs, icing me from the inside out.

What's happening?

How did I get here?

Who am I?

My chest squeezes with a choking need for air. Through the popping spots in my vision, a glassy red light shimmers above. I flail and claw toward it, only to find a layer of ice at the top, blocking me from all hope of oxygen. My eyes strain wide. I scratch along the ice until my nails snap off. It doesn't end. I pound on it until my bones crack. It won't break.

A hand seizes my ankle. My focus swings back, briefly hoping for help.

It's not.

It's an ocean full of *egui*, hungry ghosts, crawling at me through the dark water, everywhere, as far as I can see.

Their rotting hands grasp me, pile onto me, drag me down.

My mouth stretches and gapes. A shriek suffocates in my chest. The *egui* swarm around me, a writhing, stifling mass. Ice water slices up my body like razors as they haul me deeper and deeper. Dread consumes me, because there's nothing I can do—

Lines of blazing radiance ignite above, slashing through the little view I have left.

They're part of someone swimming down to me. Water boils in streams around him. The lines converge in his chest as a pulsing orb of light.

I desperately lash my arm through the *egui*. He takes it. With a mighty heave, he wrenches me out of the swarm. Our other hands lace together. His blaze-lit features are so familiar they hit me with a painful shock, yet no matter how I rummage through my sloshing mind, I can't remember who he is.

He tugs and guides me all the way to the ice layer. He puts his hand on it. The lava-like lines under his skin melt the ice in a widening circle. Pieces splinter off and drift apart.

We rupture through the surface. I gasp for air like I've never had it, so ferociously that it dizzies me.

But the *egui* are still onto us. They latch onto my legs. I kick them off while scrambling onto solid ice. My wet palms freeze upon contact, and I have to rip them off before each movement.

The blazing boy pulls himself out entirely and then helps me do the same. I tumble over the ice, so weighed down with the cold that I can hardly move. The sky is red as blood, red as fire. Monstrous hands splash out of the hole we barely escaped, skimming my arm.

"*Mei-Niang!*" The boy draws me away from them, shaking my shoulders.

Charming Lady? Why is he calling me that?

"Come on!" He scoops me into his arms, letting me lean into the warmth of his glowing chest, then breaks into a run.

The *egui* pour out behind us, giving chase. Legions and legions of them, moaning, clawing, shaking the ice. Cracks fissure out, spreading dangerously under the boy's racing steps.

Bobbling in his arms, I stare at his tense profile. The hollow in my head where I should know him, know *myself*, makes me want to scream.

How could I have forgotten him?

What does he mean to me?

Why does the sight of him make my heart ache like it might burst?

The *egui* scuff and tear at his back. I'm slowing him down, having to be carried.

"Drop me!" I shove at his shoulders.

"No." His grip grows firmer. His irises burn a vicious red, yet his gaze is tender and gentle. "You have to get out of here. You have to."

Just as I'm about to cry out in frustration, the sight of the ice beneath us trips something in my mind. A vague memory flashes through my head.

We've been on ice together before. Speeding along it.

I blink. In the next moment, he's gliding on skates, blades scraping in smooth curves. I push out of his arms. My own skates smash onto the ice. He holds on to my waist, propelling me. I loop my arm around him as well.

Yes. Yes, this feels more right.

Together, we race away from the *egui*, drawing a considerable distance from them. A shoreline speeds into sight.

But my momentum hitches as another dark mass storms in from that direction.

More *egui*.

"We have to go there!" The boy keeps me going. "It's the only way out!"

Terror strangles my bones, but if there's one thing I'm sure of, even without any memories, it's that I trust him.

I charge with him straight into the second swarm.

The moaning of the *egui* and the madness of their grasping limbs stuff my senses full, drowning me all over again. Gripping me as if he will never let go, the boy weaves through them in a smooth, graceful, circular motion, like a leaf through a storm. He draws me tight against his chest as he does.

"Remember," he pleads. "Remember who you are. Remember *me*."

The blaze in his chest beams brighter and hotter under my cheek. My senses come apart as the ice did under his touch.

Memories flood in.

I'm striding through the sunlit walkway of a prestigious school, clutching a stack of worn, borrowed books to my chest. My limbs rustle in a set of silk robes too short for my frame. Mahogany pillars pass beside me, dropping shadows over me. I do my best to ignore the stares the other students think I can't see and the whispers they think I can't hear.

I'm studying a poem in a dim locker room as fighters roar and rich spectators cheer in the arena outside. I run my battered fingers over the ancient stanzas, determined to prove I am more than what everyone assumes.

I'm on my knees in a circle of drone lights and shouting soldiers, holding my bloody, shaking hands to the back of my head, forever losing the chance to be anything but a prisoner.

I'm screaming in a Chrysalis, the girl who tried to love and heal me dead in my arms.

I'm on the floor of a cold, damp cell, my blood full of liquor, writhing like I'm burning alive. A muzzle clamps back my screams.

The girls scream instead.

So many of them.

I'm being pulled across a misty docking bridge yet again. The soldiers have another cuffed-up girl waiting at the end. My vision is too blurry to discern her features, but the iron calm of her first words shocks me.

"*Hey, at least have the guts to look me in the eye before you kill me.*"

She's offering me her hand over the back of the yin seat after the battle, bleeding from her nose, but alive and smirking.

She's putting her head to gunpoint in a room lit by a large screen, fearless with abandon, even as everyone around explodes into panic.

She's glaring at me on a shuttle racing over the Great Wall, her features finally clear to me. Her face is stunning, yet her eyes seethe with the deepest, blackest hatred.

I come to my senses. To my existence. To my reality.

"Shimin . . ." I take his face into my hands. We are now on the steps of something that looks like how I imagined the Great Wall as a kid, a man-built dragon coursing over whole mountains. The heat of the fire-red sky ripples over us. We've outrun the *egui* for now, but their moans persist in the distance.

"Zetian." His mouth curls into a smile that sends my heart aflutter.

But as the truth rises in me, so does panic. A stark red *o* intrudes into my head.

Cracks fracture from the qi meridians in his face, gaining an ember-like glow, raging hotter. Too hot. With a weak sigh like steam, he collapses to his knees over the Great Wall steps.

"No!" I drop with him, trying to hold on. He's flaking into ash and sparks. I shake my head over and over. "Stay, please stay. Please."

His smile turns sad yet serene. He strokes my cheek with a finger like heated metal. "You are the Iron Widow. This was our destiny."

"I don't want it!" I cry, squeezing his hands, shaking his shoulders, anything to stop him from vanishing. "Don't go! Don't you dare go!"

"I'm not going anywhere." He takes me into his arms, resting his chin on my head. "Don't you get it? I came from within you. Everything I was now lives on right here." He touches my temple, then kisses my forehead. "I will always be a part of you."

"No! No, no, no—!"

His lips meet mine.

Molten heat unfurls into me. I grasp him as tightly as I can, but I can't hold on. He disintegrates into cinder and soot in my arms. They drift off on the furnace-hot wind until there's nothing left but a single charred butterfly, one with both yin and yang wings.

I double over with a soundless sob.

But I know that every second I stay here is a second I'm wasting.

"*Wu Zetian*," a medley of voices whispers in my head. Not just Shimin's, but Big Sister's as well. And Yizhi's. And my mother's. And my grandmother's. And so, so many nameless girls who have suffered under the lies I must expose. "*Be their nightmare.*"

The moans from the *egui* sweep closer, like a haunting wind.

The battle is not over. This realm is still trying to consume me.

Even though everything feels impossible, even though I will never be the same, even though all I want to do is lie down and give up, I make myself keep going. I half crawl, half stumble over the Great Wall steps.

At its highest point, a throne comes into view. Breathing heavily, I stagger upright. I stare down at the cold-eyed boy sitting on it.

Qin Zheng lifts his head in surprise. The hand he was leaning on falls into his lap.

"Huh." He lets out a single, scoffing laugh. "This is new."

CHAPTER FORTY-SIX

IRON WIDOW

When my consciousness bursts out of Qin Zheng's mind realm, it's like breaking from the depths of a roiling ocean only to meet nothing but toxic, noise-filled air. Anguish and panic bear down on me, so fiercely it's unnatural.

I never panic like this.

Qin Zheng's spirit form sits before me in the yin-yang realm, cross-legged on the black yin side, while I'm shaking on the white yang side. His eyes are shut in concentration.

Surprisingly, he makes no effort to hold me back when I scramble higher with my mind, reaching into the Yellow Dragon's senses. The unnatural emotions grip me harder. My awareness of the outside world wavers so much it takes me several seconds to figure out what's going on. Qin Zheng has burrowed the Yellow Dragon out of wherever it was buried and made it to the battle. The Dragon has cornered the Water Emperor in the valley, its long, serpentine body lying in a full loop over the scorched mountainsides. No matter how the Water Emperor shifts in shape, it can't get out. The Dragon drains it of qi at every point of contact, like a clay sculpture soaking up water. The extreme emotions must be coming from the Water Emperor as it loses this hopeless battle.

Fire may be weak to Water, but Water is weak to Earth.

"Stop it . . . spare us . . . please . . ."

I swear the thoughts are coming from the Water Emperor, but that makes no sense. How could a Hundun know our language? I can't even understand the nomads properly.

Just when I'm close to fleeing back to Qin Zheng's mind realm to escape this nightmare, the emotions finally cut off, and it's like I can breathe again. The Water Emperor falls still, now a massive mound of lifeless spirit metal. It could probably be made into another Emperor-class Chrysalis.

Qin Zheng's features relax ever so slightly, but he doesn't open his eyes or acknowledge me in any way. His spirit form has manifested with the murkiest under-eye circles I've ever seen, though they make his features all the more striking in an icy, unapproachable way, bordering on beautiful. A pattern of ghostly scars laces one side of his face. This must be how he looked before the pox.

As he slithers the Dragon farther through the mountains, smashing Hunduns with its many pairs of claws, I get a better feel for this Chrysalis. The Dragon has decayed quite a bit over the centuries, but Qin Zheng repairs it with an iconic ability no other pilot has achieved since: assimilating other Earth-type spirit metal.

Usually, spirit metal from different Hunduns can't function together, but the Dragon's lengthy body picks up Hunduns like magnets as it rampages through the remaining herds. Their startled minds collide with ours upon contact, but their emotions are nowhere near as intense as the Water Emperor's, and they snuff out quickly. Their spirit metal becomes part of the Dragon, reinforcing and extending it indefinitely. New claws pop out whenever it gains a certain new length.

Swarms of bigger noble Hunduns charge at us like the *egui* in Qin Zheng's mind realm, but the Dragon destroys them effortlessly. Nothing can stop us from clearing a path to Mount Zhurong's volcano opening. After that, the battle will basically be won.

But maybe I shouldn't wait until then to make a move.

The other Chrysalises scurry behind us through the mountains. They must've reacted with screaming elation when the Dragon first appeared, yet they're eerily silent now. When tiny camera drones buzz ahead of us, I realize the Dragon's eyes must be shining different colors, a telltale sign of a Balanced Match. And one of them must be Metal white. You'd have to be missing a brain not to suspect that I'm inside.

I can almost hear the strategists in the other pilots' speakers, telling them to be cautious of the very Chrysalis that's saving their lives.

Fresh anger blazes through me. I bet they're planning to "handle" me as soon as the battle ends.

Then I'd better strike first.

Qin Zheng doesn't object when I take full control with the excuse of "having to do something." It's strange; I expected more of a power struggle. I can't figure him out. Somehow, I didn't get a single memory from his mind realm. I can only guess that his mind isn't at its clearest after waking up from a two-century sleep.

As I crush noble Hunduns like eggshells, I look right into a camera drone.

"The army has lied to us all!" I shout through the Dragon's long snout. I spew out the truth of the pilot system, emphasizing how it's dragged the war effort down by repressing half of potential pilots. People will care about something only if they realize it affects them in a real way.

"I do have proof, and I'll show it soon, but you know it makes sense! You know gender has nothing to do with spirit strength, because *I* exist! Yes, this is Wu Zetian, the Iron Widow!"

I pop open the Dragon's cockpit, showing all of Huaxia the arrangement inside. Me in the yang seat, subjugating a boy who is clearly Emperor Qin Zheng.

The army and Sages must be freaking out and shutting down livestreams by now, but I've said what I needed to. I don't waste another second. With several bounding leaps, I propel the Dragon into flight. Qi of all types, which Qin Zheng must've gleaned from the magma underground and the Hunduns he assimilated, courses through its hollow body, lifting it like a paper lantern. It feels like I'm wielding the life force of the world, not just my own.

Undulating the Dragon, I soar past the pillar peaks to where the last neat, convenient line of radio trucks is. There are more among the mountains, but destroying these will be easier.

I land the Dragon over them, flattening most. The ones I missed I crumple and lacerate with the Dragon's many claws, ensuring that the pilots are cut off cleanly from the strategists.

After I turn back, seeking out the volcano, the other pilots have clearly finished the job without us. The smoking husks of half-formed Hundun larvae pile along Mount Zhurong's incline. It's a total victory. The counterattack has succeeded.

Yet confusion dominates the battlefield. No more zipping camera drones, no more strategists shouting in cockpit speakers.

No one celebrates. The other Chrysalises simply stare up, looking lost, as the Dragon slithers in through the air. Some tap their heads out of some pathetic hope that the strategists might reconnect.

I smash down in front of the Black Tortoise near the top of Mount Zhurong. Dirt showers audibly into the volcano opening.

The Tortoise is so much smaller than me again, a puny height that makes me feel like I'm looking down at an actual tortoise.

"*How could you?*" I howl.

The battlefield hushes.

"Zetian, I'm so, so sorry." The Tortoise crawls backward down the mountain, crying with Xiuying's voice, both eyes dimming black. "Our kids . . . they were going to . . ." The Tortoise hitches to a stop. She growls. "I wouldn't do anything out of line, or *your* family will be in danger too!"

My fury mellows like a wind-chilled flame, then roars back so brilliantly and violently that it takes me an extra beat to react.

Is this the real reason she urged me to make up with my family? So they could be used to *control me?*

I can't believe I've done the one thing I've raged at everyone else for doing: underestimating a woman.

I lean close to the Tortoise, almost touching it with the Dragon's extended snout and long, golden whiskers. My words pour a silver-white glaze over its black surface. "Please. You already killed my real family."

I squash a claw through the Tortoise's head, tearing it clean off its neck. I crush and grind it. Streams of blood, so thin they're nearly invisible, trickle down the claw. The thought of Shimin going through the same thing flashes through my head, and I clench even tighter, gritting the Dragon's teeth.

Cries of shock rise from the other Chrysalises, but none of them budge from their positions among the Hundun husks.

That's how I know they won't get in the way of my next move.

Besides, it'll take them hours to get back to the undefended Sui-Tang frontier, while I can fly there in much less.

In the yin-yang realm, Qin Zheng's eyes swing open for the first time, regarding me in astonishment.

"You wish to take over your world," he breathes in his centuries-old dialect. His words are slightly slurred, as if he's drugged or drowsy.

"Yes." I choose my words carefully. This boy was an actual ruling Emperor; he won't cooperate if I make him feel like a mere tool. "There's something you should know about the role of pilots nowadays: we're not leaders anymore. If you stop me, you'll come back as nothing but a celebrity, a spectacle. People will ogle you, but they won't bow to you. If you want them to do that again, we'll have to make it happen by force."

"All right, then." He shrugs, closing his eyes again. "Let us embark."

I laugh. The sound is hollow, devoid of joy, and goes on for way too long, to the point of madness.

Redemption story, they said?

There will be no redemption. It is not me who is wrong. It's everyone else.

CHAPTER FORTY-SEVEN

EVERYTHING I DESERVE

C hang'an, the City of Everlasting Peace, is now anything but peaceful.

A wall of human noise rushes up through the cooling air, growing louder as we approach in the Dragon. A final flush of sun drains beyond the mountains framing the valley of skyscrapers. Under the descending night, the neon-peppered streets are flooded with people, as if the over-packed buildings have vomited themselves clean. The shadowed crowds fall to their knees and prostrate themselves over and over. They must have heard from the villages and cities we passed over that we were coming.

Once I took Yizhi back from the White Tiger's cockpit, I left the army of Chrysalises at the Zhou frontier. I'll deal with them later.

After it's too late to reverse what I've done.

Qieluo and Yang Jian's fed-up attitudes—and the fact that Yizhi and I owe them our lives—make me trust that they won't try to stop me. But even if they do trek back to the Sui-Tang frontier, they'll find that I've destroyed the Kaihuang watchtower.

I did not care who was in there. If the strategists are as smart as they say, they would've gotten out the moment I went rogue.

This is my admittedly graceless strategy: annihilate every center of power, so everything will collapse into chaos and people will have no choice but to obey the new most powerful thing—me.

The Dragon's shadow slinks like the Wei River over the pleading and sobbing masses, straight toward the Palace of Sages on a mountain lording over the city. I remember glaring down at it the first time I flew in.

Now I'm going to do everything I wish I could've done then.

"Pilot Wu!" shouts a gravelly voice through what sounds like the palace's entire speaker system.

"It's *Empress* Wu!" I roar back, effortlessly louder.

There's a stunned pause before the voice keeps going. "Stop right there! Think about what you're doing! Think about the consequences!"

I just laugh. I can't believe he's even try—

"Tian-Tian!"

I stop dead in the air, almost crashing over the skyscrapers and millions of people below.

It's my mother.

I zoom the Dragon's vision in on the huge, floodlit courtyard in the middle of the palace complex's manors and pagodas. There she is, held down with the rest of my family by a bunch of soldiers. One of the Sages—I don't know which, they all look the same with their heavy robes and long white beards—holds a microphone to my mother's mouth.

My spirit clenches inside the Dragon. This is really happening. I'm really being forced to make this choice.

And I brought this on myself. Qieluo was right; this is my ass, being bitten, right now. If I hadn't fallen for Xiuying's "*A little compassion goes a long way!"* spiel, my shitty family would still be safe in our shitty frontier village.

Or maybe the Sages would've taken them here before the battle regardless, just in case.

But one thing would be different if I hadn't opened my heart to them again: I wouldn't be hesitating now.

Just when my silence threatens to betray my weakness, my father snatches the microphone.

"Please . . ." He weeps, pushing my brother Dalang out of the huddle of people. "Punish *us*, not him! Let him go—he's your *brother!*"

Something shatters inside me.

I watch in a daze as Dalang sobs harder, then stumbles back and drops between our parents again. They cry out, trying to push him away, toward some illusion of safety from his evil sister trying to take over the capital in a giant metal dragon.

So this is the capacity they had all along.

This is what they would do for their son, while they sold me and Big Sister without batting an eye.

I don't want to be here anymore. I don't want to look at them. I don't want to think. I don't want to remember, to compare, to confirm that I have always, always, *always* been nothing but water meant to be hurled out the door to these people. These people, who are the only blood family I will ever have. Who I'm expected to love and defend no matter what.

Who will forever be used against me if I don't relinquish them in this moment.

What kind of life would that be? Being tools, being leverage, for the rest of their existence?

They're the ones who taught me how horrible that feels.

I know what the real mercy would be.

"Sorry," I say, cold as Big Sister's ashes. "You're in my way."

I crush the entire palace with the Dragon's claw.

Stone, marble, and dark wood snap and crumble in blooming clouds of smoke. Screams tide through the city. Huge chunks of debris tumble down the mountain, shocking back a wave of people below.

Nothing ripples in my heart.

I can't close the Dragon's eyes, so I just stare vacantly as smoke billows away from the rubble.

It's a long time before my mind grinds into motion again, and it's only because of something absurdly pathetic: a hovercraft clattering toward me, cutting through the white noise of screams.

I raise a claw to strike it down.

"Hold on!" a voice blasts through the hovercraft speakers.

I do.

Because it's Gao Qiu.

"Hold on a second, Pilot Wu—or, no, you go by Empress Wu now, don't you?" The hovercraft hatch skates open, revealing him in a flood of fluorescence. He's surrounded by sobbing little girls clinging to his black leather robes. A few goons stand guard behind him.

In my utter horror, I find myself impressed in the most vile, disgusting way.

The Sages should've taken notes. *This* is how you paralyze me.

"Now, I understand what you're trying to do," Gao Qiu says, cool and even. "And I understand that there's no brute force left in Huaxia that could possibly stop you. So I'm here to bargain!"

"*Bargain?*" I roar, with a force that sends the hovercraft teetering back.

"Whoa, whoa, let's have a civil conversation." He laughs with maniacal abandon, hanging on to a handle on the hovercraft ceiling. The little girls shriek some more, and I hate the way it makes me instantly clamp the Dragon's mouth shut. "See, I doubt your Mama and Baba ever taught you how to run a country, so you'll need some assistance to make sure things don't spiral out of control. Make me your regent! Not only will I help you run things, I'll make sure a certain video never gets sent to my darling fifth son."

I freeze.

"Video?" Yizhi speaks up from inside the cockpit. "What video?"

"Yizhi, it's nothing," I say quickly, sounding far less assured than I wanted. I never thought Yizhi needed to find out his father made me strip nude to seal the deal, and now this . . . this is the worst possible moment!

Unfortunately, even my tiniest voice is audible to Gao Qiu.

"Oh, it's not nothing, when you clearly never told him about it!" he says, with a glee that surges me close to crushing the hovercraft in my claws.

But one look at the girls, and I clench them back. I do have limits to what I can consciously do, and Gao Qiu has guessed them.

I internally scream at how the Dragon just *had* to be Earth type, the only one that can't do qi attacks. If it were any other kind, I could be attempting a precise qi strike at him.

"He's in there, isn't he?" he goes on. "This is perfect! Hello, son! You won't believe the footage I have!"

"What is he talking about?" Yizhi's tone sharpens.

"I'll explain later!" I growl, thoughts fraying. "Right now, just let me deal with—"

"Later?" Gao Qiu jeers. "Empress Wu, this offer has a time limit. I can't guarantee what will happen if you don't take it within the next ten seconds."

The hovercraft starts flying backwards.

"Let me out!" Yizhi shouts with sudden force. "Let me talk to him!"

"Yizhi, it's not what you—!"

"*Just do it*," he says, cold enough to crack my heart.

My world crumbles apart more than it already has, but I can't keep him locked in when he doesn't want to be.

Feeling like I'm tearing a hole out of my very soul, I make an opening in the Dragon's forehead. Yizhi steps out onto its long snout and into the whipping twilight winds.

"Father!" he calls into his wristlet.

"Son!" The hovercraft swings back. Gao Qiu taps his wristlet and speaks into it as well. "You should tell your lady friend what's good for h—"

Yellow-green lightning bursts across the air.

My qi flow stuns to a standstill. Even Qin Zheng jerks alert in my head from his half-asleep state.

Radiance beams under Yizhi's fluttering robes. A war cry scours out from the bottom of his lungs. Electric-hot Wood qi, boosted by Earth qi, bursts from his fingers, held like a gun. It streaks across the ether and into Gao Qiu. A smell of roasting flesh blows over on the wind.

It's over in less than three seconds, but shocks enough for a lifetime. The shrieking little girls scramble away from the charred, smoking shape that used to be Gao Qiu. His goons freak out as well, kicking it out of the hovercraft. It plunges into the city, splattering over a random rooftop, triggering another tide of screams.

Yizhi doubles over, panting.

When he turns around, his eyes burn both yellow and green, and so do the meridians in his face. Blood trickles from his nose. He wipes his upper lip with his thumb.

"I believe you," he says, cool and plain.

He yanks his waist sash loose and throws off his robes. The fabric billows away against the budding stars.

A fraction of my Vermilion Bird armor gleams on his bare

torso, the spinal brace like a line of blood down his tattooed back, the shoulder and arm pieces like parts of a torn bird carcass.

A single term sizzles in my mind: *Baofeng Shaoye*. Young Master of the Storm.

This could not have been what Gao Qiu imagined when he promoted Yizhi with that nonsense.

"Attention, all Gao Enterprises personnel!" Yizhi shouts into his wristlet between ragged breaths. "New bargain: defy us, and all of you and your families will die! Obey us, and you'll keep everything you have and more!"

The goons in the hovercraft exchange bewildered looks.

Then they sink to their knees among the sobbing girls.

"Now, repeat after me. Long live the Iron Widow!" he yells, pointing a finger to the sky.

"*Long live the Iron Widow!*" Their pledge is conducted through the hovercraft speakers.

Yizhi taps the comm line on his wristlet shut. He looks back at me with a cock of his head. "Looks like I just inherited one point four billion yuan."

The closest I can come to describing my current feelings is the look on Qin Zheng's face in the yin-yang realm: brows twisted, eyes scrunched, mouth open.

Then he shakes his head, blinking. "Hold on, how has inflation been? Is that still a lot of money?"

I burst into uncontrollable laughter, out loud through the Dragon. This time, I'm really not sure if I can stop. Yizhi has to rush back into the cockpit so he doesn't slip and plummet from the shaky motion. Emotions crash through me like a whirlwind: grief and exhilaration, rage and relief, pain and ecstasy.

What a day.

What a month.

What a life.

I've been told endless lies since I was born. That I was not kind enough, considerate enough, humble enough, honorable enough, pretty enough, *pleasing* enough. And that if I failed to meet the needs of those around me, I did not deserve to live.

Propaganda. All of it. Propaganda to keep me chasing after the approval of others on my bound and broken feet, as if being a good servant is the only thing I should be proud of.

Now, I see the truth.

This world does not deserve my respect. It is not worthy of my kindness or compassion.

When I gather my senses at last, I turn to the wailing and kneeling populace below. I can't believe they still have voices after screaming so much. It'll be tough to make them accept a new world order established by *me*, and I know that taking over Chang'an does not mean Huaxia belongs to me yet, but this is a start.

"So much for that cabin in the mountains, huh?" I mutter, just loud enough for Yizhi to hear.

"Fuck the cabin in the mountains," he says in the Dragon's head. "Let's rule the world."

EPILOGUE

Still in the Dragon, I touch down in the ash-filled valley where we battled the Emperor Hunduns. I had to come back to Zhou for three reasons: to recharge, to deal with the army, and to bring Shimin home.

But I do not find what I expect.

"What do you mean, '*they* took him'?" I exclaim to the White Tiger.

"I'm serious!" Qieluo speaks through the Tiger's mouth. "This giant hovercraft came out of nowhere—literally, it *materialized* in thin air—and then dropped down over here. By the time we rushed over, it was gone, and so were the pieces of the Bird's head!"

My thoughts race, tangled up by the concept of this. "Was it—was it the *gods*?"

"I mean, who else could it be?"

"But the gods never show themselves! They never intervene! They—"

Suddenly, a force hijacks the Dragon's voice.

"They never even helped *me* when I needed it!" Qin Zheng roars in outrage.

It's the first time he's spoken through the Dragon since he awakened.

The White Tiger and the few Chrysalises behind it gawk at us. I don't think they fully processed—on top of everything else—that Emperor Qin Zheng is actually back, revived from the brink of death after two centuries.

I can feel his spirit growing stronger, and I don't like it.

I don't know how much longer I'll be able to use him.

A beeping comes from the Dragon's cockpit. I'm still trying to wrap my head around what Qieluo said, but I disconnect to my human body to check my wristlet. I moved radio trucks around to keep communications open with Yizhi. If he's calling me, something urgent must have happened in Chang'an.

The notification opens to his frantic face.

"Zetian, it's all a lie! Everything's a lie!"

I blink. "I know—"

"No, it's nothing about the pilot system! It's the planet! *This isn't our planet!*"

"What . . . ?" I breathe. In the yin seat, Qin Zheng stirs sharply to attention.

Yizhi sounds so winded that he struggles to speak. "My people recovered a quartz drive of documents in the palace rubble. The entire idea that the Hunduns destroyed our previous civilization—it's not real! Our ancestors were dropped onto this planet! *The Hunduns are the natives, not—!*"

The screen flickers to black. White blocky text appears, scrolling slowly.

DEAR WU ZETIAN,

IF YOU CONTINUE WITH YOUR DRASTIC ACTIONS, YOU WILL GIVE US OF THE HEAVENLY COURT NO CHOICE BUT

TO INTERVENE. HOWEVER, WE RECOGNIZE YOUR POWER, SO HERE IS OUR OFFER:

IF YOU DO OUR BIDDING AS THE SAGES DID, WE HAVE WAYS TO BRING BACK WHAT YOU'VE LOST.

BUT IF YOU DEFY US OR REVEAL THE TRUTH, YOU WILL LOSE EVERYTHING.

Color returns to the screen. A dim video feed of a cylindrical tank, filled with bubbly fluid. Something's in it, attached to the top by a jungle of tubes and wires.

Something with a head, a heavy black oxygen mask, and a bare, broken rib cage that exposes a slow-beating heart and sluggishly breathing lungs. There's nothing else.

I can't process this as a person. I can't process this as . . . as . . .

But I know that short hair. I know those deep-set eyes.

A white noise lances through my brain, and so does the Metal Emperor's haunting wail.

"Humans . . . scourge of the universe . . ."

The memory of that, and the Water Emperor's pain, grief, and rage, tear through me. The mountain full of Hundun larvae, shattered and steaming, flashes behind my eyes, splicing with this horrific hope on the screen like a nightmare I can't escape, no matter which way I try to run.

I drag my nails down my head and scream.

ACKNOWLEDGEMENTS

It's been a weird journey, going from desperately trying to get people to read my writing to having people pay to read it. Well, if you didn't pay for this, that's fine, but please leave me a rating and a review on Goodreads or Amazon, LOL.

My wholehearted thanks to Rebecca Schaeffer, who met me when I was a baby writer writing things so problematic I wish I could scrub them permanently from my memory (glad those books never got published). Isn't it hilarious how we were so at odds with each other while sending beta feedback for the first time, yet we ended up getting along while chatting for real? Thanks for seeing something more in me when I was in my blunder years, and then being there for me every single day when my mental health hit rock bottom. I probably wouldn't be alive without you. This book definitely wouldn't exist without you and that life-changing conversation we had where my rants about *Darling in the Franxx* morphed into, well, THIS whole thing. (Also, check out Rebecca's *Not Even Bones* trilogy, about a girl who dissects supernatural creatures for her mother to sell on the Internet before getting sold into the supernatural black market herself!)

To Rachel Brooks, the most thoughtful and attentive agent any author could ask for, who had to deal with me suddenly throwing her this book even though I was supposed to be revising something else, then had to tell me in a four-thousand-word letter exactly why that draft of this book was waaaay too dark to sell as YA. Sorry about that; 2019 was my last year of university and I was mentally a mess, but I'd say things worked out pretty great, didn't they? ;)

To my amazing editors, Peter Phillips and Margot Blankier, for believing in me and challenging me to take this book to another level. My copyeditor, Catherine Marjoribanks, for catching all my grammar blunders (English is such a weird language, I swear . . .). My publicist, Samantha Devotta, for being as eager to hype this book as I am. Shana Hayes, for proofreading this book with an eagle eye and catching inconsistencies I never even thought of. Shenwei Chang, for their valuable sensitivity notes. And Ashley Mackenzie, for going above and beyond when doing the stunning jacket illustration and reading the whole book to ensure that the design is faithful to the story.

To the Canada Council for the Arts and the British Columbia Arts Council, for the grant that made working on this book possible.

To Rebecca Kim Wells, who changed my life forever when she chose me as a mentee in Pitch Wars 2018. I was on the verge of giving up on writing when my name was posted on that announcement. (Buy her angry bisexual feminist dragon fantasy duology *Shatter the Sky* and *Storm the Earth*, out now everywhere books are sold!) Also thanks to Brenda Drake for creating the amazing opportunity that is Pitch Wars.

To the beta readers of this book, especially those who suffered through the straight-up R18-rated first draft: Rebecca Schaeffer, Tina Chan, Meg Long, Mary Roach, JR Creaden.

To the Squaaaad: Lee Martin, Natalie Heaman, and Megan Poland, who witnessed my entire journey from messy wannabe writer struggling to get an agent to legit author with multiple book deals. The term Ride or Die was invented for friends like you guys. If I were Fergie and this were the song "Glamorous," you guys would be the ones getting Taco Bell with me, drive-through, raw as hell.

To Jen Low, who triggered the sequence of events that led me to start writing when she introduced me to . . . a certain anime . . . , and to Dylan Hayes Cross, for being the one to get me into writing for real. I almost want to curse you for all these years of stress and agony, but I guess it worked out eventually.

To Vander. Wherever you are, I hope you're doing okay.

To VRAINS HELL, for being the chaotic light in my life when I was at my rock bottom. Ari, Mac, Lily, Ra, Yusei (Chrono), Treble, Masky, Cookie, Cherie, Nox, CC, Night, Mage, Hungry, I will never forget you all. I powered through writing this book to make you guys proud.

To new friends: Marco, Francesca, Enxi, and Haru. You guys make Twitter Dot Com worth it when it seems like it wouldn't be.

To the producers of *Darling in the Franxx*: thank you for inspiring the boy-girl pilot system in this book and the idea that mechas can be used as a literary device to explore adolescence, gender, and sexuality.

To my family, for finally accepting my writing career. I still wish you would've had faith in me since the beginning, but I guess you could bring me a plate of cut fruit, and all would be even.

Finally, to the historical Empress Wu, for being a gender-role-shattering icon who managed to become the only female emperor in Chinese history. Although Zetian is a re-imagining who lives in a completely different world under completely different circumstances, I hope her spirit and schemes have done you justice.

IRON
WIDOW

XIRAN JAY ZHAO

A Rock the Boat Book

First published in Great Britain, Ireland & Australia by Rock the Boat,
an imprint of Oneworld Publications, 2021
This mass market paperback published 2022

Published by arrangement with Penguin Random House Canada Young Readers,
a division of Penguin Random House Canada Limited.

Text copyright © Xi Ran Zhao, 2021
Cover art copyright © Ashley Mackenzie, 2021

The moral right of Xi Ran Zhao to be identified as the Author of this work has been asserted
by them in accordance with the Copyright, Designs and Patents Act 1988

ISBN 978-0-86154-211-6
ISBN 978-0-86154-210-9 (ebook)

Printed and bound in Great Britain by Clays Ltd, Elcograf S.p.A.

Oneworld Publications
10 Bloomsbury Street
London WC1B 3SR
England